Relentless
IN A KILT

Other Books by Anna Durand

Dangerous in a Kilt (Hot Scots, Book One)
Wicked in a Kilt (Hot Scots, Book Two)
Scandalous in a Kilt (Hot Scots, Book Three)
The MacTaggart Brothers Trilogy (Hot Scots, Books 1-3)
Gift-Wrapped in a Kilt (Hot Scots, Book Four)
Notorious in a Kilt (Hot Scots, Book Five)
Insatiable in a Kilt (Hot Scots, Book Six)
Lethal in a Kilt (Hot Scots, Book Seven)
Irresistible in a Kilt (Hot Scots, Book Eight)
Devastating in a Kilt (Hot Scots, Book Nine)
Spellbound in a Kilt (Hot Scots, Book Ten)
Incendiary in a Kilt (Hot Scots, Book Twelve)
Lachlan in a Kilt (The Ballachulish Trilogy, Book One)
Aidan in a Kilt (The Ballachulish Trilogy, Book Two)
Rory in a Kilt (The Ballachulish Trilogy, Book Three)
The American Wives Club (A Hot Brits/Hot Scots/Au Naturel Crossover Book)
Brit vs. Scot (A Hot Brits/Hot Scots/Au Naturel Crossover Book)
One Hot Chance (Hot Brits, Book One)
One Hot Roomie (Hot Brits, Book Two)
One Hot Crush (Hot Brits, Book Three)
The Dixon Brothers Trilogy (Hot Brits, Books 1-3)
One Hot Escape (Hot Brits, Book Four)
One Hot Rumor (Hot Brits, Book Five)
One Hot Christmas (Hot Brits, Book Six)
One Hot Scandal (Hot Brits, Book Seven)
Natural Passion (Au Naturel Trilogy, Book One)
Natural Impulse (Au Naturel Trilogy, Book Two)
Natural Satisfaction (Au Naturel Trilogy, Book Three)
Fired Up (standalone romance)
Echo Power (Echo Power Trilogy, Book One)
Echo Dominion (Echo Power Trilogy, Book Two)
Echo Unbound (Echo Power Trilogy, Book Three)
The Mortal Falls (Undercover Elementals, Book One)
The Mortal Fires (Undercover Elementals, Book Two)
The Mortal Tempest (Undercover Elementals, Book Three)
The Janusite Trilogy (Undercover Elementals, Books 1-3)
Obsidian Hunger (Undercover Elementals, Book Four)
Unbidden Hunger (Undercover Elementals, Book Five)
The Thirteenth Fae (Undercover Elementals, Book Six)

Relentless IN A KILT

Hot Scots, Book Eleven

ANNA DURAND

JACOBSVILLE BOOKS JB MARIETTA, OHIO

RELENTLESS IN A KILT

ISBN: 978-1-949406-94-8 (paperback)
ISBN: 978-1-949406-95-5 (ebook)
ISBN: 978-1-949406-96-2 (audiobook)

Manufactured in the United States.

Jacobsville Books
www.JacobsvilleBooks.com

Publisher's Cataloging-in-Publication Data
provided by Five Rainbows Cataloging Services

Names: Durand, Anna, author.
Title: Relentless in a kilt / Anna Durand.
Description: Marietta, OH : Jacobsville Books, 2021. | Series: Hot Scots, bk. 11.
Identifiers: ISBN 978-1-949406-94-8 (paperback) | ISBN 978-1-949406-95-5 (ebook) | ISBN978-1-949406-96-2 (audiobook)
Subjects: LCSH: Bounty hunters--Fiction. | Man-woman relationships--Fiction. | Scots--Fiction. | Americans--Fiction. | Romance fiction. | Romantic suspense fiction. | BISAC: FICTION / Romance / Contemporary. | FICTION / Romance / Romantic Comedy. | GSAFD: Love stories.
Classification: LCC PS3604.U724 R45 2021 (print) | LCC PS3604.U724 (ebook) | DDC 813/.6--dc23.

Prologue

Magnus
London, England
Seventeen Months Ago

I survey the street for the tenth time, scanning the vicinity with care to make certain I don't overlook a sign that my quarry is nearby. Hiding in an alley affords me the cover of darkness. I'd waited until nightfall to attempt to snare my quarry for that very reason. My body stays taut and ready. All my senses remain on high alert. This is my favorite part of the hunt—the moments just before I seize a fugitive.

No one visits this part of London unless they want to buy drugs, hire a prostitute, or steal something. Dilapidated warehouses and abandoned shops occupy the street. My quarry must think she can hide here and escape under the cover of night, but no one gets away from me.

My mobile pings.

I check the new text message. *Do you have her yet?* My client has grown more agitated with every passing hour. He hired me this morning, and already I have a bead on the fugitive. Piper Lang will not be free for much longer. So I type my response: *In custody by midnight.*

It's now eleven forty-five.

Stuffing the mobile back into the interior pocket of my leather jacket, I scan the area yet again. Any moment, she will show herself. The information my client had sent made it clear the lass knows nothing about evading the law—or a hunter like me. She's a museum archivist, not a ninja.

A flash of movement catches my eye peripherally.

My pulse beats faster, and adrenaline courses through my veins, triggering a dark sort of excitement. Aye, I love the hunt. Whatever that says about me, I donnae care. Turning my head slowly, I catch sight of a figure hustling out of an abandoned warehouse and turning left down the street.

Heading straight for me.

I consider pulling my gun out, but I doubt I'll need that. The wee lass cannae fight me. I'm much taller, stronger, and deadlier.

She crosses the street and swerves this way, jogging toward me at a good clip. Her clothes betray her lack of skill in sneaking around—light-blue jeans and a matching jacket, a grey T-shirt, and white running shoes. Well, at least she chose footwear that will let her flee, but their color hardly blends into the background. She's an amateur, and no match for me. This will be too easy. Hardly satisfying.

Piper Lang watches the street as she hurries along, but she ignores what's right beside her—me, hiding in this alley.

I wait until she takes two steps past me, then I rush out to wrap my arms around her torso from behind, pinning her arms to her sides. She yelps and tries to break free, but I'm far stronger than the wee lass. "Stop fighting. It's over. Piper Lang, you are coming with me to the Met. That's the Metropolitan Police, just to be crystal clear."

"No. Please don't do this. I'm innocent."

"That's for the court to decide." I squeeze her a wee bit tighter. "I'm the hunter, not the judge."

"If you take me in, I'll die. Someone wants me dead, just like Archer Caldwell."

"Donnae care. You are accused of murder, and now you're caught."

"Please, listen to me."

I reach behind my back to pull the handcuffs out of my pocket, keeping one arm around her.

She seizes my *slat* and twists hard.

My jeans cannae protect me from that. The minx has tried to rip my cock in half. As pain erupts, I suck in a breath and lose my grip on her just enough that she wriggles away and takes off down the street.

Bod an Donais.

It's not the devil's penis that throbs with pain, though. I need a few seconds to get over the agony, then I race after her with my heart pounding and every inch of my body electrified by the thrill of the chase. Piper veers around a corner, and I lose sight of her. Even when I swerve onto the side street, I can't catch up to the woman. My client hadn't mentioned she can run like an Olympic sprinter. She races down an alley, and just as I come within ten feet of snaring her, she leaps onto a dumpster and uses its height to vault over the six-foot chain link fence behind it.

Piper Lang vanishes into the night.

Mhac na galla. I do not let anyone get the better of me, especially not a woman. That's why I cursed myself as a son of a bitch in Gaelic. The fact that she did get away impresses me—and makes me randy. My *slat* has finally stopped throbbing as I clamber onto the dumpster and climb over the fence, a feat I manage with far less agility than Piper had done. I pelt down the alley, coming out on another street. This one hosts a motel, the seedy kind that charges by the hour. But the business has clearly gone bust. The sign is tilted to the side, the interior is dark, and no vehicles occupy the car park. Its asphalt has cracked, and the lines that demarcate the spaces have faded.

A figure slips inside one of the rooms.

Piper.

I slow to a walk and steal across the street to the motel, molding my back to the wall as I inch toward the room she had entered. The door is closed. I sidle up to it and grasp the knob, twisting it carefully so I won't make any noise, then I ease the door inward.

Someone shouts, and a weight slams into the door.

But I'm ready for her this time. I use my entire body as a ram, knocking her backward though I cannae see the lass as more than a darker shape within the shadows inside the room. I rush inside and kick the door shut. As I switch on the pocket torch I always have on me, the sudden brilliance of its bulb blinds me for a few seconds. My eyes adjust quickly, though, and I set the torch on a scarred and filthy tabletop so the light spreads through the small room.

Piper Lang lies sprawled on the floor.

She glares up at me. "You bastard."

I seize her arm and force her to stand up. She faces me, but rather than trying to flip her around, I pull her into me and cuff her hands behind her back. "No getting away this time. You've shown me all your tricks, which means ahm ready for ye."

"Please don't take me to the cops."

"You are a fugitive. Donnae bother telling me your sad story about how you're innocent and someone framed you. I've heard it all before." With her body pressed to mine, I cannae help that my *slat* starts to rouse. It's a natural response to the thrill of the hunt and the satisfaction of the capture. "I would rather not tie your feet. Needing to carry you over my shoulder will slow me down."

"Oh, I'm so damn sorry I've inconvenienced you."

"Ye haven't. And ye won't."

She wriggles in a vain attempt to get free of me. The action rubs her stiff nipples against my chest. Even though she smells of sweat, the lass is beautiful. Her shapely body is molded to mine, her whisky brown eyes remain riveted to my gaze, and her chestnut hair glistens with coppery highlights. She's breathing hard thanks to our chase and the barnie we had a moment ago, but our tussle got me even more aroused. I dip my head to let her hair brush against my cheek, needing to know if the locks are as silky as they look. They are. I want to bury my face in that hair, but I won't do it.

Piper is a criminal.

But aye, she has the kind of body I'd love to explore while we're both naked. The adrenaline from the chase always leaves me on edge, needing the sort of release only a woman's body can provide. But I cannae shag Piper Lang.

I slide my hand down to her erse.

She gasps. Her eyes have widened, her gaze drawn to my mouth, and she glides her tongue across her bottom lip.

Bod an Donais. I want her.

To distract myself from the feel of her body pressed against mine, I survey the room. A small suitcase lies on the floor beside the bed, and a lantern—battery operated, I think—sits on the nightstand.

Piper rubs her body against me. "If you won't let me go, maybe we could have a little fun before you take me in."

Her voice has turned sultry. The lass is up to something. I don't trust her, but fuck, I crave her.

"Come on," she almost purrs. "I need to have sex one more time before I go to prison. You're amped up too, I can tell. Let's blow off some steam together."

Though I know what she's doing, because it's dead obvious, I cannae stop myself from massaging her erse and groaning when she rocks her hips into my growing erection. I can have a poke with her, then take her in. She's handcuffed, which means she willnae get away from me.

I hoist the lass off her feet, keeping that body molded to mine, and stalk over to the bed. I can see a single sheet of fabric covers the bed. "Where did you get a blanket?"

"Stole it from a washing machine at a launderette."

A thief and a murderer. Yet I still need to shag her.

I toss Piper onto the bed. "Donnae try anything."

Then I shut the door and turn off my torch, switching the lantern on so its glow is the only source of illumination. I willnae undress. That would leave me vulnerable, and a hunter never allows weakness to get in the way of the hunt. So I unzip my trousers and dig a condom out of my pocket.

Aye, I always need a release after a capture. Not hard to find a willing lass.

Piper's breasts rise and fall with her labored breaths. She stares at my *slat* while I stalk toward her and get the condom on.

I unzip her jeans, hook my thumb inside the waistband, and drag them and her knickers down to her ankles. She shimmies to get into the middle of the bed. I kneel between her legs, planting my hands at either side of her shoulders.

"Please uncuff me," she says. " I want to touch you."

"No."

I push inside her, groaning at how good her body feels wrapped around me.

"Oh, yes," she moans. "But please, let me touch you. I can't get away when we're having sex."

"No."

She rolls her hips, driving my cock deeper into her soft, wet flesh. When she squeezes her inner muscles around me, my eyes roll back in my head and I groan deeply.

Maybe it's lust making me drunk, impairing my decision-making. Whatever the reason, I find myself unlocking the cuffs and tossing them onto the battered nightstand. She throws her arms around me while I start pumping into her, hard and fast and rough, consuming her body with every thrust.

We shag for an hour, and it's the best sex I've ever had. But then I do the last thing I ever imagined I would. I fall asleep. A hunter knows better—I know better—but something about this woman erases everything I've learned about tracking fugitives. All I could think about was having her.

I wake up alone. All I can do is get dressed and leave.

But I notice a piece of paper on the nightstand beside the lantern.

Grabbing the sheet, I read the words Piper wrote on it. Thanks, I needed that. But you will never catch me again, Magnus MacTaggart. PS, I know your name because I peeked in your wallet.

I growl and crumple the paper, tossing it away.

For the next seventeen months, I hunt Piper Lang. Many times I get close, but she always evades me. How does a museum archivist know so much about hiding from the law? I am not the law, though. I can do things the police can't, take risks no sane person would, and capture fugitives even law enforcement failed to find.

I always get my man. Yet one woman has outwitted me.

Chapter One

Piper
Montijo, Portugal

Life as a fugitive sucks. I'm stuck on that thought as I wander down the sidewalk to stop in front of a clothing store. My stuff is getting old, and I'd really like to buy something new. Gazing through the store's window, I see lots of pretty, feminine things. But I can't wear pink or yellow or any color that might stand out in a crowd. I can't wear perfume either, or go to a dance club. I need to blend in and disappear.

So yeah, being a fugitive sucks.

I'd love to blame Magnus MacTaggart for all my troubles, but he didn't frame me for murder. Someone else did. Someone I haven't identified yet. Maybe I've gotten damn good at evading Magnus, but I've had no luck trying to identify the person who killed my boss and pinned the crime on me.

A young couple breezes past me, laughing and smiling, their arms around each other. They chatter in Portuguese. I don't speak the language. Being on the run means I don't have time to download a language instruction app and learn how to speak the native tongue of every country I've visited. So I stumble along the best I can. I've stuck to European countries because they seem the most likely to have enough English speakers that I can get by.

My gaze veers back to the store window. Pretty clothes. Cute shoes. Shiny baubles. Those things are not for me, no matter how much I want them. No, I'll have to choose nondescript stuff. I glance down at my current ensemble—khaki pants, a brown shirt, and beige tennies.

I turn around and walk back to my motel.

The red clay tiles of the roofs in this town are beautiful, but I can't muster any enthusiasm for admiring the scenery. I'm thinking about how long I can stay here. That damn Scot has pursued me relentlessly, giving me little time to investigate and discover who framed me. I think about that bastard at least a dozen times a day, though I wish I didn't. It's hard not to think about him since the man refuses to give up on catching me.

After a five-minute walk, I approach the door to my motel room. This isn't a picturesque establishment, but it's clean and cheap and the desk clerk speaks English. I'd kill for one of those auto-translate devices they had on *Star Trek*. The online translators I've found do a crummy job, and I wind up saying things the not-quite-right way. It's no wonder people think I'm nuts.

I hesitate with my hand on the doorknob. A shiver trickles down my spine. I sense… No, it can't be. My paranoia has reared its head again, that's all. Seventeen months on the run wreaks havoc with a girl's sense of security. So I shove the key into the lock. Yeah, this place doesn't have keycards, just the old-fashioned kind made of metal. As I push the door inward and shuffle into the room, that feeling tickles my senses again.

The door slams shut.

Whirling around, I gape at the man standing there. "How—"

Magnus MacTaggart aims his squinty-eyed stare at me, his lips flattened and his body tensed as if readying for a fight. "How do ye think? You're clever, but not as clever as I am."

He always dresses like a reject from a biker gang, with a skull-and-crossbones shirt, dark jeans that match his dark hair, and a well-worn leather jacket, not to mention that scruffy goatee. But I can't deny he has gorgeous blue eyes and hot muscles.

He whips out a pair of handcuffs. "Piper Lang, you are coming with me."

"Like hell I am." I stumble backward, shaking my head so hard my hair flaps around my face. I keep gaping at him, the demon who won't give up. "I'm not going anywhere with you."

"Did I suggest you have a choice?"

No choice? I've gotten away from him before, dammit, and I can do it again. Besides, I've got a secret weapon he doesn't know about. It's my turn to squint at him. I sneak a hand behind my back and pull my revolver out of my waistband, raising it in front of me. "Get out of my way, MacTaggart."

Okay, yeah, my secret weapon is a weapon.

My hand shakes a touch, despite my best efforts to remain calm. I don't understand how he found me, but the bastard probably has a team of psychics helping him. Not that I've ever believed in the paranormal. But this man seems to have a supernatural ability to track me.

He takes one big step toward me, and my gun grazes his chest. "Last chance. Come willingly, or I'll do it by force."

I poke the gun into his chest. "Get out of my way, or I'll shoot you."

"Been shot before. Stabbed too." He slants closer, pressing the gun's muzzle into his chest. "A wee lassie doesnae scare me."

"I got away from you once, I'll do it again." He kept chasing me, sure, but he didn't catch me again—until today.

Magnus snatches the gun from my hand so fast I don't have time to react. He drops it onto the floor and snares my wrist, spinning me around before I realize what's happening, using his big hand to bind both of mine behind my back. He tugs me backward into his body and lashes his other arm around my waist. "Willnae get away this time."

His gaze flicks down to my chest. The low neckline of my shirt gives him a good view of my cleavage. He slides his hand up my belly, grazing the underside of my breast.

I suck in a breath. Try not to, really I do. The creep has some kind of voodoo sex power that turns me into a weak-willed moron whenever he touches me. He might be big and mean and grizzled, like a beast from the depths of hell, but I can't deny one simple fact.

He's hot in bed.

"Let me go, please," I say, like that will work. Desperate times and all that shit. I spoke those words in a huskier voice, though I hadn't meant to do that. Maybe my sultry tone will get him horny enough that he'll slip up, and I can get away.

My nipples have tightened and started to ache, but that's irrelevant. I will not let him screw me again. No way.

"I don't let murderers go," he growls into my ear. "Ye should've considered the consequences before ye poisoned your boss so you could get a promotion."

"That's insane. I was an archivist at a museum, not next in line to be CEO of a mega-corporation."

"Greed is universal. And you should've wiped your fingerprints off the glass after you gave the man champagne laced with strychnine. But ye aren't that clever, are ye?"

"Outsmarted you, didn't I? The great Magnus MacTaggart screwed up."

I can feel his dick stiffening against my backside. Now if he'll just make one little mistake…

"I'm innocent," I say, breathing harder for some stupid reason. "Someone framed me. I had to run because the cops wouldn't believe me. Please, you can't take me back to the UK. Everyone there thinks like you do, that I'm an American slut who tried to advance her career by seducing and killing her boss."

"Not my problem. I bring in fugitives, I don't try their cases in court."

"Just listen. Let me explain—"

"Donnae give a damn if you're guilty or innocent. I'm doing my job, full stop."

"But—"

He drags me to the bed and tosses me onto it, reclaiming my wrists before I realize what's happening. Magnus restrains my hands over my belly. I squirm and glare at him, but I can't get free. He hooks one handcuff around my right wrist, then slides the other cuff through the rails in the headboard, snapping it tight around my left wrist. "No slithering away from me this time."

"What are you going to do?"

If I have sex with him, maybe he'll fall asleep like he did last time. Then I can escape. The fact that I really, really want him to screw me has no bearing on anything. I've been celibate for too damn long. A fugitive can't go trolling the clubs for a lover. So I'd taken care of my urges on my own, mostly. Under no circumstances will I ever admit to Magnus that I fantasize about him while I get off.

Magnus crawls onto the bed, straddling my legs, and bends over me to brace his palms on the mattress at either side of my shoulders. "Ye want me to fuck ye."

"Ugh. I hate you." But yeah, I want that. And I despise myself for it.

"Donnae care if ye like me." He molds one hand to my breast, and my breath hitches. "But we both know you want me inside you."

"You are evil."

He chuckles, the sound rough and dark and sexy as hell. "Aye, but you like that. Wouldn't have seduced me last time if ye didn't."

"Maybe I…kind of like it. But I still hate you."

"Good." He scrapes his tongue up my throat. "Then ye'll be wanting me to take ye now."

Breathing hard, I bite down on my bottom lip and struggle to quell this dangerous lust. I hate him, I'm afraid of him, and yet I need his dick inside me.

"Say it," he growls. "Tell me what you want—really want—right here, right now."

I can't stop my back from arching when he squeezes my tit. "Just hurry the hell up and do it, MacTaggart."

"Not until you beg for it."

Of course he wants that. He's a sadistic jerk, after all. But I glare at him instead of speaking the words he wants me to say. "Told you to do it already."

He pinches my nipple and rubs his hard-on into my groin.

My hips thrust up as if my body has a mind of its own, and I can't stop the words that tumble from my lips. "Please, you bastard, fuck me."

Magnus pulls out a switchblade and grips the neckline of my shirt. He slices it open, the halves gaping away from my breasts. No, I'm not wearing a bra. I have two that I wear sometimes, but today I'd gone without extra support because my shirt is tight enough to hold my tits up. That means the bounty hunter can see all of my breasts. He's staring at them, licking his lips.

He shoves the knife back into his pocket and yanks my pants and underwear down to my ankles, effectively shackling me with my clothes. Then he pauses, roving his gaze over my body while he strokes himself through his jeans.

My mouth decides to override my common sense again. "Please let me touch you."

"No." He unhooks his belt and unzips his jeans, freeing his dick, and wraps his fist around it to skim his palm up and down his length. "You're at my mercy, and I mean to keep it that way."

I writhe, grasping the headboard rails, so ready that it's humiliating. The fact that I'm wet and tingly between my thighs means nothing. I'm doing this to get away from him, nothing more. Yeah, hot sex is an escape strategy.

Magnus pushes my legs apart and plunges his cock inside me.

Oh God, this feels incredible. Just for a little while, I'll forget about who he is and what I am. I need to feel good, if only for a brief time.

Then I'll sneak out while he's asleep.

Magnus hovers over me while he thrusts in and out, slowly at first, then faster and faster until the bed starts to shake. His erection is big and thick and hot, just the kind of dick every woman needs to experience once. Or twice. This will be the last time. His clothes rasp against my bare belly and breasts, the sensation amping up my lust until I can't catch my breath. He pumps harder, pounding into me at a rough and almost manic pace. My cream dribbles down my thighs because I'm wetter than I've ever been in my life, even more than the first time I'd had sex with Magnus. He grunts and gasps, bends his head to latch on to my nipple, and suckles it so fiercely that I know I'll come any second.

He pulls away. My cream glistens on his dick, but he just sits there, kneeling at my feet while struggling to regain his breath.

I try to kick his thigh, but my own pants prevent it. "Don't stop. I was about to come."

"Aye, I know."

He curls his fingers around his length and pumps himself so vigorously that he starts grunting and gasping while the bed shimmies. Squeezing his eyes shut, he throws his head back and…milky liquid jets out of his cock. It sprays onto my belly. He steps off the bed and zips up his jeans.

The bastard got himself off but left me hanging.

"You can't do this to me," I say, trying to sound nasty but failing. A thwarted climax is torture. "Are you really going to leave me here with your…excretions all over me?"

"Excretions?" He chuckles. "Never heard it described that way before."

"Finish what you started."

"What if I don't?"

"At least clean this off my tummy. Don't want your crap glued to my skin."

He studies me for a moment, then saunters into the bathroom, shutting the door.

That asshole is going to leave me like this. What, is he marking his territory?

Oh, that man is going to pay for this.

<h1 style="text-align:center">Chapter Two</h1>

Magnus

I stand in front of the bathroom mirror with my fingers curled over the counter's edge, studying myself because I feel like someone else has taken over my body. I fucked Piper—again. Though I have a condom in my pocket, like I always do, I'd needed to feel her body wrapped around mine with nothing between our skin except her cream. The scent of it had intoxicated me. But at least I had the sense to pull out before I came inside her. Never have I left a lass wanting. I always make sure my lovers come, but I…needed to get away from her.

Why did I have another poke with the fugitive I'm meant to transport home? After seventeen months of pursuing the woman, I'd finally caught her, and the adrenaline rush hit me harder than ever. That's why I did it. Not because I want her, specifically. I needed a release. She gave it to me.

But I left her on the edge of climax. Have I become the sort of *bod ceann* who does that to a woman?

I grab a towel and wet it with warm water, then I march back out into the bedroom.

Piper is writhing as if she means to get out of her handcuffs. When she sees me, she stops and glowers at me. "You sick, twisted son of a bitch."

"Call me whatever you like. Nothing you say will fash me because I've heard much worse."

"You are so evil there's not even a word for it."

I sit on the bed alongside her hip. Her body is still exposed from her neck down to her ankles, and I cannae resist admiring her breasts. The hunger to touch her grows powerful, but I need to clean up after myself first. So I wipe the warm, damp towel over her belly to clean off my "excretions," as she called it. While I do that, she watches me with a puzzled expression.

"There," I say, tossing the towel onto the floor. "Ye won't have any of me glued to your skin."

"Am I supposed to thank you for that?"

The lass is still angry because I didn't give her the climax she needs. Maybe I shouldn't care about that, but I do. My parents raised me to be a good man, but I threw all that out the windae when I decided to become a bounty hunter. This profession has no room for sweetness. Not that anyone ever called me sweet, even before I became a rotten ersehole. Well, one person had called me that, but it's not an accurate description of me.

I climb onto the bed and lie down between Piper's thighs, my head poised above her mound.

Her glower disintegrates, replaced by a blank look. She doesn't blink, her attention riveted to me. "What are you doing?"

"Giving you what you need." I slide two fingers between her folds and stroke them up and down until she starts writhing again. "Beg me for it."

"No." The word came out breathless, and she grips the headboard rails.

"Beg for it." I drag my fingers down to her opening and tease it with their tips, rewarded by her soft whimper. "Ye know ye want me to make ye come, so do what I said."

"Please, Magnus, please."

The way she said my name made my cock twitch, but I willnae shag her again. I scrape my tongue up her flesh from her opening all the way to her clit. She thrashes like a wild thing. The taste of her cream drugs me, and I cannae think anymore. I close my lips around her nub and suck it hard, earning a gasp from her, but when I flick my tongue over the tip repeatedly, she cries out. I feel her body tense and see her gripping the rails even more tightly, solid clues that she's about to come. While she gasps and thrusts her hips up, silently begging me for more, I keep licking and suckling her clit until her entire body goes still, caught in the moment before climax. I thrust two fingers inside her.

She cries out.

Her body pulsates around my fingers while I thrust them into her over and over, not stopping until she's done. Then I rise to my knees at her feet. Her cream coats my fingers and my lips, the scent of it enveloping me. Piper watches, biting down on her lower lip, while I lick the taste of her off my fingers and mouth, doing it slowly while I gaze straight into her eyes.

"You taste like honey," I say. "Honey and whisky."

"Are you going to uncuff me?"

"Do ye think ahm that stupid? You will try to run if I do that."

She tries to kick me, but her trousers prevent it. "You ruined my shirt, and now you're going to leave me here practically naked until…when? Maybe you'll drag me out of this room that way."

Though I dislike admitting it, she does have a point. I cannae leave her lying there virtually naked, in large part because looking at her body makes me want to fuck her again. Though I would prefer to take her back to the UK tonight, I need rest. Hunting her takes more effort than any other job I've done, and I still have no idea why. She's an academic, not a hardened criminal.

I need to understand how she keeps evading me.

Getting the truth out of her might take an hour at most. I know how to interrogate a fugitive. So aye, spending the night in this room with her has nothing to do with lust and everything to do with uncovering her secrets to ensure I never lose track of her again. If we happen to shag one more time… *No, you bleeding ersehole, you cannot touch her ever again.*

But Piper Lang is my obsession—and my weakness.

I tug her trousers and knickers up to cover her lower half, then yank the zipper up. Her shirt has been ruined, and I'll need to take care in how I go about getting another one on her without the lass escaping. She's wily and not above using sex to distract me. I remove my belt and shackle her ankles with it, careful not to cinch it up too tight.

"Why did you do that?" she demands.

"I'm restraining the fugitive."

"You're that scared of me, huh? Some tough bounty hunter you are."

The lass means to harass me until I lash out, but that will never happen. I'm immune to that sort of tactic.

How can I get another shirt on her without uncuffing her hands? While I consider the options, I let my gaze travel down to her chest and those bonnie tits. They're on the smaller side, but I like that. I know from experience that one mound will fit nicely in each hand. Not that I'll ever touch her again except in the commission of my duty.

I decide on a method for replacing her shirt and stalk over to her suitcase that lies on the floor. Rummaging through the contents, I find a loose-fitting short-sleeve shirt and a bra. Aye, I've removed plenty of bras in my life, but I've never tried to get one onto a woman before. *Mhac na galla.* That means I'll need to adjust my plan so she can do up the bra herself.

My gaze veers to Piper and her naked torso. I rub my jaw, failing in my attempt to avoid noticing her breasts and the way the rigid tips point up to the ceiling. The last time we shagged, I loved the taste of her skin when I pulled her nipple into my mouth, but more than that, I loved the flavor of her cream. When I tasted her again moments ago, I loved the flavor even more.

I toss her shirt and bra onto the bed and lean over the lass to unhook one cuff and attach it to the headboard rail. "Donnae try anything, or you'll regret it."

She huffs.

After one last look at her breasts, I let go of the handcuff. Her right arm is free. I know she's right-handed. That's why I chose to undo that restraint. "Get dressed."

"How? You've still got my left arm immobilized."

"Not immobilized. I know for a fact you're agile and flexible. You can get your clothes on even with one arm restrained. Be creative."

She throws me a scowl.

I shove my hands under her arms and lift her into a sitting position. "Do it now, Piper."

The lass grabs her bra and manages to drop one strap over her shoulder. "I can't do the rest when my hand is strapped to the headboard."

"Of course you can. Pull the shirt over your head through the right arm. Then I will switch the cuffs to let you do the rest."

She narrows her gaze and puckers her lips.

I lean over her more until our eyes are inches apart. "Do it now, Piper."

She complies.

And I hook the right cuff onto the headboard again. When I unhook the left cuff and attach it to the headboard, she manages to get the bra over her shoulder, the shirt too, but she struggles to do up the bra's clasps behind her back. The lass makes frustrated noises. After a minute or so of struggling, she lets out a growl and glares at me.

"I can't do it," she says. "The bra is the problem."

"No, it isn't." I reach behind her to secure the tiny clasps, which brings my mouth too close to hers. The second I've finished, I pull away. "Time to put the right cuff back on."

"Please let me have one hand free. If you're holding me hostage, I'll need to eat and drink."

"All right. You can have one hand free."

"It should be my right one. That's my dominant hand."

She is demanding, which turns me on even while I want to toss her into her own suitcase and zip it up to stop her from harassing me. I switch the cuffs to leave her right hand free.

"Thank you," she says.

If she's expecting me to say "you're welcome," the bloody woman can wait for that until eternity ends. Her gratitude must be another ploy, anyway. Piper Lang will resort to anything, up to and including seduction, to get away from me.

No, she will never get away again.

I walk over to the table by the window and sit on one of the chairs that flank it. I can see a glimpse of sunshine through the minuscule gap between the halves of the curtains. We will not leave this room until she gives me answers, starting with a question that might seem trivial, though I know it's important.

"How do you get money to pay for everyday expenses?"

"I found a rainbow with a pot of gold at the end."

"Donnae play games with me. I want the truth, and I'll get it out of you by whatever means necessary."

She leans back against the headboard. "Really. What exactly do you plan on doing to me if I refuse to answer your questions?"

"Whatever I need to do."

"That's not an answer." She lifts her chin and smirks at me. "I think you're bluffing. You won't hurt me."

I hook one ankle over the other knee and link my hands over my belly. "Ye donnae know me, so maybe you shouldn't assume you understand what lengths I might go to."

"You dress like a badass and snarl at me like a bastard, but you made sure I came after you rudely spewed all over my tummy. You even cleaned me up after that."

"What is your point?"

Her lips kink up on one side. "You're an asshole, but not totally evil."

If she assumes that means I'm weak and she can manipulate me, the lass will learn a harsh lesson soon. I know ways to make a person talk without resorting to the vulgarity of torture.

"Why are you quizzing me?" Piper asks. "What happened to 'I bring in fugitives, I don't try their cases in court'?"

"Ahmno interested in your case. Just answer my questions, and this will be over soon. We are not leaving this room until I get the information I want." I steeple my fingers under my chin and give her my hardest stare. "Answer my question. And donnae tell me you found a pot of gold under a rainbow."

"No, it wasn't a rainbow." She adopts an expression of false sincerity. "I found a unicorn. It let me shave some magic off its horn."

"*Magairlean*. Stop lying to me."

The lass wrinkles her nose. "Maga-what? Are you speaking another language?"

"Scots Gaelic. And *magairlean* means bollocks."

"Uh-huh. Whatever."

"Tell me the truth *right now*, or I will punish you."

She rolls her eyes. "Yeah, sure you will. Go for it, asswipe."

I fly out of my chair and stomp over to the bed. My hands have fisted, and my teeth are clenched, though I made no conscious decision to do either. Why won't this woman just tell me what I need to know?

She stares at me with defiance in her eyes.

And I want to fuck her again right now. But I willnae do it. No one gets the better of me. No one.

Except for her.

Chapter Three

Piper

Magnus towers over me from inches away, his legs almost touching the mattress. The look on his face reminds me of the actor Audie Murphy, who had the deadly stare down pat. I used to watch a lot of old western movies with my dad, and Audie Murphy was always my favorite. A hot guy in cowboy duds? Yeah, I like that way more than a greasy jerk who dresses like a reject from the ninth level of hell.

The Scot does not scare me.

But the thought of being arrested again does.

Why does he care how I keep evading him? I guess it's a macho pride thing since he claims never to have let a fugitive get away from him—until I did it. Though I'd love to claim I'm so smart that I outwitted him, I won't lie to myself. To him, sure. But not in my own mind. I got lucky when I escaped from Magnus the first time. Then I learned how to protect myself the hard way, making more mistakes than I care to remember and stumbling along until I figured things out.

I'm far from an expert fugitive. I get away from Magnus over and over because I'd studied the bastard up close during our first encounter in London, and I paid attention to his actions every time he caught sight of me again. I doubt the jerk realizes I've made studying him my pastime. What else do I have to occupy myself when I'm not running from him? I've had loads of time to analyze his every move.

Since I'm the only fugitive who ever slipped away from him, I wonder if that means no one else ever tried to understand him. Not as a person, but as a bounty hunter. I might kind of admire his dedication and determination, but I don't appreciate it when he focuses all of that on me.

Well, I do appreciate it when we're naked and writhing under the sheets. But that's irrelevant.

"Start talking," Magnus hisses. "Explain yourself."

"Don't think I will. If you can't keep track of me, that's not my fault. I'm under no obligation to tell you anything."

He bends over to stare into my eyes, which places his mouth a hair's breadth from mine. "If ye ever want to leave this room—"

"Come off it, MacTaggart. You don't scare me, and we both know you'll never hurt me physically."

"Ye know nothing. I can hurt you in ways that will damage you far more than a slap or a knife cut."

I roll my eyes. Honestly, he is the stubbornest person I've ever met. "Not telling you a damn thing."

He glances down at my chest, and his tongue snakes out to moisten his lips.

The cretin helped me do up my bra, and I thanked him for it. Why did I do that? I owe no gratitude to the jerk who cuffed me to the headboard. At least I have one hand free, but my feet are tied together by his leather belt. I could pick the handcuff lock if I had a paperclip or something like that. But even if I could reach the bedside table, I don't see any useful objects on it. I suppose I could grab the phone and whack Magnus on the head with it, but I doubt that would stop him.

Well, I do have one trick I've used before. He might expect it, but giving it a try could be fun.

Magnus is still staring at my chest.

I lay a hand on his cheek and exert light pressure until he lifts his head to look at me. "Can't deny you're fantastic in bed."

"Not falling for that trick again."

"Maybe I've tricked you before, but my lust for you is real." I push my hand into his hair. "Can't fake how hot you make me feel."

He doesn't move, doesn't blink either.

I drag my hand down his chest to the button on his pants and unhook it.

Magnus groans deeply.

Can't help myself. I tug his zipper down and shove my hand inside to grasp his dick.

He mutters something that I assume is Gaelic. Then he bolts upright and staggers backward a few steps. His chest is heaving. "Willnae work this time. Better get a new trick."

Magnus zips up his jeans and grabs my suitcase, shoving all my belongings into it. He even snags the stuff from the bathroom and dumps that in with everything else. Then he marches out the door, slamming it shut.

Did he just steal all my stuff? If he came here to capture me, the jerk won't leave me lying here cuffed to the headboard with my feet shackled.

Seconds tick by, turning into minutes.

The door bursts open. Magnus stomps over to the bed and unties my feet, then unhooks the cuffs—but only to bind both my wrists in front of me. Now fully cuffed, I glare at him.

He throws an arm around my waist to hoist me off the bed, depositing me on my feet. "Donnae try anything. I have the legal right to take you, but a fugitive has no rights."

"Bullshit. I'm innocent until proven guilty."

"Your innocence or guilt is not my problem."

He snares my arm and hauls me outside. A gray sedan sits beside my beige car. Magnus hauls me over to the gray vehicle, rips the passenger door open, and roughly pushes me inside. Screw this. I'm changing tactics.

Eyes wide, I pretend I see something behind him and yell, "Watch out!"

"Nice try, but ahmno that easy to fool."

"Okay. Then how about this."

I grab his waistband and yank hard, which makes his forehead smack into the car's roof. Then I swing my legs out to kick him in the gut with both feet.

Magnus staggers sideways and stumbles over the curb.

I seize the opening and leap out of the car, wriggling past him so quickly that he doesn't have time to react. I run as fast as my legs can stand and risk only one glance back, seeing that Magnus has just noticed what happened and is hurrying after me. Then I focus on veering around obstacles, human and inanimate, as I rush toward freedom, though I have no idea where I'm going. People glance at me with surprise, but no one tries to stop me.

Just as I swerve around a pedestrian, the man turns and steps into my path, clearly not having seen me barreling toward him. I trip and fall to my knees, gasping for breath. Coffee from the man's cup slops onto my chest, but thankfully, it's not scorching hot.

The man helps me up while speaking in a language I don't understand, probably Portuguese.

I shake my head and hunch my shoulders. Then I notice the hard plastic coffee stirrer sitting inside his cup. *Eureka.* I snatch up the plastic stick and bolt again. Shouts from further down the street alert me to Magnus's approach. I might have a minute or two at most to free myself, so I dash into an alley and crouch behind a dumpster. Having my hands cuffed in front of me helps. I manage to slide the coffee stirrer into the lock to pick it. The task takes me longer than I would've liked, but I have to stay here while I do it. Picking a lock while running won't work. I've practiced this operation many times, which means I can get the lock open.

At last, it pops free. I ditch the cuffs and jump out from behind the dumpster.

The damn Scot slams into me.

I stagger backward half a step. No time to think. Instinct takes over as I raise my arms and ram my palms into his nose in alternating strikes. Just as he reaches for my wrist, I bend my knee and swing it up, straightening my leg at the second it strikes his groin. Thank goodness I watched those self-defense videos online.

He shouts and stumbles sideways.

And I sprint toward the end of the alley, where a chain link fence bars my way. I leap up, grabbing onto the metal bar on top of the fence, and hoist myself up and over it. The second I touch down on the other side, I break into a dead run.

Behind me, I hear the racket of someone much larger attempting to surmount the fence.

Don't look back, don't look back. I focus on what lies ahead of me—another street. The moment I race out of the alley, I whirl and run down the sidewalk. A group of people up ahead sound like they're speaking English. I slow down and try to calm my hectic breathing as I approach the group. But maybe I can use my flustered state to my advantage.

"Excuse me," I say, which causes all five members of the group, three men and two women, to stare at me. "Sorry to bother you, but I just heard my mom is in the hospital. Car wreck. I got the call a few minutes ago, and I don't have my wallet on me, so I haven't been able to get a taxi. I was wondering…"

"Let me help," one of the men says. Thank heaven he's American. The man hails a taxi, even opening the door for me. As soon as I've climbed in, the man gives me a fifty euro note. "Hope your mom's okay."

"Thank you." I hold up the banknote. "But this is too much."

"Don't worry about that. Go be with your mom."

He shuts the door for me.

I always feel horrible when I have to resort to lying. But I cannot let Magnus catch me. He'll haul me back to the UK, where everyone thinks I'm an evil, murdering bitch. I let the taxi driver take me to the hospital, strictly to avoid seeming suspicious. I use what's left of the money that nice man gave me to buy a bus ticket to Huelva in Spain and suffer through a very long ride in a vehicle that has seen better days. But the fare was cheap, so I can't complain.

Once in Huelva, I head for the port and barter my way onto a shipping vessel that's headed for Tunisia. I hang out there for a few days, then I need to get moving again. I have no belongings, since Magnus put them in his car. I have no money either. So I barter my way to Naples and start the merry-go-round again, working off the books for whoever will hire me, cleaning toilets or busing tables, whatever it takes.

Will Magnus find me again? Who knows.

But a tiny part of me hopes he will.

Chapter Four

Magnus
Dùndubhan Castle, Scotland
Three Months Later

I stand inside the great hall in Dùndubhan, the medieval castle owned by my cousin Rory and his American wife. Couples wander around the dance floor while an up-tempo song plays and children's laughter echoes through the cavernous space. Tonight, it's a dance club. I see the bairns at their special table in the corner, eating and having a good time. Everyone is enjoying the wedding reception for my cousin Kirsty and her American husband, Luke.

All the men wear kilts, including the Americans.

This is the first time I've attended a wedding. Most of my family thinks my job makes me just shy of being a criminal, and they find me…intimidating. Well, a few of them don't. Kirsty calls me "sweet" and "such a dear." I donnae correct her misconceptions because I love the lass. Everyone does. No person on earth could not feel that way about Kirsty MacTaggart.

But now she's Kirsty Turner.

I catch sight of the newlyweds on the dance floor. Kirsty notices me and smiles brightly. The best I can offer is a tight smile and a nod because I expect the anger and recriminations to begin at any moment. After all, Kirsty insisted on inviting my parents to the wedding.

Callum, another of my cousins, approaches me. The lad slaps me on the back and grins. "Quite the do, eh? Our stinking-rich cousins went all out for this wedding. I think they spent more on Kirsty and Luke than they did on Jack and Autumn."

"I hear congratulations are in order. You've gotten engaged to an American lass, haven't ye?"

"Aye. Kate is the bonniest, cleverest, most pigheaded lass on earth. We're perfect for each other."

"Sounds like you are."

"Donnae worry. You'll find the perfect woman too, someone who fits you like a glove." Callum leans in to whisper, "Might be easier to find her if ye get out there and mingle."

"This room is full of my cousins, aunts, and uncles. I don't date relatives."

"Kate's sister is here."

"I thought she had a boyfriend."

"Oh, aye, that's right. I forgot." Callum pats my back. "Your girl is out there somewhere."

Kirsty hurries up to us and holds out her hand to me. "Ye havenae danced with me yet, Magnus."

Callum thumps me on the back again. "Aye, Magnus, you do that. Don't want to disappoint the bride."

He knows bloody well I intensely dislike dancing. But I love Kirsty like a sister, so I take her hand and follow the lass out onto the dance floor. While we navigate around the other pairs who shuffle about in time with the music, Kirsty regards me in a way I recognize. It means she's tapping into her "second sight," or as she likes to call it in Gaelic, her *da-shealladh*. I have never subscribed to that rubbish, but I respect her beliefs. What I can't stomach is knowing that she means to share her supposed insights with me. Any second she'll tell me, whether I like it or not.

"What is it?" I ask. "Get it over with, Kirsty."

She smiles, and I cannae be annoyed with her when she does that. My wee cousin has the sweetest smile on earth. "You always know when I'm tapping into my *da-shealladh*. Maybe you have a touch of it in you too."

"*Magairlean*. Whatever celestial powers that be who gave you second sight did not grant me anything."

"Donnae say 'bollocks,' not even in Gaelic. Or do you think my *da-shealladh* is nonsense too? Because I know you've got a wee sliver of the second sight."

"A few seconds ago, you said 'maybe' I have it. Now it's a certainty?"

She smiles again, her cheeks dimpling, and taps a fingertip on my nose. "The more you fight it, the more certain I am that you have a touch of the second sight."

"I wish I did. Supernatural insight would be a bloody great help when I'm hunting fugitives."

Then I could find Piper again without searching the whole world for her.

Aye, for the past three months, I've spent every waking hour doing just that—and wondering what I will do if I track her down. Piper got away from me twice. Cannae let the hunt go on for seventeen months this time. I need to have her. To find her, that is. Bringing her to justice is my only goal.

Why, then, do I have erotic dreams about her every night?

I need to capture her, detain her, and drag the lass back to the UK to stand trial. That's it. My fantasies mean nothing except that it's been too long since I shagged anyone.

Except for Piper.

Kirsty's eyes light up, and her lips fall open even while they curl up a wee bit. "You've met your soul mate, haven't ye?"

"That's bol—It's nonsense, Kirsty. Donnae try to talk me into believing in rubbish like soul mates."

She rises onto the toes of her shoes and leans in to whisper in my ear. "Donnae be a grump when you see her again. Show the lass who you really are—a good, sweet man with a heart of pure gold."

"You do realize that every time you say that to anyone other than me, they think you're off your head."

"Why should I care? It's the truth."

Only Kirsty views me that way. Piper thinks I'm evil. I suspect she sees me more clearly than my wee cousin does.

The songs ends, and our cousin Iain asks the bride for a dance.

I amble back to the corner where I'd been standing. But I only make it to the buffet table in front of that spot.

My father steps in front of me. "What d'ye think yer doing? Coming to a family event? Yer no more a MacTaggart than ye are my son, which means not at all."

"Let's not do this at Kirsty's wedding."

My father spits in my face, but since he's a foot shorter than I am, the saliva lands on my throat. "Never come back here again. '*S e plàigh a th' annad*.'"

Aye, I am a plague. Nothing good ever comes from knowing me.

My mother races up to us and grasps my father's arm. "Baltair, what are ye doing? Please donnae make a scene tonight."

"It's all right," I say. "I'm leaving, anyway."

Does my mother seem almost sorry about that? No, I must have misread her expression.

Turning away from my parents, I stalk out of the great hall.

In the morning, I receive a call from the man who has paid for my twenty-month-long search for a single fugitive. Royce Hammond demands I meet with him in person. He's flying in from London, and I'm meant to meet him at a hotel near the Inverness airport. Considering how much he pays me, and for how long he's done that, I feel obliged to meet the man and hear what he has to say.

But aye, I expect to be sacked. Even if that happens, I will still hunt for Piper Lang.

When I knock on the door to Hammond's room, it swings open seconds later. Royce Hammond gives me a haughty look, his chin raised. "Get your arse in here, MacTaggart. I don't want to stay in this rubbish heap one moment longer than necessary."

Rubbish heap? It's a nice hotel, though not five star. Working for an arrogant Brit never appealed to me, but Hammond offered me such a generous daily stipend that I couldn't say no. Maybe I should have. Donnae like Royce Hammond and donnae trust him either.

But I get my erse into the room.

Hammond slams the door and commands me to sit on one of the two beds. "This bloody hovel doesn't even have a living room, much less a jacuzzi."

"Aye, you're really slumming it here in Inverness."

My client doesn't sit down. He stands directly in front of me and scowls. "Why haven't you found Piper Lang? She's a museum archivist, not a criminal mastermind. I was led to believe you are the best bounty hunter in the world, but now I'm wondering if you could find a mouse in a cheese factory."

"Donnae get shirty with me, Hammond. I know you've hired other hunters to find Piper Lang, but none of them got within a hundred miles of her. I've been within sight of the woman dozens of times." And I captured her twice, but I won't tell him that. "We both know I'm your only shot at bringing her in."

He scowls at me a bit more, then blows out a breath that relaxes his whole body. "All right. I'm giving you one more chance. Bring Piper Lang to me within two weeks."

"You mean bring her to the Met."

The arrogant erse doesn't respond. Instead, he picks up an attaché case from the floor and drops it onto the bed, then pulls out a slim packet. He hands it to me. "I've arranged for you to fly to London. Perhaps you need to confer with the Met a bit more to acquire new leads. But you won't have the luxury of flying on my fastest jet anymore. You'll take the 757 to Montijo and start your search from the last place you saw her."

As if I couldn't have figured that out on my own. *Pòg mo thòin*, I want to snarl at him. But telling the man who pays me to kiss my erse won't help matters. I also won't tell him I've seen Piper since Montijo, though I didn't catch her.

I accept Hammond's packet. He's arranged for me to stay at a chain hotel that seems nice enough to me, though Hammond undoubtedly thinks sending me there is a punishment. The packet he gave me includes an itinerary that states I will depart this evening via Hammond's 757. That barely gives me enough time to drive home and pack, then hurry back to the airport.

This time, Piper Lang will not get away from me.

Barcelona, Spain
Three Days Later

I park along the street, a block from the location where I expect to find my quarry. This afternoon, I heard from my contact at the Metropolitan Police in London. Thanks to that conversation, and the CCTV footage my contact acquired from the Barcelona police, I know exactly where to find the fugitive. I'd hired a car at the airport, then used the map on my mobile to find the area where the camera footage was taken. Will my quarry still be here? Or was she just passing through?

With Piper Lang, who knows.

Maybe I should worry that I've spent so much time and money on hunting one woman. While the time is mine to burn, the money belongs to Royce Hammond, who seems as anxious to capture Piper as I am. That makes me wonder about his true motives, based on the fact he seems to have no connection to Piper, but I need to concentrate on tracking her right now.

Night has fallen. The shadows help to conceal me, especially since this part of town seems to have fewer streetlights and most businesses have closed for the night. I notice a motel about a block away from the CCTV camera that caught a snapshot of Piper two days ago. On both previous occasions when I'd found her, she was staying at a by-the-hour place.

I jog across the street and walk into the motel office. After a brief conversation with the desk clerk, who speaks just enough English that I don't need to try out my paltry Spanish vocabulary, I learn which room houses a single American woman. I show the clerk a photo of Piper, and he confirms she is the woman residing in Room 8 under the name of Patty Jones.

I also learn the clerk saw her leave the room earlier, heading for a takeaway restaurant two blocks away. She'd asked for directions.

Once again, I end up hiding in a motel room waiting for the lass to return. This time, though, I sit in a chair by the window, beside the door instead of hiding behind it. She left the blinds shut and the nightstand lamp off, so I have plenty of cover. The meager glow of the bathroom light doesn't reach me.

A key chunks in the lock, and the doorknob rotates.

I hold still, barely breathing, the anticipation chasing over my skin like electricity.

The door swings inward. Piper shuffles across the threshold, pushing the door shut with her erse.

She freezes for a moment, then spins toward me.

I surge to my feet and clamp a handcuff around her wrist before she realizes what's happening. Then I haul her over to the bed and toss her onto it. Once I've secured her to the headboard with the other half of the cuffs, I use my belt to bind her ankles the way I had the last time I caught up with her. Maybe I should have cuffed both her wrists, but I doubt she can pick the lock. Am I underestimating the lass? She has gotten away from me multiple times. But no, she won't get out of the cuffs.

Now that I have her secured, I take one step backward. "You're mine, Piper. As soon as you tell me what I need to know, you are flying back to London with me."

She struggles against her bindings and gives me a nasty look. "You bastard."

I lean over the lass to stare into her eyes. "Before I take you back there, I want the answers you never gave me. Tell me how you kept getting away from me."

No, I shouldn't care. But after what Royce Hammond said, I need to know. And she is going to tell me.

Tonight.

Chapter Five

Piper

Magnus stares into my eyes like he thinks he can hypnotize me into confessing all my secrets. Why should I do that? He'll drag me back to England the second I've told him what he wants to know, and I am not that stupid. My power comes from not sharing. If he wants answers from me, I need a promise from him.

I slant toward the jerk, which makes our lips brush against each other. I swear I didn't do that on purpose. "Want to know how I survived on the run? I'll tell you—if you promise to listen to my side of what happened when my boss was murdered."

"Your side means nothing to me."

I lean back against the headboard. "Then I guess you don't really want answers."

He snarls something that must be Gaelic, and it must be sweary words too.

"Tell you what," I say. "Feed me, and I'll answer your first question. But if you want to ask me more things after that, you'll need to give me that promise."

Magnus drills his gaze into mine, and his jaw works like he's grinding his teeth. Then he straightens, his expression abruptly neutral. "I could stand to eat too. I'll ring room service."

I laugh, probably with a little too much enthusiasm. "Are you nuts? This is a by-the-hour motel, not a swanky place. Room service consists of a candy vending machine in the lobby and a maid scrubbing the toilet once a week."

"Fine. You will remain here while I find some food for us."

"Don't forget the key. It's on the nightstand."

He grabs the key and marches out of the room, slamming the door.

Magnus left me here with one hand shackled. Well, I guess the great hunter isn't infallible after all. I have one hand free, which gives me leverage. Only a teeny bit. But yeah, I should be able to do something with the leverage I've got. What, exactly? I need to get out of the other cuff. That's all I know.

Twenty months on the run taught me a thing or two. But I doubt Magnus realizes just how much I've learned.

I slide my legs off the bed. Since the jerk bound my ankles, I don't have much chance of running away—unless I can free my other hand. Then I could undo the belt he strapped around my ankles. One step at a time, that's how I need to do this. With my feet on the floor, I shimmy sideways until I bump into the nightstand, then I use my free hand to hunt for what I need. I could pick up the phone and call for help, but my Spanish is limited to saying hello and ordering food. Making a fuss while I try to communicate with the desk clerk doesn't seem like a good idea.

Okay, I need to think.

I root around in the nightstand, searching for anything I might use to free myself. I find a notepad and a flimsy plastic pen, plus a bible. Yeah, that's super helpful.

Magnus might come back any minute. I can't waste time.

So I hunt around behind and under the nightstand but don't find anything useful. Just lint.

I suddenly realize one important fact. Call it a "duh" moment. Why am I sitting here with my feet bound? I have one hand free, which means I can undo the belt Magnus tied around my ankles. So I do that. Freeing my feet comes with an unexpected bonus. The skinny thingy that hooks into the belt holes is made of metal. Maybe I can use that. I start working on the handcuff with the metal thingy. It's bulkier than what I've used before to pick locks, but it might work. I grimace while I struggle with the cuff, and I'm starting to sweat a little too.

The door swings open, and Magnus strides into the room, kicking the door shut. He holds a paper bag in one hand.

His attention lands on me. "What the bloody hell do you think you're doing?"

Oh, shit. How did he get food so fast? I thought it would take him a lot longer.

The jerk tosses the bag onto the table. "Are ye wanting me to take you back to the UK right now?"

"No. Please don't do that."

"You disobeyed me. Freeing your feet is one thing. But picking your cuffs? That's not acceptable."

"Actually, I didn't disobey anything. You never told me not to try to get out of these cuffs."

He points at the bag of food. "Are ye not wanting to eat, then? I don't feed fugitives who circumvent my orders."

"Get over yourself, MacTaggart." I can smell the food—burgers and fries, I bet—and it's making my mouth water. Yes, I want and need to eat. But I won't tell him that. "If you starve me, I'll be too weak to answer your question."

"After this, you'll be needing to answer more than one question to get the food."

Damn that man. I hope he gets bitten by a poisonous snake. Oh, wait. That would mean he bit himself.

But once again, I have no choice. "Okay, I'll tell you what you want to know. One answer, then you let me eat."

"After that, you will answer all my questions."

Yeah, he can think that all he wants. As long as I don't say yes or no, he can't claim I owe him information. The issue is up in the air, floating above our heads, waiting for a chance to smack him in the face.

Magnus walks to the bed and reclaims his belt, which I had dropped when he entered the room. Then he sinks onto the chair by the table. "Tell me how you managed to pay for your life on the run."

I've paid for it more than he could possibly imagine. "As soon as I realized someone was framing me, I emptied my bank account. Got cash. It was enough to keep me going for a while, but I've had to find, um, creative ways to beef up my funds."

"Such as what?"

"Selling my clothes, my jewelry, everything I'd been able to stuff into my bags before I left my flat in London. When that was gone, I took off-the-books jobs doing whatever I had to do to survive."

"Does 'off the books' include criminal activity?"

"No, of course not. I want to prove my innocence. Don't you think becoming a criminal would negate that?"

He grunts. "You *are* a criminal. A murderer, in fact."

"Excuse me? That is not a fact. I'm accused of murder, but I haven't been convicted."

"Because you ran away. Being a fugitive is a crime."

"You called me a murderer, not a fugitive."

Magnus rises and stalks up to me, bending from the waist to glare into my eyes. "Donnae care if you murdered your boss or not."

"Then why call me a murderer? You clearly assume I'm guilty."

"Whether you are or not doesnae matter to me."

Yeah, he keeps saying that. But he acts like he does care and he assumes I'm guilty. The man has a weird fixation with the fact I'm accused of murdering my boss. He seems to be obsessed with me, or at least with the crime I've been accused of committing.

He glances at chest—my boobs, of course—then returns his attention to my face. "How do you keep getting away from me?"

Oh, so that's his problem. How dare a woman outwit the great Magnus MacTaggart. Not sure if anyone else would call him "the great," but I'm sure he thinks of himself that way. The unstoppable bounty hunter. The infallible, scruffy, incredibly hot bastard.

"Guess your tracking skills aren't as amazing as you think," I say. "A lowly archivist managed to steer clear of you for twenty months. What does that say about you, hey?"

His lips peel back from his gritted teeth when he speaks. "It says only that you are a conniving con artist and murderer who has undoubtedly wormed her way into a criminal syndicate."

"A syndicate?" I can't help laughing because what he said is ridiculous. "Now I'm the mastermind of a nefarious mafia run by museum employees. That's probably what you think. Jeez, you are one paranoid, conspiracy loving jackass. Let me guess. You think the curator of the Smithsonian shot JFK, not Lee Harvey Oswald."

"Haud yer wheesht," he hisses.

"What?"

"It means shut up."

Well, if he wants me to shut up, I will accommodate him. After all, I can't answer his dumb questions when he just ordered me not to speak.

I make a zipper motion across my closed lips.

He squints at me. "Tell me how you—"

Shaking my head, I point at my zipper-sealed lips.

"What the bloody hell are you doing?" he demands. "You are going to answer my questions."

I grab the pen and notepad from the nightstand and scrawl a note: *You told me to shut up.* Then I hand him the little piece of paper.

Magnus reads the note. He stares blankly at it for moment, then lets out a feral snarl. Crumpling the paper, he hurls it across the room, where it lands on the opposite side of the bed. The jerk growls a string of unintelligible words that must be more Gaelic curses.

He stomps over to the chair and drops onto it so hard that it jumps backward an inch or two. "You can speak."

"Thank you so much. Caught by your own nastiness, weren't you?"

"But you knew I didn't mean you shouldn't answer my questions."

"Yeah, I did. You needed to get knocked down a few pegs, though."

He just sits there studying me, his expression inscrutable, for so long that I start to wonder if he's a robot and I broke all his circuits with my defiance. I will never succumb to that man. If he wants to take me back to England so I can stand trial, I will fight him every step of the way. Maybe I used to be a mild-mannered archivist, but now I have become a fighter.

I doubt Magnus gets that. He's a sexist jackass, I'm sure.

He tosses the bag of food to me. "Maybe I did bring that on myself."

Wow, he just admitted he's not perfect. That's what I heard, anyway. I listened between the lines.

I open the bag. "Two hamburgers? One must be for you."

"Aye."

Once I've pulled out the hamburgers and two containers of french fries, I look at him. "I could throw you a burger, but not fries. You'll have to come get the food yourself."

Magnus approaches the bed and sits down beside me. He takes a package of fries.

I grab the last two items in the bag—two cups of coffee, housed in a cardboard holder—and offer one cup to him. It has letters printed on its lid in marker.

"That's yours," he says, taking the other cup out of the bag. "This one's mine."

God, the coffee smells so good. I need caffeine. When I take a sip, I realize something. "You got me a caramel macchiato?"

"Aye. It's your favorite."

I gape at him. Seriously, I do. My jaw drops, and I stop blinking, my eyes wide. "How do you know what kind of coffee I like?"

He sips his drink. "I learned everything about you. A good hunter always understands his prey before he tries to capture them."

Maybe I should be offended that he called me prey, but I don't care. Back in the UK, everybody thinks I'm a vicious bitch who seduced and killed my boss in cold blood so I could get his job. "Prey" is probably the nicest thing I've been called in a long time.

"But I still don't understand," I say. "Who told you my favorite coffee is caramel macchiato?"

"No one told me." He takes a huge bite of his hamburger and devours it before he explains. "I searched your flat. There were two empty cups in the rubbish bin. When I sniffed them, I could tell they had both contained caramel macchiato. My sense of smell is legendary."

"Oh, please. You expect me to believe you're famous for being able to sniff out caramel flavored coffee. It's hardly a superpower. If I sniffed you, I bet I could tell a lot of things about your habits."

"Go on, then. Sniff me."

I walked right into that one, didn't I? "No thanks. I'd rather eat."

We both start eating and don't speak while we consume our burgers, fries, and coffee. I'd been hungrier than I realized, and I think I could've eaten his burger too. A fried apple pie would've been awesome. Actually, I would kill for a crate of those right now.

Not literally. I don't murder people.

Magnus dumps our garbage in the trash can under the nightstand and returns to his chair. "Where did you learn to pick locks?"

Oh, what the hell. Can't hurt to tell him.

"I learned that from a French cat burglar," I say. "Not long after I got away from you the first time, I bumped into Oscar Thibault on the streets of Limoges. He was charming and sexy, and we had lots of fun together. When I told him about my, um, problem, he offered to teach me how to pick a lock."

"You fucked him so he'd teach you that."

"No. I slept with him only after he taught me lock-picking. I liked him a lot."

"Why didn't you stay with the ruddy frog?"

"Don't you know it's rude to call a Frenchman a frog?"

Magnus grunts.

"I'll answer your question anyway," I tell him. "Oscar got caught breaking into an heiress's château. He's currently serving a prison sentence."

The Scot chuckles.

Chapter Six

Magnus

That's what ye get for having a poke with a frog." Aye, I know that's a nasty insult, and I have nothing against Frenchmen. But the thought of Piper sleeping with another man makes me… No, I'm not jealous. What am I, then? Disgusted. Aye, that's it. I'm disgusted that anyone would have a poke with her. That includes me. I should never have done it the first time, much less the second time, and it will never happen again.

"Poke?" she says. "I assume that means sex."

"That's right. Any woman who sleeps with a frog and a Sassenach gets what she deserves." I lean toward her. "A Sassenach is an Englishman. I was referring to Archer Caldwell. I've read everything about your case, and I know ye shagged him."

"You are the rudest, most obnoxious, vilest, meanest, ugliest cretin I've ever met."

"Am I?" I lean forward, elbows on my knees, and speak in a deeper, rougher tone. "You seem to like rude, obnoxious, vile, mean, ugly cretins. Ye shagged me twice."

"Yes, we had sex twice. You started it both times."

"No. *You* seduced *me* back in London."

"Aren't you supposed to be bulletproof? Immune to my seduction? Not much of a bounty hunter, are you, if I could trip you up just by suggesting we get it on."

Maybe she makes a valid point. And maybe I have been off my game a wee bit lately. Hunting Piper has become the sole focus of my life. Though I still take other jobs for paying clients, I capture the blokes in question without much trouble. None have escaped from the UK. I've pursued only one woman in my entire career, and she has become the only fugitive ever to get away from me once, much less over and over. How does she do it? Piper still hasn't explained that. I caught her scent, so to speak, last year in France. But I never got a glimpse of her. The lass does leave breadcrumbs, though she's clearly unaware of that fact. I'd gotten close enough to look her in the eye multiple times in other locations, but she always slips away.

Did she love that Frenchman? I shouldn't care. I don't care, and it makes no difference to me.

So naturally, I ask, "Were you in love with Oscar?"

"None of your business."

I shouldn't have asked, but my obsession with the lass pushes me to discover everything about her. Not because I care for Piper. I hardly know the woman. But somehow she has put a spell on me, capturing my soul to turn me into an obsessed eejit.

"Your lover does not interest me," I say. "Tell me how you've stayed one step ahead of me for twenty months."

"If Oscar doesn't interest you, why did you ask if I loved him?"

Though I know glaring at her won't help, I do it anyway. Cannae stop myself. And my curiosity gets the better of me. "How many lovers have you had since you became a fugitive?"

"Forget it. I'm not discussing my sex life with you, unless you feel like sharing the details about your lovers."

"I fuck strangers. There's nothing to tell."

"You're an antisocial loner. Big surprise."

"So are you." I grip the arms of my chair, though I donnae mean to do it. "I know more about you than you think."

"What do you mean? Were you spying on me before I got arrested?"

"Ahmno a private investigator. No one hires me unless an accused criminal jumps bail or runs before they can be arrested. That's what you did."

She eyes me with a strange expression, seeming almost curious. "How much do you think you know about me? My trash isn't that informative."

"I read your diary."

"You did what? That's a horrible invasion of privacy."

"Fugitives donnae have privacy." I relax into my chair, feeling oddly better now that I've shattered her belief that I know nothing about her. "I also read every file in your office at the Fernsby Museum as well as the transcript of your interview with the Met, and I searched all the government records related to you."

"Whuh—How can that be legal?"

"Because I am a bounty hunter. People hire me because I have access to private information and can dig into my quarry's personal matters without a warrant."

"Quarry? I'm not a rabbit."

No, she is not. But I will hunt her to the ends of the earth.

"Why are you so determined to take me in?" she asks. "Are you that hard up for work?"

Should I lie or refuse to answer? No, I think the better tactic is to tell the truth. "My client offered me an obscene amount of money to find you."

"Who is your client?"

"Cannae tell you that. It's confidential."

"I have a right to know who wants me locked up."

"No, ye don't." I stand up and peer through the gap in the curtains to check the vicinity. It's a longtime habit. I don't even think about what I'm doing anymore because watchfulness has become second nature. When I face Piper, she still sits there on the edge of the bed, one hand shackled to the headboard, and seems to be waiting for my response. "You have no rights. A fugitive gives up all of that when they go on the run. Whatever interest my client has in seeing you tried for the crime you're accused of committing has nothing to do with me."

"You can't honestly believe I have no rights."

"As far as my job is concerned, you don't. I will do whatever it takes to get you back to the Met." I approach her and bend down to meet her gaze. "Make it easier on yourself. Give up."

"Like hell I will."

I straighten. "We're leaving now. A jet is waiting for us at the airport."

"Jet? You must make a lot of money off the suffering of innocent people."

"I have never hunted an innocent person. They're always guilty."

"Even the mighty Magnus MacTaggart can be wrong."

I unhook the cuffs and secure them again behind her back, with both hands shackled this time. I press my mouth to her ear. "You're caught, Piper. Give up the fight. Ye cannae seduce me again, which means you have no tricks left to try on me."

"Do I at least get to know how you found me this time?"

"No."

I gather all her things, including the toiletries, and set her sole bag on the floor beside the door. "You will come with me willingly. Making a scene won't help, but it will draw the attention of the local authorities. Do you understand?"

She nods.

Fortunately, I parked my car two spaces down from the door to this room. That means I can carry her bag to the vehicle and stow it in the trunk quickly enough that she doesn't have time to try anything. Maybe she's given up. I donnae care. She shuffles her feet as I escort her to the car and gesture for her to climb into the passenger seat.

"If you behave," I tell her, "then I will cuff your hands in front. But you need to earn that privilege."

"You are so—Ugh. Never mind."

She climbs into the car.

I shut the door and get in on the driver's side. As the engine revs up, I try to focus on the plan I had devised before I located Piper and took her into my custody. Aye, I did have a plan. Drive to the airport. Fly back to England. Hand her over to the authorities. Then I can go home, for whatever that's worth.

My mobile chimes. I have a new text.

Checking the message, I see it's from my cousin Kirsty. Callum and Kate have set a date for their wedding. Will you be there?

Not sure, I type. Busy with work.

Please try. Callum wants you there.

He's my cousin too, and aye, at Kirsty's wedding Callum invited me to be there when he marries his American fiancée. He invited me to their engagement ceilidh too.

Say yes, Kirsty admonishes.

I give in and tell her, *Maybe is the best I can do.*

Kirsty responds with an emoji of a grinning face.

She is an adult, a mature business owner, but sometimes she acts like an excited teenager. I love her, though. No one could dislike the sweet lass, and I've always had a soft spot for her. I don't see Kirsty that often, since my job keeps me busy and I know I'm not welcome at home by most of my family. But I always look forward to seeing the lass whenever I do go home, and I also don't mind seeing her brother and the small group of other cousins who aren't afraid of me.

Aye, I make everyone uncomfortable. But only one person refuses to speak to me—except when he called me a plague at Kirsty's wedding reception. Maybe my father is the real reason I rarely go home.

See you soon, Kirsty types. Emojis of hugs and kisses punctuate her message.

I tuck my mobile back into my pocket.

Piper leans toward me, squinting like she's studying my face. "Are you almost smiling? I think I saw your lips twitch up the teeniest bit for half a second."

I might have smiled, briefly, but I will not admit that to Piper. "You're daft."

"Calling me crazy? Sounds like you're defensive. Almost smiling embarrasses you."

"Nothing embarrasses me."

She opens her mouth, and I know she wants to tell me what a flaming ersehole I am, but I gun the engine and swerve backward out of the parking space, the noise drowning out anything she might've wanted to say.

I navigate the streets of Barcelona on the way toward the airport. Fortunately, Piper stays quiet and focuses on the scenery outside her window instead of harassing me. I donnae care that the scenery consists of a highway and trees with clusters of buildings breaking up the greenery until we reach the airport. As we navigate the enormous complex of buildings, we get the occasional glimpse of a sliver of the ocean.

"Hey, wait," Piper says, vaguely gesturing toward who knows what. "I want to see that."

"See what?"

"The ocean. Drive over there. I want to see the ocean before you drag me off to my doom."

"You are not getting out of this car until we're on the tarmac."

She puckers her lips. "All you have to do is drive past the water so I can see it. My last glimpse of freedom before I go to prison forever. Please."

"No."

"I'll harass you for the whole plane ride back to England unless you show me the ocean. Five minutes, that's all I'm asking for."

Aye, I have no doubts she will make the journey home a miserable experience. Cannae hurt to drive past the ocean, strictly to shut her up.

I bypass the airport and head straight for a road that seems to skirt the water. As the road curves to the right, the view comes into, ah, view. Piper sits up straighter and leans forward to crane her neck, determined to see the ocean. Her excitement makes her look younger and bonnier, not at all like the fugitive who seduced me and has evaded me for so long.

Not anymore. I have her at last.

A tingle sweeps over my skin. I cannae be excited to have Piper in custody. It's ridiculous. I must've gotten a sudden, brief chill. Then again, I have hunted this woman for a long bloody time, so a wee bit of excitement wouldn't be unprecedented.

"Look," she says. "Palm trees. And a beach. I'd love to sink my toes into the sand."

I can't let her do that, so I turn the car around and drive back toward the airport.

Piper keeps craning her neck, to look out the back window this time, as if she cannae make herself give up the view yet. But finally, she faces forward. "I wish I could've walked on the beach."

"You could have visited a beach whenever you liked. Haven't you lived in this city for some time?"

"Six weeks. But I didn't go sightseeing, and I never saw the ocean when I got here because I came from the north."

"How much of Barcelona did you see?"

"Only the streets I drove down to get here and the area immediately around the motel." She freezes, then slowly turns her head toward me. "My car. It cost money, and now it's abandoned at the motel thanks to you."

"You have worse problems than the loss of your vehicle." I swerve onto another street, and the momentum throws her sideways. "You are an accused murderer. Worry about that for a while."

"I worry about it every second of every day. I dream about getting caught and going to prison and never being able to prove I'm innocent."

She dreams about it? I shift in my seat, suddenly uncomfortable—because of the lack of sufficient cushioning, not because I feel bad for her. "You deserve to have nightmares."

Piper falls silent, though she keeps watching me.

I swear I can feel her attention focused on me like the tickle of a feather on my skin. "What do you want now?"

"Let's make a deal. I will not try to escape if you listen to my story."

"What story?"

"How my boss died and what part I played in the events before and after that."

I grunt. "It's a fairy story, then."

"Will you listen or not?"

"Since ye willnae get away again, I donnae need to listen to anything you say."

"Maybe you should listen just so you can tell me it's bullshit. If you hear me out, I promise not to talk about it anymore. I'll do whatever you say—after you hear me out."

I grip the steering wheel harder, my attention riveted to the road ahead, and consider her offer. The chance to make her stop pestering me and instead do whatever I say? That's too good to pass up. But I don't know if I can trust the lass to keep her word. It can't hurt to agree to her suggestion. And I will have control over her. She'll do anything I tell her to do.

Another tingle sweeps over me. The thought of having her under my control… Aye, it's making my cock stiffen.

I take a deep breath and make my decision. "We have a deal."

Chapter Seven

Piper

Magnus accepted my deal. He's going to listen and let me explain what really happened. Whether he will ever believe me, I don't know. The man is stubborn and heartless, and I can't imagine him feeling any emotions other than anger. Of course, I'm biased by the fact he has hunted me for twenty months, ruthless in his determination to capture me.

I've always wondered why he chose me as his number one target. Magnus must have worse fugitives to track, but he aimed all his hatred at me instead of drug dealers and child murderers and all sorts of other people who committed truly heinous crimes. I haven't even been convicted.

So why me?

That question will have to wait. First, I need to tell my story and hope I can convince him I don't belong in prison. I won't live to see that happen, anyway, because the real killer is out there somewhere and will never let me stay alive.

The obnoxious Scot pulls over so he can move the cuffs to shackle my hands in front of my body instead of behind me. We don't speak again until we get to the airport. As private jet passengers, we get to avoid security and head straight for the plane. When I see the jet, I halt and stare at it.

Magnus gives me a little shove. "Move. Now."

"Who owns that jet? It looks like a commercial airliner without the company logo on it."

"It's a Boeing 757. And it is privately owned, by the man who hired me to find you." He gives me another shove. "Get moving."

A super rich man wanted Magnus to bring me in. Why am I that important? It doesn't make sense. But I follow Magnus up the steps and into the gigantic jet. Why two people need an airliner to take us to the UK, I don't know. A plain old private jet, the kind that costs millions instead of hundreds of millions, would've done just fine.

Once we're inside the plane, Magnus directs me to sit on a sofa that backs up to the windows. He stands between the sofa and the coffee table, right in front of me. Arms barred over his massive chest, he stares at me with that steely expression I've gotten to know too well.

A pilot comes out to close the door. He nods to Magnus, then returns to the cockpit. A few minutes later, I hear the jet engines ramping up, their whine getting louder and louder.

Magnus keeps staring at me.

My skin itches like I've got invisible ants crawling all over me, but I know that's just nerves.

As the jet starts to roll down the runway, Magnus sits down on the coffee table. And he keeps staring at me. I know he likes to try to intimidate me, so I won't let him succeed. I turn sideways to lean against the sofa's back and gaze out the window, watching the tarmac zoom by faster every second as the jet heads toward takeoff. When the wheels lift off the runway, I watch Barcelona race by beneath us and eventually disappear from view.

"You have approximately two and a half hours to tell your story," Magnus says. "Best get started."

I face him, absently rubbing my wrists.

He glances at my hands, and I swear he winces the tiniest bit. Then he removes the handcuffs.

"Thank you," I say. "Not worried I'll try to jump out of the plane, huh?"

"You aren't that insane."

"Gee, thanks for the ringing endorsement."

"Donnae waste your breath on sarcasm. Tell your story."

"Okay." I tuck my feet under me cross-legged and clasp my hands on my lap. "I admit I made a lot of mistakes, but I did not kill Archer Caldwell. Yeah, okay, I slept with him—once. We'd gone to a fund-raising gala for the Hugo Wyatt Fernsby Museum of History, where Archer and I both worked. We went as a couple because neither of us wanted to go alone. I drank a little too much. We both did. Then he asked me to spend the night with him, and I said yes."

"Just like that? Well, ye did fuck me twice. And I didnae even take you to a posh party."

I want to lash out at him for implying I'm a slut, but that won't help anything. So I take a breath and exhale it slowly, letting the anger sift out of me. "I'd been working with Archer for two years. We weren't exactly friends, but we got along well at work. He was also attractive, sexy, and charming. Smart too."

"He also dressed posh." A muscle ticks in his jaw. "I saw pictures of him."

Is Magnus jealous of Archer? If so, I have no idea if that's because Archer was "posh" or if it's because Magnus doesn't like that I slept with someone other than him. No, he can't care about that. He hates me, though he has no problem with screwing me. I have no problem with that either, though I wish I had the self-control to tell him to go to hell instead of practically begging him to take me.

Why can't I resist that damn Scot?

"Yes, Archer dressed well," I say. "We exchanged some flirty banter once in a while before that night. I liked him, but we only had sex the one time. Things got kind of awkward between us after that. I'm sure that's why the cops thought our relationship was suspicious. My co-workers, the people I'd thought of as friends or at least friendly acquaintances, told the police all sorts of stuff about how I seemed nervous in the days leading up to the murder."

Magnus stares at me with the same steely expression he'd worn earlier, the inscrutable facade I can't read.

Whether he believes me or not, it's time I told him everything.

Twenty-One Months Ago

I exit the elevator onto the tenth floor of the high-rise where my boss lives. Maybe I should have said no when Archer asked me to come to his flat, but he swore he just wants to talk and clear the air between us. Our one-night stand has created a lot of tension and awkwardness, and I hope talking it out with him will make things better at work.

At his door, I pause to collect myself. Jeez, I haven't felt this nervous since the day I interviewed for the archivist position at the museum. But I steel my nerves and just do it.

I ring the doorbell.

The door opens a moment later, and Archer nods, not quite smiling. "Good evening, Piper. Thank you for coming."

He steps aside, waving for me to go inside. Then he leads me into the living room that has a stunning view of the River Thames and the gigantic Ferris wheel known as the London Eye. Even at night, the view is breathtaking. Archer invites me to sit on the sofa while he drops onto an armchair across from me. He rests his elbows on his knees and gazes at the floor.

After a moment, he lifts his head to look at me. "The night I spent with you was the best thing that's ever happened to me. I'd love to keep seeing you, but I won't be working at the Fernsby anymore. I plan to hand in my resignation tomorrow."

"What? I thought you loved the museum."

"I do. But, well, I can't stay there anymore." He shifts in his chair as if he can't get comfortable and almost winces. "I want more time with you. But I have to leave London, have to leave the country, as soon as possible. I'll be moving somewhere far away, not sure exactly where yet, possibly an island in the middle of the Pacific Ocean. I've always dreamed of doing that. I need you, Piper. Will you come with me?"

"For the weekend?"

"No. Forever."

Archer had been giving me little signals lately that he wanted more, things I noticed because I pay attention to other people's tells. I always have. That's just the kind of person I am, though my hyperawareness doesn't grant me any special ability to know when things might go sideways. Men often stun me with their abrupt attitude shifts. But Archer has done more than surprise me. I'm so shocked I don't know how to respond. I can only stare at him.

"I've overstepped, haven't I?" Archer says. "Sorry. It's just that I've had these feelings for you for quite a while, and after that night, I thought—hoped that something had changed for both of us."

"Nothing has changed for me. I'm sorry, Archer. I really do like you, but not the way you want. Certainly not enough to move to a desert island with you."

He bows his head. "I understand. Had to try, didn't I?"

God, I feel horrible for rejecting him. I should never have slept with Archer, but I can't undo that mistake. Did he really think I'd run away with him on a moment's notice? This whole conversation has been bizarre.

Archer straightens and gives me a tight smile. "Let's forget about what I said. I do have another reason for asking you to come here. It's brilliant news. We've secured the Assyrian exhibition. The museum in Ankara will loan us a significant number of items from their Assyrian collection for a three-month run."

"Wow. That's amazing."

"Yes, it is." He doesn't look thrilled, but I guess the way I rejected his desert-island proposal has dampened his mood. "We should celebrate. This is your achievement, after all. You spearheaded the campaign to bring this exhibition to the Fernsby. I have some champagne chilling, and I think we should drink to your success and the good fortune of our whole institution."

Archer hurries out of the living room, disappearing into what I assume is the kitchen. Did he buy champagne because he thought I'd become his girlfriend tonight and run away with him? Just the thought that he might have makes me feel awful. I hadn't meant to lead him on.

He returns to the living room carrying a silver bucket filled with ice that holds a bottle of champagne as well as two glass flutes. Archer sets all of that on the coffee table between us, then plucks the bottle out of the bucket and pops the cork. While he pours the bubbly into the two flutes, I clasp my hands and try not to wring them. Though I'd rather go home, now, I don't want to offend Archer—especially after I rejected his romantic gesture.

I accept the flute he offers me and take a dainty sip.

"Here's to you," he says, tipping his flute toward me. "You deserve to become the next director of the museum."

"Director? But I—This is all very sudden."

"I know. But I will recommend you for the position. I'm sure the board will agree."

He's only forty-three, so I can't figure out why he would give up his entire life this way. Now he wants me to take over his job.

I set my glass down on the table. "I'm so confused, Archer. Why do you need to leave? Everybody loves working with you, and you're a great director."

He bows his head again, scratching the back of his neck. "There are things you don't know about, things I wouldn't want you to know because it might put you in a precarious position. Please accept that I'm leaving for good reason, to protect all my employees, but particularly you."

"I don't understand. What's going on?"

"Let's forget about all of that rubbish and toast to your success." He thrusts his flute toward me but bumps his knee into the table, making the flute slip out of his grasp. It thunks down, spewing champagne across the shiny wood surface. "Bollocks. I should clean that up."

He rushes into the kitchen, returning seconds later with a dish towel in his hand. As he wipes up the champagne, his flute rolls across the smooth surface and dumps the remainder of its contents onto my shoes as the glass falls off the table's edge. "Bloody hell. I'm sorry, Piper, so sorry."

"It's okay, really." I pick up the flute and set it on the now-dry tabletop. "Mind if I go into the bathroom to clean my shoes?"

"Of course. And I am so terribly sorry." He pours himself another glass of champagne.

"You can stop apologizing now. It was an accident."

I hurry into the bathroom and dry my shoes off as best I can. While I'm doing that, I hear the doorbell ring. Then two voices start speaking, softly at first but gradually escalating. Though I can't hear what they say, I can tell Archer and the visitor, who might be male or female, are now having an argument, based on their tone of voice. Should I go out there? Or stay here until the argument ends? I have no idea what the etiquette of a situation like this is.

The door slams.

I open the bathroom door a sliver, just enough to peek out into the living room. Archer seems to be alone now. So I walk back out there. The scent of warm, woodsy cologne wafts in the air, diminishing quickly.

Archer stands in front of the chair he'd sat in earlier, looking rather pale.

"Are you okay?" I ask.

"Fine, yes." He snatches his glass off the table and guzzles it. "But you should go. I apologize for the ruckus."

"No problem." I study him, wondering if I should say anything else, but I decide it's not my business. "Well, good night, Archer."

"Good night, Piper."

I walk out of his flat—and never see him alive again.

Chapter Eight

Magnus

Why should I believe your story?" I ask. "You admit to having an affair with Archer Caldwell and to being in his flat on the night he died. I've read every bit of information about your case, and I understand how strychnine poisoning works. You didn't need to be there when he died to have killed him. All you had to do was drop some strychnine into his champagne glass and walk out the door. You could've been long gone before the poison kicked in."

"Anyone could have put the poison in his glass. It wasn't me."

"Only your fingerprints were found on the champagne flute."

"Because I touched both the flutes. His fell on my shoes, and duh, I got my prints on it when I picked the thing up."

"Your hairs were found in his bed."

She lets out a frustrated growl. "Because I had sex with him the week before. I guess he's a typical guy who doesn't wash his sheets very often."

"He had traces of your lipstick on his shirt collar."

"I have no idea how that happened. But I left my purse in the living room when I went to bathroom, so it's possible the real killer found my lipstick and somehow put traces of it on Archer's shirt. It's a common color, anyway. Or maybe somebody doctored the evidence after the fact." She narrows her gaze and flattens her lips. "Isn't lipstick on a man's collar a total cliche? I would've thought cops wouldn't fall for that, much less the great Magnus MacTaggart."

She calls me "the great" whenever she wants to fash me. The lass is transparent in many ways, but she hides much more, that's for certain.

"Now you claim the police were in on the crime," I say. "That's bollocks."

She rolls her eyes. "Yeah, because there are never any crooked cops. I wouldn't even know how to get strychnine or how much to use. But you probably think I went to Poisons 'R Us and got advice from the resident strychnine expert."

"No, I donnae think that. But I know you are clever and resourceful. You evaded me for seventeen months and then another three months, and no other fugitive has ever done that."

"Woo-hoo, I hold the world's record for hiding from you. Did anybody alert Guinness? I'm sure they want to put my mug shot in their book."

I slant toward her to look straight into her eyes. "Your story has enough holes in it to qualify as a golf course."

"Oh please. You're not going to believe me no matter what evidence I provide because you want me to be guilty. You're a misogynist."

Why does she insist on calling me names? I grasp her chin. "On the contrary. I love women, just not you."

"But you screwed me twice." She shakes her head free of my grip. "Do you always fuck women you despise?"

No, I have never done that—except with her. I cannae explain why Piper drives me to the edge of sanity and the only way to regain my self-control is to shag her. Maybe I feel a sort of kindred connection with her, but that's rubbish. I have nothing in common with the lass. She's a fugitive, and I'm a bounty hunter. We are enemies.

I rise and stalk over to the nearest chair, then crash onto it.

"Are you pouting?" she asks. "Or thinking about my story so you can come up with a lame-ass debunking theory? Probably both."

"Haud yer wheesht."

She laughs with enough sarcasm that I swear I feel it dripping down my nerves. "That's the best comeback you can muster? Well, I guess wit isn't in your wheelhouse. You're nothing but a brute who loves to kick people when they're down."

I want to snarl at her, but that would be giving her what she wants. Instead, I prop my feet on the chair across from me, lay my hands on my lap, and shut my eyes.

"Taking a nap, huh? Great strategy, MacTaggart. You might wake up to find I've seduced the pilots and convinced them to tie you up and let me escape. After all, I'm a witch who casts lust spells over men."

Aye, she does that to me. But she's not a witch. My cousin Kirsty is a Wiccan, so I never use the word witch as an insult.

Piper finally stops talking.

That woman is going to drive me barking mad. I've dealt with all sorts of criminals, but none as vexing as Piper Lang. Do I believe her story? Not yet. Maybe I never will, but certain aspects of her tale make me wonder if she might be telling the truth. Proving her innocence is not my job. I will take her to the authorities and walk away.

I try to sleep, but my mind keeps replaying Piper's words. Her voice echoes in my ears. *You're not going to believe me no matter what evidence I provide because you want me to be guilty.* Maybe I do, or maybe something else biases my opinion of her. No idea what it is. The lass torments me with her sarcasm, arouses me with her body, and triggers a growing sense of unease in me. Have I misjudged her?

That's not my problem. Catch the villains, don't converse with them. I've always stuck to that rule—until now.

Piper said Caldwell poured champagne into two glasses, then gave one to her. If I believe that, it means the champagne was poisoned either while she was in the bathroom or after she left. The argument she overheard suggests the killer laced Caldwell's drink during that time rather than after she left, and that's what the police believed happened. But I need to double check the information from the Met as well as Piper's original statement. Luckily, my cousin Evan created a private online database for me that includes digitized copies of all the relevant information for every case. The more I know, the better prepared I am to track my quarry.

I log in using my mobile phone and navigate to the collection of documents related to Piper. Her official statement matches what she just told me. That doesn't prove she's telling the truth. Next, I reread the reports compiled by the detectives at the Met, but it's exactly the way I remembered it. Trace evidence was found including fingerprints, which Piper never denied were hers.

Who was the mysterious visitor?

No one but Piper claimed someone else had entered the flat. The police couldn't find any witnesses who saw another man—or woman. Since Caldwell's flat lay at the end of the hall right next to the stairwell, anyone could have sneaked in and out without being seen. Most residents took the lift rather than coming and going via the stairwell, which opens into the car park. The murder happened at night, so it would've been hard for a witness to identify the mystery person even if they'd been seen.

Am I actually starting to believe her? Piper might be seducing me in a different way now, convincing me to believe her story by looking anxious while she related the supposed events of that night. The only fact that cannot be refuted is that Archer Caldwell was poisoned using strychnine.

I've wondered since the day my newest client hired me why he needs to find Piper so badly. The bloke offered me far more money than anyone else ever had, which made me suspicious. But my research into him assured me the man is indeed a billionaire who can afford to pay higher than the going rate. No amount of research helped me figure out why he's determined to have Piper brought back to the UK. He seems to have no connection to the museum, Caldwell, or Piper.

Mhac na galla. I shouldn't care why the man wants to see her punished. I shouldn't care if her story is true or not. I hunt fugitives, that's all. I've never cared whether they were innocent or guilty.

So why am I wondering about that now?

The most important part of my job involves listening to my instincts. If I'm having doubts, there must be a reason. Taking Piper back to London will result in the authorities locking her up again, and that will make it more difficult for me to unravel the mystery. I need to keep her with me until I find the answers to all my questions.

Piper is sleeping on the sofa, so I sneak up to the cockpit and ask the pilots to drop us off in Limoges. Aye, I've chosen the city where Piper met that French laddie who romanced her. I have not chosen Limoges because I'm jealous of her relationship with Oscar Thibault. I don't know Piper, therefore I cannae be jealous. But I had to think of a destination, and Limoges sprang to mind. It seems like as good a place as any to begin the hunt for the truth.

I've probably spent too much time with my honorable cousins. They've rubbed off on me. Aye, I'll blame them for the quest I mean to undertake. It certainly has nothing to do with Piper.

The pilots balk at my request. They worry their employer will be angry when he learns I talked them into taking a detour. But a stack of euros changes their minds. I always carry extra cash in the appropriate currency with me wherever I go. Aye, my client will be annoyed—but with me, not the pilots. I told them to claim I held a gun to their heads.

I'm exactly the sort anyone would believe might do something like that.

We've just touched down at Limoges when Piper rouses from her nap. The lass must have been exhausted. Life as a fugitive must be nerve-racking. In my own way, I am a fugitive too—from my family—so I know how much that life can drain a person.

Piper glances out the window as the jet taxis down the runway, about to park on the tarmac. "Where are we? That doesn't look like London."

"We're in Limoges."

She jerks her head to stare at me. "Limoges? Why?"

"Thought you might want to catch up with your true love."

"My what?" She pushes up off the sofa and plants her hands on her hips. "Did you really bring me here because of Oscar? I don't need to see him. He's in prison."

"You must want to see him, even if you don't need to."

"No, I don't want that. Why are you obsessed with Oscar?"

That's a good question. Rather than answering it, I grab her suitcase and mine, then head for the jet's door. One of the pilots has just opened it for us. I glance back at Piper. "Hurry up. Or do I need to restrain you again?"

She gives me a mulish look but hurries after me while I stomp down the stairs and onto the tarmac. Piper follows me. She doesn't try to run away, though she could since I haven't cuffed her wrists again. For whatever reason, she comes with me as we bypass airport security to head straight for a car hire agency. I secure us a vehicle—a nondescript four-door model—and stash our belongings in the trunk.

"Where are we going now?" she asks.

"Donnae know yet."

"That's comforting. The great hunter has no clue what he's doing."

"Get in the car."

I jump in behind the wheel, slamming the door hard enough that the vehicle shimmies.

Piper climbs into the passenger seat.

Maybe I rev the engine a wee bit more than is necessary, and maybe I veer onto the street too hard, making Piper yelp and slap her hands on the dashboard. Thoughts of that French erse keep tormenting me. I feel a strange possessiveness toward Piper—her body, not the woman herself. That's the only reason why I donnae want to think about her fucking someone else.

"Where did you live while you were in Limoges?" I ask.

"In a tiny apartment."

"Tell me how to find it."

"Why? Someone else lives there now, I'm sure."

I swerve around a corner, having no bloody clue where I'm going. "Just tell me the address. I want to see your apartment."

She huffs but gives me the address.

Ten minutes later, I park the car along the street in front of the apartment building. It's a small, two-story structure that probably dates back to the nineteen twenties, but I'm not an expert on French architecture. Piper tells me she lived on the second floor, so we sneak inside and climb the stairs.

"Right there," she says, pointing to a doorway.

I approach the door and try the knob, but of course, it doesn't open. Pulling out my lock-picking kit, I work on the lock until it pops open. Then I shove the door inward and wave for her to enter the apartment. "Fugitives first."

Piper rolls her eyes but walks inside.

And I shut the door behind us. "Does it look the way you remember?"

"Yes and no. Somebody else's stuff is all over the place." She rounds on me. "Why are we here? This has nothing to do with the murder."

I have no answer to that question. Piper once lived here, and I needed to see the place. My obsession with knowing everything about her has intensified now that I have her in my custody, and I suppose that explains my somewhat irrational behavior.

"You don't have a clue, do you?" Piper says. "Where I've lived since going on the run won't solve the mystery of who killed Archer."

"Aye, I know that."

She flaps her arms. "Well, that's just great. You dragged me here for no damn reason."

"Not no reason." Just nothing that won't sound insane. But I need to make up an excuse for our trip to Limoges. "Only I know you ever lived in this city. That means we can find a place to stay while I comb through the evidence to come up with a plan to determine who killed Archer Caldwell—you or someone else."

"Of course I'm still on your list of suspects. You want me to be guilty."

"I have no stake in the outcome."

"Bullshit. You've hated me from day one, but I have no idea why. What did I ever do to you?"

What did she do? Piper got away from me. I need to know how, but she still won't tell me.

Suddenly, I have an idea. To get answers from Piper, I need to take her to a secluded place where no one will interrupt us. No, I donnae want to get her alone so I can shag her. Why did I think about that? My subconscious knows I want her, for reasons I cannae understand. But I will not give in to the lust. Getting her alone so I can properly interrogate her has nothing to do with the dangerous desire she provokes in me. I could have interrogated her back in Barcelona. But I gave up on that. Now I've given up on earning the bounty I've spent twenty months struggling to earn.

I grab her arm. "Let's go."

"Where?"

"Just come with me and stop asking questions."

"You don't want me to ask anything because you have no clue what you're doing."

Aye, but I won't admit that to her.

Chapter Nine

Piper

Night descends on the world as Magnus drives out of the city, heading into a rural area. At first, we pass by large houses with swimming pools and other signs that the occupants have mucho money. But gradually, the houses give way to countryside, and we see only the occasional dwelling that seems like something an average person would live in. Lights burn in some houses while others are dark.

He ordered me to shut up and not ask questions. Like hell I'll do that. The jerk can't possibly believe I'll obey that command—or any of his orders. Not unless he explains himself.

I wish the man weren't so hot and incredible in bed. Though I've never liked grizzled biker types, I have this bizarre and intense attraction to him—to his body. Well, his voice too. If he never spoke again, maybe I'd get over this lust. But every time he speaks in that rough voice with his Scottish accent, I want to rip his clothes off and climb all over his body.

We stop in a quaint village to eat dinner and buy some groceries, then we get back on the road. Magnus checks a map on his phone every so often as if he actually has a clue where he's going. I remain skeptical.

Our journey takes us to the middle of nowhere, at the end of a very long driveway where a house that's seen better days awaits us in the darkness that's broken only by our headlights. The grass all around the house is overgrown, and the driveway has become nothing more than a two-track through the weeds.

Magnus parks in front of the house. "We're here."

"Uh, where? This place looks like it needs to be demolished."

"The structure is sound, but the owners abandoned the property. A real estate investment firm bought it. They haven't done anything with the place yet, so we can safely hide out here for a while."

"How long is a while?"

The jackass glares at me. "You've been on the run for almost two years. What difference does it make to you if we stay here for a day or a month?"

I take that to mean he still has no plan whatsoever. Perfect. Maybe I didn't have a clear strategy when I went on the run, but at least I had a good excuse. A museum archivist doesn't get training in how to evade the law. Magnus is a bounty hunter, which means this is his job. He ought to have an actual plan.

The Scot climbs out of the car, then leans through the open door to give me his favorite hard stare. "Donnae bother trying to run. It's ten miles to the nearest sign of civilization, and that's nothing more than an empty holiday house."

"How do you know that?"

"Because I do."

Every time he says something like that, I want to grab the most convenient blunt object and whack him with it.

He holds our two bags of groceries in one arm and strides toward the house, carrying a flashlight in his free hand. Since I have no choice, I follow him inside. The front door is unlocked, and it opens easily with no squeaking. I hope that means this place is in decent shape on the inside, if not the outside, though I kind of doubt it has running water or electricity. Luckily, the house does have a lot of windows that provide natural light to illuminate the space—natural moonlight right now, since it's dark out. I don't like dark places anymore. I'd hidden in too many of those during the early days of my flight from the police.

Magnus shuts the door and leads me into what looks like a living room. It has furniture in it. Stuff that looks relatively clean, if old. Maybe I can sit on the sofa without getting fleas or contracting malaria or whatever. I guess malaria is only in tropical climates. So at least I don't need to worry about that.

The jerk sets the grocery bags on the wooden table situated between the sofa and an armchair. He sets the flashlight on a table too, standing it upright so it serves as a makeshift lamp. Then he announces he's going out to get our bags. When he comes back, he sits in the armchair staring at me across the table, where I relax on the sofa, and we enjoy a snack of nuts and fruit. Well, "enjoy" might be an overstatement. Right now, I would prefer something sweet and unhealthy, but I won't complain about the food. At least the Neanderthal is feeding me.

Once we've finished our snack, Magnus leans back in his chair and hooks one ankle over the other knee. His arms rest on the chair, and his gaze remains glued to me with an intensity that both annoys and unnerves me.

He tips his head slightly to the side. "Why didn't you peek out into the living room while Caldwell had his argument with a stranger? You waited until after the other person had left."

"What?" It takes me a moment to realize what he's talking about. "Oh, you mean on the night of the murder. I don't spy on people. It's rude."

"But fleeing from the police is good etiquette."

"I had no choice."

He lifts his brows. "No choice? That's rubbish."

Though I do not trust him, no way, I think it's time I told him something I've kept to myself until now. "Someone tried to kidnap me. That's why I ran."

"You should have told the police."

"I did. They wouldn't believe me." I sink into the sofa, my feet tucked under me. "It happened the day before I was arrested. Someone broke into my flat and tried to put a cloth over my face, I assume to chloroform me. I managed to knee the guy in the balls and run away before he regained his composure. But the attacker ran after me, chased me for three blocks. He only gave up because I went into a crowded bar and slipped out through the back exit."

"Why would someone want to kill you? If you were framed, the real murderer should want you alive to take the fall."

"Though I hadn't been arrested yet, the cops believed I was guilty. All the evidence pointed to me. They were just waiting for confirmation. I think the killer wanted me dead so no one would bother looking closely at the evidence and maybe finding proof I'm innocent. A dead killer ends the investigation, right?"

"Usually."

"The cops found me the next day and arrested me."

"But you escaped. Used your knee-to-the-*bagais* trick to disable the detective sergeant who was about to handcuff you. His partner was on the other side of the car and couldn't get to you in time."

I stare at him. "Knee to the what?"

"*Bagais.* It means balls."

"Okay. Yes, I did that to the cop. Honestly, shouldn't trained police officers be prepared for something like that? Well, anyway, I ran and managed to hide—until you found me." I can't help smirking. "You were even easier to get away from than the cops. All I had to do was wait until you fell asleep. Some amazing bounty hunter you are."

He averts his gaze and shoves a hand through his hair. "Aye, that was an amateur mistake."

Did he just admit he screwed up? Never thought I'd hear him say that.

"But it was your fault," he says. "You wanted to have a poke twice, and you liked to make things…very energetic. I was jeeked after that."

The context makes it clear the word jeeked means wiped out. "So now it's my fault you screwed up and fell asleep. That's the lamest excuse I've ever heard."

"Not an excuse. It's a fact. Donnae ye remember how hard we shagged and for how long? We were both covered in sweat after that."

Oh yeah, I remember our athletic sex and the way sweat glistened on his rippling muscles. I saw him naked twenty months ago, but the second time, I only got a glimpse of his dick. He saw all of me. That's not fair.

But I can't complain about the orgasm he gave me.

On that other day so many months ago, I had wanted to sleep with him—actually sleep. But I couldn't. My plan to get away from Magnus depended on him falling asleep first. Having sex with a stranger and then skulking out is not my thing.

Since he wants to interrogate me, I should get to grill him too. If I ask permission first, he'll say no. "How old are you?"

"Doesnae matter."

"Oh, yes it does. You say you've read every scrap of information about me, which means you know I'm thirty-six. Probably know which brand of tampons I use too. I deserve to know something about the man who dragged me out into the middle of French nowhere."

He puckers his lips, then sighs and relaxes. "I'm forty-one."

"Do you have any family?"

"One question is all you get."

Like I'll let him get away with that. I slide my legs off the sofa to lean forward and stare at him the way he stares at me. I doubt I look as menacing as he does, but a girl can't have everything. "You know all about me. That's what you said. What did you learn about my past?"

"Enough to do my job."

"Oh, so reading my diary was work-related. How did my innermost thoughts help you catch me?"

"Understanding my quarry gives me an edge."

More vague responses. Jeez, having a conversation with Magnus is like trying to tow a boat through a frozen lake. "Why bring me to this remote house? How did you even know it was here? And don't give me another murky response. I want a clear answer."

"You have no leverage to make me do anything."

Damn, he's right. How can I get some leverage? The only thing I know will knock him off balance is if I seduce him. No, I will not do that again. Never. Uh-uh, no way.

It's weird that we've had sex twice, but we have never kissed.

He props his feet on the table, crossing his ankles. "How does it feel to be alone in the world?"

"Why would you ask me that?"

"Because I know all about you, Piper. Your parents are divorced and live in America, though in different states, and they have never visited you in England, not even when you were arrested. After finishing your bachelor's degree, you went on to earn a master's in archival studies. You worked at three different museums in America before you got your job in the UK two years ago as head archivist."

A chill shivers over my skin. He knows way too much about me, and I know nothing about him. I can't trust this man. Nobody who has that much information about me could possibly be an ally. But I am so tired of living on the run, alone, struggling to survive. My only hope is Magnus MacTaggart. Before I can even think about trusting him, I need to learn more about him and figure out if he will ever believe I did not kill Archer.

"Please tell me something about you," I say. "If you really want to find out the truth about Archer's death, we need to trust each other. That can't happen when you're an enigma."

He drums his fingers on the arms of his chair, his gaze riveted to mine. Seconds tick by, then minutes. I know because there's a clock on the wall that counts the seconds and minutes. Finally, he speaks. "I have a family, but I don't see them often. I'm estranged from my parents, and though I have cousins who have become mates, I'm not particularly close to them either."

"You really don't have one close friend."

"Do you?"

I hunch my shoulders. "Thought I did. But my friends at the museum assume I'm a murderer, so no, I don't have anyone I'm close to." I bite my lip, afraid to ask the next question because it's embarrassing. "Does this place have a working toilet? I really need to, um, relieve myself."

"The house has a toilet, but it depends on the well—which needs electricity for its pump to run." He jerks a thumb toward the area behind him, outside the sliding glass doors. "Go outside to take care of whatever you need to do."

"Outside? Somebody might see me."

"We're in the middle of sodding nowhere, as you've repeatedly pointed out."

"Are there wild animals around here? Don't want to get eaten while I'm emptying my bladder."

He stares at me again, his lips compressed. Then he grabs the flashlight and jumps up, stalking over to the sliding glass doors that open onto what looks like a patio. I can sort of see that now, since his flashlight sheds light through the glass.

"What are you doing now?" I ask.

"Escorting you to the outdoor *taigh beag*."

"You're speaking gibberish."

"Not gibberish. *Taigh beag* is Gaelic for privy."

I can't stop the laughter that bubbles out of me. "Privy? This isn't Shakespearean times. Or do Scots like to use ancient terms for things?"

"Do ye want to relieve your needs or not?"

"Yeah, I do."

And I let Magnus lead me outside. This might be the most embarrassing moment of my life, but at least he didn't order me to hold it in until the next time we visit civilization. Yeah, I've been reduced to feeling grateful that a sullen jerk lets me pee.

Being a fugitive bites the big one.

Chapter Ten

Magnus

I let Piper decide where she wants to relieve herself, and she chooses a stand of trees not far from the house. If anyone should stop nearby and glance this way, I doubt they would see us. She insists I turn my back to give her "a teeny bit of privacy." She won't run away. There's nowhere to go. I chose this house for that very reason, and I will keep her here until I figure out what to do next.

Just as we walk back into the house, my mobile chimes. I stop behind the chair I'd sat in earlier and read the text message: *Have you betrayed me?*

No, I type. Royce Hammond wants to know why his jet arrived in London without me or the fugitive on board. But accusing me of betraying him does not make me like him any better. I donnae care for the *cacan* at all. He paid me to do a job. Liking him was not a requirement. He thinks his status as a billionaire means everyone will kneel at his feet and beg for his favor.

I do not beg for anything.

Another text appears. *Where is she?*

PL is in my custody.

You were meant to bring her to me.

When I'm ready.

Several seconds elapse without a response. I've just decided he gave up when my mobile rings. The caller ID tells me it's my client. I don't bother to say hello. "I told you I have what you want. I'll bring you the prize when I'm ready."

I'm being careful because Piper has just sat down on the sofa. She can hear everything I say.

"That's not how it works," the British ersehole says. "I paid you to find Piper Lang and transport her to me. If you don't comply by 10 p.m., you will regret it."

"Donnae be threatening me, ye *cacan*. Your money doesn't scare me."

"But my power and influence will. I warned you from the start that I do not tolerate insolence. And I've been enormously patient for the past twenty months." His voice becomes a harsh whisper. "There will be consequences for a betrayal of this magnitude."

"Sod off, ye *bod ceann*."

I hang up.

Piper watches me with wide eyes. "Who were you talking to? Did that have anything to do with me? I'm guessing the prize is me."

Should I lie? Since my client has turned out to be a *tolla-thon*, I no longer feel any loyalty to the ersehole or any need to maintain discretion. The bastard means to scare me? That's rubbish. Anyone who threatens me will regret it far more than I'll regret whatever consequences he claims he'll dole out.

"Aye, that call was about you," I tell Piper. "The man who hired me to find you is annoyed that I didn't take you to him today."

"What will he do? Based on what I heard you say, he threatened you and tried to scare you."

"Do I seem like the sort who gets frightened easily?"

She almost smiles. "Not really."

I settle onto the chair. "Donnae worry about that *cacan*. I can handle him."

"What does *cacan* mean? You also said *bod ceann*."

"*Cacan* means wee shit, and *bod ceann* means dickhead. Those are Scots Gaelic words."

She does smile this time, and the lass looks even bonnier with her cheeks dimpled. "Gaelic sounds like a fun language."

"Aye, it is. But it's good for more than cursing." I rub my chin as I rake my gaze over her body. "Gaelic also has a dirty side."

"Sounds interesting—and hot." Her sultry tone makes blood rush into my cock. "Maybe you can teach me naughty Gaelic sometime."

I want to do that right now. Does this house have a bed? But I can shag her anywhere, even on the floor or the table. The sofa would be softer, though. "Aye, maybe I will teach you that sometime."

"Do you realize we've never kissed?"

"What's your point?"

"That we had sex, but you haven't kissed me. I've never been with a man who didn't want to kiss me at least once before we got naked."

I wish she hadn't spoken the word naked or implied I should kiss her because now I want to ravish her mouth and strip her bare to fuck her on the sofa. Aye, I know I shouldn't do that. But I can kiss her. That wouldn't drive me off my head. One kiss, just to prove to the lass… something. I have no idea what I'd be trying to prove, but I want to taste her lips. I need to do it.

So I walk over to the sofa and sit down beside her. "One kiss."

The lass bites her lip, releasing it slowly, and her eyes light up.

I slide a hand into her hair and tug just enough to bring her face closer to mine, then I tip her head back and seal my lips to hers. She exhales a breath that tickles my upper lip and moans softly. I wrap my free arm around her and pull the lass's body into mine, allowing myself to enjoy the simple sweetness of feeling and tasting her lips, but I need more than that.

When she clutches fistfuls of my shirt and wriggles, rubbing her tits against me, I cannae stop myself. I thrust my tongue between her parted lips and get my first taste of her mouth. The velvety softness of her tongue, the way she teases me with light strokes, and the flavor of her make my cock twitch as all the blood in my body floods into my *slat*. If I donnae stop kissing her, we will be fucking on the sofa in a matter of seconds. I want to keep going, but I force myself to pull away. Still, I keep my hand in her hair. The strands feel as soft as silk on my skin.

Her cheeks have turned a pale pink, and her lips are slightly swollen.

Bod an Donais, Piper has never looked bonnier.

She glances sideways at my hand, where it still cradles her head. "Um, that was nice."

I yank my hand away. "Nice?"

"Yes. Thank you for that, Magnus."

What had I expected her to say in response to my kiss? I don't even like her, but I enjoyed kissing her. I'd love to do it again. But that would send the wrong message. Maybe I'd hoped she would be breathless and swoon into my arms after our kiss. No, I didn't want that. Even if I had wanted it, she didn't swoon.

She thanked me.

I can honestly say no woman has ever done that after a kiss. After a shag, aye. But what they say is more along the lines of "oh, Magnus, you're a god, thank you." Well, something like that. I might not be remembering it verbatim. I have perfect recall of the moment when a lass I'd just fucked for an hour collapsed on the bed after her third orgasm and she announced, "I don't know how you did that, but I think you must be an alien sex god because nobody else has ever made me come like the world is exploding."

Maybe I should tell Piper about that, so she won't think our kiss was just "nice." But I have a feeling she would laugh at me.

"You're scowling," Piper says. "I gave you a compliment, but you're acting like I insulted your manhood."

"My manhood? Ye know bloody well how good I am at shagging you."

"Really. The first time was good, but you didn't even get naked the second time. And you spewed all over me."

"Stop saying that. You make it sound like… Donnae know. But I don't like the word 'spew.' It's ridiculous." I throw both my arms around her and drag the lass into me. "And I made ye come for me, so ye've got nothing to complain about."

"Gimme a break. You are not as hot as you think."

"You're only saying that to fash me. It willnae work."

"Fash? I don't know what that means. You probably made up the word."

I clasp her to me more tightly, our lips millimeters apart. "The word fash means bother, and it is not made up. It's a Scottish term. Donnae be insulting my country."

"Oh, I get it. You're allowed to insult me and call me a murderer, but I can't poke fun at your silly Scottish words."

My cock is hard now. Why arguing with her always gets me randy, I cannae explain. How she makes me lose control of all my senses, I can't explain that either. But I'm breathing harder, my *slat* is throbbing, and I'm balanced on a razor's edge, about to fuck this woman who I cannae stand.

This will make three times. *Mhac na galla.*

I crush my mouth to hers and plunge my tongue deep, groaning when she slings her arms around my neck and hooks one leg around my hip. I flip her onto her back. My entire body covers hers, and she wraps both legs around me. We devour each other's mouths while she thrusts her hips as if she means to fuck me with our clothes on.

A noise makes me freeze. It sounded like a click.

Pushing up on my elbows, I whisper, "Did you hear that sound?"

"What sound?" She's breathing hard and seems a touch dazed, but still manages to whisper.

"It was a click."

"Sorry. I didn't hear anything."

Rising into a crouch, I peer into the shadows in the hall.

Piper opens her mouth to speak.

I hold one finger to my lips, and she closes her mouth. Though I haven't heard anything else, my hunter instincts have kicked in, warning me that something isn't right. Someone might have come to check on the house, but I can't imagine why they would skulk inside instead of just walking in and stumbling onto us. I gesture for Piper to stay put, and though she frowns at me, she does what I silently asked.

I slide off the sofa and creep toward the hall while keeping my back to the wall.

A dark shape within the shadows moves just enough that I can tell someone is there.

I have a Glock in my bag, but I'd assumed I would never need that weapon so I left my bag in the entryway along with Piper's. Now that I need the gun, I can't get to it without crossing paths with whoever has sneaked into the house. Doesnae matter. I can find other ways to disable an attacker. Flexibility is the key to a hunter's success.

Piper huddles on the sofa, peeking over its top with her eyes wide.

The shuffling of shoes on the wood floor draws my attention back to the hall. I peer into the shadows, tilting my head slightly to the side to improve my chances of hearing any wee noise the intruder makes. Breathing. More shuffling. The figure has moved closer, and the light of the full moon casts a faint glow on the intruder, just enough that I make out his entire silhouette and the shape of the gun in his hand.

No more waiting. It's time to pounce.

I rush toward the figure and slug him in the gut. While he doubles over, I knee him in the groin, slam my fists down on his back, and throw him into the living room. The bastard grunts and cries out as he hits the floor on his side, curled up in an almost fetal position. I turn on the lantern so I can get a good look at my enemy.

The man seems quite young, probably in his twenties. His face is wrenched by agony, and he cups his groin while hissing breaths through his clenched teeth. His shaggy hair has fallen over his eyes. The *cacan's* gun lies on the floor near the sofa.

"Who is that?" Piper asks. "Do you know him?"

"No." I grasp the back of the man's coat and hoist him off the floor, letting his feet hang a few inches in the air, but I now look him straight in the eye. "Who the fuck are ye?"

The *cacan* flicks his gaze back and forth between me and Piper. "I'm nobody. This was just a job, I swear it."

He speaks with a British accent, but that doesn't tell me what I need to know. "What is your name?"

The lad bites the inside of his cheek, making it pucker.

I pull him closer. "Tell me your name or I will reach down your throat to tear your larynx out."

Chapter Eleven

The man's eyes flare wide, and he holds perfectly still as if he's digesting Magnus's threat and trying to decide if the bounty hunter can actually do what he described. Can he do it? Would he do it? Maybe stoking the man's fear serves Magnus's purpose, whatever that might be. The Scot has been nasty to me, but nothing like the way he's acting right now.

It's surprisingly hot.

"Charlie Burton," the intruder mumbles. "My name is Charlie Burton."

Knowing his name doesn't matter as far as I can tell, but I think demanding it gave Magnus the chance to demonstrate he's stronger and tougher than the intruder. Now the kid will comply.

"Who sent ye?" Magnus snarls.

"I-I don't know his name. The geezer offered me ten thousand pounds if I would come here and take the woman. I got a free trip to France and a room at a posh hotel."

"Take her?" Magnus gives him a hard shake. "Stop lying to me. Who sent you and why? Only an eejit would take a job like that without knowing who hired him."

"Well, that's me. I'm an idiot, for sure."

Oh yeah, no one would disagree with that statement.

"Last chance," Magnus says. "Explain yourself, or I will squeeze the information out of you."

"All right, calm down." Charlie raises his hands while still dangling from the Scot's grip. "It's true I don't know his name, but he picked me because I'm a 'tosser who doesn't have a conscience.' That's what he said. I couldn't turn down all that money. Kidnapping a girl sounded easy. The man who hired me didn't warn me about you."

"Describe the man."

Charlie's brows furrow. "Describe him?"

Magnus gives the kid an even harder shake that jostles his head. "Aye. That means tell me what the *bod ceann* looked like."

"He, uh, looked like the sort who has women chasing him all the time. He's tall and has muscles, though nothing like yours." Charlie swallows hard enough to make his Adam's apple jump. "I think his eyes are brown, but I can't remember for sure. He had, ah, thick lips. I noticed that because they made me think of my uncle. He's got lips like that."

"Fascinating." Magnus drops the twerp. "Royce Hammond hired you."

"Royce who? Never heard of him."

"Hammond wanted you to capture the woman. How did you get here so fast?"

"Been here since this morning. On call waiting for my orders. That's all I know."

"What did he tell you to do with me?"

"N-nothing. He said you didn't matter because he terminated your employment and you won't get paid. That's your punishment. You're nothing but a filthy bounty hunter, so he doesn't need to bother getting rid of you." Charlie holds his hands up again. "His words, not mine. I swear, that's all he told me."

Magnus glances over his shoulder at me. "Get his weapon."

I leap off the sofa to snatch up the gun. "What now?"

"Hold on to it." Magnus glares at Charlie. "Might need to shoot off a few fingers if he doesn't cooperate."

Charlie flaps his head. "No, no, please. I'm no threat to you. I'm just a bleeding coward and a petty thief. Told you everything I know."

"No, ye haven't." The Scot drops him, and the twerp crumples into a heap on the floor. "How did you find us?"

The whiny thief winces. "That man said he'd kill me if I told you anything."

Magnus kneels beside him, leaning forward to stare into his eyes. "What do ye think I'll do to ye if ye refuse to tell me?"

Charlie starts trembling. His teeth chatter when he speaks. "Oh God, please don't hurt me. I wish I'd never taken this job."

"Willnae hurt ye if I get the information I want."

A dark spot blooms around his groin, spreading outward. Charlie just wet his pants. That's how much Magnus terrifies him.

"Tell me," Magnus growls through clenched teeth.

"Okay, okay," Charlie whines. "That guy—Hammond, I guess—told me how he put malware on your mobile that lets him track you. Gave me an app for my phone that helps me follow your movements on a map."

Magnus hisses something I can't understand. Must be Gaelic. And based on his tone, I'm pretty sure he's swearing a blue streak.

"Can you remove the malware?" I ask Magnus.

"Not sure." He zeroes his gaze in on Charlie. "Do you know how to remove it?"

"Me? I don't know anything about that technical rubbish."

I come up beside Magnus, who still kneels next to Charlie. I keep holding the gun the bumbling kidnapper had dropped, and I make sure to keep the muzzle aimed at the floor and my finger off the trigger. "What now? If Hammond can track you—"

"Donnae worry about that." Magnus rises and pulls out his phone. "I know someone who can help."

He dials a number and holds the phone to his ear, his gaze still nailed to Charlie. "Evan, it's Magnus. Sorry to bother you, but I have a technical issue that I hoped you could help me solve. I understand if you donnae want to do it." He sighs as if he's relieved by whatever the mysterious Evan said. "Aye, thank you. The bloke's name is Royce Hammond."

While Magnus listens intently to whatever that other man is saying, I watch Charlie. The twerp doesn't seem likely to try anything. I mean, he peed his pants. He's terrified of Magnus, and I don't blame him. But Magnus has never scared me that much. Sure, I panicked the first time he caught me, but only for a few minutes. Then something strange happened. I knew—just *knew*—he would never hurt me. Yeah, he snarls and growls and says nasty things. That's all he does, though. Despite his bad-boy attitude and biker chic outfit, he would only follow through on a threat if the other person deserved it.

I shouldn't believe that, but I do. Call it woman's intuition.

Magnus says goodbye to his caller and pops open the rear panel on his phone. He fiddles with something, then snaps the panel back into place. With a smug smile, he holds up the thingy he'd removed from his phone. "The SIM card. Cannae track my phone when it's deactivated."

He drops the card on the floor and stomps on it several times until the thing no longer resembles any kind of electronic doohickey. It's a tiny pile of garbage now. He repeats the process with my phone.

Charlie's entire body quivers, and tears dribble down his cheeks. "Please don't kill me."

"I willnae do that," Magnus tells him. "Unless you try to follow us. We're getting in our car and driving away. You will stay here until ye cannae see our vehicle anymore, then you'll get in your car and drive in the opposite direction. Understand?"

"Y-yes."

Magnus grabs Charlie's arm and helps him get up off the floor. "I'll be keeping your gun, laddie."

"Fine. I don't want it."

"Stay in the house, but watch out the window to see when we're gone. Then do as I said."

"Yes, I will." Charlie sags into Magnus and starts to sob. "Thank you for not killing me."

Magnus lifts his gaze heavenward and shakes his head. After giving Charlie's back a few light pats, he steps away from the kid and looks at me. "Time to go."

He takes the gun from me and tucks it into his waistband, nestled against his spine. Then he grabs our bags and leads me outside. We climb into the car, and Magnus steers the sedan onto the road.

"What now?" I ask. "Are you sure Hammond can't track us anymore?"

"Not sure of anything. We need to get far away from here."

"How far?"

"Switzerland, for a start. By the time we get there, Evan should have the information we need."

"Um, how far is it to Switzerland?"

Magnus navigates around a corner onto a wider road. "Probably a wee bit more than seven hours by car."

"Who is Evan?"

He glances at me sideways. "Doesn't matter."

I won't waste my breath on trying to make him tell me things, not right now. Our encounter with Charlie has left me shaken. Maybe it's the crash after an adrenaline rush, but I feel uneasy and can't help worrying whether we can ever get away from Royce Hammond. If the guy can install malware without Magnus knowing it, I wonder if we can be safe anywhere.

After a while, I can't keep my worries to myself anymore. "If there's something on your phone that makes you trackable, shouldn't you throw the phone away?"

"Not yet."

"Should I get rid of my phone?"

"Not yet."

Oh, he's in a mood now. Repeating those two words doesn't seem like a positive sign that he knows what the hell he's doing. Why couldn't I get caught by a bounty hunter who's a computer expert? No, I get the gruff, rude Scot who didn't bother to check whether his phone had been compromised.

I shouldn't blame him, though. Right? I mean, I didn't think about malware either.

Magnus pulls over to the side of the road in a deserted area. No houses, no fences, nothing that suggests anybody lives out here. I suppose that's why he stopped in this spot.

"Listen to me and donnae interrupt," he says. "Nod if you agree to do that."

After what happened back in that house, I think I should obey him—for now. So I nod.

"The man I spoke to earlier—Evan—is a computer expert," Magnus says. "He can help us find a safe way to communicate with him and anyone else we need to contact. He can also provide us with tools that will stop our enemies from tracking us again."

Sounds awesome. But I don't say that because he wants me to just listen.

Wait. We have enemies? I thought it was only Royce Hammond. But Magnus used the plural. That implies we've got more bad guys hunting us or might soon have more of them.

I open my mouth to ask him about that but shut it again. I promised not to speak. *Damn.*

Magnus sighs and gives me a long-suffering look. "Go on. Tell me your latest complaint."

"Not a complaint. I'm wondering how many 'enemies' you think we have out there."

"Donnae know. But if Royce Hammond wants you, I have no doubts he will employ more people to hunt us." He runs a hand through his hair and sighs again. "This time, he willnae hire a bumbling petty criminal. He'll get it right."

"What are you suggesting? Hammond might hire assassins or something?"

"Told ye, I donnae know." He grips the steering, his gaze now aimed straight ahead. "But I'm going to find out."

"How?"

Magnus ignores my question and starts off down the road again.

I sink back in my seat and try not to think about who Hammond might hire and what they might do to us. I've never met Royce Hammond, never heard of him either, but he's determined to put me in jail or maybe even kill me. Oh God, how did I end up in this mess? Having a few sips of champagne with my boss shouldn't have triggered a catastrophe.

The person who murdered Archer needs to pay. I am not that person. Does Magnus still believe I am? I don't care what he thinks of me, except that his opinion might interfere with tracking down the real killer.

I "haud my wheesht," as Magnus would say, for about an hour before I can't take it anymore.

"Do you still think I killed Archer?" I ask.

He shrugs one shoulder.

Great. Now he won't even speak to me. Guess I'll "haud" my whatever for a while longer. Why did Scots make up so many bizarre words? "Be quiet" works fine for the rest of the English-speaking world. I might think that wheesht thing is weird, but I can't deny Gaelic is a lovely language—even when Magnus is cursing at me in that tongue.

Eventually, we come upon a quaint village. Magnus pulls into a parking lot behind a bed-and-breakfast and shuts off the engine.

"Are we stopping for the night?" I ask.

"Yes."

"Oh, thank goodness. I need a nice soft bed to sleep in, not a bucket seat."

We go inside to check in, and Magnus speaks to the desk clerk in French. He knows that language? What other secret talents does he have? Well, we aren't exactly best buddies, so I imagine there are lots of things I don't know about him.

"They have one room available," Magnus tells me. "We'll need to share."

"Fine. Just don't handcuff me to the bed again." That was unbelievably hot, but I will not have sex with him tonight. I'll swear to that on a bible or phone book or whatever.

He smirks. "Cannae promise I willnae do that."

I wish he hadn't spoken in a deep, sexy rumble that made my nipples ache. Yes, fine, the man is outrageously hot and so good in bed that some-body should bronze his dick. But I don't like him. Even if he is kind of helping me now.

"How many languages do you speak?" I ask.

"English and Gaelic. Some French, but only a few phrases in Spanish."

"That's more language skills than I have."

Once he's gotten us signed in, we head upstairs to our room.

It has one bed. Not a Magnus-size one either. No, I'll have to sleep right next to the damn Scot. Well, it's not like I'll lose control and rip his clothes off. He's the one who tore my clothes off back in the motel. But I won't let him do that again.

I swear I won't.

Can I sleep tonight? Not with Magnus beside me.

Chapter Twelve

Magnus

I've brought Piper to a hotel. We have one bed. I'll need all my self-control to keep my hands off that woman. No, I won't. We're both too jeeked to even think about sex. I feel that way until Piper kneels to open her suitcase, facing away from me so I cannae help staring at her bonnie erse. I want to walk over there, drop to my knees behind her, and fondle those cheeks.

Bloody hell. I shouldn't think that, much less do it.

Piper rises, holding an armful of clothes, and hurries into the bathroom. She shuts the door behind her.

No, I didn't hope she'd leave the door open so I could watch her undress.

I get ready for bed and lie on the mattress, pulling the covers over me while I wait for her to come out. Tomorrow, I need to contact Evan and find out what sort of plan he has devised. When I spoke to him today, he vowed to come up with a "roadmap to safety." I didn't point out that Piper and I might never be safe as long as Royce Hammond lives. I cannae say I've never taken a life, but I didn't do it because I wanted to become a killer. I had no choice.

Piper emerges from the bathroom wearing pink pajamas that have cartoons of ice cream cones all over them.

"Is that what you call blending into the background?" I ask. "Cannae see how you avoided getting captured if you dress that way."

She drops her dirty clothes on the floor. "I don't wear pajamas in the daytime, obviously. And I must be a master fugitive since I managed to stay out of your grasp for such a long time, then I got away again for three more months."

Mhac na galla. She's right. Either I've lost my touch or she learned quickly how to hide from me. Piper is clever. Beautiful too. And sexy. Even in bloody silly pajamas, she makes me want to fuck her right now.

I pull the covers back. "Get in bed."

She freezes, not even blinking. Her attention stalls on my cock.

Aye, I'm lying here naked. I always sleep that way. It doesn't mean I intend to seduce her.

"Why are you naked?" she asks, her voice hushed.

"Get in bed, woman."

She puckers her lips and lodges her hands on her hips. "Woman? I have a name, you know. If you're going to call me 'woman,' maybe I should start calling you 'jackass.' That sounds right to me."

"Do what you want." I roll over onto my side, facing the wall. "Sleep on the floor if ye cannae handle the fact I'm not wearing any clothes."

"Ugh. I hate you."

I chuckle. "Except when I'm fucking you."

The bed jostles as she climbs onto it and tugs the covers over us both. When I glance at her over my shoulder, I see she's facing away from me.

Maybe I should be nicer to her since Royce Hammond sent someone to abduct her today. But I cannae comfort her. I have no idea how to do that. My lifestyle doesn't afford me the opportunity to develop normal relationships with anyone, not even my family. I've made a wee bit more of an effort lately, because of Kirsty. She wants me to become a real member of the MacTaggart clan, and some of my other cousins have tried to do that. I donnae make it easy, though that's not on purpose.

Do I believe Piper is guilty? Royce Hammond wants her badly, which makes me suspicious. I should've listened to my instincts about him and refused the job. But then I would never have met Piper. That would be a good thing, wouldn't it? Now I'm on the run with a woman who inflames my lust and makes me break every rule I created for myself.

But no, I donnae believe she killed Archer Caldwell.

I have no evidence to the contrary, yet I no longer accept the official version of events. To get answers, I'll need help from Evan—though I will do whatever is necessary to keep him from getting entangled in this mess. He has a wife and bairn who need him far more than I do.

What if Hammond goes after my family?

I stay awake for hours while that thought ricochets in my mind, but eventually, I grow so exhausted that I cannae stay awake anymore. I sink into a slumber haunted by dreams of what might happen to the people who matter to me, the cousins who have tried to bring me into the fold because they care, though I've given them no reason to feel that way.

When I wake in the morning, Piper lies beside me with her back pressed to mine. The soft material of her pajamas brushes against me.

She exhales a soft sigh. "Are you finally awake?"

"Aye. What time is it?"

"Eight o'clock."

I spring upright, my pulse racing. "Why did ye let me sleep for so long? We need to be on the road, not lounging in bed."

"How is that my fault?" She flips onto her back, arms barred over her chest. "You oversleep, and I'm to blame. Typical."

"In what way is that typical? I've never shared a bed with you before."

"Of course you have. That night when you screwed me and then fell asleep."

She's right. But only sleeping with her feels different, and my mind refused to connect this event with what happened the first time I found her.

"We need to get moving," I say. "Grab some food and go."

"You still plan on going to Switzerland."

"Aye. But we'll make a stop first."

"Stop? Where?"

I shift onto my hands and knees, intending to climb over her body to get off the bed. But I stop with my knees at either side of her thighs and my hands bracketing her shoulders. My gaze travels over her body, from her tousled hair down to her pajama top that has stretched tight over her breasts and strains the buttons, then further down to her hips.

"Move your ass, MacTaggart."

"What if I don't?"

Her gaze drops to my groin where my *slat* is already firming up. It has nothing to do with her. I get an erection most mornings. But Piper licks her lips and wriggles just enough to make my cock harden even more.

I don't have time to shag her right now.

But I cannae resist brushing my *slat* against her, which makes the lass suck in a sharp breath. She arches her back, lifting those bonnie tits, and licks her lips again, slower this time, dragging her tongue across her flesh while she gazes directly into my eyes.

"How about a morning pick-me-up?" she asks.

"Donnae think I'll fall for you seducing me again."

"But you're so easy, Magnus. I didn't even have to try yesterday."

The husky tone of her voice doesnae bolster my willpower. Why can't I resist this woman? Maybe I haven't done it so far, but the rules change today. No more giving in to my lust.

She closes her fingers around my *slat*. "Sure you don't want a quickie before breakfast?"

I groan when she starts gliding her hand up and down my length. "Not this time."

With more willpower than I've ever needed before, I peel her hand away from my flesh and jump off the bed. Then I rush into the bathroom and shut the door. *Bod an Donais*, I'm so hard I cannae think. Piper did this to me on purpose, though I have no idea why she wanted to get me this randy. The woman who despises me cannae want me to take her body again. But I need to relieve the pressure before that lass tempts me again, so I grasp my cock and start pumping.

Someone knocks on the bathroom door.

I stop in the middle of rubbing one off and roll my eyes at my own numpty thoughts. Someone? It's Piper, of course. She wants to torment me more, but since I cannae see her body, she will not get what she wants.

Not right now.

She knocks again. "Will you hurry up? I need to pee."

I can't walk out there in this condition. An alternate strategy seems appropriate. "Give me a moment."

"Make it a quick one. My bladder is about to burst."

"Aye, I'm hurrying." I slide the shower door open and step inside, turning the water on. The cold spray does nothing to alleviate my problem. "Come in and do what you need to do."

"What? No. You have to leave the bathroom."

"Use the bog while I'm in here, or wait until later. Your choice."

She makes a frustrated noise, something between a whine and a growl. Then she throws the door open and stalks over to the toilet, flipping up the lid. The frosted glass of the shower stall lets me see her as only a blurry figure, but I hear it when she starts to relieve herself.

I turn the water temperature up until steam starts to roil around me. Hot water doesn't help either. "Aren't ye done yet?"

"Yes. But I need a shower too, you know. Some damn Scot dragged me away from my motel room yesterday and took so long to get me to another one that I didn't have time to shower last night."

"Why do ye always have to talk so much and complain about everything?"

"Maybe I wouldn't do that anymore if you stopped acting like a bastard."

Cannae stop the chuckle that rumbles out of me, though I donnae make that noise because I feel lighthearted. It's a dark sound. "I am a bastard. But ye love that about me, don't you? Wouldn't beg me to have another poke with you otherwise."

"Excuse me? I have not begged for it. Well, maybe I did yesterday—but only because you wouldn't let me come until I pleaded."

I should never have mentioned sex. My erection won't go away until I stop thinking about her body and the way it felt to have her slick flesh molded to my *slat*.

"You're an evil son of a bitch, MacTaggart."

"Aye." Though I shouldn't do it, I slide the shower door open. With one hand flat on the tile wall and the hot water sluicing over me, I look at Piper. "Step in here and I'll make you come. That's a certainty."

She stares at my cock, breathing harder while her stiff nipples show through her pajama top.

I rub my *slat*. "Ye want this inside ye again. Donnae deny it."

The lass clears her throat, straightens, and meets my gaze head-on. "Yeah, I want that. But it will never happen again."

She spins around and marches out of the bathroom, slamming the door shut.

I close the shower door and start pumping again. It only takes a few seconds, then I come. A strangled shout explodes out of me. I take a moment to catch my breath, but after that, I finish my shower.

When I step out of the bathroom, Piper scowls at me. "May I have a shower now? Or are you planning to withhold cleanliness to punish me for not screwing you?"

She can't think I would do that. Even I'm not that much of a *tolla-thon*.

"Have your shower," I say. "But make it quick."

"Thank you so much for your benevolence."

She marches into the bathroom and shuts the door.

I can't decide if she's angry just for the sake of being fashed or if unfulfilled lust has her tied up in knots. It doesn't matter. We have serious problems to deal with, and her body ranks low on my list of things to do today.

By the time she emerges from the bathroom, I've gotten dressed.

She put on clothes too and now holds her pajamas in one hand, neatly folded.

"I rang room service," I tell her. "They've made us a takeaway breakfast. We need to get on the road immediately."

For once, the bloody-minded woman doesn't argue with me. We carry our bags downstairs and pick up our food, then jump into the car. During my mostly sleepless night, I wondered whether Charlie might've attached a tracking device to our car. But I discarded the idea. The lad was terrified of me, and he swore he didn't know anything else. Still, I think we should switch cars before we cross the border into Switzerland.

I make a detour, turning off the main road and into the town of Montchanin.

"Where are you going?" Piper asks. "Shouldn't we stay on the main road?"

"Haud yer wheesht, woman."

"Oh, I absolutely will not 'haud' my anything. Especially not when you order me to do it."

I swerve into the car park of a large building and slam on the brakes, halting the vehicle in a parking slot near the front doors of the establishment.

"What is this place?" Piper asks. "Looks like some kind of store."

"Because it is some kind of store." I throw my door open and jump out, then lean over to peer at her. "You can stay in the car if you want, though I'll probably handcuff you again to make sure you don't try to run."

I won't do that. Why did I say it? The lass drives me off my head. What fashes me more is that I no longer want to restrain her and I've stopped worrying that she might run away. I cannae…trust her. No, it's not that.

Piper climbs out of the car and follows me into the store without complaining.

Aye, a miracle has happened.

Chapter Thirteen

Piper

While we explore the aisles of merchandise, I grab whatever food items I see because who knows when Magnus will feed me again. Most of what I grab is not nutritious food. Who cares? I'm falsely accused of murder and some guy I've never met wants to abduct me. Stress makes me want to stuff my face. Maybe if I get fat, Magnus won't try to have sex with me anymore. Right, because I can gain fifty pounds in the next hour or so. The jerk does not help me carry my armload of potato chips, candy, and prepackaged fried fruit pies. No, of course he doesn't. Magnus must've been born in a pigsty because he certainly behaves like a pig.

I snag another food item—beef jerky, this time. I'm not a fan of that stuff, but I can't be choosy when I'm on the run with a rude Scot.

Magnus eyes my latest treasure. "If you mean to kill me with cholesterol, you'll have a long wait."

"This is *my* food. You can starve for all I care." Jeez, now I'm acting like a spoiled teenager. I blame the Scot. He drives me crazy.

Magnus glowers at me, then stalks off down another aisle. He apparently finds what he'd been looking for—a cell phone, the pay-as-you-go kind—and nabs two of them.

"You need two phones?" I say.

"One is for you."

I blink rapidly, unable to comprehend the words he spoke or what they mean. Finally, my brain catches up. "You bought me a phone. Why? I figured you'd lock me in the trunk so I'll stop pestering you. But I guess the phone is so I can call to tell you when I need a pee break."

"Willnae ye ever stop harassing me?"

I can't help it. My lips curve into a self-satisfied smile. "Is the great Magnus MacTaggart letting a wee lassie get him riled up? I don't harass you, anyway. I ask legitimate questions and ask for clarification when necessary."

"Ask? Ye donnae request anything. Whenever you say the word please, it's either a sarcastic comment or a plea for sex."

We've just reached the checkout aisle, and I toss my armload of junk food onto the conveyor belt. "I don't plead for sex. You aren't that good."

He drops the cell phone packages on top of my pile of food. Then he slants toward me so he can hiss under his breath, "Of course I'm that good. And ye do beg me for more, even if only with your eyes."

"My eyes?" I say with a snide laugh. "Get over yourself, MacTaggart. No part of me pleads for anything from you."

"Ye want my *slat*."

The cashier is staring at us wide-eyed and says something in French.

I never learned the language, so I can't respond to the girl.

Magnus mutters something that's not English or Gaelic, as far as I can tell, and the cashier starts ringing up our purchases.

Once we're back in the car, Magnus brings out his old phone and holds out his hand to me, palm up. "Your mobile. Now."

"Why?"

His nostrils flare. I swear they do that, just like an angry bull. "Give me your mobile, or I'll strip you naked to find it."

I might kind of like it if he did that, but I won't admit it out loud. So I dig my phone out of my pocket and hand it to him. "You're welcome."

"Didnae say thank you."

"Exactly."

His lips flatten, but he turns his attention away from me to the four phones he now has balanced on his lap. He opens the packages of the new phones and plugs one into the cigarette lighter. "Once this one is charged, we'll do yours and get both set up."

"Gee, thanks. I almost think you're being nice." I squint at Magnus like I'm analyzing him. "Nah. You accidentally acted like you might not be a total jerk, but the moment passed."

His nostrils flare again. He rolls down his window and tosses our old phones onto the asphalt of the parking lot. Then he starts the car, backs up, and drives over our old phones.

"What did you do that for?" I ask.

"Donnae want anyone to track us. The only way to be sure is to destroy the mobiles we'd been using."

I've had just about enough of the snarling bull seated beside me not telling me anything. Just about? Oh no, I careened off that cliff hours ago. Maybe yesterday, actually.

"Time to explain who Evan is," I say. "No more 'haud yer wash' or whatever that saying is. And no more 'it's none of your business' either."

"It's 'haud yer wheesht.' And who Evan might be is—"

"Uh-uh-uh. What did I just say? You weren't listening, were you? Nope. If you had listened, you'd know I said I won't stand for you saying everything is none of my business."

He growls like an irritable bear. Yeah, now he's a pig-bear. That term suits him perfectly.

"I want info," I say. "Cough it up, MacTaggart."

The damn Scot floors the accelerator and swerves out onto the street, roaring down it like we've got a horde of fire-breathing demons chasing us. He barrels through the town and veers onto the main road so fast that the tires squeal. Once we're back on the road to wherever we're going, he slows down to an almost normal speed.

"You're insane," I snap.

"Aye."

"Got any other stops to make? If so, I need to buy a parachute. You're driving this car like it's a jet plane."

He grips the steering wheel so hard I expect his knuckles to shatter. "Do not speak to me. I need a break from your incessant havering."

I face forward and fold my arms over my chest. "Fine. Let me know when you've decided to become a human being again. What am I saying? You aren't human. You're a demonic pig-bear."

Magnus glances at me, his brows raised, and his lips tick up at the corners a smidge. "Pig-bear?"

"Never mind. It's my private nickname for you, and I don't feel like explaining it." I look at him. "You didn't object to the demonic part."

"I don't object to any of it, though I do think 'pig-bear' is bloody silly."

"Can't call you a teddy bear, that's for sure."

He grunts. "No one would call me that. Except maybe—no one."

"Except maybe no one? That doesn't make sense. And since you paused between saying maybe and no one, I think you're lying."

The pig-bear grunts again.

He continues driving down the four-lane highway without speaking or acknowledging I exist, instead staring straight ahead. After a few more miles, he turns off onto what seems like an access road. A bridge crosses the highway here, but we turn right onto a regular street. Magnus pulls over to the side of the road and stops.

"Is there a problem?" I ask. "Maybe you're lost."

The jerk doesn't even bother to grunt. He seems to be pretending I don't exist while he fiddles with his new phone. The charging cable is still connected to the cigarette lighter, but he manages to do who knows what on the phone's screen anyway.

"Get out of the car," he commands as he keeps fiddling with his new phone.

"Excuse me?"

"I said get out of the car. I need to make a private call."

"Screw that. You get out of the car, Pig-Bear." Yeah, I've decided that's his new name. Why not? He decided to stop speaking to me until he delivered his command. And I decided to give him a stupid, insulting nickname. We're even.

But I do feel a little foolish, like a spoiled kid having a hissy fit.

Magnus glowers at me.

"I'm sorry I called you Pig-Bear," I say. "That was childish. But you can't seriously expect me to stand on the side of the road while you make your call. It's not safe."

He squeezes his eyes shut and rubs them with his thumb and forefinger. "Aye, you're right. I'm sorry."

Did the great Magnus MacTaggart just admit he made a mistake? He definitely apologized. I didn't hallucinate it.

"Thank you," I say. "I appreciate that."

"I need to ring—" He scrunches up his whole face like it pains him to finish that sentence. Then he sighs and relaxes. "I need to ring my cousin Evan. He's a billionaire tech mogul and one of the cleverest people I've ever known."

Holy shit. He gave me a few crumbs of personal info. I might pass out from shock. "Okay. I could plug my ears if it will make you feel better."

"That's not necessary."

"Your cousin is really a billionaire?"

"Aye. He's the CEO of Evanescent Security Technologies Limited, the company he started."

"Wow, that's impressive. Do you think he can help us?"

"I hope so." He messes with his phone again, and I hear the line ringing through the speaker. "If you could be quiet while I talk to Evan, that would be…helpful."

He's trying not to be rude, isn't he? That's weird, but I like it. I realize he's using the speakerphone because the charging cable isn't long enough to let him hold the phone to his ear. But I can't help wondering, or maybe hoping, that he finally decided to bring me into the loop.

"Evan MacTaggart," a voice says on the other end of the line.

"It's Magnus."

"Good morning. How are you and your lass today?"

"She's not my lass." Magnus grits his teeth while he says that, but then he seems to force himself to relax a smidgen. "We destroyed our mobiles and bought new ones, the sort that aren't connected to any account."

"Good. Now you need to get a clean vehicle. Logan advised me on how you can do that, but you might want to ring him for more advice. He is a former MI6 agent, after all."

"Piper is sitting beside me listening to this call."

"Nothing I've said is confidential information."

"Go on, then."

He glances at me, though I can't figure out why since he maintains a neutral expression.

"Why don't I text you the details," Evan says. "It's a wee bit complicated. If you have questions, you can ring Logan."

"Aye, I'll do that. Thank you, Evan."

He recites the phone number to Evan, then ends the call.

I might be gaping at him. He can't blame me for that. I mean, he went from being a snarling jerk who wouldn't tell me anything to sharing info about his family in the space of twenty minutes by my estimation.

"Now you know who Evan is," he says. "Does that make you feel better?"

"Yes. But now I'm curious about Logan."

"Can we talk about him later?"

"Sure."

We sit here in silence, apparently waiting for the text Evan promised to send. Cars rush past on the highway beside us. Wispy clouds drift by, and I find myself relaxing. My muscles soften, and the tension inside me melts away little by little. Why should I feel so much better just because Magnus apologized and sort of introduced me to his cousin? It's crazy.

His phone makes a bloopy noise.

Magnus grabs the device and squints at the screen. "Evan sent the information."

"Is it really complicated? Just switching cars doesn't sound that difficult."

With his head bowed, he glances at me sideways and smirks. "Ye donnae know the MacTaggarts. This is more than just acquiring another vehicle. It's a plan."

"For what?"

"You'll see."

He starts driving again, pulling out onto the highway and heading off through the French countryside. This time, I don't mind that he didn't share all the details with me. I get the feeling he wants to surprise me with the plan his cousin came up with, and that makes me feel…good. Which is weird. But I like it.

As I watch the scenery whizzing by, my mind travels back to yesterday when I'd pointed out Magnus and I have had sex twice but never kissed. Then he kissed me. I shouldn't assume that means he, um, likes me. But I want to believe that.

Yeah, I've lost my mind. And it feels good.

Chapter Fourteen

Magnus

Piper keeps glancing at me with a soft, sweet smile on her lips. It's somewhat disturbing. An hour ago, she called me a pig-bear. Now she looks like she wants to crawl onto my lap and curl up there. I might not mind if she did that, but it would send the wrong message. We are not dating. I don't do that anymore, and she's a fugitive. Two reasons I should never give her the impression I feel anything for her, not even sympathy.

Why, then, am I leveraging all my contacts to help her?

"I could drive for a while," she says. "You must be tired."

My first instinct is to snarl at her that I donnae need her help. But I didn't sleep well last night, and I feel like I might fall into a trance while traveling down the highway. Instead of behaving like a pig-bear, which is a bloody ridiculous nickname, I should act like a mature adult. Only Piper has ever made me behave in such an irrational manner.

"All right," I say. "You can drive for a wee while."

"Yay! Thank you. I love driving."

My lips twitch like they want to form a smile, but I can't allow myself to do that. I pull over on an access road and switch places with Piper. "Donnae drive too fast. We want to avoid running into law enforcement."

She salutes me. "Aye-aye, captain."

I don't understand the silliness so many women like to engage in. It serves no purpose other than to fash men. Well, it fashes me. I suppose other blokes might not mind. My cousins who have married Americans seem unfazed by the antics of their wives, who love to meddle in other people's lives. I won't tell Piper about them yet. Maybe never. She won't need to know unless I take her home with me, which I cannot do.

"Mind if I turn on the radio?" Piper asks. "I need some upbeat tunes."

"Do what you like. I'll be asleep, so it willnae fash me."

She switches the radio on and flips through stations, which are all in French, until she finds one that plays some sort of pop music. "You probably prefer death metal, huh?"

"No. I prefer bagpipes."

"All the time? Come on, you must like some other kind of music." She pulls out onto the highway. "Your music preference isn't information I can use to seduce all your secrets out of you."

I ignore her comment and tilt my seat back until I'm almost lying down, then I fold my hands over my belly and shut my eyes.

"Sleep tight," she says. "Don't let the bedbugs bite."

"This isn't a bed, so there can't be bedbugs."

"Jeez, you're such a grump."

"Aye. Wake me in an hour."

"Sure thing."

Fortunately, she gives up on talking to me. Despite the annoyingly cheerful music she chose, I fall asleep. Sometime later, I rouse and glance at the dashboard clock, which tells me I've slept for an hour and a half.

"I told you to wake me in an hour," I say. "Ye cannae follow any directions, can you?"

"Of course I can. But you seemed like you needed more than an hour's rest."

"Cannae trust you to do anything I say."

She huffs. "Excuse me for being nice and considering your well-being."

Why would she care about that? Since I prefer not to think about the answer to that question, I move my seat back into the upright position and glance at the surrounding landscape. "Have we crossed the border into Switzerland yet?"

"No."

"Well, at least ye didn't cock that up."

She shakes her head. "I should've known a nap wouldn't improve your mood. You like being grouchy and nasty."

No, I don't like that. But it's a necessary part of my job.

I grab my new mobile phone and bring up a map program, typing in the name of a particular airport.

"What are you doing?" Piper asks.

"Pull over at the next convenient place. I need to drive the rest of the way."

The lass salutes me, just like she had earlier. "Aye-aye, captain."

"Stop saying that."

Once we've switched places, I take a moment to have the maps program give me the quickest route to our next destination.

Piper leans over the center console to peer at my mobile's screen. "Montbéliard? Why are we going there?"

"Haud—" I grumble and try to restrain my frustration with the bloody woman. "Just sit back and watch the scenery. I know where I'm going and why, but you don't need to know yet."

She makes a derisive noise, but at least she sits back and aims her gaze out the window as I told her to do.

Maybe I should explain my plan—or rather, the plan Evan and Logan devised for me—but I've gotten accustomed to keeping things to myself. It's hard to change a lifelong habit. Not sure if I want to change, anyway.

We reach the Montbéliard Courcelles Airport fifteen minutes later, and I steer us off the highway, onto a two-lane paved road that leads us to our destination.

Piper leans forward to stare through the windscreen, jerking her head left and right before she settles her gaze on the flat, well-mown area surrounded by a fence. "Is that an airport? Are we flying somewhere?"

"No. But aye, that's Montbéliard Courcelles Airport. We are going there, but not to fly."

As we draw closer to the airport, Piper's eyes widen. She points at the long runway. "Look at that. Somebody's parked a private jet there. Looks like a fancy one, not that I'm an expert on airplanes."

"It is a fancy one." I turn onto the road that accesses the airport's car park and pull into a slot. "My cousin Evan owns that jet."

Her expression goes blank. For a moment, she just stares at me as if she's slipped into a coma while sitting upright. Then her lids flutter. "Are you saying I get to meet your cousin?"

"Evan isn't on the jet. He sent our cousin Logan to help us."

"Logan? That's the ex-MI6 guy, right?"

"Aye." I throw my door open. "Get out. We'll retrieve our bags after we talk to Logan."

I lead Piper into the airport terminal, where we find my cousin leaning against the wall rather than sitting on a chair. He wants to surveil the area, I'm sure. Logan's time in MI6 molded him into a consummate spy. Maybe that's why I get on best with Logan, though I do fine with my other cousins too—the ones who will speak to me.

Logan raises his brows when we approach him. "Didnae mention the lass you had with you was so bonnie."

"Her looks are irrelevant."

My cousin eyes me in the way I've come to understand means he's assessing the situation or maybe just me. "Why are you going to Basel?"

"I know someone there. A trusted contact."

"With a man like Royce Hammond hunting you, it might not be wise to trust anyone outside the family."

"Donnae worry about that. I trust this contact with my life—and so do you."

"Ye wouldnae be going to see…him. Would you?"

"Aye, I am. So ye know he can be trusted."

Logan smirks. "You must be desperate. He's not a black sheep the way you are, but everyone in the family knows asking for his help is like wishing for a wildfire. Scorched earth is his favorite approach to everything. But I will alert the lad you're on your way and need his assistance."

"I know what he's like. Not saying I'll ask for his help, but I can trust him to give us a safe place to hide while I figure out our next move."

"A good plan, provided the lad cooperates." Logan reaches inside his jacket and pulls out a small rectangular object, then offers it to me. "This flash drive contains all the information we could gather on Royce Hammond. I've contacted some trusted sources who haven't gotten back to me yet, so I'll update you if I get more from them. This is a tangled web of data, Magnus. You'll need expert help."

He means I might need the fire starter's help.

I accept the flash drive, tucking it into my trouser pocket. "Thank you, Logan."

"Rory and Lachlan are leveraging their contacts too."

Why would they do that? I haven't done anything to show them I want to be a part of the family. But that's the MacTaggart way. We step up to help each other no matter what. I've never done much for my family, though, except to help Kirsty.

Logan looks at Piper, and his lips curve into a sly smile. "You must be the lass who keeps getting away from Magnus."

"Yes, I am," she says. Then she holds out her hand to him. "Since Magnus won't introduce me, I'm Piper Lang."

My cousin shakes her hand. "Logan MacTaggart. I'm one of the few family members who will speak to Magnus. The others will come to their senses, though, once they realize he's not a craven criminal."

"Why would anyone think that?"

He shrugs. "I should let Magnus explain that to you."

"We should go," I say. "No time to waste."

"Be careful," Logan tells me. "The information we've gathered so far is not encouraging. Royce Hammond seems like a dangerous man."

"I've dealt with worse."

"Maybe." Logan leans toward me, nailing his gaze to mine. "Or maybe not."

He wouldn't try to frighten me. Logan knows better. For him to issue that sort of warning makes me wonder what he and our other cousins have dug up concerning Royce Hammond. I don't have time to look through the information right now. We need to get to Switzerland.

Logan hands me a keyring with a single key on it. "We procured a clean vehicle for you and passports, which are in the car. Donnae ask how we did that. Best not to know these things."

Piper seems confused, but I am not. Logan means the car might not have been acquired legally, but it has all the requisite papers if we should get stopped by a law enforcement entity. I accept the key and hook the ring around my middle finger.

"Try not to get yourself killed," Logan says. "It would ruin Callum and Kate's engagement ceilidh."

"I'll try not to disappoint them."

We say goodbye to my cousin and head back outside. I see two other vehicles in the car park. When I push a button on the keychain Logan gave me, the headlights on a grey four-door car flash. That's our ride.

I instruct Piper to get into the new vehicle while I retrieve our bags and stash them in the trunk. For once, she doesn't complain. She follows my orders without even giving me a dirty look, not even when I insist on driving. Within five minutes after we left Logan, we're exiting the airport car park.

Piper tips her seat back and props her feet on the dashboard. "I like your cousin. He's hot."

"Logan is married."

"I can appreciate a man's physical attributes without wanting to jump his bones."

"You said you like him because he's 'hot.' That means you're attracted to him."

A laugh snorts out of her. "Oh please. I like Logan because he's clearly a smart, tough, efficient man."

"You met him for five minutes."

"I can tell a lot about someone in the first few minutes after I meet them." She leans sideways toward me. "When I first met you, I knew you'd be a tough-as-nails, uncompromising, rude and obnoxious jackass."

Well, I cannae argue with that assessment. But I doubt she figured that out on the day we met. She's had nearly two years to reach that conclusion.

"This wildfire guy we're going to meet," Piper says. "Is he another mysterious cousin?"

"You'll find out when you meet him."

"Gee, thanks for not telling me squat, as usual." She tips one foot side to side as if she's counting out a rhythm. "I know we're on the run, but I wish we could take a few minutes now and then to enjoy the scenery, maybe visit a landmark or something." When I open my mouth to speak, she holds up a hand. "I know, I know. Life or death situation, no time to enjoy anything. It's just that after twenty months of running, I miss the little things like seeing the Eiffel Tower."

She sounds melancholy, and when I glance at her, she looks that way too. Defeated might be a better word. I've chased her for so long, but I never wondered how her life as a fugitive has affected her. She's lonely, I think. Lonely and scared.

As we reach the traffic circle at the end of the airport's driveway, I stop and study the options. Turn right to get back on the highway. Or I can turn left.

"How long are we going to sit here?" Piper asks. "I don't see any other cars. What are you waiting for? A heavenly sign?"

"No." I make my decision, though I cannae explain why I do it, and turn left.

"Isn't the highway over there?" She points in the opposite direction. "That's how we got here."

"We are not going directly to the highway. We'll make a stop first."

"But I thought we urgently needed to get to Switzerland."

"It can wait a wee bit." We cross under a railroad bridge, and I turn right onto another street. "I'm taking you to the Château de Montbéliard. We're sightseeing."

Chapter Fifteen

Piper

Sightseeing?" I say. "Seriously? You kept saying we don't have time for anything except getting to Switzerland to meet a guy who I assume is another of your mysterious cousins. But now we're stopping off at a landmark or something."

"I thought you would like to see the Château de Montbéliard."

"Wow, thank you." I experience a bizarre and inappropriate desire to hug him and kiss his cheek. He'd probably flip out if I did that. "I can't wait to see this place. What is it?"

"A castle."

"I've never seen a castle before, not in person. This will be amazing."

He grunts. "Aye, it will be a thrill for me too."

Yeah, his tone makes it clear he doesn't think it will be fun at all.

I study his profile. "You know, it wouldn't kill you to loosen up now and then. I get that you have a dangerous job, but it's not healthy to stay on high alert all the time. Everybody has to relax once in a while."

"Not me."

"During my time as a fugitive, I learned that relaxation is critical to maintaining my mental and physical health. So I spent thirty minutes every day practicing meditation."

"If you're expecting me to meditate, you'll be disappointed."

"Massage is also a good way to de-stress." Why did I say that? He might think I want to give him a massage. Maybe I would like that. I mean, rubbing down that big muscular body could be fun. But I would wind up screwing him again. So no, I won't offer to give him a massage. "You could buy an electric massager."

He ignores my comment as the street winds around sharp curves and he focuses on his driving.

I can see what look like turrets up ahead. "Is that the castle?"

"Aye."

The closer we get to the structure, the more excited I feel. I've always enjoyed sightseeing, but I don't usually get this worked up about it. After so long on the run, to do something normal feels like winning the lottery. Magnus parks along the street and guides me toward the castle. It has two big round turrets as well as two smaller rectangular ones, and the building seems to have multiple wings. The high walls make me think of medieval knights battling their enemies to save a princess who hides inside the massive stone structure.

"Can we go inside?" I ask.

"Aye."

He's reverted to monosyllabic mode. Well, I intend to enjoy this excursion no matter what he acts like.

Magnus takes my hand to lead me into the castle.

I stare at him, stunned by this simple act of affection. That must be what it is, right? He wouldn't hold my hand to make sure I don't run away. Well, maybe he would. But this doesn't feel like the bounty hunter keeping control of his quarry. He continues holding my hand while we explore the two museums inside the castle, but when we exit the building, he lets go of me. Though I want to ask him why he wanted to hold my hand, I decide not to poke the bear.

Then we're back on the highway, racing toward the Swiss border.

We have no trouble crossing into Switzerland thanks to the fake passports Logan had procured for us. I already had a phony passport, but Magnus told me I should not use that one. Royce Hammond might know about it. His cousin gave us "clean" passports. That's what Magnus said. Since he hasn't let me see those documents, I have no idea what alias his cousin gave me. Maybe I'm now Hildegarde Munchkin.

I peer out the windshield. "Are we in Basel now?"

"Aye."

"Will we go straight to your mysterious cousin? The one Logan never mentioned by name?"

Magnus throws me a sharp look. "Stop looking for mystery under every rock. His name is Errol Murdoch, and yes, we'll go directly to his home."

"Don't you think Royce Hammond can find us there?"

He chuckles. "Ye donnae know Errol."

"But I will soon. Right?"

"No, I mean to chase him away before you see him." He shakes his head and sighs. "What do ye think? Of course you're going to meet him. Errol makes Logan seem boring."

This sounds more intriguing every minute. A mysterious cousin who makes an ex-spy seem boring and who lives in Switzerland. "Why does your cousin live here in Basel?"

"He doesn't live here. Errol has a base of operations in Basel, and I happen to know he's in the city right now."

"Um, how do you know that for sure?"

"I used the hotel's phone to ring him this morning while you were in the shower."

"Oh. Aren't you worried someone might've found out about that conversation somehow?"

Magnus gives me a look that I interpret as meaning "oh please, you're talking to the great Magnus MacTaggart here, lassie." I have to trust he knows what he's doing. He and his cousins are all I've got.

"We might need to warn your parents," he says.

"About Hammond? I hadn't even thought of that." I hug myself, though I didn't consciously decide to do that. Talking about my family always makes me uneasy.

"How often do you have contact with your parents?"

I wrap my arms around myself more tightly. "They kind of disowned me."

"Before or after you were charged with murder?"

"After. I called to tell them, and I guess I hoped they would rush to England to support me. Instead, they shut me out and announced I'm no longer their daughter."

Magnus glances at me. "I understand how you must feel."

"How can you? I've met your cousin, and it's clear you have family who care about you."

"I do, but my parents are a different story." He focuses on the road, gripping the wheel with both hands. "The last time I saw my father, he told me never to come back. Said I'm a disgrace and a plague, and that he's ashamed of me."

"Oh God, Magnus, I'm so sorry. What did your mom say about that?"

"Ma said nothing. She always lets Da make the decisions."

"I guess they don't like what you do for a living, huh?"

"Aye." He rests one elbow on the window and scratches his cheek. "My father thought I should join the local police force after I left the army. Instead, I became a bounty hunter. Da sees that as tantamount to becoming a criminal."

Though I want to ask him a question, I feel like it's not my business. He just gave me more answers than I've ever gotten out of him before, so I don't want to push too hard.

"I can tell ye want to ask me something," he says. "Go on."

Well, now that I have permission… "Why did you become a bounty hunter?"

"To catch criminals. After my time in the army, I didnae want to take a job where I'd have to work with other blokes and get along with them. I'd been through hell in Afghanistan, and I just wanted to be alone."

"I get it. But you are friendly with your cousins."

"Never used to be. I'm the black sheep of the clan, and most of my relatives are afraid of me." He turns a corner, heading down a narrower street. "But recently, my cousins have tried to bring me into the fold. I've let them. Before that, I was only friendly with Logan and his sister Kirsty." He parks the car along the street and shuts off the engine. "You're about to meet Errol. He's a strange lad, but don't let that put you off. He's clever underneath the barmy rubbish."

Barmy rubbish? Yeah, that sounds fabulous.

As we climb out of the car, I tip my head back to look at the building in front of us. The four-story structure has a boxy shape, taller than it is wide, and has been painted a pale green color. Despite the brick parking lot, I would definitely call the style of the building modern, not old world. I've never been a fan of modern architecture since I'm more comfortable with the past. Compared to my present, the medieval world sounds like heaven.

"Move your erse," Magnus says from the other side of the car. "Donnae want to stand out here on the street."

"Then go stand on the steps." I point to the building's entrance, which has steps that look like marble with a darker stone flanking the doors. Above the entrance, a sign announces the building's name—Céleste. I don' know what that means, but it's a beautiful word. "Is this where Errol lives?"

"No, I brought you here for no reason."

"You don't need to get snippy with me. I'm asking a simple question."

"Aye, Errol lives here."

I point at the sign. "Do you know what that French word means?"

"Heavenly. Errol told me that last time I saw him, and I'm sure he will explain his theory about the name when you meet him. He loves to haver."

Magnus walks over to my side and lays a hand on my back as we approach the entrance and climb the stairs. As we push through the doors, I see mailboxes along one wall and and a door labeled "bureau."

"It means office," Magnus says. "Since you're gawping at the door, I assumed you'd want a translation. I'm not fluent in French, so donnae be asking me to translate what anyone says."

"Don't worry. I will never ask you to do anything ever again."

He smirks. "I'll believe that when the sun disintegrates."

I can't keep up with his moods. He runs hot and cold, alternately teases and insults me, and just grunts if he doesn't feel like answering my questions. I suppose his job has made him a loner, and so has his estrangement from his family. I can relate, but I haven't turned into a grump because of my personal issues. Jeez, I'm a fugitive and yet I stay upbeat. Mostly.

We take an elevator to the third floor, then Magnus leads me down a long hall to the unit at the far end. He knocks on the door. I hear the distinctive sound of a security chain being disengaged.

The door swings inward, revealing an attractive man who seems young, though I can't tell that for sure. He might just have one of those faces.

He's wearing a cowboy hat and a kilt—nothing else.

Magnus groans. "Errol, put some trousers on, would ye? A shirt too."

He tosses his hat onto a nearby rack. "Why? I love swinging free, as Aidan likes to say."

"You're too old to act like a bairn."

Errol moves aside, waving for us to enter. "Logan texted me that you'd be coming, so I made tea for us."

"Oh, how nice," I say. "Thank you. I'm Piper Lang, by the way, since Magnus is allergic to introducing me to anybody."

"I was about to do that," Magnus growls. "Didnae give me the chance."

We amble down the entryway into a spacious living room while Errol shuts the door and hurries past us.

"Sit here, Piper," he says, gesturing toward a puffy armchair. "I haven't had a lass in my apartment since at least…" He scrunches up his face like he's trying to remember. "Last Thursday. It's a pleasure to host you."

Magnus drops onto the sofa. "Did Logan inform you of the situation?"

"Aye," Errol says as he settles onto a padded wooden chair. "Anything I can do to help? I assume so since you're here, but I cannae guess what you might need from me."

"For now, a place to stay."

"Of course. My home is yours." He glances sideways at me. "But I only have one bedroom."

"We'll share."

"I'd rather sleep with Piper than you."

Magnus throws his head back, shutting his eyes. After a couple of seconds, he faces his cousin again. "I meant Piper and I will share the bedroom. You can sleep on the sofa."

"Oh aye, that is a better plan, I suppose."

The surly Scot hoists his body off the sofa. "I need the bog."

He starts to head for a door beside the open kitchen but stops when Errol says, "It's not there anymore."

Magnus slowly turns halfway toward us. "Where the bloody hell is the bog, then?"

"I meant I don't use that bathroom anymore, so I shut off the water to it. You'll need to use either the full bath in the bedroom or the toilet in the office."

"Why do you have a toilet in your office?"

"Because I'm in there more than I'm in the bog. Donnae like to walk far when I need to relieve myself."

Grumbling, Magnus strides down the hallway and disappears into a room.

Errol chuckles softly. "Donnae worry, Piper. I was telling a porky about the toilet in my office. This flat has two bathrooms, but no freestanding toilet. I'm just harassing Magnus."

"Um, why are you harassing him?" I know he's rude to me, but he's been rather polite to his cousin.

"Magnus is too uptight. He needs a wee bit of bothering." Errol tilts his head to the side, studying me. Then he smiles. "I bet you bother him plenty."

"Yeah, I do. He deserves it."

Errol laughs again, louder than before. "I like you, Piper. We need to get better acquainted."

He jumps out of his chair and scoops me up in his arms.

Chapter Sixteen

Magnus

"Put her down, Errol," I snarl as I stomp out of the hallway and straight to my barmy cousin. Though I don't know Errol well, I've employed his skills a few times over the past year, though even he couldn't help me capture Piper. How does the woman evade everyone? How does she outwit me? I still have no answers to those questions.

Aye, it fashes me. I need to know.

Errol still has Piper in his arms.

"What the bloody hell do ye think you're doing?" I demand.

"She looked uncomfortable in that chair, so I was moving her to the sofa."

"The lass can walk. She doesnae need you to carry her." My hands ache, and I glance down to find I've been clenching my fists. Given the tightness in my jaw, I know I must have gritted my teeth too. "Put her down."

Errol finally sets Piper on her feet.

But he cannae help himself. He takes hold of her arm and guides her toward the sofa. "Let's sit here together so we can blether about Magnus."

I try not to growl, but my cousin is testing my patience. "Donnae be gossiping about me—in front of me."

"So it's all right if I do that behind your back?"

"No."

Piper and Errol settle onto the sofa with no more than a foot between them. I donnae like my cousin sitting that close to her, especially when he's half-naked.

I aim my hardest glare at Errol. "Get dressed."

"What's wrong with my kilt? At least I don't dress like a Satan worshiper."

"There's nothing wrong with my clothes."

My cousin rolls his eyes. "All right, Magnus, no need to get up to high doh. Ye must have a big crush on the lass to behave this way."

Piper's eyes flare wide, but only for a moment. Then she stares down at her lap, smoothing her hands over her jeans.

Will Errol never stop talking? He's embarrassed Piper, not that I should care about that. I can't help noticing her clothes, though. She always wears bland outfits, and I've assumed she does that to blend in and make it harder for me to track her. It worked. But I doubt her clothing is the main reason I hadn't been able to catch her until yesterday.

My cousin finally ambles down the hallway, disappearing into the bedroom.

I collapse onto the armchair, exhausted by Errol's antics. The lad will turn me into a bampot, for certain, but I need his help. Still, I'm no longer sure I should ask him to get involved in this mess—because Royce Hammond is dangerous, not because Errol keeps flirting with Piper.

Can my barmy cousin handle that sort of situation? He might love to start fires, metaphorically, but life-threatening risks are a different matter altogether.

Piper is watching me with a curious expression. "Why does your cousin have a different last name? Was his mom a MacTaggart and she married a guy called Murdoch?"

"Yes. If ye know the answer, why ask the question?"

"For confirmation." She grasps her knees, which seems like a nervous movement. "Are you sure he can help? Errol seems kind of…flighty."

"I told ye he's very clever underneath all the barmy rubbish."

My cousin emerges from the hallway dressed in grey trousers and an off-white long-sleeve dress shirt as well as black loafers. He saunters over to the sofa and sits down beside Piper again, though this time he leaves an arm's length between them. He combed his hair too—and he's wearing bright purple socks with gold stars on them.

I stifle a groan. At least he doesn't have aluminium foil on his head.

He slants toward Piper and speaks in a ridiculous fake whisper. "So tell me, Piper, are you and Magnus getting married?"

"No," I say. "We are not. Stick to the issue at hand, Errol."

"Which is what? You havenae told me yet."

"I thought Logan would have briefed you."

He touches Piper's thigh, just above her knee. "Magnus hasn't participated in the family life in so long that he's forgotten how we do things."

"Errol, ye *cacan*—"

"All right, all right. Donnae get your kilt in a twist. Of course, you aren't wearing a kilt…" He removes his hand from Piper's leg and faces me. "Logan knows better than to tell me everything over the phone or the internet. Even the most secure system can be hacked. But he did ring to let me know you were coming and that you need my special brand of help."

"We do." Assuming he has enough marbles left in his brain to do what I need him to do. I think I can hear those wee balls rolling around between his ears. As much as Errol confounds and annoys me, I know he does have a full complement of marbles. It's just a matter of encouraging him to use them.

Piper glances at me, then looks at Errol. "Are you a computer expert or a security specialist or something?"

"Oh, no," he says with a chuckle. "I'm a treasure hunter."

She grins and laughs. "A treasure hunter? I didn't think anybody really did that."

"That's because we're a secretive lot. Donnae want someone else nicking our treasures because we had a drink together and relaxed a wee bit too much, then blurted out the location of a bloody great hoard."

"So, are you like Indiana Jones?"

"Oh, aye." He winks. "But I left my fedora and my bull whip in the bedroom. Care to come with me to see them?"

"No, she doesn't," I say with slightly too much volume. "Why donnae you explain to Piper what you can do?"

"I am kind of confused," she says. "Treasure hunting doesn't sound like something that will help us."

Errol touches her leg again. "It's not the job that matters, it's the skills. A treasure hunter needs to be creative, intelligent, curious, and so much more. I have a photographic memory, I can read lips, I speak twelve languages, I'm bloody good at reading people, and I practice magic tricks."

"Um, how do magic tricks help?"

"Sleight of hand is a useful skill when you're trying to outwit someone. I'm also a risk-taker and a puzzle fanatic. Crossword, sudoku, anything that tests my mental prowess." He leans closer to Piper. "And I have all the prowess you could want."

The *cacan* is flirting again.

Despite his bizarre behavior, Errol is everything he just said. I've seen him in action, though never for a job like this one. I need to make sure he understands the stakes.

"Errol, I need to explain the situation," I say. "This won't be an exciting hunt for treasure. We're in serious trouble. A dangerous man wants to capture Piper or possibly kill her and me too. Royce Hammond is not a man to be trifled with."

"I never trifle, Magnus. But it would be helpful if you told me how I can be of assistance."

"Evan and Logan gave me a flash drive with a trove of information on it related to Hammond. We cannae wait while I try to sort out the details. But you have the skills to do it faster."

"Aye, I do."

He's not being arrogant. Errol might behave like a barmy flirt, but I've seen him reassemble an intellectual puzzle. He knows what he's doing.

I dig the flash drive out of my pocket and toss it to him. "If you want the job, it's yours."

"Danger *and* a puzzle?" He tosses the flash drive in the air and catches it. "Of course I'm in."

"Good. Let's go into your office."

Errol shakes his head. "I need to be alone while I fit all the pieces into the jigsaw. Why don't you and Piper go sightseeing? Basel is a bonnie city." He smiles and winks at Piper. "But not as bonnie as your lass."

"I'm not his lass," she says. "Nobody owns me."

"Didnae mean to imply ownership. But I've never seen Magnus with a woman before. We all assume he shags lasses when he's away, but he doesn't bring them home—or take them on his missions."

I resist the urge to snarl at him. "That's enough, Errol."

My cousin slings an arm around Piper's shoulders and employs his phony whisper again. "Donnae let Magnus the Beast fash ye. It's all an act. Our cousin Kirsty says he's the sweetest man on earth, next to her brother Logan."

"Sweet?" Piper says as if that's the most insane thing she's ever heard.

"You'll see," Errol tells her. "He cannae hide it as much as he likes to think he can. Not when he's with family."

I spring up from my chair. "Piper, let's go…sightseeing. If Errol wants privacy to do his job, we should give him that."

She hops up and grins. "More sightseeing? That's fabulous."

"Donnae get too excited."

The lass rushes around the coffee table to me, raises onto her toes, and kisses my cheek. "Thank you, Magnus."

"It was Errol's idea, not mine."

"But you agreed to do it, and I'm grateful for that."

My cousin is watching us with an expression I've seen before. It means he thinks he understands something that had confounded him. Whatever he thinks he understands about me and Piper, he's wrong. I can't trust her. The woman got away from me again and again, and she might have used talking about her life as a means of getting under my skin. It didn't work. No one gets inside me.

Errol hands me a keyring that has one key on it. "So you can get back inside the flat without knocking."

Accepting the key, I lead Piper out of the flat.

In the lift, she turns toward me. "Are you sure Errol's apartment is a safe place?"

"Ye donnae know him. Errol has become rather paranoid about protecting his secrets from other treasure hunters. To accomplish that, he hired our cousin Evan to install a high-tech security system that not only prevents anyone from breaking in, but also blocks electronic signals and does a lot of other technical things that I don't bother to understand."

"But if Errol lives here, Royce Hammond could find us."

The lift doors open, and I usher Piper out into the entryway. "There's no paper trail. I don't know how Errol managed that, but I doubt he did anything illegal. I might not know my cousin that well, but I trust Logan's opinion, and he swears Errol is clever and trustworthy. He uses his Basel flat as a base of operations."

"Does he live here full-time?"'

"No. He has a house in Scotland."

"Logan said Errol starts wildfires."

I lay a hand on her back. "Donnae worry. That was a metaphor. Errol likes to get people up to high doh as a way of distracting them. It's a strategy, not a sign of instability."

As we walk out the main doors, Piper asks, "Couldn't someone follow him to find out where his secret home base is?"

"Logan taught Errol how to evade his enemies. The lad is very clever and very careful. Besides, I don't think Errol owns the flat, and I'd be very surprised if his name is connected to it in any way."

"How old is Errol? I've been curious about that."

"Thirty-seven. Do you have any more questions about my cousin? Or can we get on with the sightseeing bollocks?"

"Wow, you make it sound like so much fun."

At our car, I open the passenger door for her.

She climbs in while eying me with a strange expression, almost as if she's confused.

I'm confused too. What the bloody hell am I doing? Opening doors for her? Getting angry when another man flirts with her? I donnae ever do that. Piper might get the wrong idea and think I care about her, which I don't. For twenty months, I've hunted the woman. She became my obsession. The lust I feel for her has nothing to do with the lass herself. It's losing the game that fashes me and drives me to fuck her whenever we're alone.

But I didn't touch her last night. Which means nothing.

Piper is still gazing at me through the passenger side window with that same puzzled expression.

Why am I standing here like a ruddy statue? I stalk around to the driver's door and jump in. Suddenly, I realize what I need to do to get rid of this obsession. "I want to know how you kept slipping away from me, and you're going to tell me. Right now."

"You really can't handle the fact a woman got the better of you. Male pride will bite you in the ass, MacTaggart."

"Aye. But I need to know."

She slants over the center console toward me, and her voice becomes a sensual whisper. "You strike me as the hands-on type. So instead of telling you, let me show you."

"In what way?"

Piper opens her door. "I'm going to run, and you will chase me."

"Donnae be ridiculous."

"Well, if you aren't up to the task…"

"I'm up for it."

My pulse is beating faster, and my breaths have quickened too. A sensation like electricity races over my skin. This is rubbish. I don't get excited because a woman speaks to me in a husky whisper. But chasing Piper has always been my obsession and the most exhilarating experience of my life.

I want to hunt the lass again.

To find out how she evades me. That's all.

"Go on," I say. "Run."

She leaps out of the car and bolts.

Chapter Seventeen

Piper

I've gone completely insane. Show Magnus how I kept getting away from him? If that's not poking a bear, I don't know what is. But the risk amps up my adrenaline and gives me a weird kind of high that I've never experienced before. As I pelt down the street, heading who knows where, my heart pounds—and it's from more than exertion. An excitement like nothing I've ever experienced before rushes through me, tingling on skin and making me so wet that my panties feel damp.

I glance back.

Our car is still parked in front of Errol's building, but I don't see Magnus.

He's on the hunt. For me.

I race down a different street, one full of houses that all bump up right next to each other. Though I want to glance back, I know I should stay focused on the road ahead and what I will do next. One house has a wooden fence behind it. I swerve down the narrow allow between that house and the next one, then I vault over the fence. My feet slip, and I crash to the ground. But I haven't injured myself, so I spring to my feet and race to the other side of the yard, vaulting over that side of the fence into an open area behind the neighboring house. I'm not a superhero. I got over that wooden fence because it was only as tall as I am.

That means Magnus could see me, if he's close enough.

Slowing to a jog, I zigzag between houses and other buildings as I make my way to anywhere that's not close to Errol's apartment.

I hear footfalls behind me and risk a backward glance.

Magnus is sprinting after me, though I have a two-block lead.

Up ahead, I notice a shop. The lights are on, so it must be open. While Magnus's footsteps grow louder, I slow to a fast walk and duck inside the shop. Clocks of various types and sizes cover one wall while a glass case filled with watches and jewelry forms a counter along the back wall.

The gray-haired gentleman behind the counter smiles at me and says something in French. I have no idea what the words mean.

I approach the counter and put on a cheerful front. "Do you speak English?"

"Of course," the man says. "How may I help you?"

"Well, I—" How should I explain this? I've done similar things before to get away from Magnus, but suddenly, I feel weird about it. *Suck it up, girl, and do what you have to do.* "This might sound strange, but my ex-husband is chasing me. Our divorce was finalized today, and he's very angry about that. I'm afraid of what he might do if he catches up to me. Could you, um, call the police for me?"

"*Oui.*" He reaches for the phone but hesitates, instead turning to holler into the back area I can see through an open door. "François! Henri! *Pourrais-tu m'aider?*" He flashes me a smile. "I asked them to help me."

Two young men trot out of the back room and converse with the older man in French. Then they march out the door to stand on the sidewalk, arms barred over their chests.

"François and Henri will keep your husband away," the older man tells me. "If you need help, I can drive you to a house for abused women."

"Oh, thank you so much." I engage in a touch of melodramatic acting, sniffling and making my voice quiver just a touch. "I'm so grateful for your help."

"Follow me. My car is parked behind the shop. My name is Gaston."

"I'm Emily."

Yeah, I hate lying to a nice man who offered to help me. But I can't tell him the truth. After so long on the run, I've gotten used to lying—but I will never like needing to do it.

Gaston ushers me out to a small gray car, and we start off down the road, luckily in the opposite direction from where Magnus was. Will he catch up? That electric excitement tingles through me again when I think about what he might do if he finds me. The two times he caught me, we had sex. Hot, incredible sex. But I shouldn't do that with him again. No, definitely not. I will resist his growly, snarly, sexy voice and his naked, muscular, tattooed body.

"You can drop me off right here," I say. "You've already gone to too much trouble for me. I can find my way to the safe house."

"Are you sure, *cherie*?"

"I am. Thank you for all your help."

He pulls over, and I hop out.

Once Gaston has driven away, I start walking again. Running would seem suspicious now that I've traveled beyond the somewhat deserted area where Errol lives and into a part of town that bustles with activity. I pass by a hotel, but I can't hide there. The two times Magnus found me, I'd been holed up in motels. He'll expect me to do the same thing this time, which means I need to devise a different strategy. I pass by what looks like a trolley station, and the tracks in the street suggest I'm right about that. Should I ride a trolley? No, that's too slow.

My legs have started to feel stiff and sore, and sweat trickles down my temples. My tummy grumbles too. I spot a bar up ahead that might serve at least snacks. Since I need a restroom too, the bar looks like my best option. Will Magnus find me here? Guess I'll find out how good a tracker he really is.

I go into the bar and order water and food, then head for the restroom. Now that my bladder is happy, I chow down on cheese fondue and a plate of sausage. Though I've never been a big fan of either of those foods, I'm so hungry that I don't care what I'm eating as long as it fills my tummy. Once I've finished my snack, I look out the window—to enjoy the view and to check for large, angry Scots approaching. I don't see Magnus, but I have the strangest feeling he's not far away. After paying my bill, I exit the bar and start walking again, in the opposite direction from where Errol's building lies. Part of my escape involved a car ride, so I can't tell for sure how far I've gone.

As I travel through the city, I keep an eye on my surroundings. Magnus has a knack for catching me off guard, and to win this game we're playing, I need to stay alert. It's exhausting. My brain hurts from thinking so much. Maybe I'm just tired from the stress of knowing a billionaire wants to abduct me or maybe even kill me.

A flash of movement draws my attention to the other side of the street.

I slow down and glance over there peripherally, keeping my head aimed forward. I get a glimpse of a figure dressed in black, but not a good enough look to identify the person. Should I turn my head to look? That would tip my hand if it's Magnus. He'll know I saw him. But I'm not ready for the game to end just yet. So I turn left at the next intersection, and once I'm beyond the mystery man's view, I break into a jog. A quick glance back reveals no one following me—yet. If Magnus has tracked me down, he will come this way. I run faster and veer around a corner into an alley. A dumpster sits tucked against the wall of one of the buildings, and a tall chain link fence blocks the other end. Damn. I've locked myself in. But maybe that's not entirely a bad thing.

Can I leverage my mistake to get the upper hand? I've done it before, though not in this way.

Since I can't climb over the fence—it's too tall—I dash over to the dumpster and climb inside it, letting the lid fall shut above me. Yeah, okay, it stinks in here. *Really* stinks. But this is hardly the worst place I've ever hidden. I push the lid up just enough that I can peek out into the alley. No sign of the Scot yet. My breaths have shortened, and my pulse thumps in my ears while that old tingle comes back, exciting my skin and making me horny. It's inappropriate, but I don't care. This game is too much fun.

Footsteps clap outside the alley, coming down the sidewalk.

I lower the lid a teeny bit more, though I can still see whoever might enter the alley. With one hand, I root around until I find what I need and grip it firmly.

A shadow falls across the alley's entrance.

Magnus. I know it's him.

"Come out, Piper," he says, though I still can't see him. Only his shadow. "It's over. I've caught you."

Not yet he hasn't. Until he drags me out of this dumpster, the game goes on.

He takes two steps toward the entrance, though I can't hear his footfalls. I see his shadow moving.

Then it vanishes.

Magnus left? No, he wouldn't do that when he was so close.

It's a trick. Has to be. I won't fall for that. Minutes tick by, but I can't count them because I would need to turn my phone's screen on, casting a light that Magnus might see. So I stay here, frozen and barely breathing, wondering when he will make his move. Even when I'd been legitimately fleeing from the Scot, I'd experienced this same kind of thrill. What that says about me, I don't know. Don't care either.

A noise above me makes me flinch, but I don't lift the dumpster's lid to see what happened. This must be part of his plan to catch me.

Whump. A figure dressed in black sails down to land right in front of the dumpster, facing away from me.

I spring up, lash an arm around his neck, and hold my weapon to his carotid artery. "Don't move, MacTaggart. Your ass is mine."

He glances at my weapon and chuckles. "A plastic spoon willnae hurt me."

"No, but this was a game to see if you could catch me. You didn't. I win."

"Do you?" Magnus grabs me under my arms and flips me over so I'm standing in front of him. He lashes his brawny arms around my torso, pinning me there. His scruffy goatee rasps against my cheek as he speaks in a rough whisper. "I will always win, Piper. You're never getting away from me again."

I wriggle my ass against him. His dick is already firming up. "I got you first. If I'd had a real weapon, you'd be dead. I won."

"Must be wanting me to fuck ye in this alley. Why else rub yourself into my *slat?*"

Oh God, I do want that. Right now.

He sniffs my hair. "Ye smell like rubbish."

"Because I hid in a dumpster. Duh." I manage to push my hand behind me, even while he keeps me pinned, and clasp his cock in my fingers, rewarded by his soft gasp. "See? I win. You always need to fuck me after the chase. Unless the scent of garbage turns you off."

He rushes forward and crushes me to the brick wall of the building across from the dumpster. With his entire body mashed to mine, and his erection pressing into me like a steel bar, I can hardly catch my breath.

A phone rings.

Magnus groans and, without moving away from me, answers his phone. "Errol? What? Oh, aye." He shoves the phone back into his pocket. "We'll have to wait for that poke. Errol has information we'll want to hear. His words exactly."

He takes my hand and leads me out onto the street. We walk until we manage to catch a taxi, then head straight for Errol's place.

Damn. I really needed a good "poke."

Chapter Eighteen

Magnus

I needed to fuck Piper in that alley. Needed it so badly I couldn't breathe. Though I can't explain it, this woman always knows how to shift my lust into overdrive and make me do things I shouldn't. Our game got me so randy I thought I'd *caith* in my trousers. During the taxi ride back to Errol's building, I suffer from an overpowering need to shag her right here in the backseat, despite the driver watching us. Donnae care. Being inside Piper again has become the sole focus of my thoughts.

She slides a hand up my inner thigh. Leaning against me, she whispers, "I want you so bad. Promise you'll screw me soon."

"Not until after we hear what Errol has found out."

"Can't wait that long."

"You'll have to." Not sure I can wait either, but whatever Errol learned must be important or he wouldn't have told me to come back. I pick up her hand, setting it on her lap. "Donnae test me, or you'll find out what sort of animal I am."

"Already know that."

She doesn't bother me for the rest of the taxi ride, or in the lift on our way up to Errol's flat.

Hunting Piper for twenty months had been the most exciting bounty of my life, but even now that I have her in my custody, I still feel an erotic thrill when I chase her. Maybe a wee part of me wondered if she might take the chance to flee the country, but I don't honestly believe she would have. She enjoys the hunt as much as I do.

When we walk into Errol's flat, the living room is empty.

"I'm in the office," he shouts to us. "Come in here, please."

Piper lifts her brows at me, but I just shrug. Who knows what Errol thinks he's found. But I know it must be important. So I take Piper's hand, heading down the hall and into the office.

My cousin sits at a long desk that holds three computer monitors and several box-shaped devices that I assume are CPUs or whatever tech experts like Evan would call them. All three monitors display different things, though I can tell it's spreadsheets and text documents.

Errol gestures toward two office chairs tucked into the corner. "Grab a seat. We have a lot to discuss."

We do what he said and wheel our chairs up to his desk.

"You must be a tech whiz like Evan, hey?" Piper says.

Errol chuckles. "No, not at all. I learned enough to do my job, but I have no interest in becoming a whiz at computer bollocks. My interests lie in uncovering lost treasures, which involves solving riddles. That's the skill you need today."

"What have you found?" I ask.

He smiles with smug satisfaction. "I know who Royce Hammond really is."

"Do you mean he uses an alias?"

Errol shakes his head. "He was born Royce Gilbert Hammond, but his persona as a billionaire corporate mogul and philanthropist is pure rubbish. Well, more precisely, it's a distraction."

"In what way? He clearly has an obscene amount of money."

"Aye. But he didn't amass that fortune through hard work and innovation." Errol points to a spreadsheet on the screen directly in front of him. "These are Hammond's real financial records. He uses cryptocurrency transactions on the dark web to anonymously funnel illicit funds into shell companies around the world. His empire encompasses far more than what he shows the public. Your billionaire mate is, as Gavin Douglas might say, one bad dude."

"Hammond is not my mate."

"Good. Then ye won't be upset to learn he's as bent as an Englishman's dick."

I won't comment on his slur of Englishmen. One of my newest relatives is a Brit who married my cousin Catriona. I've never heard anyone use the phrase Errol just invoked. He must have invented it himself.

Piper whispers to me, "Who is Gavin Douglas?"

"The husband of my cousin Jamie. He's American."

Errol points at the monitor to his left. "This screen shows the encrypted text messages Hammond has sent to various people who are, shall we say, not of the highest quality. Nothing in the texts is criminal, but if you read between the lines, they're conducting illicit business."

"Can we use this information to take him down?"

"Not through proper channels. None of this was acquired via warrants, and it's not exactly clear-cut evidence."

I slouch in my chair and sigh. "Then it's useless."

Errol makes a derisive noise. "Did I say that? No. If you want to get under his skin and tickle him good, we can do that quite easily."

"Would ye mind speaking English?"

Piper snorts out a laugh. "English? You don't speak that language."

"I speak Scots English. Which is much sexier than the British or American versions."

"Oh, aye," Errol chimes in. "Much sexier. Just ask my girlfriends."

"How many have you got?" I ask.

"Just one at a time, but there are seven days in a week."

My cousin's love life has no bearing on our situation, so I ignore his comment. He can shag as many lasses as he wants as long as I don't have to hear the details.

"Donnae frown, Magnus," Errol says. "I'm good at puzzles, remember? I see patterns and trace them to their source. That's how I track down treasures everyone thought had been lost thousands of years ago. If I can uncover the forgotten tomb of a supposedly mythical Chinese emperor, I can help you. This task was beneath my skills."

His tone of voice tells me he doesn't believe that. Errol seems like the sort who will take any job, however small or seemingly insignificant, because he loves the hunt as much as I do.

"Tell me what patterns you've found," I say. "And please explain it in some version of the English language, not technical jargon."

"Chill out, Magnus. I'm going to explain." Errol grins. "I learned 'chill out' from Luke Turner."

"Kirsty's husband," I say for Piper's benefit. "She's our cousin too, and her husband is American. They just got married."

"Your family sure is complicated."

I groan. "You have no idea."

"Here we go," Errol says. "The explanation. I mentioned Hammond's use of cryptocurrency. Among the files Logan and the lads managed to acquire, I found Hammond's crypto wallet. It's basically an app that holds all the information about his transactions—the blockchain, which is a type of ledger."

"Donnae need a crash course in this crypto rubbish. Tell me what I need to know."

"Pardon me for trying to enlighten you." Errol leans back in his chair and rotates it toward me. "I noticed patterns in Hammond's cryptocurrency transactions when I downloaded the blockchain data and compared it to his crypto wallet. He sends a great deal of money to three locations—Istanbul in Turkey, Lima in Peru, and Sydney in Australia."

"Hammond's company has offices in those countries."

"Aye, and he's using crypto transactions to funnel illicit funds into his corporate coffers without anyone knowing."

Piper raises her hand. "Um, how does any of this help us find out who really killed Archer Caldwell?"

"Because the information Logan provided also included data about Caldwell, which let me trace the patterns of his interactions with Hammond."

"They knew each other?"

"Aye. Your friend Archer employed cryptocurrency too. Hammond sent him funds that way fourteen times in the year before Archer was killed."

"If those transactions are anonymous, how can you tell who sent money to who?"

Errol taps his temple. "Patterns, *gràidh*, patterns. I have the blockchain information and Hammond's crypto wallet. Wasn't too hard to find the pattern that helped me reach the right conclusion."

I give Errol a hard look. "How can you be sure your assumptions are correct?"

"When I say I reached the right conclusion, I mean it's the logical inference from the data I have. The patterns match up." He points to the center screen. "This data strongly suggests that Hammond uses cryptocurrency funneled through his foreign offices to enrich his company. All the funds eventually wind up at a bank used by his London headquarters."

Tracking fugitives, I can do. But tracking money that has no visible source? *Bloody hell.*

"The money trail is interesting," I say, "but I donnae see how that helps us identify who really killed Caldwell."

Errol crosses his arms over his chest. "Would it help you to know that Caldwell traveled to Istanbul, Lima, and Sydney within the last year? Every time he returned to the UK, he received a large crypto payment."

"Hammond paid him off. But for what?"

"I examined another pattern too."

"Are you going to tell me, or do I need to guess?"

My cousin smiles. "Thought I'd drag it out for a wee while, just to watch you scowl and seethe. It's fun to poke the monster and see what happens." He holds up a hand when I start to speak. "Relax, Magnus. I'm having you on. You're too serious."

"Oh, yeah," Piper says. "He's definitely got a stick up his ass. Magnus is very uptight."

"You'll be good for him," Errol declares. "But I should explain the other pattern before the beast erupts. Caldwell's travel patterns were easy to track, especially since the police did a lot of forensic analysis on his mobile phone. Logan's contact at the Met gave him a copy of the data, which means I now have it too. During the eleven months before his death, he traveled to a dozen locations around the world, but he always started and ended his jaunts in one of the cities where Hammond has corporate offices."

"Which means what?" I growl. I'm getting bloody sick of waiting for the answers he claims to have.

"Caldwell was trafficking in stolen artifacts."

Piper jerks forward, her wide gaze locked on Errol. "What? I can't believe he would do that."

"Did ye know him well?"

"Not really. We worked together and sort of, um, dated very briefly. But we weren't good friends."

Dated briefly? I think that's her way of sidestepping the fact she shagged the man once. Not wanting my cousin to know that is understandable.

"I can't prove what he did conclusively," Errol says. "But the patterns indicate he did traffic artifacts. I've given you two all the information I have and my interpretation of it. The rest is up to you."

"Thank you, Errol," I say. "You've been a great help."

"Yes, thank you so much," Piper says. "But aren't you worried about letting us stay here with you? I mean, Hammond sounds like a very dangerous man who has no scruples."

"Donnae worry about me. My business partner owns this building, through various shell companies. I'm not entirely sure the name he gave me is his real name, but it doesn't matter. I trust the lad with my life, and we've been through harrowing situations together. The life of a treasure hunter is as treacherous as a bounty hunter's job, maybe even more so."

I want to point out that's rubbish, but I can't swear it is. Errol seems like a barmy lad who loves to solve puzzles, but Logan seems to think our cousin has many hidden facets to his personality. In the time I've known Errol, I have gotten the same impression.

"There's much more data on the flash drive," Errol says. "I'll need more time to assess the information from the Met. They did a thorough job of collecting evidence and witness statements, but I doubt they have a treasure hunter on their team. We lot have a unique way of looking at things."

He does, for dead sure. And I think I'm finally beginning to understand him and appreciate the strange way his mind works.

"You should eat lunch before getting back to work," I say. "Piper and I will make the food. You need to take a break and let your mind rest."

Errol stares at me without expression for several seconds. Then he grins and slaps my arm. "I knew you weren't a demon biker after all. Not even a Satan worshiper."

"Demon biker?" Piper says. "I don't get it."

"That's what Luke Turner likes to call me," I say. "He has no idea Kirsty told me about it. She thinks it's funny that her husband calls me that."

"So you don't ride a motorcycle."

"I know how to ride one, but I prefer cars. My cousin Callum is the biker."

"A demon biker or a regular one?"

I almost smile. "Regular. Evan gave Callum a Harley for his birthday last year."

"Your family sounds cooler all the time." She leans over me to pat my cousin's cheek. "You're a sweetie-pie and a brilliant riddle-solver. I've only met three MacTaggarts, but I think you're my second favorite."

"Who's the first?" Errol asks. "Cannae be Magnus. Nobody likes him."

Since my cousin is smirking, I decide I don't need to batter him senseless.

"Kirsty thinks he's a sweetheart," Errol says, "but we all know she's off her head. The lass is a witch who claims to have psychic powers."

I shake my head. "You love her as much as the rest of us do."

"Aye, everyone loves Kirsty. Will you be going home for Callum's engagement ceilidh?"

He wants me to be there, but I'm not sure that's a good idea. My father will go ballistic if I turn up at the wedding. But I tell Errol, "We'll see."

"You were there for Kirsty. Do try to be there for Callum too."

I roll my chair backward and stand. "Let's get out of this room. All three of us. We need food."

Chapter Nineteen

Piper

Magnus and I are making lunch together. I feel like I've accidentally slipped through a magical doorway into an alternate world without even realizing what happened. The so-called demon biker wants to whip up a meal with me while his cousin watches from the living room. Since it's an open kitchen, we can see Errol. He's sitting in an armchair in front of the windows with his attention focused on us. A slight smile curls his lips. I can't imagine why he thinks watching us make lunch is fun, but he clearly enjoys the show.

We don't make anything fancy, but it tastes so good that I think I might have orgasmed when I first tasted my sandwich. That's insane, but yeah, I haven't enjoyed a really good meal in so long that it feels like a miracle. My fondue and sausage snack didn't satisfy me the way this food does.

"You're a good team," Errol says. "Like Sherlock Holmes and Dr. Watson."

"Which one of us is Sherlock?" Magnus asks.

"Piper, naturally."

I like Errol even more now. He might have become my favorite person in the world. Nobody has ever described me as being like Sherlock Holmes, the genius detective. Not sure Errol is right about that, but I appreciate the compliment.

After lunch, Errol returns to his office. Magnus and I sit on the sofa, at opposite ends.

"We need to discuss our options," I say.

"No, we don't. I make the decisions."

"Like hell you do. We're partners, remember?"

He grunts. "Errol said that, not me. You are still my prisoner."

"But you won't get a bounty for bringing me in. Hammond will never pay the hunter who betrayed him. You'll be lucky to get out of this alive."

"We both might die."

"Aren't you a ray of sunshine, Lord Satan the Demon Biker."

Magnus twists his mouth into a grumpy expression, but when he speaks, his voice is pure seduction. "Call me whatever you like. We both know ye love the way I fuck ye."

"Which has no relevance whatsoever to the current situation."

"Of course it does." He slides across the sofa to sit beside me with his muscular thigh pressed to mine. Resting an arm on the sofa's back behind me, he shimmies closer to tuck me against his hard body. "You'll get a better night's sleep if I make ye come so hard ye see stars."

"You aren't that amazing in bed."

"No, I'm better."

I huff. "Get over yourself, MacTaggart. I've had better lovers than you."

He hooks a finger under my chin, tilting my face up to his. "Donnae lie, Piper."

"Why should I tell you the truth? You'll use it against me."

Of course I'm lying. Magnus is so incredible in bed that he's probably ruined me for other men. I might as well go to prison. If Magnus is my only option for sex, I'd rather stay celibate for the rest of my life. Well, okay, not really. But I can't imagine anyone else will ever make me feel the way he does—in bed. The rest of the time, he makes me want to slug him, stab him, shoot him, and dump his sorry ass into a ditch. I am not a murderer, but I'd make an exception for him.

Magnus shifts his hand up to cradle my nape and slants in to feather his lips over mine. "Tonight, you'll beg me to take you."

"Dream on, Pig-Bear."

He flicks his tongue out to tease my lips. "Beg me to kiss ye."

"Never." So what if I can't catch my breath? It means nothing. "You should beg me to have sex with you."

Magnus brushes his scruffy goatee over my mouth. Then he gets up, stretches, and ambles into the bedroom, shutting the door.

I sit here waiting for my heart rate to normalize and my skin to stop tingling. I wish I could say I want that jerk only because he showed me some kindness today. But that man has been my sexual Achilles heel for nearly two years. If he takes me into the bedroom, shuts the door, and strips naked…I will never be able to resist him. My weakness annoys me, but I won't deny the truth.

Errol emerges from his office and drops onto the armchair across from me. "Is Magnus having a wee lie-down?"

"I have no idea. He went into the bedroom without telling me why."

"Donnae be hard on him. He's been the black sheep of the clan for a long time, and his own parents won't speak to him. He needs friends."

"Like you, Logan, Evan, and whoever else."

"Aye. We want to be his mates, but Magnus doesn't always cooperate."

No shit. The man treats his brooding loner status like a badge of honor. But I've seen hints of what he really feels, the sadness he hides under all that gruffness. I understand what it feels like to be abandoned by your own parents, treated like a criminal, cast aside. I am a criminal, according to the authorities. My parents decided to believe the cops instead of me.

Do they care that I'm on the run? Do they even know about that? Maybe they've written me off so completely that they don't want to know what becomes of me.

"Why are you sad?" Errol says, and he sounds genuinely concerned.

"It's nothing. Personal stuff." I know I shouldn't ask, because it's none of my business, but I can't help myself. "Why do you think Magnus wants to look like a hardcore demon biker? I don't buy that he just wants fugitives to think he's super bad or whatever."

"Cannae answer that question. Only Magnus knows." Errol studies me for a moment. "You have feelings for him, don't you?"

"What? No. I mean, I can't stand him. That's the only feeling I have for the jerk."

"Are you sure about that?"

"Yes. I don't like men with scruffy goatees who wear skull-and-crossbones T-shirts and who treat me like I should be tarred and feathered."

"Hmm." Errol studies me some more, then rises and heads for the hallway. "Back in a moment, lass."

I crane my neck to see where he's going. Into the bedroom, it looks like. Weird. Magnus is in there, so I guess Errol urgently wants to talk to him.

My curiosity gets the better of me, and I tiptoe over to the bedroom door. I can hear muted voices in there, so I plaster my ear to the wood.

"If ye want Piper, ye best make a few changes." That's Errol's voice.

"Changes? You're off your head if you think I want her. I willnae change myself to please a fugitive."

I should walk away. Right now. Eavesdropping on a private conversation is rude. Well, so is the surly Scot.

"Donnae need to completely renovate yourself," Errol says. "Just spruce up your appearance a wee bit. Let the lass know ye care enough to at least trim your goatee. Lasses donnae like being kissed by a man whose face feels like a porcupine's backside."

Magnus growls something that I can't understand. Maybe it's Gaelic.

The doorknob turns.

I race to the sofa, leaping over its back to land on the cushions.

Errol ambles into the living room and sits on the armchair again. "What's wrong, lass? Ye look winded."

"No, I'm fine."

"Are ye sure?"

"Uh-huh."

Magnus saunters out of the bedroom and sits down on the sofa an arm's length from me.

He trimmed his goatee. Brushed his hair back too so it no longer resembles the untamed locks of a wild beast. And he exchanged his skull-and-crossbones shirt for a dark gray one that has the words Scotland the Brave written on it below a stylized image of a lion.

Did he take Errol's advice and spruce himself up to impress me? No, he wouldn't do that. There must be some other reason for the changes he made.

"I'll get back to work," Errol says, "and leave you lot to do…whatever you do together."

Magnus's cousin disappears into his office.

"Why did you change your shirt and trim your goatee?" I ask.

"Felt like cleaning up a wee bit."

"But why now? You could've done that this morning, or last night."

He scowls at me. "Donnae need to explain myself to you."

"Will you ever stop snarling at me? I'm getting damn sick of it."

Magnus grunts.

Oh yeah, I'm damn sick of that too. I thought monosyllabic Magnus was the most annoying version of him, but grunting Magnus is even worse. "Use your words, Pig-Bear."

"You want words? All right." He grabs me around the waist and hauls me into his body. "Tonight, we will fuck."

"Try being slightly less crude when you seduce me."

He smirks. "That means ye want me to shag you."

"No, I—Ugh. Let's talk about something else."

"Such as?"

"What's our next move?"

He pulls me onto his lap so I'm straddling his thighs with his hardening dick pressed into my groin. "I know plenty of moves that will make you scream and claw my back like a wild thing."

"You are obsessed with sex, aren't you? I meant what's our next move in terms of finding out who framed me."

Magnus tosses me onto the cushion beside him. "You're wanting the boring talk, then. Filthy is much more fun."

"I agree. But we don't have time—"

"Aye, we do." He slides his hand between my thighs, moving up inch by inch. "Our game left me wanting more—of you."

"Yeah, me too. But your cousin is twenty feet away."

He tips his head back and hollers, "Errol! Go somewhere else for a while."

Errol trots out of his office, halting near the sofa. "I know you're wanting to shag in private, but I have information I think you'll want to hear right away. And it might change your plans."

Magnus waves toward the chair across from us. "Sit down and tell us how brilliant you are."

"Very, that's how much." Errol sits on the edge of the chair. "When I compared the patterns of the encrypted texts with Caldwell's travel habits, the answer became clear."

We both wait for him to go on, but he just sits there tapping one foot on the floor, seeming excited.

Magnus glares at his cousin. "What became clear? Ahmno the Mac-Taggart who has psychic powers."

"Well, at first I assumed Caldwell traveled to those three corporate offices as part of his smuggling operation. But Logan sent me a bit more information, and that's when I had my eureka moment." Errol taps his finger on the coffee table while he speaks. "Istanbul is the key. I'm fair certain that's the central hub for the antiquities smuggling. Now that Caldwell is dead, I cannae say whether Hammond has found another person to take over the everyday operations. He doesnae seem like the hands-on sort."

"No. He prefers to keep his hands clean on the surface. But underneath, he's covered in blood."

I glance from Errol to Magnus. "So, we're assuming Hammond killed Archer?"

"Not sure. I think finding those answers means taking a trip to Istanbul."

"I've never been there."

"And you never will. I'm going alone."

"What?" I turn toward him, giving him a look I hope conveys the fact I will not be left behind. "What if Hammond wants me dead? I'm sure he's not sitting on his hands, eating bonbons and watching his favorite show on TV."

"He can't sit on his hands and eat. Unless he's licking the food off his desk."

"You know what I meant."

"It's too dangerous." He stares straight ahead while gritting his teeth. "I can't take you with me."

"What, has it become physically impossible for me to leave this apartment? Unless you've erected a force field around me—"

"Stop acting like a bampot."

"A what?"

Errol chuckles. "He called you a raving lunatic."

I slug Magnus in the arm. "Stop insulting me without explaining what your crazy Scottish words mean."

"If you insist. Here's a plain English one for you. I don't need a woman I can't trust going on a mission with me. You'll probably run away again."

"No, I won't. You have my word." I stand up. "Can't believe you still don't trust me. I had a hundred chances to run, and I didn't do it. I'm trusting you with my life. But you still expect me to run away? Come on. I deserve better than that."

Without waiting for his response, I whirl around and stalk into the bedroom. Then I slam the door shut behind me. And I sag against it. Tears burn in my eyes. I feel kind of nauseous, and I want to collapse into a heap on the floor to sob until my stomach hurts. Since the day Archer was killed, I've had no one on my side. *No one.* What a fool I was to think Magnus might believe in me. Even my parents don't.

Maybe I should run, but I'm too exhausted to do that anymore. I am alone.

Chapter Twenty

Magnus

Mhac na galla. Why did I tell Piper I don't trust her? I no longer believe she wants to run away, yet I told her the opposite. But I can't think about that right now, not with my strange cousin watching me with a disappointed expression while shaking his head a wee bit as if he can't believe what he sees.

I'm a raging ersehole. That's what he sees.

"Go on and say it," I tell Errol. "Whatever you're thinking about me, I can take it. And you'll be right."

"I was thinking you're the bampot. Only a lunatic would talk to a woman that way and upset her so much that she hides in her room to cry."

"You don't know if she's crying."

He lifts his gaze toward the ceiling, shaking his head again. "The only thing that will break through your skull is a diamond-tipped saw."

"What are you implying?"

"Piper is a bonnie, sweet lass who shares your love of danger. She wants you, ye numpty, and ye just told her to sod off."

"No, I did not."

Errol slumps in his chair. "You think you didn't. But Piper heard it that way."

"When did you become an expert on what women think?"

"Years ago, that's when." He shuts his eyes briefly as he exhales a long, groaning breath. "I pay attention to what women want and think and hope for. That's how I can have a girlfriend for every day of the week, if I want that. But you…" He looks at me and twists his mouth into a disgusted expression. "You are a bloody stupid *bod ceann.*"

"So much for us being good mates."

"I am your mate. That's why I feel free to tell ye the truth."

My gaze wanders to the bedroom doorway. Is Piper in there crying because of what I said? *Bod an Donais.* This is why I shag women but don't get entangled with them. Relationships are too bloody complicated.

"The truth is," Errol says, "you know how to seduce women, but you pay no attention to what they really want. You have to read between the lines. Care about what they feel."

"Become a woman. That's the only way I could do what you're suggesting."

Errol covers his face with his hands and lets out a loud groan that's almost a growl. "I give up. You're a hopeless case."

Maybe I am. But mostly, I've gotten bloody sick of sitting here waiting for something to happen—for Hammond to send another lackey or someone worse than the *cacan* Charlie. If Hammond murdered Archer Caldwell, I need to find proof of that. I need to act, not sit here havering with my cousin.

Errol stands and stretches, yawning loudly. "I'm going to make some coffee, then get back to work. If I study the patterns more, maybe I can narrow down the search area to a specific location in Istanbul." He starts for the open kitchen, then pauses to glance back at me. "I'll make enough coffee for everyone, if you and Piper want some later."

"But you won't let me drink it now."

"Aye, ye can. But we both know what you really need to do right now."

He might be barmy and irritating, but Errol clearly understands women better than I do. Should I take his advice? I need to keep Piper with me—to ensure she doesn't run, and to protect her. The best way of doing that is to show her a wee bit of...kindness. Or something like that. I'm not famous for that sort of behavior.

I push up off the sofa and turn toward the hallway, but I can't make my feet move.

"Look like ye need a bit of encouragement," Errol says. "Just remember how you treat Kirsty. That's all you need for inspiration."

Kirsty is like a sister to me while Piper is the woman I want to shag, but I understand what he means. I don't scowl, growl, and snarl at my cousin.

I stride up to the bedroom door and raise my hand to knock, but I freeze. Piper is still crying. I can hear it, and I think she might be standing right in front of the door on the other side. I'm a *tolla-thon* of the worst sort, making a lass cry and refusing to show her any kindness. Not sure I ever knew how to handle a situation like this. But I need to try now.

"Piper?" I say. "May I come in?"

The door shifts a little as if she'd been leaning against it. "Uh, sure. Just gimme a sec."

Sniffling follows her statement. Then I hear shoes scuffling across the wood floor, the sound retreating from me. Piper blows her nose—quietly, but I still hear it—and silence follows.

"Piper?"

She clears her throat. "Yes, you can come in now."

I go inside and shut the door behind me. Halfway to the bed, I stop. What is wrong with me? I can't move because I'm paralyzed by…fear. I donnae let fear stop me. Never. Yet here I am frozen in place because of the woman who sits slumped on the bed with her feet tucked under her cross-legged, her eyes red and her cheeks stained with tear tracks.

Piper snatches a tissue from the box on the nightstand and blows her nose again. "Don't worry. I'm not expecting you to console me or anything like that."

But I want to do it. *Bod an Donais.*

I settle onto the bed beside her, leaving a small gap between us. The time has come to do something I've never tried before. "I'm sorry for what I said."

"Sorry you said it or sorry you meant it?"

"What's the difference?"

"If you don't know the answer to that question, you're even more clueless than I thought."

"Aye, that's true. I have no bloody clue how to make you feel better." I rest my elbows on my thighs and cradle my face in my upraised hands. "I wish I had a clue, but I don't."

She says nothing.

Well, I cannae blame the lass. I'm not the sort of man any woman wants to get involved with except for a night of sex.

"You want to make me feel better?" she says.

"Aye."

Piper starts laughing, the sound soft and gentle, almost affectionate. "Maybe there is hope for you after all."

With my face still in my hands, I peek sideways at her. "What's so bloody funny about that?"

She throws an arm around my shoulders, touching her cheek to mine. "I never would've guessed you could be so adorably clueless."

"Adorable? Ye must have me confused with someone else. I'm the pig-bear demon."

She laughs again and kisses my cheek. "I was wrong about that. You're a sweetheart in disguise."

"Only my cousin Kirsty ever calls me sweet. The rest of the family thinks she's off her head to describe me that way."

"Guess I'm crazy too, because I meant it. You have a sweet streak I never would've expected to find in a tough bounty hunter."

I lower my hands and slip an arm around her. "Didnae like hearing you crying all alone in this room."

"So you would've been okay with me crying alone in a different room?"

"No. I donnae want you to cry at all."

"There's a simple way to make sure that never happens again." She tickles my cheek with her fingertips. "Don't say nasty things anymore."

"I didn't mean what I said about you wanting to run. I know you won't do that."

"Why did you say it, then?"

As bad as I am at understanding and comforting a woman, I'm worse at explaining my feelings. "Can we talk about that later? I need to do something right now."

"Errol must have more info to share."

"This has nothing to do with my cousin." Well, it does in a way. But I won't tell Piper that Errol helped me figure out what I need to do to make up for my *tolla-thon* behavior. Instead, I turn toward Piper and pull her into my arms. Then I brush hair away from her face and touch my lips to hers. "I want to make love to you, *gràidh*."

"What does that mean?"

"Make love?" I close my hand over her breast. "It means I want to fuck ye, but in a sweet way this time."

She pokes my belly with her finger. "Very funny, Pig-Bear. I know what 'make love' means. But you said another word I don't understand, though I heard Errol say it earlier."

"*Gràidh* means darling. It's Gaelic."

"Are there dirty Gaelic words too?"

"Aye, of course. We Scots know all sorts of ways to drive a woman wild, with words and actions."

"I bet you do." She splays a palm on my chest, then glides it down to my waist. Her fingers toy with the button on my trousers. "Show me how a Scotsman does that."

"Works best if I'm wearing a kilt, but I donnae usually pack one when I'm on the hunt."

"Mm, I would love to see you in a kilt." She curls her tongue around my earlobe, then draws it into her mouth, releasing it slowly. "Make love to me, Magnus. Please."

"Donnae have to beg. I need this as much as you do."

Piper pulls the covers back and crawls backward on her knees until she kneels at the center of the bed. Then she unhooks the top button of her shirt.

Bod an Donais. Watching her undress sends blood rushing into my *slat.*

She unbuttons her shirt with deliberate slowness, fully aware of how her striptease affects me. I'm breathing harder by the time she gets rid of her top. But when she unhooks her bra and slides it off her shoulders, I stop breathing altogether. Aye, I've seen her body before. The last time, I had her handcuffed to a bed. This time, she's free to leave whenever she wants—but I know she won't. Piper will never run from me again.

The lass lies down on her back to shimmy out of her jeans and knickers.

"Leaving your socks on?" I say. "Maybe I should take them off for you."

"Please do."

"Need to do something else first."

I remove my boots, then stand and face Piper. She watches while biting her lip as I pull my shirt off and toss it away.

"Wow," she says. "I love your muscles and your tattoos. Wanna trace those patterns with my tongue."

"Later, *gràidh.* I have plans for your body first."

She tracks my every movement with her gaze while I unzip my trousers and pull out the condom packet I always have in my pocket. I toss it onto the nightstand, then get rid of my trousers and socks. My cock springs free, attracting Piper's attention.

She licks her lips. "Mm, yes. I want that."

I crawl onto the bed, crouching between her feet. "Time to get rid of your socks, *leannan.*"

The lass wiggles her feet as if she cannae wait for me to do what I said.

For a moment, I just gaze at her. Though we have shagged before, I never took the time to appreciate the beauty of her body, from the perfect mounds of her breasts to the swell of her hips and lower to the curly hairs on her mound. I settle my hands on her hips, then drag my palms down her legs, shifting them to her inner thighs as I make my way down to her ankles.

I remove her socks and begin to massage her soles.

She writhes and moans.

While I keep rubbing her soles, I meet her gaze. "Need to taste ye, *gràidh.* Right now. Need to feast on your cream until I'm drunk from the flavor of you."

"Oh God, Magnus. I want your mouth on me." She grasps the headboard rails. "Then I need your cock inside me."

"Aye, I need that too."

I lie down between her legs, and she bends her knees to frame me with her thighs. The scent of her desire surrounds and intoxicates me while I spread her folds with two fingers and lap up the slickness that glistens on her flesh. Piper bucks her hips and cries out. I lick my way up her skin until those curly hairs tickle my face, then I seal my lips around her clit and suck.

She throws her head back and lets out a sharp cry.

I stroke her folds with my fingertips while still suckling that nub, and I keep my gaze riveted to hers, unwilling to glance away for even one second because I might miss the look on her face when she comes. Piper's breaths quicken and shorten into gasps. She thrusts her hips up, silently pleading for me to make her come.

Cannae deny her anything she wants.

So I thrust three fingers inside her, fucking the lass with my mouth and my fingers until her body goes rigid. I know she's about to tumble off that cliff.

"Yes, Magnus!"

Her inner muscles contract around my fingers, over and over, while I keep suckling her clit until she's done.

Piper lies there, limp and breathing hard, a look of sheer satisfaction on her face.

She's never looked more beautiful.

The lass pats the mattress beside her. "Lie down, please. I have plans for you."

<h1 style="text-align:center">Chapter Twenty-One</h1>

Piper

Magnus flops onto the mattress on his back, making the bed shake. I do have plans for him, but first I need to recover from the amazing climax he just gave me. The man knows how to treat a woman in bed. He's getting better with the not-in-bed parts of life too. I can't expect him to change overnight, which means I need to be patient.

According to his cousin Kirsty, Magnus is a sweetheart. I've seen glimpses of that side of him too. But I realize he's walking a fine line with me, trying to balance doing his job with figuring out who really killed Archer. I don't think he's ever collared a fugitive who made him doubt that person's guilt. But he thinks I might have been framed.

So yeah, he has a lot of stuff to deal with.

Once I can breathe without my ears ringing, I sit up and get into a kneeling position beside Magnus. "Do you trust me?"

"Aye, Piper, I do. Should never have said I don't."

"It's okay. I get that you're in a difficult and confusing position, wanting to help a fugitive instead of just dragging me back to the UK."

He runs a hand up and down my thigh. "Let's not talk about that right now."

My gaze flicks to his cock. That thick, long, beautifully veined erection takes my breath away. I rise to my knees and swing one leg over to straddle his hips. Then I reach into the nightstand to grab the item I need.

I dangle the handcuffs from my index finger. "How much do you trust me?"

"All the way, *gràidh*."

"Glad to hear it." I hook one cuff around his left wrist, then thread them around the headboard rails to secure his right wrist too. I've bound him to the headboard the way he'd done to me once. "Still trust me?"

He lifts one leg to rub my ass with the sole of his foot. "Aye, all the way."

Since he already has a condom on, I don't need to wait a second longer. I rise to my knees, then sink down onto his length inch by inch, reveling in the firmness of him and the way he fills me up so deliciously. The other two times we had sex, it was scorching hot and out of control. As much as I enjoyed that, I love this even more because I get to feel him, really feel him, while we gaze into each other's eyes. To experience every sensation to the fullest feels...so good I can't describe it.

With him seated deep inside me, I lay my palms on his chest and bend my arms to bring our faces closer. "Thanks for using ribbed condoms. Never used to think much of those, but sex with you has made me love them."

He rolls his hips, spurring me to suck in a breath. "Glad ye like it, *leannan.*"

I'm amazed that a man like Magnus cares about giving his partners the best experience possible, but like it says on the box, those condoms are ribbed to increase a woman's pleasure. Getting to know Magnus is shattering all my preconceptions about the Satanic biker.

Straightening my arms, I start to move, lifting myself a little with every stroke. Magnus tilts his hips, urging me to rock forward every time I sink back onto his length, and he groans when I increase the pace. That sound, so deep and rough and rife with hunger, gets me so hot that I need to move faster and rise up higher so I can slam down on him even harder. He bends his knees and thrusts his hips up in time with my movements. Soon, I'm bouncing on his cock while I lean backward to plant my hands on his thighs, and the slapping of flesh on flesh fills the room. My wetness dribbles down my inner thighs, and my heart pounds so hard and fast that I can barely breathe.

I don't care. This feels too incredible to stop.

And damn, he has strong legs.

He straps those powerful thighs around me and flips us over so his body now pins me to the mattress. Doing that twists the handcuffs, making them tighter, but he doesn't seem to care about that at all. He keeps thrusting into me, driving in deeper, pumping faster, while the wet sound of our bodies merging echoes inside the room along with our grunts and gasps.

"Please, Magnus, yes," I moan while I grip his biceps and lash my legs around his hips. "Please, more, deeper, make me come."

"*Dé an doimhneachd?*"

I have no clue what he said, but the meaning of the words doesn't matter. The rough, growly tone of his voice tells me it was something dirty, and that knowledge ramps up my need so much that my clit throbs and I whimper like an idiot. Only this man has ever turned me into a nympho-maniac, but I absolutely can't get enough of him.

Magnus wriggles his hips, somehow parting my folds without using his hands. The sensation of his balls rubbing against my most sensitive spot pushes me over the edge. My entire body stiffens, and I can't breathe or move or think, frozen in the second before my climax hits. So close. I'm about to—

He lunges his head down to take my nipple between his teeth and suck on it.

I fly off that cliff, my orgasm thundering through me with every spasm of my inner muscles. The way my body milks him makes me feel his hard length more than ever while electric bolts of pleasure fire down all my nerves, and I can't stop myself. My head snaps forward, my back flattens into the mattress, and I scream his name.

Magnus pounds into me harder, then freezes on the last thrust with his cock buried deep inside me. He squeezes his eyes shut and roars.

Holy shit. That was even better than the other times we had sex. This time was…mind-blowing.

He drops on top of me, but swiftly rolls us over so he's beneath me again. He also managed to do that so the cuffs aren't twisted anymore. Damn, he's got skills.

I grab the handcuff key and release him. When I see his wrists are a little red, I grasp his hands and kiss the irritated skin. "I'm so sorry. Didn't mean for you to get hurt."

"Ahmno hurt, lass. I've been shot and stabbed before, so a little chafing is nothing."

Yeah, he'd mentioned before that he'd suffered those kind of injuries. He really is one badass bounty hunter. Has he ever killed someone? I want to know the answer, but I also don't want to know. We can talk about some-thing else right now.

"What did you say a minute ago?" I ask. "I'm guessing it was Gaelic."

"*Dé an doimhneachd.* You begged me to go deeper, so I asked how deep."

"Well, you did just fine without my input."

I move off him and toss the condom into the trash can beside the bed. Then I lie down and cuddle up to him with my cheek on his chest. It feels weird to snuggle with the man who ruthlessly pursued me for al-most two years, determined to bring me in no matter what, but this also feels right. I kind of expected him to pull away when I tucked myself against him, but he hasn't done that. Instead, he curls an arm around me, and with the other hand, he combs his fingers through my hair.

Tender Magnus? My brain is having trouble processing that change.

His fingers massaging my scalp relax me so much that I find myself blabbing things to him that I probably shouldn't. "You said you trust me. All the way. I trust you like that too."

"Good. We need to trust each other if we're going to survive this."

"Survive sex? Or survive whatever Hammond might do next?"

"Hammond, of course. Even I'm not deadly in bed—unless my lover turns out to be an assassin who I have to kill to save myself."

I lift my head to look at him. "Has that ever happened to you?"

"No."

"But you mentioned you've been shot and stabbed."

"Aye, by fugitives who were desperate to escape. Desperation drives people to do all sorts of things they might never try otherwise."

"Yeah, I'm well acquainted with that phenomenon." I rest my cheek on his chest again and absently trace the lines of his tattoos with my fingers. "I had to learn a lot of skills I never imagined I'd need, like lock-picking."

"Your French thief lover taught you that."

"Uh-huh. Are you jealous of Oscar and Archer?"

Magnus grunts. "Why would I be? They couldn't have satisfied you as well as I do."

"True." I bite my lip while I focus on the swirling lines of one particular tattoo. Its abstract design fascinates me. Or maybe I'm just avoiding his gaze while I ask my next question. "Do you believe I'm innocent?"

"Aye."

"Really? You've been so dead-set on taking me in, and you swore you don't care if I'm guilty or not."

"Because I didn't know you then. I might not know you well yet, but I've seen enough to convince me."

I'm afraid to ask, but I have to risk it. "Are you saying you're convinced I'm innocent? That I didn't murder Archer?"

He kisses the top of my head. "Aye, lass, that's what I'm saying."

A warm glow sweeps through me from head to toe, but the warmest part settles in my chest, over my heart. He believes me. For twenty months, I've had no allies other than Oscar, and he cared more about getting his next big score than helping me. To be fair, I never asked for his help. Somehow I knew he wouldn't risk his own safety for me. Hot sex doesn't automatically lead to a meaningful connection.

"You really believe me?" I say, my voice tight from the emotions overwhelming me. Tears sting in my eyes, and I let out a single sob. "You have no idea what that means to me."

He rolls onto his side, facing me, and pulls me into his arms. My face is tucked against his throat. "Hush, *mo leannan*. You're not alone anymore."

I burst into a fit of sobbing, my tears dribbling down his throat. He probably thinks I'm crazy, but I can't help my reaction. My own parents had rejected me when they found out I'd been arrested. I'd thought Oscar might become a trusted partner, but I realized quickly that he would never be that for me no matter how much I liked him. But the man who hunted me, the bastard who cared only about capturing me, has become the one person in all the world who believes in me.

Magnus just holds me until I stop crying. Then he picks me up and carries me into the attached bathroom, where he sets my bottom on the counter. I watch him turn on the shower and test the temperature until he seems satisfied with it.

He waves a hand. "Come, lass. It's time to have a shower."

I don't even think about it. I go to him, and we step into the shower stall together while steam rises around us. He uses a damp washcloth to wipe the tears away from my eyes and cheeks, then he uses his hands to rub soap all over me before he grabs a bottle of shampoo and washes my hair, massaging my scalp with his deft fingers. It feels wonderful, and I close my eyes and lean into him, exhaling all the tension inside me. Once I'm clean, he plucks up the soap, clearly intending to get himself clean too.

But I snatch the soap from him. "Let me do this for you."

He nods.

No other man would've wanted me to help him get clean unless it was foreplay. Magnus isn't like anyone else. I hated him and did everything I could to keep him from finding me. Now, I don't want to escape. I need to skim my hands all over that gorgeous body, so I pour liquid soap into my palm and rub my hands together to suds it up before I start gliding my fingers over his skin to spread the soap. I can't resist exploring every muscle with my fingertips, but when I bump into a scar that slashes across the right side of his pecs, I pause to feather one finger over the furrow of that wound. It healed long ago, but I have a feeling the emotional scars haven't disappeared.

When I finish getting him clean, he clasps both my hands, enveloping them with his. He gazes into my eyes for a moment without speaking. Then he kisses me. It's a sweet, sensual kiss that makes a warm glow burgeon inside me again. He peels his lips away from mine, shuts off the water, and leads me out of the shower stall.

After we dry each other off with a plush towel, he touches his lips to mine. "We should get dressed. Errol will want us to have dinner with him."

I can't speak. A dreamy feeling I've never experienced before has taken control of my mind and body, and all I can do is follow him into the bed-room. We get dressed, and head out into the living room. The man I hated has become more than a lover. He gave me a gift I never expected. Magnus MacTaggart has made me feel safe and cherished.

And I will follow him anywhere.

<h1 style="text-align:center">Chapter Twenty-Two</h1>

Magnus

We sit around a small table tucked into the corner of the living room and eat the meal Errol insisted on making for us. I hadn't known the lad could cook. But then, I don't know him well, though the time I've spent with him today has let me learn much more about him. He's not a bampot, as I'd first thought. He has the cleverest mind of anyone I know, including Evan the tech genius.

But Piper might be the cleverest of all. She eluded me, after all.

Now, Errol and Piper are laughing. He just finished telling her another story about his adventures as a treasure hunter. She loves every tale he weaves for her, but I cannae focus on what either them says. My thoughts keep returning to the bedroom, when I told Piper I believe she's innocent, then I took her into the shower and didn't even try to shag her again. We didn't just shag this time, though. Something happened that I still can't explain and don't understand.

She cried, and I comforted her.

No one who knows me would believe I could ever behave that way. But I donnae like it when Piper gets upset, and the longer I'm with her, the more it fashes me.

Piper waves her hand in front of my face. "Are you paying attention?"

"No."

"Well, you missed some really important info while you were off in la-la land."

I glance at her, then Errol.

My cousin sits there with his arms crossed and a smug smile on his lips.

Bloody hell, I must have missed something pivotal if he's looking at me that way. "What were you two talking about?"

Errol rolls his eyes and speaks in a sarcastic tone. "Only the most vital piece of information in the history of the universe. But I cannae say it again. These words were so important that I had to forget them the instant I spoke them."

"You're full of rubbish. Just tell me."

"Not sure I want to. If you're having concentration issues, I might need to tell you five times, and I'm too jeeked for that."

"Stop being cheeky. Maybe I need to batter sense into you."

"All right, Magnus," Errol says while raising his hands, palms out. "No need for violence. I will tell ye again, but try to listen this time."

"Go on." I lean toward him until only inches separate us. Then I speak in the voice that usually makes people cringe. "I'm listening now."

My cousin chuckles. "Aye, ye are so bloody frightening."

Piper laughs too. "Isn't it cute when he talks that way?"

Cute? I decide to ignore that ridiculous statement. "Start talking, Errol."

"I was digging through all the data from the Met," he says, "and I found a pattern nobody else noticed. To be fair, it's not obvious that the information is important. I only realized what I was looking at when I meditated while staring at the computer screen."

"Meditation? That's bollocks."

"Have ye ever tried it? The technique can be very helpful in washing away the grime so you can finally see what lies beneath it."

I revert to the voice Piper had called cute, strictly to avoid battering my cousin. "What did ye find? No more games, just tell me."

He chuckles again. "Piper's right. You are cute when you try to intimidate us. Anyway, here's what I found. Royce Hammond and Archer Caldwell were funneling illicit antiquities through the Fernsby Museum."

Piper jerks forward, her hands clamped over the table's edge. "They did what? Are you sure? I worked there, and I never saw any evidence of that."

"Did ye think they'd make it obvious?" Errol asks. "Wouldn't have taken me hours to figure it out if they'd been sloppy."

I sit back in my chair and tap my fingers on the tabletop. "How do we prove that's what they did?"

"You need to start in Istanbul," Errol says. "I'm sure that was the hub of their operations."

"How sure are you?"

"Dead certain. But you'll have to trust my instincts. I cannae prove it."

I trust Errol, despite his often barmy behavior. He has helped me before, but this hunt will be the toughest and most dangerous I've ever undertaken. Do I have enough faith in Errol's hunches to act on the information he's given us?

Aye, I do.

"Give me a summary of what you've figured out," I say to Errol. "Then Piper and I need to get moving."

"Cannae do that."

"Why not?" I might be snarling again. Piper probably thinks that's adorable.

Errol frowns at me. "Because I haven't written it down. Keeping vital information in a notebook or on a computer is not the safest way to prevent your enemies from getting hold of it."

"*Mhac na galla.* What are you driving at?"

He taps his temple. "It's all in here."

"But you can write it down for me."

"Aye, I could do that."

"Brilliant. Do it now."

"Cannae. Or rather, I willnae do that." He pushes his chair back and stands up. "I'm going with you and Piper."

"Like hell you are. It's too dangerous."

"But you're taking Piper with you. I have more experience in the field than she does." He gives the lass a polite smile. "No offense, *gràidh.* I know you've been on the run for a long time, but dealing with antiquities thieves is more in my wheelhouse."

Before I can bark another command at him, Piper speaks up. "You're right. We do need your help, if you're sure you don't mind the potential for being tortured or murdered, possibly both."

"No worries. I can handle anything Magnus can, though he clearly thinks I'm a barmy eejit who can barely use a steak knife and certainly can't fight villains." He smirks at me. "Havenae looked in my bedroom closet yet, have ye? Go on, take a look. Then you'll understand."

Piper jumps up. "Let's go look together, Magnus."

I groan and get up, following Piper into the bedroom.

She pulls open the door to the walk-in closet. "Holy shit."

Leaning around her, I peer into the space. Then I stomp to the bedroom doorway and shout, "What the bloody hell, Errol. You've got an arsenal."

"Aye," he shouts back to me. "Glad I'm a bampot now, aren't you?"

I return to Piper, and we both shuffle into the closet. It contains every sort of weapon a man could want, everything from firearms and grenades to bows and arrows, even slingshots. Some of these weapons, I can't even identify, and most are illegal to possess. I see Kevlar vests too.

Errol steps onto the closet's threshold. "Want me to go with you now?"

"Aye, you're coming with us." I grasp his arm and drag him out into the hall. "But right now, Piper and I need to go to bed."

"Oh, aye. You two have a good lie-down." He makes a lie-down sound like we're going to shag each other all night. "See you in the morning, bright and early."

I shut the door.

Piper and I do not have a poke. We don't talk either. All we do is undress and crawl into bed together, with me lying on my back and Piper curled up against my side. I tuck my arm around her, holding the lass close. I've never slept with a woman like this. Never wanted to do that. The day I first caught up to Piper, everything changed—though I didn't realize it at the time, and I'm not sure what it means. Am I still obsessed with her? Can obsession turn into something real and intimate? I have no fucking idea.

But I sleep better than I ever have before.

When I wake in the early morning, the sun hasn't risen yet and Piper still lies tucked up against me. Neither of us moved all night, apparently. I didn't wake up even once, which has never happened to me before. Since I donnae want to disturb her, I lie here mulling over our problems and the information Errol gave us. Maybe I shouldn't have agreed to let him come along on our journey to who knows where, but I no longer see him as a barmy lad who has unusual skills. He's a very clever man who has clearly seen battle, though not of the sort I'd seen in the army. I believe he can be of use to us, and I have no doubts he understands how to protect himself and others.

Donnae care what happens to me. But I will do anything to protect Piper.

The lass curled up against me stirs, exhaling a soft breath that tickles my skin.

I glance at the clock on the nightstand. It's ten after five. Errol wanted us to get up by six thirty. Should I let Piper sleep a wee bit longer? She looks bonnie and sweet with her features relaxed and her lips curled into the faintest of smiles. I wonder what she dreams about, but I willnae ask her. The lass's dreams are none of my business.

She stretches while still lying beside me, and her breasts brush against me.

My cock is getting hard, but that happens most mornings. The fact that Piper just rubbed herself against me... Well, I won't claim it has nothing to do with my growing erection. My *slat* got a head start before she did that, though.

Piper stretches again and yawns, then her lids flutter open. She aims a sweet, sexy smile at me. "Good morning."

"Aye, *madainn mhath.*" When her brows wrinkle, I explain, "That's Gaelic for good morning."

"You Scots can't help yourselves. You've just got to complicate every conversation with those Gaelic words."

"Women love it when I speak the old tongue. It makes them randy, especially when I say dirty things."

She slides over to lie half on top of me with her tits crushed to my chest and her *ròmag* brushing my cock. Donnae mind that. But I will need to fuck her before breakfast.

"Tell me some dirty Gaelic," she says, her tone husky. "Might as well make use of your morning wood."

"I might be stiff on most mornings, but I only get this hard when a sexy woman drapes herself all over me and rubs her *ròmag* into my *slat*."

Piper props her chin on her folded hands. "Do I have to handcuff you again to get a translation?"

"No, lass," I say with a chuckle. "I said you rubbed your genitals into my cock."

"Keep going. I want to hear more."

"If yer wanting *drabastachd*, ahm willing." I push a hand between her erse cheeks until I feel her slick heat on my fingers. "I mean to pet your *boicoinn* until yer so *musaidh* that ye cannae stand it, then we'll *reitheachas* until ye scream. Maybe I'll *caith* all over yer belly instead and make ye suck my *ball-fearghais*. But donnae worry, I will always make sure ye come."

She stares at me.

Aye, confusion is the response I expected. "Let me translate. If you're wanting obscenity, I'm willing. I mean to pet your folds until you're so randy that ye cannae stand it, then we'll fuck until ye scream. Maybe I'll come all over your belly instead and make ye suck my manly limb—my cock, that is. But donnae worry, I will always make sure ye come for me."

I thrust a finger into her opening.

The lass gasps and pushes up on her straight arms to aim a halfhearted scowl down at me. She slaps my chest. "You better not get yourself off without me. Especially not after telling me what all that dirty Gaelic meant. I'm so horny I can't stand it, so you better make good on your promises."

"Oh aye, you can count on it."

She sits up and straddles my hips. "Did you seriously call your dick a 'manly limb'?"

"I did."

"That sounds like something a prissy Victorian would say."

"Careful, *gràidh*." I shove a hand between her thighs to cup her mound. "Calling a Scotsman a prissy Victorian is a serious insult. I will need to punish you for that."

"Go on, I dare you. Try to punish me." She slides off my body and grasps my cock. "We both know you can't catch me."

"Not every time, but I always find you."

She pumps my *slat*. "Two out of a hundred isn't a great track record. You kinda suck at hunting me, MacTaggart."

I surge up to grab her around the waist and flip her onto her back, with me on top of her. "I said donnae be insulting a Scotsman. And I caught you three times."

"The last one doesn't count. You don't want to take me in this time."

"But I want to take ye—right now."

Three knocks rattle the door.

"Wakey-wakey," Errol calls out. "Time to rise and shine and catch the villain. With the world's premier treasure hunter and puzzle solver on your side, you're sure to be victorious."

"Haud yer wheesht, ye *cacan*. I'm trying to shag Piper."

"Sorry. No time for that." The doorknob wriggles. "Do I need to come in there and separate you two?"

I slide off the bed and offer my hand to Piper, helping her up. "We're getting dressed, Errol."

"Good. Breakfast is ready."

His footfalls recede.

Piper wraps her arms around me. "Wish we had time for a shower, but that would lead to sex."

"Aye. Today, we'll have to be celibate—until I find a way for us to have a poke when Errol's not around."

"The great Magnus MacTaggart is afraid of his cousin overhearing us?" She wags a finger at me and clucks her tongue. "Don't turn into a prissy Victorian."

I chase her into the bathroom—and this time, she lets me catch her.

Chapter Twenty-Three

Piper

After a hearty breakfast that included enough food to feed five Scotsmen and their lasses, the three of us jump into Errol's "hot ride." He called it that. Magnus is not impressed with his cousin's car, though. It's a perfectly nice vehicle, but I think Magnus was hoping for a Jaguar or a Ferrari. The four-door sedan Errol drives lacks sex appeal. When I tell him that, Errol laughs and says, "Wait until ye see the plane."

Our host packed a ton of weapons into two metal trunks and stuffed those into the backseat, which left me squished in beside them. Our luggage takes up the entire "boot" of the car. That's what the Scots call it—the boot, aka the trunk—though that's a British term. Errol promised the ride to the airport wouldn't take long. He also said the weapons will be "no problem, lass" because we're flying private, not commercial.

"You own a plane?" I ask as Errol swerves around a corner. He insisted on driving, of course. Men. They just can't stand to let a woman take charge of their cars.

"Aye, I have a plane. It's not as posh as Evan's jet, or even the ones owned by Lachlan and Rory. But mine will get us where we need to go."

"You must be rich. No offense, but your apartment doesn't give that impression."

"Donnae need a posh flat. But a plane is essential in my line of work. Cannae have my competitors getting to the treasure before me." Errol slams on the brakes as we reach an intersection with a red light. "But ahmno rich. I have enough money to support my needs. That's all I want."

"Yeah, I don't need fancy stuff either. Got used to living with less during my time on the run."

"That time is over now, aye? You have Magnus."

He makes it sound like I'm dating his cousin. I've had sex with Magnus, and maybe we shared some personal stuff, but I have no idea if we could ever be a normal couple. Guess that depends on whether I go to prison. Would Magnus visit me behind bars? Not sure if convicted murderers get conjugal visits.

I cling to my seatbelt while Errol careens around another corner.

"You're going to kill us all," Magnus tells his cousin. "Slow down, Errol."

"Would you go slow if you were driving?"

Magnus conspicuously says nothing.

Errol smirks. "Didnae think so."

Somehow, we arrive at our destination without crashing or getting concussions from our heads hitting the roof. None of us is bleeding either. Hallelujah. Errol drives us right up to the plane, parking so close that I think it will crush his car when we take off. Behind us, I see a big gray hangar that has two much smaller aircraft inside it.

Errol's plane isn't quite what I expected.

We climb out of the sedan—and Magnus growls when he sees our new ride. Seriously, he growls. The man really is a bear or a wolf or something. "Errol, ye damn erse, what the bloody hell is this?"

"My plane. Well, more specifically, my partner's plane. He lets me use it whenever I like."

"We need to get to Istanbul today, not next month."

Errol makes a rude noise. "Donnae insult the plane. She's a beauty, and Marilyn will get us there."

He named the plane? And he called it Marilyn? I'll have to ask him about that later since my curiosity demands to know. But right now, I need to keep Magnus from beating the tar out of his cousin.

"Get us there when?" Magnus snarls. "By the next millennium?"

"No," Errol says with a laugh. "Sixteen hours give or take, depending on how long our three fuel stops take."

"Sixteen?" Magnus shouts that so loudly it echoes off the hangar behind us.

"Do ye want speed or stealth? Marilyn will get us there without the need for the kind of long runway private jets require." Errol saunters up to the huge silver plane and caresses its gigantic wheel. "She's a Douglas DC-3. Might not be a youngster, but she's a good girl."

"Do you talk to your plane?" I ask.

"Aye." He reaches up to pet one of the propellers. "You're a bonnie lass, aren't ye?"

If he kisses the plane, I'm running away again. Rather be a fugitive than fly with a guy who thinks his plane is his girlfriend.

Luckily, Errol gives us a sly smile and says, "I'm having you on. Donnae think my plane has a mind of her own. And before ye ask, Magnus, I know a DC-3 isn't alive. But it's common practice to call a plane 'she.' All right?"

Magnus nods, then he eyes the aircraft as if he thinks it might fall to pieces any second. "Are you sure this thing will get us to Istanbul? We'll have to cross the Alps."

"I know the best route to take. Stop worrying and trust me."

The man I slept with last night grunts.

Errol lifts his brows. "I'll take that to mean yes, ye do trust me."

"Just get us on the plane, ye *cacan*."

I scan my gaze over the huge aircraft, from the nose that stands high above my head to the tail that almost touches the ground. I notice dings and large scratches on the plane's body, and I swear the tires are bald. The silver paint job seems a little tarnished too. Yeah, the "bonnie lass" has seen better days, but I have to trust that Errol knows what he's doing. Magnus trusts him. That gives me hope that we won't die in a fiery crash. Or any kind of crash. I'd rather not die at all, actually.

A short ladder stands below an open door or hatch. Not sure what the proper terminology is. Errol approaches the ladder and sets a hand on its top rung. "Hop on in."

I move toward the ladder, but Magnus pushes in front of me. He climbs into the plane and turns around in a circle like he's examining the interior. Then he nods to me. "You can come in. Donnae see any obvious signs the bloody thing will fall apart."

"Gee, you're a fantastic flight attendant. Thanks for the words of encouragement. Will your safety speech involve telling me that in case of emergency, I should return my seat to the upright position and kiss my ass goodbye?"

Magnus squints at me, then jumps out, landing on the dirt runway. He makes a vague gesture that I assume means he wants me to board the aircraft. When I start to climb the ladder, Errol places a hand on my ass. I can't decide if he did that to help me or if he just wanted to feel me up.

Magnus helps his cousin carry the two big trunks up to the plane and toss them inside. Though Errol needs to drag his trunk over to the ladder, Magnus picks up the other one and carries it on his shoulder. He chucks the thing inside without even climbing the ladder.

Wow. I want him so badly right now. All that dirty Gaelic he told me earlier doesn't help me squelch my lust.

Errol pushes the other trunk halfway up the ladder, then Magnus pulls it all the way into the plane. His cousin retrieves our other bags. Then he jumps in and shuts the door while Magnus secures all the luggage using ratcheting straps attached to the floor rails.

"Are you sure this thing is air-worthy?" I ask Errol. "The tires looked, um, kind of bald."

"No, they're not bald. Just well-worn."

Really well-worn.

I must look terrified because Errol squeezes my shoulder and says, "She's air-worthy. I wouldnae bring you on this plane if I thought there was even a slim chance we would crash."

I'm no expert on aviation stuff, so I have to believe him. Errol wouldn't lie about that.

Now that we're all on board, I survey the interior. The floor of the empty space angles up toward the cockpit, which means I'm standing on a kind of steep grade. Feel like I'm leaning sideways, but I'm not. Rails form lines that stretch from the cockpit all the way down the length of the interior. The cockpit door hangs open, or maybe there is no door. I can't tell for sure. Along both walls hang canvas slings that almost look like seats, though they have nothing in common with the airline version. No, these seats resemble lawn chairs.

"Do passengers sit on those sling things?" I ask.

"Aye." Errol waves toward the cockpit. "But you can sit up front with me."

Magnus eyes the sling seats. "You expect me to sit in one of those."

"You can take the jump seat, if you'd rather."

Errol strides up the slanted floor with ease, but I have to slap a hand on the wall to keep from falling down. Magnus picks me up and carries me to the cockpit. He has to set me down at the doorway, though. We won't both fit through it. Errol is already strapped into the right-hand seat. I climb into the chair beside his, avoiding instruments or some kind of doohickeys that fill up the space between the seats. Errol shows me how to strap myself in with the lap belt.

Magnus leans over Errol's seat, one hand gripping its top edge, and snarls into his ear, "The jump seat is sized for a fairy, ye *cacan*."

"Then take one of the slings."

"Ahmno letting Piper out of my sight."

Since he said he trusts me, all the way, I decide he's just being overprotective.

Grumbling, Magnus drops onto the very small sling-like seat behind my spiffy pilot chair—which sports bits of stuffing that poke out from tears in the leather covering. The jump seat looks less beat up, probably because no one ever wants to sit there. After fussing with his lap belt for a minute or so, Magnus gets himself strapped in.

Then he slants over to peer between our seats. "Where's the radio, Errol?"

"It broke a few months ago. Haven't gotten round to replacing it."

"You better have GPS or radar."

"Nah, I donnae need those." Errol taps his temple. "The navigation data is stored in the best database on earth—my head. A compass is all I need."

My pulse is racing so fast I think my heart could burst out of my chest and sprint back to the UK all by itself.

Errol manipulates controls I don't understand. The engine sputters.

"Are ye sure this thing flies?" Magnus asks.

"Calm down, mate. Just give Marilyn a minute to warm up."

The engine sputters a bit more, then finally catches and escalates into roaring.

"Now we're ready," Errol says. "Prepare for takeoff. That means hold on to your erse, Magnus."

I grip my seat, which has no arms, and pray we aren't about to die.

The plane rolls down the dirt runway, bouncing over rocks or potholes or who knows what. My teeth clack. Vibrations rattle my skull. The aircraft keeps rolling, faster and faster, until the tail rises and the floor levels out. We've lifted off. I see the earth dropping away from us as we soar into the sky. I blow out the breath I'd been holding and sag in my seat. We didn't die.

Not yet, anyway.

We are in the air, on our way to Istanbul. I've never been there. Maybe I'd feel excited about visiting a new country if we weren't heading toward a confrontation with a potential murderer. But I doubt we'll see Hammond in Istanbul. Magnus told me his former client is at a conference in Dublin for the next three days as the keynote speaker. So I can rest easy knowing he probably won't show up to abduct or murder me, not in the next few days, at least.

Magnus stretches his legs out, sideways to the seats Errol and I occupy. "Why couldn't ye find a jet? If you'd told me this was your plan, I would've called to have Evan send his Gulfstream for us."

"Do ye want the villain to know where we're going?" his cousin asks. "Hammond can't know about this plane since it belongs to my partner. Marilyn might not give you the most luxurious ride, but she'll get us there safely."

I glance at Errol. "Are we really going the whole way in this plane?"

"Aye. But we'll make three stops to refuel and stretch our legs. Should be in Istanbul by nightfall."

When I glance back at Magnus, he has his ankles crossed and his eyes closed. I don't believe he's sleeping. The canny Scot wants to listen to me and Errol chatting without letting on that's what he's doing. During our long journey, Errol shares more stories with me, all about his adventures in treasure hunting. The guy knows how to weave a good tale, and I have no idea if everything he tells me is true or if he likes bullshitting me. Either way, I love hearing about his adventures.

"Sounds like you're not home all that much," I say after he finishes his third story. "Must get lonely."

"If you're offering to be my girlfriend, I'll fight Magnus for ye."

"You'll lose that fight. Your cousin is wicked strong." And wicked hot, but Errol doesn't need to know that. "Seriously, do you have a girlfriend? I'm not buying the story that you have a different woman for every day of the week. You seem like the one-woman man type."

He stares straight ahead out the cockpit window, and his expression tightens. "Not many lasses can put up with the sort of life I lead."

"I'm sure you'll find someone." For a moment, neither of us speaks. Then I remember something. "You know, when I was in Archer's apartment after his argument with a stranger, I smelled that woodsy, spicy scent. I assumed it was a man's cologne, but now I'm wondering if it might've been a woman's perfume."

"Could've been," Errol says. "Some lasses like that sort of scent."

I want to say something else, but I don't get the chance.

"Time for our first pit stop," Errol announces. "Hold on to your erses. We're coming in for a landing."

Chapter Twenty-Four

Magnus

We survive the long journey to Istanbul, though not in comfort. Our three refueling stops at least give us a chance to unbend our knees and massage out the kinks in every muscle in our bodies. I understand why Errol thought this type of plane would be the right choice—it has no GPS or other electronics that could be tracked—but understanding doesn't make my neck hurt any less. Christ, the lad is off his head. Traveling by DC-3? I'd rather have walked all the way to Turkey.

Our third pit stop takes much longer than the first two since we decide to stay the night—in a hangar that has what look like bullet holes in the corrugated metal walls. Errol assures me it's "leftover from the war."

"Which war?" I ask. "The Battle of Bannockburn?"

"No," he says with a chuckle. "World War Two."

I can't remember which country we're in, and it hardly matters. Piper looks exhausted, and I donnae blame her. Errol at least had sense enough to suggest we stop to get some sleep before we finish the last leg of our journey.

It's after eight a.m. by the time we touch down on a dirt airstrip just outside Istanbul. Errol converses with the owner of this wee airport, in Turkish, and strikes a deal with him to sell us an old Land Rover the man has no use for anymore. It's in decent condition. Better than "Marilyn," that's for dead certain. Cannae believe Errol named the airplane. No, actually, I can believe it. But I am not referring to that plane by its name. And I willnae be calling it "she" either.

How did we get into the country without showing our passports? When I asked Errol that, he told me to "relax and stop worrying" because this is "a back door operation."

Errol retrieves several items from his trunks. He hands me a Glock 9mm pistol as well as a switchblade. Though he takes a handgun too, also a Glock, he seems more concerned with three electronic devices that he tucks inside his suit jacket. Aye, the lad changed into a suit just after we landed. Piper and I change clothes too, but we're stuck with what my cousin chose for us.

Piper wears blue trousers and a peasant blouse, both of which look bonnie on her. I'm stuck with khaki trousers and a ruddy Hawaiian shirt.

"You're on holiday," Errol says when I give him a nasty look. "That's your cover. I'm an executive, and you two are my brother and sister-in-law who tagged along on my trip to Turkey. Try getting into character."

"I could be a tourist without looking like a bloody moron in a flower shirt."

Piper runs her hands up and down my shirt. "I think you look damn hot."

Aye, I feel much better about my clothing now. Even if she is full of rubbish.

Errol closes the plane's door and pulls out what seems like a remote control device similar to the sort used to operate a television. He punches a button. I hear a buzzing sound, but it dissipates quickly.

"What is that?" I ask, pointing at his wee device.

"Nothing to worry about. We should get moving."

The Land Rover rattles and stutters as much as the plane had, but we finally get it running. Errol wants to drive again, but I order him to sit in the backseat. He can give me directions. After his performance on the streets of Basel yesterday, I will not let the lad operate a motor vehicle ever again. But he does give me directions, and soon we're rolling down a divided highway that has three lanes in each direction. The scenery reminds me of parts of Scotland, but this region is more arid than my home.

Eventually, we pull into the parking lot of a five-story box of a building. Small trees mark each corner. The only sign on the structures declares this to be "Sovereign World Industries"—in Turkish, of course. Errol needs to translate for me. The name assures me we're in the right place—in Hammond's domain. The building isn't large. I would've thought a billionaire's corporate offices abroad would resemble his headquarters in London. But this is the most nondescript office complex I've ever seen.

As we walk into the building, I suddenly realize I'm holding Piper's hand. Maybe I should let go, but I can't convince myself to do that. I like the feel of her soft wee hand in mine.

My attention shifts to the space we've walked into, which seems deserted. Open walkways line three sides of the interior on all five floors, leaving the central atrium open all the way to the top. A counter just ahead of us looks like it was meant to be the reception desk or a security checkpoint. I see no one manning the counter, but bland music plays through speakers I can't see.

"This place is giving me the creeps big time," Piper murmurs. "I feel like we stepped into a horror movie where all the people on earth have vanished except for us."

"Aye, it is strange."

Errol throws his head back and shouts, "Hello! Is anyone here?"

His voice echoes in the cavernous lobby.

The clicking of heels alerts me that a female someone is approaching, though I can't see the individual yet. Instinctively, I move in front of Piper to block her from the person coming toward us.

A dark-haired woman marches out of a corridor and halts several yards away from us. "Welcome to Sovereign World Industries. I am Dilara Terzi. How may I assist you?"

She has a British accent but a Turkish name, which suggests she was educated in the UK. The lass dresses in what seems like designer clothes. I'm no expert on women's fashion. But my suspicion is confirmed when Piper whispers to me, "Her clothes cost more than my last new car."

Errol strides up to the woman and offers his hand. "It's a pleasure to meet you, Ms. Terzi. I'm Andrew Blackwood from Scotland, and those two are my brother and his wife."

"Please call me Dilara." She shakes Errol's hand. "What can I do for you, sir?"

"It's Andrew, not sir. My brother has been wanting to visit Turkey for ages, so I gave him a holiday in this country as his birthday present this year. Dick and Jane just got married, so it's their honeymoon too, and I'm their tour guide."

Did he just rename me Dick? I'll have choice words for him later, the *cacan*. And Jane doesn't do justice to Piper. It's too plain.

"You've been to Istanbul before?" Dilara says to my cousin.

"Aye, several times. It's a beautiful city—and country." He pulls out a business card and hands it to her. "We're on holiday, but I thought I could do a bit of business while I'm here."

The woman studies his card, then smiles brightly at him. "Please, come with me to my office."

Errol keeps throwing bollocks at the poor woman, and she keeps devouring it. I had no idea my cousin was a consummate actor, but he plays his role to the fullest, never once tripping over his own lies or even hesitating when Dilara asks him a question. He coughs up all the right answers and sounds like a real executive or whatever he's pretending to be right now.

Piper and I follow Errol and his new mate down a long corridor.

I can't wait any longer to ask the question I've needed an answer to since we walked into the building. "I was wondering why no one else seems to be here. Are you working alone, Dilara?"

She glances over her shoulder at me. "Most of our staff went to a corporate retreat in Ankara. A skeleton crew stayed to man the offices."

"How did you know we were here?" Surveillance cameras, I'm sure, but I want confirmation. "This is such a bloody huge building."

"It is. But we have cameras that alert us whenever someone enters the lobby."

This all seems a wee bit too convenient for my liking. We just happened to show up on the day when virtually the entire staff has gone on holiday. Coincidences make me suspicious. Errol and Piper must feel the same way. They're both too clever to believe we got this lucky.

Could Hammond or his minions have tracked us? Errol believes his mate's apartment building is well protected from spies, but nothing is perfect. Or maybe the gent at the airport was paid to put a bug in the Land Rover. It's also possible I've gotten a touch paranoid, but I know something isn't right here.

Dilara ushers us into an elevator and up to the top floor, where she takes us to a massive corner office that has a spectacular view of the city. The woman is bonnie, and I can't help wondering if that's why Hammond told her to stay here while everyone else left. If she were a man, I'd wonder the same thing. Attractive, friendly strangers who express eagerness to serve my needs always make me uneasy. It's the bounty hunter in me, suspicious of anyone who seems overly solicitous.

Once we've all sat down, with Dilara behind her desk and the rest of us on the other side, our hostess folds her hands on the desktop. "Andrew, I'm sure we can come to an agreement that will benefit your company and ours."

I clear my throat. "My brother didn't mention what your company does. I'm curious."

"We manufacture and market semiconductor chips."

"Really? That's very interesting. I had no idea British companies did that sort of business in Turkey."

"Oh, we have close relationships with native companies. Sovereign believes in leveraging local assets as much as possible."

I'd already known Hammond got rich from his chip business, but I wanted to make this woman say the words out loud. She didn't flinch when I asked. If she's involved in any of Hammond's shady dealings, she does a fine job of covering it up.

Errol chats to Dilara about semiconductor rubbish as if he honestly does want to partner with Sovereign to buy their chips for his fictitious mobile phone business. While he feeds the lovely woman a load of bollocks, I examine Dilara's office. No photos, not of her family or her associates. No plaques either. Most offices have something personal somewhere on the walls or the desktop, but this place looks like it could belong to anyone. It's generic.

Piper clasps my hand under the table and gives me a tight smile.

She must worry about what we're doing here. It's dangerous, infiltrating the enemy's territory when we have no idea what Hammond is up to here in Turkey or back home. If Errol is right about the illicit antiquities, we might have walked straight into trouble. We have no choice. To uncover the truth, we must take risks.

Even ones that might kill us.

"Let me show you some of our chips," Dilara says, rising from her chair. "I can take you into the clean room, Andrew, but I'm afraid your brother and sister-in-law will need to stay here. It's a security issue."

No, I donnae like this at all. Errol should not go anywhere with anyone alone. But I cannae speak up without drawing suspicion. I have to let him do it. Well, the lad does have a closet full of weapons. I know he has a gun and sneaked a few more items onto his person before we came here. I need to trust him.

I've never needed to trust anyone. It's not my strong suit.

"Please wait here," Dilara says. "I will need to find guest badges for all of you."

The woman walks out of the room.

Piper, Errol, and I exchange glances and wait. We have no choice. I need to explore this building, but with security cameras and who knows what else, I cannae just start poking around. Not yet.

Dilara returns and hands us each a badge that has the word guest printed on it. "Dick and Jane may wait in the atrium or make use of the cafeteria, which is on the other side of the atrium. Andrew, please come with me. I will be delighted to show you our operation."

The legitimate part of their operation, she means. I have no doubts illegal things happen here too.

I hold Piper's hand again as we exit the office. Errol goes off with our hostess, while Piper and I make our way back to the atrium.

Two armed security guards now stand watch at the counter.

Aye, we need to be very careful.

Chapter Twenty-Five

Piper

This building gives me the creeps, and I feel like invisible insects are crawling over every inch of my skin. At least Magnus keeps holding my hand. That contact eases my anxiety a little, though nothing will make me feel safe until we get the heck out of here. I worry about Errol too. We let him go with a strange woman who works for the man who might have killed Archer Caldwell and who definitely has criminal tendencies.

I trust Magnus and Errol, but we're three people against who knows how many bad guys.

As we amble across the atrium like tourists admiring the architecture, those two security guards trail behind us. How can we investigate with armed nannies on our tail? I need to talk to Magnus, but not in front of an audience.

He stops us halfway across the atrium, pretending to admire a fountain that has multiple layers with water trickling down to the bottom. I can't get interested in that, and I doubt he cares either. Magnus slips an arm around my waist and nuzzles my cheek like he wants to snuggle or make out or something. Only when his lips meet my ear do I find out his plan.

"Pretend we're being affectionate," he murmurs. "And listen without reacting to what I say."

"Oh, honey, I love it when you say sweet things." I make an appropriate facial expression, which seems to convince the guards.

"We cannae investigate with those blokes on our erses."

"I agree. This is a beautiful fountain."

"Need to find Errol. But to do that, I'll have to disable the guards." Magnus kisses my neck. "Follow my lead."

"Mm-hm." I feign embarrassment. "Please, honey, not in front of those nice men."

Oddly, I am getting turned on by what Magnus is doing to my neck. The whispery tone of his voice gets me even hotter.

We need to get rid of those guards. I have an idea, one Magnus will hate. But I doubt he has a better one.

I leap into the fountain and start dancing around, splashing water onto the floor. Then I kick things up a notch by bursting into song and spinning around and around like a crazy person.

"Out of the water," a guard snaps. "Stop this now."

"But it's so much fun," I announce as I scoop water into my hands and fling it at the guard. "Let's all dance and sing and get soaked."

While the guards gape at me and move forward like they want to grab me, Magnus creeps up behind them. He grabs one guard's weapon and smacks it into the man's head. Just as he collapses, Magnus strikes the other guard. Both men are down. Magnus tosses their guns onto the floor and drags one unconscious man into an unlocked office, then drags the other one in there. After searching for a locking mechanism on the door for a couple of minutes, he gives up.

I rush into the office and rifle the desk drawers, where I find two big rolls of clear packaging tape. "Let's tie them up with this, huh?"

Magnus frowns briefly but then takes my advice. He tapes the men to office chairs and tapes their mouths shut too. He slams the door behind us and seizes my hand. As we hurry away from that office, he snags the two handguns from the floor and offers one to me.

I take it. But God, I hope I never need to use the thing.

"Didn't you already have a gun?" I ask as he tows me back toward the reception counter. "Errol gave you one, right?"

"Aye. But it never hurts to have multiple weapons."

"Where are we going now?"

"To find Errol."

"Shouldn't we, um, ransack offices or something? We need evidence."

Magnus stops dead. He turns his head toward me slowly. "We should go to Dilara's office."

"Why? We've been there already."

"It's a hunch."

"Okay. If you think that's a good plan, I'm on board."

His mouth curls upward at one corner. "You honestly trust me, don't you?"

"Yes. I've told you that already."

"Aye, ye did." He pulls me toward the elevators. "We're going up."

"Guess you're not worried this is a trap anymore."

"I'm dead certain it is a trap. But we need to take the chance we might find something useful before they come after us. Your life is on the line, Piper."

Because Hammond or someone he hired framed me for murder. Yeah, I'm totally on board with risking everything to find proof I'm innocent.

A few minutes later, we exit the elevator and jog toward Dilara's office. The door stands open, but no one seems to be inside the room. The creepy-crawly sensation returns, but I have to ignore it—for now. Magnus tells me to search the desk while he tackles the file cabinets. All the drawers in the desk and cabinets are locked, but that hardly stops us. We have no reason to worry about stealth since we disabled those two guards and we're pretty sure this whole thing was a setup. But we agree to use the quietest means of accessing the locked containers so we won't alert the bad guys any sooner than necessary. I use a letter opener to pry the drawers out. Magnus prefers to bash the heel of his Glock into the cabinets.

We find nothing useful. Damn.

I let Magnus decide where we should search next, and he marches down the hall while swiveling his head left and right as if he's looking for a specific door. His longer legs move him faster, leaving me lagging behind.

"What are you doing?" I ask.

"Searching."

"Aimlessly, it seems like."

"Not aimlessly." He halts abruptly, and I bump into his backside. Then he points toward a door. "There."

"Can you read the words on that door? It's Turkish."

"I have a hunch." He whips out his phone and takes a picture of the door. Then he fiddles with his phone. "It's the janitorial closet."

"How do you know that?"

"Thanks to an online translation site. I uploaded the image I just took and had the site analyze it."

"I'm impressed, except..." I point at the door. "That's a janitorial closet. Are we looking for incriminating mops?"

He gives me an annoyed look. "I chose this door because it's the smallest and most unassuming we've seen. Maybe they've hidden something important in plain sight, inside a janitorial closet."

Since I don't have a better idea, I follow him in there. But it's just a closet. We hunt for secret openings or anything that might suggest this room is more than a place to store mops and brooms, but we find nothing. Magnus clenches his jaw tight and clenches his fists too as we exit the closet and start down the hall again.

I grab his arm. "Stop, Magnus. Please."

He halts but doesn't look at me.

So I step in front of him. "We can't keep wandering through this building. We need a plan."

"I thought the closet was—I'm a bloody stupid erse."

"No, you are not. You were wrong, that's all. Maybe we should go find Errol and just get out of here." I rub my arms, though I don't feel a chill. Well, not the physical kind. My intuition shivers a ghostly chill through me. Something about this place just doesn't feel right. "Do you honestly believe virtually all the employees of this large building have gone to a corporate retreat?"

Magnus compresses his lips. "No. I'm fair certain this was a setup, though I cannae figure what Hammond is trying to accomplish."

"Let's get out of here. Please."

"All right. We'll go downstairs and wait for Errol." He brings out his phone again and taps the screen as if he's typing on it. Then he shoves it back into his pocket. "I texted Errol. Told him you're not feeling well."

"Secret code for 'get the hell out of there'?"

"Aye."

Magnus starts back the way we'd come, heading for the elevator.

As we wait for the car to arrive, I remember something and have to ask. "Why aren't you worried about your cousin?"

"I am. But Errol can handle himself. I'm more worried about what he might do than what our enemies will do to him. They'll never get the chance."

"Logan said asking for Errol's help is like wishing for a wildfire. He also mentioned Errol's favorite tactic is scorched earth."

"Aye."

"But he seems kind of goofy—smart, yes, but goofy—not the scorched earth type at all."

One corner of Magnus's mouth kicks upward. "Just wait."

We ride the elevator down to the ground floor and hurry toward the atrium. But Magnus halts at the door to the room in which we'd tied up those two guards. The door now hangs open, and the men are gone.

Oh shit. This is not good.

Magnus clamps his hand around mine and races for the entrance. He tries to open one of the glass doors, but he can't do it.

"Locked," he hisses. Then he drags me backward, releases my hand, and pulls out the handgun Errol had given him. He fires two shots. The explosive noise reverberates through the building and hurts my ears.

But the glass does not shatter.

Magnus snarls something I can't understand, so it's probably Gaelic cursing. "The door is bulletproof."

"What should we do?"

He surveys the atrium and the hallway. "Wait for Errol. We have no other choice."

"If guns can't open these doors, how can Errol help?"

"The lad has more than a few weapons. Not sure exactly what he does have, but I guarantee it's not legal or subdued."

Scorched earth? I have no idea if Logan meant that literally, but I'm about to find out.

Alarms blare, the harsh noise echoing in the atrium and making my ears hurt. Recessed lights in the walls, which I had taken for decoration, suddenly begin to pulsate with alternating red and yellow. A clearly recorded voice emanates from speakers I can't see, the calm tone in opposition to the flaring emergency lights.

No idea what the voice is saying, but I don't imagine it's a welcome message.

The sound of pounding feet echoes from the far end of the long hallway Dilara had led us down earlier. Errol comes barreling around a corner, heading straight for us.

"Run!" he shouts. "Outside! Now!"

"The doors are locked and bulletproof," Magnus hollers to his cousin.

"Bloody hell!"

As Errol races toward us, the noise of more pounding feet erupts behind him as well as to our right, at the other end of the atrium. Just as Errol stumbles to a halt beside us, figures come into view down the hall and in the atrium. Armed guards are about to swarm us.

Errol grasps his midsection, breathing so hard he seems to almost be hyperventilating.

"What did you do?" Magnus asks.

"Something bad." He manages to smirk while still trying to catch his breath. "Well, bad for them. Good for us."

"We're trapped, ye eejit."

"Oh, I wouldnae worry about that."

A horde of guards now surrounds us. We're penned in front of the glass doors. Time to kiss our asses goodbye.

I glance at Errol, and he winks.

The alarms fall silent.

From further across the atrium, the clicking of high heels echoes in the large space. The guards move aside to create a path for the woman to walk through to reach us.

Dilara plants her hands on her hips. "Royce warned me you would be difficult. That's why I locked all the doors. You will not get away, but you will be transferred to an alternate location to await transport back to the UK."

"Royce Hammond is going to kill me," I say. "He framed me for murder and wants to stop me from proving he committed the crime. Do you really want to help a murderer get away with it?"

Dilara's resolute expression falters. She stops blinking, her gaze fixated on me. "You are Piper Lang."

"Yeah. But you must've known that already. Why else lock us in and threaten to send us back to the UK?"

"I didn't expect—" She tugs her suit jacket down, swallows hard enough I can see it, and clears her throat. "Royce wants you returned to the UK. I will do my job and only my job, full stop."

My mouth goes dry. My heart pounds. I clutch my belly, though I have no idea why I do it. There's no way out, and I'm about to be delivered straight to Royce Hammond. If my voice would work, I'd spit out a slew of curses.

Because we are screwed.

Chapter Twenty-Six

Magnus

Aye, things have taken a turn for the worse. And aye, we seem to have no way out. But I've never let the obvious get in my way. What appears to be inevitable often turns out to have hidden loopholes, and it's just a matter of locating those weaknesses so I can exploit them.

I'm standing between Piper and Errol, so I lean toward my cousin and whisper, "What did you do?"

No, I donnae believe he just ran away from Dilara and the guards. That alarm indicated something amiss, a worse problem than one Scot fleeing the building.

"Donnae want to ruin the surprise," Errol says. He checks his watch. "Might want to take a deep breath and hold it."

"Why?"

Rather than replying, my cousin sucks in a breath and holds it.

I whisper to Piper, and we both follow Errol's instructions.

"What are you doing?" Dilara asks, eying us with suspicion. "Why would you hold your breath? It won't save you from whatever Royce has planned."

A boom reverberates through the building. That alarm starts screaming again, and the entire structure trembles around us, beneath us, as if someone has set off a bomb.

Dilara shouts orders to the guards. All but six of them rush off—to assess the situation and the damage the explosion caused, no doubt. The remaining guards raise their weapons and form a semicircle around us, with Dilara in the middle.

"Why did we have to hold our breath?" I whisper to Errol.

"It's more dramatic that way."

Bloody Errol.

"Your friend has done something," Dilara says. She ought to sound annoyed, but instead, I get the impression she's anxious. "Tell me what he did."

Errol raises his hand. "I can explain that to you, since I'm the one who did it. I placed a very small electronic device on the exterior of your main server. It just had a meltdown."

"Do not lie to me. You triggered an explosion."

"No, I caused your computer system's brain to explode. The cooling units would have shut down first, which made the server heat up to a dangerously high temperature." Errol's lips tighten into a smug smile. "Nothing exploded. But lots of things short-circuited, and an electrical surge will have burnt out all the electronics in your clean room."

Dilara's eyes widen.

Errol leans in, speaking in a pseudo-whisper. "Donnae think it's clean anymore, love. Scorched is more like it."

The woman fists her hands. "Seize them."

Oh aye, that will work. We'll just stand here waiting for those blokes to grab us.

I glance at Errol, and he nods.

The guards take half a step toward us.

And we rush them. Errol pulls out a stun gun and zaps one guard who crumples to the floor, then he hits another one. That guard stays upright but loses control of his weapon. It clatters to the floor.

I slug one man, making him double over, and ram my knee up into his chin. The lad stumbles backward, trips over his own feet, and falls to the floor.

A guard tries to seize Piper, but she executes a groin kick and slams her elbow into the man's throat. He manages not to fall, but he stands there stunned and immobile.

One guard left. I punch him in the stomach and rip the gun out of his hand. Errol has pulled out zip ties, and he tosses some to me. We begin binding the stunned men.

Dilara lets out a primal scream and throws herself at Piper.

I spin around, about to rush to Piper's aid, but I donnae need to bother. Piper slugs Dilara, then grabs the woman's wrists to cuff them behind her back. I toss the lass a zip tie, and she secures it around Dilara's wrists.

"More guards will be coming," Dilara says, and I swear I hear a note of fear in her voice. "You cannot escape. The doors are locked and resistant to firearms."

Errol chuckles. "Firearms? Aye, those doors are bulletproof. But they cannae withstand my secret weapon."

Dilara's lower lip trembles faintly. "Royce never lets anyone escape his clutches, and his punishments are severe."

My cousin unbuttons his shirt from the waist halfway up his chest, revealing rectangles of a white substance taped to his belly. He peels one rectangle away from his skin and turns toward the door.

"What are ye doing?" I ask. Then I bend toward him so I can see what he has. "Is that C-4?"

"Aye." He pastes the rectangle to the glass using the tape and inserts a wee object that looks similar to a mobile phone card. "Time to step back."

He moves away from the door while gesturing for all of us to follow him. I herd the guards while Piper manages Dilara, and we don't stop until we reach the fountain in the middle of the atrium.

"This should do," Errol says as he pulls out his mobile and poises his finger over its screen. "Might want to plug your ears."

"Just do it, ye *cacan*."

Errol taps his mobile screen.

The glass doors explode. The concussion rattles the windows in the atrium.

Footfalls pound from elsewhere in the building, probably that long hallway down which Errol had fled moments ago.

"We need to go," I say. Then I seize Dilara's arm. "You are coming with us."

I drag the woman with me as Errol and Piper follow me out, each of us hopping over the pile of shattered glass that used to be a door. When the bloody woman stops walking and digs her heels in, clearly hoping that will make me release her, I throw her over my shoulder.

And we run for the car.

Errol is sitting in the driver's seat and has the engine running before Piper and I reach the vehicle. That lad can run like a gale-force wind. I tell Piper to take the front passenger seat while I toss Dilara into the backseat and climb in.

My cousin floors the accelerator. We rocket across the parking lot and out onto the street, violating every traffic law in the city of Istanbul, I'm sure. He slows down slightly as we swerve out onto the three-lane highway, headed back to the airstrip.

Piper twists her torso to face the backseat. "You want to interrogate her, right?"

"Aye. She's coming with us."

"On the plane?"

I pull out a zip tie and secure it around Dilara's ankles. "She knows more than she wants to admit. So aye, the bitch is coming with us until I wring every bit of information from her."

"Will you torture her? If so, I'm cool with that."

Piper is joking, I think. But the lass has proved to be far tougher and more cunning than anyone else, man or woman, I've ever hunted. Maybe she wouldn't mind if I use physical force to coerce Dilara to talk. But I doubt that will become necessary. My usual techniques will do.

I manhandle the woman to get her into an upright sitting position. She had been sprawled across the backseat with her legs on my thighs. I strap the seatbelt across her lap for an extra layer of restraint. She cannae jump up to try anything.

Turning toward her, I lay an arm across the seat's back behind her. "Tell me what that building really is."

"Oh, it's a chip factory," Errol says. "I saw enough of the place to be sure."

I slant toward Dilara. "That's not all you lot do there. Tell me the rest."

She turns her head away.

And I grasp her chin, forcing her to look at me. "Do I need to start cutting? Small nicks will bleed and hurt like the devil, but they won't kill you."

No, I willnae do that. But she believes I will. I can see it on her face and in her eyes. The woman fears what I might do, but she still doesn't speak.

"I need your tie," I tell Errol.

"Let me get it," Piper says. She undoes the tie and hands it to me. "Here you go."

"What are you doing?" Dilara asks, her voice hushed.

I wrap the tie around her head as a blindfold, knotting it in the back. "Now, tell me what I want to know."

She bites her lip hard.

The woman is stubborn, but not nearly as strong as Piper. I pull out my pocket knife and hold the dull side of the blade to Dilara's throat. She can feel the cold metal, but I doubt she can tell I'm not using the sharp edge, not even when I skim it across her throat.

"No, please, don't," she cries. "I wish I could tell you everything I know, but Royce will have me killed if I do."

"What do you think I'll do to you?"

She bows her head, her shoulders shaking as if she might cry. Then she hauls in a deep breath, blows it out, and raises her head. "All right. I'll tell you."

"Go on."

"I normally work at the London headquarters, but Royce sent me here yesterday. He believed you might come to Istanbul because it's the closest Sovereign location outside of London. I was to detain you and Piper Lang. Royce never mentioned a second man." She takes a shallow, shaky breath. "He wants the woman. She's a fugitive."

"Tell me something I couldn't find out on the internet."

"We were instructed to keep you on the premises until the extraction team arrived. Royce doesn't care about you, only the woman."

"What was he planning to do with us?"

She wriggles, but I don't think she means to attempt an escape. Dilara is uncomfortable, which is exactly how I want her to feel. "Piper Lang is to be taken back to the UK. I have no idea what he has planned for you and your friend, but it wouldn't surprise me at all if he had you killed."

Oh aye, he would love the chance. Hammond wants Piper alive but me dead, and he gambled on where we might go—gambled and won. But I'm positive Hammond never counted on Errol destroying his chip factory and had no idea the lad came with me. I doubt he knows anything about my cousin. "Did Hammond kill Archer Caldwell?"

The lass flinches so minutely that I can't be sure I didn't imagine it. "Archer who? I have never heard of anyone by that name."

"But you know about the illegal antiquities Hammond has been acquiring and selling."

Dilara goes perfectly still, her face now a blank mask.

"I'll take that as a yes." I drag the knife across her throat again. "I'm getting weary of this. Start talking or I'll forget about the blade and bring out a much more painful weapon."

A single sharp sob racks her body. She sucks in a breath and lifts her chin. "I know nothing about that. But Royce often has packages delivered to the Istanbul office that employees are ordered not to open. They're held until a parcel shipping company comes to take them away."

"Bring out the thumb screw," I say. "We'll start with that, and if she still willnae cooperate, we'll try the saw."

Piper wrinkles her brow and mouths, "Thumb screw?"

I guess the saw doesn't fash her. She probably has no idea know what a thumb screw is and that's why she looks confused. It was a medieval torture device. Honestly, ahmno sure what the thing looks like or how it works. But my statement has the desired effect.

Dilara cringes, and tears dribble down her cheeks. "Please, I've told you all I can."

Mhac na galla. I was hoping this woman could provide useful information, but Hammond undoubtedly keeps most of his minions in the dark on purpose. Only a select few would know everything. I suspect Dilara is holding back out of fear of what Hammond might do if he found out she confessed everything. Then again, maybe she genuinely doesn't have the answers we need. Either way, I won't risk keeping her with us. Hammond might have bugged her mobile or put a tracking device on her person.

"Pull over on a side street," I tell Errol. "This woman is of no further use to us."

Dilara bursts into a fit of sobs.

Let her think I mean to kill her. The bitch obeys the commands of an evil bastard, which makes her as guilty as Royce Hammond.

Errol turns off the highway and stops along a deserted street.

I open the door and push Dilara out, then lean down to cut her bindings. "Count to sixty, then remove the blindfold."

We get on the road again.

Just as we swerve back onto the highway, Errol sighs. "Ye gave her my tie. It was from a posh store, ye know."

"I'll buy ye a new one."

Piper glances at Errol, then me. "What do we do now? Our grand plan was a bust."

"Not entirely," Errol says. "I copied the contents of the Sovereign servers onto my watch."

"Your watch?" I say. "How the bloody hell does that work?"

"Microminiaturized electronics." He waves a dismissive hand. "Never mind the details. All you need to know is that I have all their data, and I programmed my mobile to search the files for any mention of antiquities or similar phrases."

"When did ye have time to do that?"

"On the drive to Sovereign's offices. I knew I'd be able to hack their servers and acquire all their data."

"You did what? I thought you were just a treasure hunter."

"Oh, I'm always looking to learn new tactics. Evan's hacker mate taught me how to do all of that last year. He's an ethical hacker, in case you were wondering, not the bad sort."

Will I ever understand Errol? It seems unlikely. But I'm bloody grateful he came with us.

I pat his shoulder. "Good job. Now get us back to the plane without blowing anything else up."

Chapter Twenty-Seven

Piper

Life on the run can't compare to traveling with Magnus and Errol. He has explosives taped to his tummy. Seriously. Errol Murdoch is not the goofy nerd I took him for when we first met. He's more like a Scottish Indiana Jones with a touch of James Bond thrown in for good measure. The guy doesn't care about his personal safety and is willing to take risks that seem insane to me, the fugitive.

Somebody's phone makes a loud bloopety-bloop sound.

Errol looks at me. "Hold the wheel for a moment, will ye, lass?"

"Um, okay." I grip the steering wheel with one hand, trying to keep us on the road.

He pulls out his phone and studies the screen without expression. Then he stuffs the phone back into his pocket and retakes the wheel. "Thank you, Piper."

"Sure, no problem." As we race down the long two-lane road that leads to the airstrip, I ask, "What's our next move?"

Errol glances over his shoulder at Magnus. "I have a suggestion, but you are the big kahuna."

"Kahuna?" Magnus says. "You've been watching that American television series again, haven't ye?"

"*Magnum P.I.* That's what it's called, not 'that American television series.' Do ye want to hear my idea or not?"

"Go on."

"We should go to Göbekli Tepe."

"I have no idea what that means."

Errol twists around to look at Magnus while he speaks and somehow manages to keep the car in the correct lane at the same time, though he steers with only one hand. "Göbekli Tepe is one of the most important archaeological sites in the world. My watch just sent me a text on my mobile because my search program got a hit. The data I borrowed from Sovereign mentions that Hammond's agents made frequent trips to Göbekli Tepe. They also engaged in a lot of email chatter about that place and tried to be cryptic about it, but I saw through that. Would've fooled you, but not me."

"Are you calling me an eejit?"

"No, not at all."

"And what do you mean your watch sent you a text?"

Errol shakes his head. "Never mind the details, Magnus. Focus on Göbekli Tepe."

Magnus groans. "Never mind the details? Sounds like you're calling me an eejit again."

"You're a clever man, but our brains work differently, that's all. You're a tracker, I'm a puzzle solver."

I glance back at Magnus, expecting to see him scowling. But instead, he wears a slight smile.

"Aye," Magnus says. "Your brain is very different from anyone else's."

"Thank you," Errol says with a grin.

"Face forward, laddie. You're meant to watch the road ahead, not behind."

Errol obeys his cousin's command, but I think he only does that because he feels like it. Magnus doesn't intimidate Errol—or me, not anymore. He never did, actually. I was terrified of being hauled back to the UK and locked up for the rest of my life, but I never feared Magnus. I wouldn't have gotten naked with him otherwise.

Once we arrive at the airstrip, Errol parks the Land Rover behind the DC-3. We all climb out of the car and head around to the passenger door. Errol had left the ladder in place but the door closed. Just as we walk around the wing, with the door in sight, we stop.

A man lies on the ground, on his back, apparently unconscious. I don't recognize him.

Instinctively, I start to run toward the guy to help him, but Magnus grabs my arm to stop me. He makes a "stay put" gesture and slowly approaches the prone man. Errol goes with him, and both men kneel to check if the guy on the ground is injured or dead.

"He has a pulse," Magnus says. "Donnae understand why he passed out here, by the plane. Maybe he had a heart attack, but that doesn't explain what he was doing here."

"He'll be fine," Errol says. "Just a wee shock."

I trot over to the men and bend over to peer at the unconscious person on the ground. "A shock? I hope you're not implying something scared him so much that he passed out."

"No, lass," Errol says. "I meant the shock from my security system. If anyone tries to enter the plane when the system is enabled, they'll get an electric shock. Enough to knock a bloke out, but far from fatal."

Magnus shakes his head. "Electric shocks? If this man had a weak heart, you might've killed him."

"I only use the security system when I'm in a place where I cannae be sure villains won't try to steal my plane."

"Aye, this heap of rust is worth protecting."

Errol pats the unconscious man's cheek. "Wakey, wakey."

When he gets no response, Errol smacks the guy's face hard.

The stranger's eyelids flutter open, and he groans. Then he sees Errol and mutters something in Turkish. Whatever he said, it didn't sound like a compliment. Errol responds in Turkish, and the man glowers at him. Whatever Errol says next, it makes the man scramble to his feet and hurry toward the hangar.

"What was that about?" I ask.

Errol shrugs one shoulder. "I simply reminded him that he shouldn't have been trying to break into my plane and if he ever tries that again, he'll wish my security system had electrocuted him. Then I suggested he should let my mate take him into custody."

His tone of voice when he'd spoken to the old man had sounded conversational, not confrontational. Errol Murdoch is a complicated man.

"Your mate?" I say.

"Aye. The bloke who owns the airstrip and the hangar. He'll keep that scunner until I let him know the coast is clear."

"You think the 'scunner' is working for Hammond."

"That's right," Errol says. "He admitted he's working for Sovereign. Hammond paid him a hefty sum to plant a tracking device on my plane, but my security system foiled his plan."

"How did Hammond know where we parked the plane?" Not sure if that's the right word, but it hardly matters whether they park or dock or moor a plane.

"Sovereign has more sophisticated technology than I thought. After we arrived at their offices, they used the Wi-Fi on our mobiles to insert a wee bit of malware and trace the path of our car back to the airport using GPS." Errol rises and taps the screen on his cell phone. "Just shut off the security system. We should get in the air right away, before Sovereign sends thugs to kidnap us."

"Or worse," Magnus adds.

I shake my head at him and lay a hand on his cheek. "Try optimism for a change. It'll be a novel experience for you."

He smirks. "I'm very optimistic about my chances of having another poke with you."

Not anytime soon. We can't have sex in the back of a cargo plane while his cousin is watching. Well, we *could*. But I don't want to do that.

Magnus opens the human-size door, but we don't climb in yet. Errol wants to take the Land Rover with us. That means he needs to open the other side of the door to make a wider opening in the side of the plane. I hadn't realized the door could go wider. But I watch Errol fold out the other side and remove the ladder. He and Magnus drag a big metal ramp out from somewhere inside the plane and position it under the open doorway.

Now they're ready to load the Rover.

Magnus tries to assist his cousin by making hand gestures to guide him up the ramp and into the cargo hold. But Errol pays no attention to that. Instead, he gets the Rover lined up with the big door, then backs it up.

"What are ye doing?" Magnus shouts.

Once again, his cousin ignores him. Errol floors the Rover and rockets up the ramp into the cargo area, stopping inches away from the far wall and barely missing our luggage.

Forget the dangers of Errol's electric security system. I think I had a mild heart attack just watching him load the Land Rover onto the plane.

We climb aboard and manage to get airborne without any trouble, though we change into less conspicuous clothes first. The flight takes several hours, but I don't bother keeping track of the time. It hardly matters. We'll do whatever we need to do to find out the truth, however long it takes and whatever risks and hardships we need to endure. I have no choice, but Magnus and Errol could have walked away. Neither of them did. They both want to help me. Errol does it at least in part because he loves danger, I think. I've learned that much about Errol Murdoch, and I have to admit I admire his enthusiasm and fearless nature.

I sit in the seat beside Errol for the entire flight, which doesn't take nearly as long as our journey from Basel. Magnus once again insists on taking the jump seat, though it barely fits his bottom, much less the rest of him. No longer the pig-bear, he has become my partner in this adventure and my protector.

While we're in the air, I have nothing to do except ask Errol questions. "You said you're a treasure hunter. Do you scoop up artifacts before archaeologists can get there?"

"If you're implying I steal them, the answer is no. Museums around the world hire me and my partner to find treasures that have been lost to history." Just as he had in the car, he keeps one hand on the wheel while he looks at and speaks to me. It's even more disconcerting in a plane than in a Land Rover. "We're paid for the work we do. That's how we earn a living—the legal way."

"But you don't always use entirely legal means to do that work."

He smiles and wags his eyebrows. "My methods are top secret, lass. You'll have to kiss me if you're wanting more information."

Magnus kicks his cousin's arm. "Stop flirting with Piper."

"Because she's your girl." Errol grins. "Magnus MacTaggart has a crush on a lass. Wait until I tell the family about this."

"Haud yer wheesht, ye *cacan*."

Errol and I change the subject, talking about Göbekli Tepe and other ancient sites instead of his cool job. Time passes much more quickly when I have someone to talk to, especially when that someone shares my interest in history.

"We'll be landing in fifteen minutes," Errol announces. "I'll give ye a final warning, Magnus, so ye can hold on to your erse."

"Still donnae understand why we're going to an archaeological site."

"Because it's important to Sovereign. That lot must have a bloody good reason for going to Göbekli Tepe so often and discussing it in cryptic emails."

"We're basing our strategy on emails. How comforting."

"No more arguing," I say. "We'll be landing soon, and there's no point in bitching about why we're going to this site. Time to kiss and make up, boys."

"Ahmno kissing him," Magnus says.

Errol grins and winks at me. "I'll gladly kiss Piper instead."

"Where are we landing?" I ask, mostly to end the kissing conversation.

"Ten miles from Göbekli Tepe," Errol says. "That's why we needed to bring the Land Rover."

Magnus clears his throat. "On whose airstrip will we be landing?"

"I know a bloke. He's letting us land in his field."

"When did you contact him?"

"Before I blew those glass doors apart, but after I trashed Sovereign's servers."

"That's impressive," I say. "You've taken multitasking to a whole new level."

"Donnae encourage the lad," Magnus says. "He's off his head."

I don't believe him for one second. Magnus likes Errol, and I can tell he admires his cousin's determination and spirit.

We land in a barren field, but I can see a house not far away. After we get the Land Rover out, Errol secures the plane with his electrical booby trap and assures us that the "bloke" who lent us his field knows all about the security system. So if we come back to find an unconscious man lying on the ground right next to the plane, it won't be Errol's friend. It will be a bad guy.

That's not as comforting as Errol seems to think it is.

At least we don't need to ditch our phones. He removed the malware, so we can't be easily tracked.

We pile into the Rover and head across the landscape toward our destination, steering clear of roads. The red soil gives way to grassy hills, and in the distance, I see stands of trees, though it doesn't resemble the forests I've seen in America or the UK. It has more of an affinity to Spain, but even that doesn't describe the landscape here accurately. Civilizations existed in this region for more than eleven thousand years, and I can't help experiencing a sense of awe as we approach the site and the grassland becomes peppered with yellow wildflowers. We park within walking distance and trek up the hill on foot.

I swear I can smell the past in the air. Okay, I know that's dumb. But I am a student of history, so I should feel awed right now.

The main part of the site has a canopy over it to protect the ancient pillars and remnants of walls. We hike over to the large white canopy and see it has railing around it to stop tourists from going into the ruins, and a walkway surrounds the structure. If we're looking for antiquities thieves, I doubt we'll find them here among the tourists. When I mention that to Magnus, he turns to Errol.

"What now?" Magnus asks his cousin.

"I suggest we wait and watch. Look for suspicious individuals."

"So ye have no plan. That's what you just told me."

"There must be a reason why Sovereign employees come here. I'm positive this is the hub of their antiquities operation, but I donnae know where exactly to look." Errol lowers his voice to a whisper. "We should hide until after dark. Illicit things always happen at night."

"Hide where?"

I raise my hand. "I've got an idea."

Magnus gives me an annoyed look but waves for me to continue.

The three of us huddle together so the guys can hear me though I'm whispering. "We can hide down there, in the ruins."

"Down there?" Magnus says, his brows rising. "Ye want us to defile a sacred place. Isn't that what people like you think of ruins? They're not to be touched."

"We won't touch the obelisk or the columns. We'll just hide in a corner down there, concealed by the shadows. Besides, desperate times call for breaking the rules."

"Doesnae bother me. If we're all in agreement, then we need to look for a way to sneak down there."

"It's my idea, so you know I'm on board."

"So am I," Errol says.

I straighten and nod. "All right. Let's break into an ancient site."

Chapter Twenty-Eight

Magnus

We catch a bit of luck in our attempt to sneak into the ruins because we seem to have arrived during a lull in the tourist traffic. Errol and Piper keep watch while I climb over the railing around the ruins and drop down onto a steep, rocky slope. I scan the area visually until I find a promising dark area. Then I make my way over there to verify that we can hide in the space. Aye, it looks all right. We may need to crouch there to stay in the shadows, but we'll make do. So I return to where Errol and Piper are waiting for me.

"Come on," I say, keeping my voice soft enough that no one nearby will hear but loud enough for Piper and Errol to understand me. The slope I'm standing on is several feet taller than I am, so I hold my arms up and tell Piper, "Jump. I'll catch you."

The lass doesn't hesitate or question my ability to do that. She jumps.

I catch her in my arms, then set her down on the rocky slope.

Before I can offer Errol any help, he vaults over the railing and thumps down beside us. Aye, he's a showoff. But I cannae deny the lad knows what he's doing with all this covert rubbish. I might need to employ a bit of stealth when I hunt fugitives, but I haven't needed to break into an archaeological site to stalk antiquities thieves.

I haven't had this much fun in years. Maybe never.

We scramble down the slope and slowly make our way toward the shadowed alcove I'd found. Piper stumbles into me. I catch her—and realize the lass is staring at something below us, in the circle of large upright slabs at the center of the ruins.

Errol comes up behind Piper and peers down at the T-shaped pillars. "What are we gawping at? I think we need to hide, not admire the ancient artwork."

"Look at that," Piper says, sounding like she might cry. Her eyes have teared up too. She points to a large rectangular slab situated within the circle of T-shaped pillars. "It's the Göbekli Tepe obelisk. You can see the dinosaur-like creature carved into it."

"Why are ye crying, *gràidh*?" I ask. "It's just a big rock."

"Just a big rock?" Her jaw falls open. "It's one of the most ancient man-made structures on earth. Human beings carved that obelisk more than eleven thousand years ago." She sniffles, and her voice quavers. "I never imagined I'd see the Göbekli Tepe obelisk in person."

Though I should order her to get moving, I realize I need to let her experience this for a moment. She is a museum archivist, after all—or she used to be. To her, history is the most potent drug. I give her a moment, but we cannae wait too long, and I tug her arm to urge her to keep going. She nods and wipes her eyes with the back of her hand, then we continue toward the shadowed alcove. Once we've settled into our hideaway, all of us sitting on the rocky ground, we have nothing to do but wait for dusk. We've muted our mobiles to avoid making any unnecessary noise.

Tourists come and go, and the sun's position changes. We move to a different spot to keep ourselves in shadow, but no one notices us. Maybe this place doesn't usually get many tourists because I haven't seen hordes of them. I'd visited the Giza pyramids in Egypt once while tracking a particularly irritating fugitive, and that site was swarming with tourists. I'd never heard of Göbekli Tepe until today. It must not be as famous as other sites. Gradually, the number of people ambling along the walkway above us dwindles and finally stops altogether. The sun has almost set, leaving us in a twilight world among the remains of a long-dead civilization.

I climb up to the railing to check. Everyone is gone. No vehicles nearby.

Errol and Piper have been watching for me to give them a sign. I wave for them to approach. Once we've all climbed out onto the walkway, we quietly make our way toward a spot where we can view the entire area, crawling up a small slope on our bellies to lie there and wait.

Minutes tick by. A lot of minutes.

Headlights appear in the distance, bobbing slightly as they move closer.

Errol leans in to speak straight into my ear, his voice barely a whisper. "That must be them."

"Aye."

My cousin produces a small pair of binoculars from somewhere inside his clothes. That lad seems always to have an arsenal of weapons and devices on his person. He peers through the binoculars, then hands them to me. "Look."

I take the binoculars and spot the approaching vehicle. It seems like an SUV, though I can't see it well enough to identify the make or model. The vehicle stops in front of the pavilion that covers the ruins inside which we'd hidden until nightfall. My eyes have adjusted to the darkness, and the moon has risen to provide some light, though it's not quite a full moon. We parked the Land Rover in a spot where no one entering via the prepared paths would notice it, but these people don't seem to worry about discovery.

The vehicle stops near the pavilion. Two figures emerge from the car, and they seem like men based on their builds. The blokes retrieve two large suitcases from the rear cargo area of their SUV, each man taking one case. They stride down the stepped boardwalk that guides visitors to a dirt path that accesses other sites in the complex.

Where are they going? And what are they doing? Errol believes Sovereign employees are engaged in the illegal antiquities trade, but I cannae understand what they would do here in a public venue. And why bring suitcases? They can't mean to dig up artifacts right here. I trust my cousin, though, now more than ever before. I've gotten to know him better, and I trust his intuition. If Errol says Sovereign is in the business of stealing and selling antiquities, I take his word for it.

From our position on the hill to the west of the pavilion, we watch the figures as they step off the boardwalk and continue onto the wide dirt path, turning south toward a lookout point that has wooden railing. The men set down their suitcases, and one climbs over the railing so the other can hand the suitcases to him. Once the second bloke has jumped over the fence, the pair head for the nearby rocky area.

I'd seen that area in the daytime. It has a number of holes in the ground, all in a specific section of the rocky landscape. Most of the holes are relatively small, but two are large. The men approach one of the large cavities and repeat the process they'd done at the railing, with one man passing the suitcases to the other, though now they must do that while one lad is at the bottom of a hole.

We sneak down the hill, crawling on our bellies until we reach the stone wall that hems in this side of the dirt path. The strangers are still over there doing something with those suitcases, though it's too dark down there for me to tell what they're doing. We wore dark colors for this occasion, and Errol provided me and Piper with black ski masks, so we hurry across the dirt path in a half crouch.

The lads with the suitcases seem too engrossed in their task to notice anything else.

We steer clear of the area directly in front of those holes. Instead, we slink in the opposite direction where there are no barriers to stop us. Then we belly-crawl again, making our way around the smaller holes which isn't a pleasant experience. Scrubby weeds and grass offer little resistance, but the hard and rocky ground proves less hospitable. Still, we manage to reach the ledge above the hole in which those lads are at work. They seem to have hidden their suitcases down there somewhere.

Is this a drop-off point? A public site is an odd choice, but then, Royce Hammond has never seemed like the type who worries about things like that. I've always thought he must be the daredevil sort, though he hides it well.

The lads down in the hole move toward the wall as if they mean to climb out.

No time to waste on explaining my plan to Piper and Errol. I leap into the hole and run for the men, punching one so hard he falls to the ground and slugging the other in the gut, making him double over in pain. I grab him by the throat, hoisting him up until his face is directly in front of mine and his feet dangle above the ground.

Errol and Piper join me in the ancient hole.

"Keep an eye on that one," I tell them, nodding toward the bloke on the ground. "I need to have a conversation with this one."

Errol plants a foot on the dazed lad's chest and pulls out his Glock .9mm. "Donnae worry about him. I've got this laddie, and you've got that one. But it doesn't seem fair. Piper won't have anyone to assault."

The lass comes up beside me. "Don't worry about me. I love to watch Magnus throttle slimy little twerps."

The *bod ceann* I'm holding by the throat tries to pull my fingers away, but all he manages to do is scratch my skin. "Let me go. You won't get a bloody thing out of me."

A British *bod ceann*. Well, that figures since Hammond is a Brit and his company is headquartered in London. I have nothing against Brits in general, but when they threaten to kill me, I get a wee bit fashed.

I shake the *cacan*, which makes him gurgle. "I know Royce Hammond sent you. So spare yourself and tell me everything, unless you enjoy excessive pain and graphic violence."

He gives me a mulish look.

That's the best he can do? I've seen more intimidating looks from Piper.

"Dig in his pockets," I tell her, "and see if he has any identification."

Piper roots around in the man's clothing and brings out a wallet, then searches it. "His name is Anthony Gerard. And guess what he has?" She whips out an ID badge. "This asshat works for Sovereign. What a surprise."

Errol searches the bloke he's holding down with his foot, seeming not the least worried that the man is rousing from his stupor. My cousin produces a wallet and ID badge from that man's pocket. "This one is Wilbur

Cockburn. No wonder he's a criminal ersehole, with a bloody stupid name like that."

I shake my prisoner harder this time. "What's in the suitcases?"

Anthony Gerard glowers at me.

"Have it your way." I rush toward the lumpy wall of the hole we're standing in and slam Gerard into it while keeping hold of his throat. With my free hand, I pull out my Glock and press its muzzle into his temple. "Talk or die. You have five seconds to decide."

"I don't know what's in the cases. We deliver them, that's all. We get a text from Dilara Terzi giving us the day and time of the drop, then a bloke from Sovereign always meets us at a cafe in Gaziantep."

"He gives you stolen artifacts."

"Is that what's in the cases? We had no idea. Cockburn and me, we get the cases and drive here, then put them in the hole. That's all either of us knows."

Do I believe this eejit? Not quite. "Why would you do what Sovereign tells you?"

"Because they pay us. We're petty criminals, not sodding masterminds. We need the money."

Oddly, I believe him. Which leaves us with nothing.

I release Gerard, and he slumps to the ground. "Let's tie these two up and leave them as a gift for the local police, along with those cases."

Errol reaches into his coat pocket and produces two zip ties.

"Do ye always have those on you?" I ask.

"Aye. They come in handy for a lot of things."

While Errol restrains Gerard and his mate, I walk to the two suitcases tucked behind a large rock and drag them out into the open. "Let's see what's in here."

Piper kneels beside me.

Each suitcase has a combination lock built into it. I use the butt of my Glock to break them open. Shooting the locks might've been quicker and easier, but it would make more noise. I flip the cases open. Both contain objects nestled in packing foam shaped to fit each piece. Even I can tell these are ancient artifacts.

"So they are involved in the illicit antiquities trade," Piper says. "Archer must have been helping them, though I can't imagine why. He cared about protecting the past as much as I do."

"Maybe Hammond threatened him with blackmail."

"Yeah, maybe. But Archer seemed like an upstanding guy."

"Anyone can hide a dark side." I shut the cases. "Let's make sure the authorities get these artifacts."

Chapter Twenty-Nine

Piper

I thought it would be harder to get two bound men out of a rocky pit. But no, Magnus just pushed them up with his hands on their behinds and tossed them out. He did the same with the suitcases, and we left the criminals zip tied to the doors on their car and their loot stashed in the backseat.

Someone will find them before morning. Errol made sure of that by calling in a tip to the police. He used Gerard's phone to do that.

We drive back to the plane and are in the air before the cops have a chance to drive out to Göbekli Tepe. I hated leaving those artifacts behind. What if the authorities don't handle them properly? Important pieces of human history might be destroyed.

"Are you worried about the ancient trinkets?" Magnus asks from the jump seat behind me.

"Yes. How did you know?"

"Because you care about old objects and history. You care about a lot of things that donnae enter the thoughts of most people."

"It's my job to care. Or it used to be."

Errol pats my knee. "Donnae worry, *gràidh*. You'll get another museum job as soon as we prove your innocence."

"Even if I'm exonerated, I doubt I'll ever get another job as an archivist. I've been on the run for almost two years. How could anyone trust me?"

"They will if they know what's good for them," Magnus says. "Anyone who treats you like a criminal will answer to me."

I have my very own knight in shining armor. Wow. Well, he's more like a rogue warrior dressed in black leather and riding a fire-breathing steed.

Errol raises his brows. "Magnus the protector? That's new."

The rogue warrior huffs. "It's not new. You weren't there when a *tollathon* tried to ruin Kirsty's life."

"Aye, Logan told me about that. You borrowed Rory's Jaguar so you could whisk our wee cousin away to the safety of Dùndubhan."

"What's Dùndubhan?" I ask. "And why did Magnus need to whisk your cousin away in a Jaguar?"

"It's a long story," Magnus says. "Tell you later."

"We have time," Errol points out. "Six hours or so until we reach Istanbul. Plan to stop there to get breakfast. I'm fair starved."

"You're always fair starved. I've seen ye eat half a turkey by yourself, then ask for more."

"Hunting for treasure is hard work."

Magnus grunts, then stretches his legs out. When I peek around my seat to look at him, the rogue warrior has his eyes closed and his hands clasped over his belly. Guess it's nap time for the badass bounty hunter. Since we've been up all day and are now flying through the night, I should get some sleep too. But our adventure at Göbekli Tepe has left me wired. Don't think I can sleep yet.

I turn to Errol. "Mind if I ask you some questions?"

"Not at all. Conversation will keep me awake."

"Okay. Why did you become a treasure hunter?"

"At first, it was for the excitement. But I quickly realized I love digging up treasures that no one else could find or that nobody bothered to look for. It's a special kind of thrill to hold an object in your hands that hasn't seen the light of day in centuries or even thousands of years." He holds the wheel, or whatever the term is for that contraption, in one hand while he speaks to me. "I also love solving puzzles, and ancient history is one big puzzle."

"I get it. That does sound exhilarating." I wriggle around until I sit halfway facing him. "You're the only treasure hunter I've ever met."

"A treasure hunter virgin? Maybe I should show you my equipment."

"Haud yer wheesht, Errol," Magnus says without even opening his eyes. "Piper isn't interested in your equipment."

"I meant my hammer and trowel."

"Sure ye did."

Though I hate to interrupt their good-natured argument, I have an idea I need to run by them. "Did you guys notice how Dilara seemed nervous when she first saw me? Almost guilty, I'd say."

"I noticed too," Magnus admits. "Donnae know what to make of it."

Errol rubs his chin. "Hmm, that's an interesting observation. Need to think on it."

Magnus lays a hand on top of my head. "Try to get some sleep, *mo leannan*."

I slouch down in my seat, but though I don't expect I'll fall asleep, after a while I do drift away into a dreamless slumber. I only know I fell asleep when I wake up to discover sunrise brightening the sky—and that the plane is already on the ground. How did I snooze through the landing? Guess I was more tired than I realized.

No one else is in the cockpit, so I get up to yawn and stretch before I wander into the rear area of the plane. The men stand beside the Land Rover talking in hushed voices.

"Good morning, boys," I say. "What's the huddle for?"

"We're discussing our next move," Magnus tells me. "We know Sovereign is in the illicit antiquities trade, but we still cannae prove it. Even if we'd kept those two suitcases, nothing in them ties the theft to Sovereign or Hammond."

"So it was all for nothing."

"Not entirely. Errol copied everything on the Sovereign servers, which means he might find incriminating information or at least another clue that will lead us to what we need."

"Which is what?"

"Clearing your name. What did ye think I meant?"

I hunch my shoulders and wrap my arms around myself. "Wouldn't blame you guys if you want to bail. This is turning into a major operation with dangerous stakes, and I don't even know what the stakes are."

"Errol should go home. But I'm staying with you."

"Why do I have to go home?" Errol asks. "I thought we were a team."

Magnus claps a hand on Errol's shoulder. "We are a team, but I need you to comb through all that data you collected from Sovereign."

"I can do that without going home."

A phone rings. It's mine.

Digging it out of my pants pocket, I see the caller ID shows a number but no name. I turn the screen so Magnus can see it while the phone keeps ringing. "Should I answer?"

"Aye. But put it on speaker."

I accept the call and hit the speakerphone button. "Hello?"

"Still on the run, are you?" a British male voice says. "And Magnus Mac-Taggart must be with you as well."

"Who are you?"

Magnus steps closer, staring down at my phone. "What do you want, Hammond?"

"To share a bit of news with you and your slag. Have you fucked her yet? Oh yes, of course you have. I bet she's a brilliant shag."

"Cut the crap," I say. "Tell us why you called, other than to act like an obnoxious ass."

"I told you, darling. I have news." He pauses, probably thinking that will increase the drama. It just makes me want to crawl through the phone and deck him. "Mummy and Daddy are in my custody as we speak."

"Whose Mummy and Daddy?" Magnus demands.

Hammond chuckles. "Piper's parents, of course. I wouldn't bother with yours. They despise you, so there's no percentage in abducting them."

"Where are my parents?" I ask as a subzero chill rushes through me. If he's hurt them…I'll murder the bastard and gladly go to prison for it.

"I invited them to stay in the house I own in Tennessee. Luckily, I have a very fast jet, so it took me no time at all to collect Mummy from Arizona and Daddy from Vermont." He sighs with mock wistfulness. "I can see why they're divorced. Those two bicker nonstop."

"Gee, I'm so damn sorry my parents annoy you, the kidnapper."

"You should give a toss, darling. If they irritate me too much, I'll kill them."

Errol waves a hand to get our attention, then mouths, "Keep him talking."

"Come to Nashville," Hammond says. "Be here by noon tomorrow, or dear Mummy and Daddy will each get a .9mm slug to the brain."

He hangs up.

The phone tumbles from my hand, clattering on the floor.

Magnus slings an arm around me, pulling me close. "Donnae worry. We will save your parents, ye have my word on that."

"But how? This rust heap will take days to get there, if it can even make it across the ocean."

"I'll contact Evan. He won't hesitate to send his jet to pick us up. It can get to America in about eight hours."

Errol clears his throat and waits for us to look at him. "I wasn't able to trace that call, but I did record it."

"How does that help?" Magnus asks.

"It's evidence. He threatened to murder Piper's parents."

"Aye, but we cannae prove that's Hammond's voice."

Errol tucks his phone inside his jacket. "Maybe not, but it's a start. You can at least threaten the bastard with the recording, say you'll leak it to the media if he doesn't give you Piper's parents."

That's not a half bad idea. But I can't think right now. Maybe my parents abandoned me when I was arrested, but I cannot let them die because of me.

Magnus calls Evan and arranges for his cousin to send his jet to meet us in Basel. That way, we can drop Errol off before leaving for America. Errol refuels our plane, though we've stopped at a different airstrip than last time. None of us wanted to renew our acquaintance with Hammond's lackey, who deserved to get knocked with an electric shock. Errol's friend who owns that airstrip will release the criminal as soon as Errol gives him the word. With everything arranged, we climb back into the cockpit and take off, heading straight for Switzerland.

We don't speak during the long flight. After refueling twice more, we hurry to the private airstrip in Switzerland where Errol keeps his plane. Once we've exited the plane, it's time to say goodbye—for now.

I kiss Errol's cheek. "Thank you for everything. You're a sweetie and a genius."

"Don't I get a real kiss goodbye? Might never see me again, what with villains on the loose."

"That's all the kiss you get," Magnus growls.

After everything Errol has done for us, I feel I owe him more than a peck on the cheek. And I kind of want to annoy Magnus too, just for fun. So I take hold of Errol's face and kiss him full on the mouth. No tongue, though. I like him, but not that much.

Magnus grasps my arm, tugging me away from his cousin. "Enough. The laddie already thinks he's God's gift to women. Donnae inflate his ego any more."

Errol smirks and bounces on his toes. "I'm a sweetie and a genius. That's more than you'll get a woman to say to you."

Magnus rolls his gaze heavenward and groans.

I give Errol a hug, then Magnus and I take a taxi to the international airport. We bypass all the security stuff, heading out onto the tarmac where a big spiffy jet waits for us. We climb up the stairs, and a pilot greets us. He's Scottish, naturally. We don't chat with him, though. The situation is too dire to waste any time, so we sit down in a pair of big puffy chairs positioned on either side of the plane with an aisle between them. We're close enough that I can stretch my hand out to Magnus. He grasps mine, giving me a reassuring, if small, smile. Behind us, I see a long sofa across from a TV that's attached to the top of a low cabinet.

Maybe I'd enjoy my ride in private jet if I didn't know what's at stake. My parents lives are in the balance. I try to enjoy the view out the window as we reach altitude, but the landscape can't distract me from my fears of what might happen next.

Magnus gets up and kneels beside my seat. He clasps my hands, sandwiching them between his palms. "Donnae do that."

"Do what?"

"Wring your hands. I will make certain Hammond doesn't harm your parents."

I hadn't realized I was wringing my hands. Guess I'm more anxious than I thought. "Sorry. I can't help it. This is the first time someone has threatened the lives of people I love. Even though my parents shunned me, I still care what happens to them."

"You need to relax. Cannae spend the entire eight-hour flight worrying."

"Can't stop myself from doing that."

He stands up, offering me his hand. "Come with me, *leannan*. I can distract you."

I give him a dubious look. "How, exactly?"

"With sex."

"As good as that sounds, I doubt even mind-blowing sex could distract me for more than a few minutes."

He grabs me around the waist and hoists me out of my chair. Hugged to his hard body, I feel my pulse accelerating. "I know how to distract you for much longer than that. Trust me."

I do trust him. One hundred percent.

So I slide my arms around his waist. "Okay. Distract me."

Magnus sweeps me up in his arms and carries me away.

Chapter Thirty

Magnus

I used to think it was barmy that Evan's jet has a bedroom. Today, I thank every star in the heavens that it does have such a room. It's at the rear of the cabin, far from the pilots. With eight hours to kill, I'll need to pace myself if I mean to stop Piper from worrying for the entire trip. Not that I think I can fuck her for eight hours straight. We'll need to rest now and then, and pause for meals too, not to mention snacks. I mean to keep the lass well nourished.

Maybe my plan has more to do with wanting to shag Piper than needing to relax her. Since I can do both at the same time, it's irrelevant which impulse came first.

But she will come first, always, while I take her body again and again. Sex is my favorite stress-relieving technique.

I carry her into the bedroom, kick the door shut, and toss her onto the mattress.

Piper jumps up, kneeling at the foot of the bed right in front of me. "Maybe we should do some yoga instead."

"Yoga?" I say with a chuckle. "No, lass, we need to have a poke."

"But it's weird to have sex with you while my parents are being held hostage by a madman."

"Royce Hammond isn't mad. He's devious and ruthless."

"Only a crazy person would abduct people and use them as leverage."

I reach for the zipper on her jeans and pull it down. "No more talking."

"But—"

When I shove my hand inside her jeans, the lass stops complaining. But when I push my fingers inside her knickers to stroke her mound, she sucks in a breath and leans into me. I love the way she responds to my touch, always have. Maybe that's why I cannae get enough of her. She holds nothing back when we shag, but I've restrained myself with her. She probably wouldn't believe that considering the intensity of the sex we've had so far.

Piper lets her head fall onto my chest and starts to cry.

I hook a finger under her chin and lift until I can see her face. Tears stream down her cheeks. "What's wrong, *m'eudail?*"

"Mom and Dad. What if Hammond—" Her words choke off on a sob.

I enfold her in my arms and caress her hair. "He won't hurt them before we get there. I doubt he'll hurt them at all, it's just a bluff."

"You don't know that. If he killed Archer, he's capable of anything."

"*M'eudail,*" I murmur, but I cannae think of anything else to say. So I tell her the truth. "I'm sorry, Piper. All I can do is wait until we meet Hammond and then beat the living hell out of him. Donnae have a clue how to comfort someone. I want to make you feel better, but it's not in my nature."

"Bullshit." She raises her head to aim her bleary eyes at me. The tracks of tears stain her cheeks, but she's not crying now. "You've done more than anyone ever has to comfort me. You protected me, and you've done every-thing you can to find answers and try to clear my name."

"Only after I pursued you relentlessly for nearly two years. I didnae care if you were guilty or innocent."

"Why should you care? Your job is to catch fugitives. I couldn't provide any evidence to the contrary, so of course I seemed guilty. I forgive you for not believing me."

She forgives me? I cannae understand why.

"Don't apologize," I say. "I'm the one who needs to make it up to you. I used to vow to myself that I would go to any lengths to take you in. But now I realize my job means nothing compared to you. I will go to the ends of the earth and back to prove your innocence."

She stares at me for a moment, not blinking, her lips parted and her gaze nailed to mine. Then she swallows hard, the movement in her throat visible, and splays a hand over my cheek. "I know you would do that. I know you'll always be there for me, no matter what happens. I feel the same way about you."

I raise a hand to cup her cheek. "I know, *mo gaoloch*, I know."

She turns her face into my hand and kisses the palm.

What just happened? Something important, that much I know. But exactly what it means... We're both under too much stress to understand that right now. I won't even try. We'll have time for that later. And I absolutely will not think about why I called her my darling using three different Gaelic words.

I told Piper the truth. I will do anything to prove her innocence.

"As much as I love getting dirty with you," she says, "I'm too anxious and exhausted to enjoy sex. But I'd love it if you would lie down with me and just hold me for a while."

"There's nothing I'd rather do."

We lie down on top of the covers with me on my back and Piper on her side. If feels good to have her warm, soft body nestled against me and her hair tickling my chin. She draped one arm over me too, and her fingers trace circles on my chest. This must be what my cousins claim will happen when a man meets the right woman and everything clicks into place.

I used to think it was nonsense. Today, I wonder if it might be true.

"Why did you call Errol a sweetie?" I ask. "Didnae say anything like that about me."

Cannae believe those words just came out of my mouth. I don't care if she thinks I'm sweet or not.

"Are you jealous?" she asks. "Because you should know that I do think you're a sweetie. But you're also a sizzling-hot superhero with a magic *slat*."

"When did you learn Gaelic?"

"From listening to you and Errol."

"I see. But ahmno a superhero, and my cock does not have magical powers."

She laughs and kisses my cheek. "You didn't complain that I called you a sweetie."

"Donnae say it in front of anyone else. Might ruin my evil bastard image."

"Your secret is safe. But I have to correct you on the magic dick thing. Yours is definitely enchanted. As for being a superhero, you are the man who kept tracking me down time after time. That definitely takes superpowers."

"I'm no hero."

"Hmm. You're afraid to admit you are a good man, aren't you?"

"Not afraid. But it's rubbish."

She sits up, braced with one arm, and gazes down at me. Her lips curve into a soft smile. "I'll convince you sooner or later."

"You are bloody-minded, so maybe ye will."

Piper feigns shock. "Did Magnus MacTaggart, badass demon biker bounty hunter, just admit a woman might know more than he does?"

"No. I said ye might convince me. That's not the same as you being right." I spring upright and sling an arm around her waist. "Ahmno a demon or a biker. But I'll accept the badass description."

"I changed my mind. Let's get it on right now."

"Are ye sure?"

"Yes." She whips her shirt off, flinging it onto the floor. Her lacy pink bra barely covers her tits. "Promise you'll say filthy things to me in Gaelic."

"Aye, I will. And I'll do filthy things to you too."

"Thank goodness." She gets rid of her shoes and socks, then shimmies out of her jeans. Clad in only her bra and matching knickers, she crawls toward me on her knees to straddle my lap. While she unhooks my belt, she says, "Let's do something different this time. I want to swallow your dick and suck you off so good your eyes roll back in your head."

"Do it, *mo gaoloch*. But donnae make me come. I'm needing to fuck ye like mad."

"I'll get you almost there and stop." She frees the button on my trousers and drags the zipper down. "Now, start talking dirty Gaelic to me."

I know we're both using sex as an excuse to avoid thinking about our problems, but I donnae care.

Piper pulls my trousers down, then crawls backward until she kneels over my feet. The lass yanks my trousers off, throws them onto the floor, and strips off my socks too. I'm naked from the waist down. That's not good enough. I pull my shirt off and toss it away.

"You're wearing too much clothes," I tell her, my voice roughened by the need pulsing inside me.

She ditches her bra and knickers. "Better?"

"Aye. Yer so fucking beautiful, Piper, and so sensual I cannae think anymore when I see ye naked."

"Ditto." She lies down with her head between my thighs and lays her hands on my hips. "Need to eat you up."

I cannae speak anymore, not with my *slat* throbbing and the hungry look on her face stealing my breath. When she drags her tongue across the head of my cock, I gasp and fist my hands in the covers. My heart pounds, and I fight the urge to grab the lass and fuck her like a maniac. But she wants to do this, and I willnae deny her.

Oh aye, I want her to do it too.

She coils her tongue around my cock over and over while her hands travel down to my *bagais*. She cups my balls with one hand, massaging my thigh with the other, and laps up the bead of moisture on my crown. I bend my knees as if I mean to thrust into her mouth, but I force myself to hold back and let her have her way with me. She skates her palms up to my chest and pinches my nipples.

I jerk and almost *caith* just from that wee action. "Piper, ah."

She lifts her head. "Ready for the main event?"

"Aye, please." I begged. *Bod an Donais*. No one would believe it, not that I'll ever tell anyone.

Piper slides my cock into her mouth inch by inch, her eyes half-closed, moaning as if I'm the best thing she's ever tasted. I would grip the headboard rails, but this bed doesn't have any. So instead, I crush the pillow in both hands while a gasp bursts out of me. Piper takes me in as far as possible, then starts to suck and lick and slide her mouth up and down while her fingers close around the base of my erection.

And she pumps me with her delicate hand.

The pace of her movements accelerates little by little, making me squeeze my eyes shut and dig my fingers into the pillow so hard I think I'll rip the bloody thing apart. Pressure builds inside me with every lick of her tongue and pump of her hand. I'm close to the edge. So fucking close that I can't breathe anymore and my entire body goes rigid.

Piper sits up, licks her lips, and aims a sexy smile at me. "You taste better than any food. If I made you come in my mouth, I know that flavor would be even better."

I snarl a slew of Gaelic curses.

Then I surge up and sweep her into my arms. Leaping off the bed, I use one arm to flip the covers back and drop her onto the mattress. The lass bounces and makes a squeaking sound. I get the condom from my trouser pocket and sheath myself.

Then I pounce on Piper, landing on all fours straddling her body. "Ye got me so worked up, I cannae make ye come first."

"Don't care. Screw me like a demon biker."

Bloody hell. This woman has me so randy I donnae even care that she called me a demon biker again. She could call me a wee mouse, and I still wouldn't give a damn. But as I gaze down at her, the bonnie, sweet look on her face triggers a pang in my chest. I'm about to shag her, yet she smiles at me with sweetness, not carnal hunger. A lock of hair has fallen over her eye, so I tuck it behind her ear and try not to think about what her expression means or why my chest feels tight and my throat has gone thick.

I spread her thighs with my knee, then rub my length between her folds until the condom glistens with her cream. Though I'd love to rip the latex off and feel her slickness coating my flesh, I know I shouldn't do that.

She arches her neck and bends her knees, her eyes half-closed. "More, Magnus, please. I need you inside me."

A few minutes ago, she begged me to talk dirty to her. But now, I donnae want to do that. This feels like the wrong moment to whisper wicked things to her.

"*M'eudail,*" I murmur, then I cannae think of what else to say. So I show her instead.

I pull my hips back and slide into her body.

Chapter Thirty-One

Piper

Magnus drops onto his elbows, his chest brushing my breasts, while he glides in and out slowly as if he plans to spend hours doing only that. No one has ever made love to me this way, and I never would have imagined Magnus MacTaggart would be the one to show me this kind of tenderness.

Every time he pushes inside me, he feathers a soft kiss over my lips. He never looks away, keeping his focus exclusively on my eyes even when he raises onto his straight arms to thrust with more power, though he keeps the pace languid. I grip his wrists, unable to tear my gaze away from his even while my breaths quicken and my heart races. The delicious tension inside me mounts little by little, and I can't stop myself from whispering his name, moaning his name, begging him never to stop. I sense the climax coming, like a summer storm on the horizon, the pressure building until the first drop of rain falls to the earth.

And I come.

The orgasm feels unlike anything I've experienced before. I tumble over that cliff in slow motion, sailing down through a warm and sensuous sea of pleasure, my back bowing up while I lift my hips into his thrusts. A soft cry spills from my lips, and the climax fades away.

Magnus pumps into me a few more times, groaning as he comes deep inside me. But he doesn't lie down. He stays where he is, not even pulling out of my body, and keeps his gaze pinned to mine.

I graze my fingers down his cheek. "You okay?"

"Aye." He rises to his knees, wipes a hand over his mouth, and still stares at me. "That was…"

He seems incapable of completing his sentence. Did romantic sex with me short-circuit his brain? No, that can't be the problem. Well, maybe it is.

Magnus sits back on his heels between my feet, still seeming dazed or in shock or something.

I sit up and scoot closer to him. "What just happened? I thought we shared a beautiful moment, but you look like you might throw up. Please talk to me."

He shuts his eyes and bows his head, then lets out a long sigh. "I'm sorry, lass. Didnae mean to make you feel—I'm not going to throw up. All right?"

"Please tell me what you're feeling. I loved what just happened between us, but you clearly don't agree."

"*Mhac na galla*," he says softly. Then he shifts position to sit with his legs bent in front of him and rests his elbows on his knees. "This is something I've never experienced before, and I donnae know how to explain it or deal with the consequences. Talking about my feelings isn't my strong suit."

"Gee, really?" I say in a teasing tone. I smile too, to make sure he knows I'm not annoyed. "Have you ever had a steady girlfriend? A serious relationship?"

"No. I dated lasses when I was a lad, but after I joined the army, I didn't have much opportunity to date. I served in Afghanistan and saw things…no one should see. Watched my mates die when they stepped on mines, and worse things than that." He shoves a hand through his hair, still not looking at me. "After the army, I couldnae take a normal job. I wasn't normal anymore, maybe I never was. Becoming a bounty hunter felt like the right choice. I could protect the world from criminals the way I should've been able to protect everyone from terrorists. I failed at that, but I've done well as a hunter."

"Have you avoided dating because you feel unworthy of love?"

Magnus jerks his head up and aims his unblinking gaze straight at me. "Why would you ask that?"

"Is it true? If I'm way off base, just tell me. I asked because I listened to everything you just told me and extrapolated a hypothesis."

He almost smiles, but the expression can't quite take root. "You are a clever lass, *mo leannan*. I never thought much about why I behave the way I have. You changed that. Since the first time I caught you, I've sensed a sort of kinship between us. That's barmy, and I haven't wanted to believe it."

"Do you believe it now?"

"Aye. You and I are kindred spirits, aren't we? Shunned by our families, always on the run, though for different reasons. I travel the world hunting fugitives while you struggle to stay one step ahead of the authorities. We're both outlaws, of a sort."

I move beside him and rest my cheek on his upper arm. "It's okay if you're afraid of what I make you feel. The same thing happened to me. I didn't want to believe the guy who mercilessly hunted me could turn out to be a good man underneath the gruff, tough bounty hunter shell."

He glances at me sideways and smirks. "I am a gruff, tough bounty hunter."

"Yeah, I know. And that side of you is hot. But I've seen other facets of you lately, things that convince me you are a sweet man underneath." I slip an arm around him, and he wraps his arm around me too. "The way you made love to me just now proves my point. You are a good man, Magnus."

"Not sure if that's true, but I know you make me feel that way." He kisses my temple. "But we shouldn't be talking about me right now. I know you're worried for your parents."

"Yeah, I am. Would you lie down with me and just hold me?"

"Aye, we can do that."

He lies down first and stretches an arm across the other pillow as an invitation to cuddle up. I settle in alongside him and do just that. I snuggle up to the tough-as-nails bounty hunter, and he curls his arm around me. We just lie here enjoying the intimacy and the connection we forged without even trying to do that. I don't realize I fell asleep until I wake up—thanks to Magnus's mouth on mine. The gentle caress of his lips rouses me in the most wonderful way.

"Are ye awake, love?" he murmurs.

"Mm-hm." I open my eyes and yawn. Loudly. "Are you awake?"

He chuckles. "Aye, lass, I am. We'll be landing in ten minutes, so ye might want to get dressed."

"Ten minutes?" I spring upright, jabbing my elbow into his neck accidentally. "I couldn't have slept for eight hours."

"You did, Piper. Must've been more exhausted than you realized."

"Did you get any sleep?"

"I did, though only for five hours. I sneaked out to talk to the pilots and find out when we would be landing, then I came back to lie in bed with you again." He slaps my bottom. "Get dressed, *m'eudail*. Breakfast is waiting for you in the main cabin. I already ate."

"Ten minutes to dress and eat?"

"You can take as long ye like. The jet will wait."

"But my parents can't." I whip my head side to side, searching for a clock but not finding one. "What time is it?"

"Seven fifteen. Relax, we will get to Hammond's house in plenty of time. But you need food first."

I dress and eat faster than I ever have before. How could I have forgotten that my parents are in danger? But I did forget, at least for a while. Magnus made love to me and shared something of himself with me, and the threat to my family vanished from my thoughts. I could chastise myself for that—in the past, I would have—but after almost two years on the run, I've given up on self-flagellation. Letting myself relax while I waited for our jet to reach Nashville does not make me a bad person.

Now if I can just convince Magnus he's not a bad person...

Yeah, I might need months to accomplish that feat. Possibly years. The weirdest part? I wouldn't mind spending the rest of my life proving that to him.

As we walk down the stairs onto the tarmac, I see a black limousine is waiting nearby. "Did one of your cousins send a car for us?"

"No. Hammond must have done that."

Just as we reach the limo, the driver gets out and comes around to our side. He stops a couple of yards away and lifts one side of his suit jacket to give us a glimpse of the gun nestled in a shoulder holster. "No tricks. Give up any weapons you have, then I'll scan you to make sure you aren't hiding any."

Scan us? With what?

He pulls out a palm-size device that doesn't look like anything I've seen before.

"We didn't bring any weapons," Magnus says. He must mean we didn't bring them out of the jet, because I know we've got some in there. "But go on and scan us."

I glance over my shoulder and see the pilots have shut the jet's door. Magnus told me earlier that he'd instructed them to hole up in there and not let anyone in until he says so.

Hammond's driver finishes his scan and nods. "You're clean."

"May we get in now?" Magnus asks.

The driver opens the limo's back door for us. "Please do. And you should know the door locks can only be operated from the driver's seat."

We can't leap out of the car while it's whizzing down the road. Oh darn, I really wanted to do that. No, not really.

Magnus climbs in first, probably because he's in protector mode now and needs to make sure no one waits inside the limo to ambush us. I wait until he waves for me to enter, then I get in—and the driver shuts the door. The limo has two bench seats that face each other. We sit on the rear bench, but we can't see the front of the vehicle where the driver sits because a solid partition blocks our view.

On the other bench sits a strange man.

He smiles in a way that sends an icy tingle down my spine and holds out his hand to me. "We meet at last, Piper. I'm Royce Hammond."

I do not shake his hand, instead clasping mine on my lap. "May you rot in hell while demons gnaw the flesh off your body."

He chuckles. "I like a feisty woman. No wonder Magnus wants to protect you at any cost. You are beautiful, sensual, and strong."

"Gee, thanks. I'm so incredibly not flattered."

"Feisty *and* sarcastic. I love that."

I cross my legs and do not respond to his weird flirtation in any way, keeping my expression neutral. Since I'm wearing pants, he can't ogle my legs—which I bet he would be doing if I'd chosen a skirt.

We should not have come here, but we had no choice. If Hammond decides to kill Magnus and take me back to the UK without releasing my parents, I can't do a damn thing about that. I've felt powerless for so long, and all because of this man. I don't have proof he's behind all of it. My intuition tells me I'm right, and I've learned to trust my instincts.

"Take me to my parents," I say. "Then you can do whatever you want with me."

Magnus narrows his gaze on me but does not speak.

Hammond hooks one ankle over the opposite knee and smiles with creepy lust as he skims his gaze over my entire body. "Anything I want? That is an intriguing offer, but I prefer not to snack on MacTaggart's leftovers."

"What do you want? Why did you pay Magnus to hunt me for twenty months?"

"You are a fugitive, pet. And I have a strong sense of justice that won't let me rest until you are punished for your crime."

Bullshit, I want to say. But I keep my mouth shut. Royce Hammond loves to play games. I can tell that after spending five minutes with the creep. I didn't suck at reading people before I became a fugitive, but life on the run has taught me even more about noticing subtle cues.

"Where are you taking us?" Magnus asks.

"To Piper's mummy and daddy, of course. After you've seen them, we will discuss the situation."

I wish I believed he wants to chat. But no, this guy has an ulterior motive—probably layers of ulterior motives that fit together so perfectly no one can peel them apart.

"Let's have a drink, shall we?" Hammond says. "I brought a bottle of Highland whisky, Ardbeg single malt. Not my drink of choice, but I thought you might like it, MacTaggart. Scots have poor taste in drinks and, well, everything else too. Except for women, clearly."

He opens up one section of his bench seat to reveal a mini bar and brings out a bottle of Scotch.

Magnus grits his teeth so hard a muscle ticks in his jaw. "Not thirsty."

"As you wish." Hammond returns the bottle to the hidden bar and pushes the seat back down. He checks his watch. "We're ten minutes away. Then you lot will tell me why you handed my prize over to the Istanbul police." He leans forward, his expression turning hard and cold. "I do not take kindly to sabotage."

Chapter Thirty-Two

Magnus

I want to grab Royce Hammond by the throat and strangle him. But I cannae do that—yet. Once I see Piper's parents and know they're unharmed, I will make Hammond pay for everything he has done. Did he murder Archer Caldwell? Donnae know yet, but my gut tells me he did—or he at least convinced someone else to do it for him. Aye, he's that kind of bastard. If I'd known what the man was like when he hired me to find Piper, I would never have taken the job.

But I take any job I'm offered. Does that make me as bad as Hammond? I cannae investigate every fugitive to find out if they actually committed the crime. My remit is to hunt them and bring them home to stand trial. I never wondered if I'm doing the right thing, not until Piper.

No other fugitive has ever evaded me for more than a few days. I became obsessed with hunting Piper, with catching her at any cost. But now I wonder if that obsession stemmed from a subconscious recognition that she and I are kindred spirits. Maybe I'll ask my cousin Jack about that sometime. He's the psychiatrist in the family.

Assuming I live long enough to see the clan again.

No matter what happens, Piper will survive this. I'll make certain of that, even if it means I die to ensure her safety. While she slept, I arranged a backup plan for us, though I can't promise it will work. That's why I haven't told Piper about it.

The limousine rolls down increasingly less populated roads, heading toward a destination that remains unknown and an outcome that remains a mystery too. The forest along either side of the road becomes thicker and darker. Soon, we turn onto a gravel road that's barely wide enough to accommodate the limousine, and the vehicle jounces over potholes while gravel ticks on the undercarriage.

Finally, the trees open up to reveal a clearing.

A modest-size log cabin occupies the space, and through the windows, I see lights burning inside the house. As we stop near the porch, the front door opens. Two men emerge, both dressed in dark jeans and T-shirts with guns berthed in shoulder holsters. They want us to know they're armed. Hammond wants us to know. Does he think I've never seen this sort of tactic before? I've seen, done, and experienced everything in my line of work, so he's wasting his time trying to intimidate me.

Will his tactic work on Piper? I doubt it. The lass might seem like an average woman, but she has fortitude and skills no one would imagine a former museum archivist would need. Piper is strong. She won't cave when Hammond pushes her.

And he will push.

The driver gets out and opens the car door. Hammond waves for us to exit first, then follows us up the porch steps and into the house. The lads with guns bring up the rear of our wee parade as Hammond guides us through the living room and down a hallway to a closed door.

He knocks twice.

The door opens, and another armed bloke dressed in black scans his gaze over us. Then he steps aside to let us in.

We find ourselves in a bedroom. Two middle-aged people, a man and a woman, sit on the bed. Their wrists are bound with handcuffs, their ankles with duct tape.

Piper's hand flies to her mouth, and her eyes widen. Then she reasserts her calm demeanor. "Mom, Dad, are you okay?"

Her parents nod. Mrs. Lang gives her daughter a tight smile. "We're fine, dear."

"Did they hurt you, Piper?" Mr. Lang asks.

She shakes her head, the faint shimmer of tears in her eyes. But she blinks rapidly and lifts her chin. "I'm fine. Don't worry, you'll be home soon."

"Now that you've seen them," Hammond says, "we will retire to the study to discuss matters."

He leads us to another room that has a desk and chairs as well as a small sofa. His men take up positions at either side of the door, which remains open. Piper and I sit in the chairs positioned in front of Hammond's desk while he drops onto the chair behind it.

Hammond rocks gently, hands folded over his lap. "Your cousin hacked the servers at Sovereign's Istanbul office. That was not a clever thing to do. Haven't you heard about the dangers of poking a sleeping bear?"

"Didnae think you ever slept. Vampires just lie in their coffins until dusk."

He jerks his chair closer to the desk and flicks open a file folder that had been lying on the desktop, pretending to peruse the document inside the folder. "Errol Murdoch. Your twat of a cousin was the one variable I failed to include in my calculations. I am rather annoyed by his appearance."

I grunt. "Good. I'll make sure Errol keeps on annoying you."

"You want him to die, then?" Hammond slaps the folder closed and nails his gaze to me. The *bod ceann* probably thinks his stern expression and narrowed eyes will intimidate me, which only proves how little he knows. "You stole from me."

"No, your men stole those artifacts. We returned them to the proper authorities."

"They belong to me. Do you have any idea how much money I've lost because of your stunt at Göbekli Tepe?"

"Donnae give a toss about your losses. I'm dead sure you have enough money left to keep you living in the lap of luxury for the next thousand years."

"You stole from me." Anger distorts his features, and he slams his fist down on the desk so hard that it trembles. "I want reparations."

"Give us your demands and get it over with."

"I want you dead," he snarls. "But I need you to suffer first."

"You'll be disappointed. I donnae break, and I donnae cry." Though it takes intense effort, I manage to relax into my chair as if nothing he says or does fashes me. "Errol has all the information from your Istanbul servers. If anything happens to us, he will give all of it to the Met or Interpol, whoever wants it the most."

"The data doesn't matter. I own coppers all over the world, which means I will never be charged with any crime." He rises, leaning over the desk to glower at me. Spittle flies from his lips when he hisses, "I am invincible."

Insane is more accurate. He believes he has so much power and money that no one will ever catch him. But punishment comes in many forms, and I mean to demonstrate that for him.

My mobile chimes. I make no move to bring it out and check the new text. Donnae need to look. I know who it is and what will happen in a few moments.

Hammond is clueless.

"Give me your mobile," he demands. "Right now."

Casually, I pull the device out of my pocket and toss it onto the desktop. "Have a look. Scan the bloody thing with whatever equipment ye want."

He snatches up the mobile and flicks his thumb over the screen—to find the new text message, no doubt. His brows furrow. "Don't miss this special offer. Get two mobile phones for the price of one, only fifteen pounds for a limited time. Reply 'yes' to confirm."

"Not quite what ye hoped to find, eh? Text message scams are a right nuisance."

He hurls the mobile. It flies past my head to slam into the wall. If he hopes he destroyed it, that doesn't matter. I received the message, and I know what I need to do now.

Piper is staring at me.

I wink at her.

She stares at me for another second or two, then faces our host again. "Let my parents go. I'm the one you want, and you've got me."

We have fifteen minutes, which means it's time to act.

I leap out of my chair and seize Hammond's shirt, hauling him off the desk to cuff his wrists behind his back with one hand. I latch my other arm around his neck.

The guards reach for their guns.

"Donnae do that," I snarl, and the guards freeze. "With one wee movement, I can snap his neck. Now ye could shoot me in the head, but then you'll need to deal with her." I nod toward Piper. "She's been on the run for twenty months. The lass can take both of you and not break a sweat."

I might be exaggerating, but not by much.

Though Hammond tries to laugh, I choke it off by tightening my arm around his neck. He croaks, "Shoot him."

Both guards pull out their weapons.

Piper springs out of her chair, picks it up, and whacks the armed men with it. One drops his gun and stumbles into the wall, seeming dazed. The other aims his weapon at the lass, but she swings her chair again, and the gun flies across the room to land on the sofa. The bloke grabs Piper, pinning her to his body. His lips curl into a smug expression.

Ah, he doesnae know the lass.

"Need a hand?" I ask while Hammond tries to wriggle free of me. I'm bigger, stronger, and meaner. He hasn't got a chance—especially when I choke him again.

"No thanks," Piper says. "I've got this."

"I've got *you*," the guard tells her.

She rolls her eyes, then grabs his *bagais* and twists so hard I wince. The guard gasps and loses his grip on Piper. She seizes her chair again and smacks it into the laddie's head. He crumples to the floor, unconscious.

The other guard is rousing from his dazed state.

"Watch the other one," I tell Piper.

She whirls around and whacks him with the chair, the crack of the blow to his head assuring me she succeeded. The man slumps on the floor.

I squeeze my arm around Hammond's neck just enough to make him pass out, but I maintain my hold on him. "I have zip ties in my pocket. Get them for me, *gràidh*. The other guard might've heard the barnie in here, so we need to move fast."

Piper hurries over to get the zip ties out of my trouser pocket. We have enough to restrain all of Hammond's men, so I instruct her to bind his wrists and ankles to make sure the *bod ceann* can't move. I snatch up the guard's weapons and hand one to Piper.

"Watch them," I say. "And if they so much as bat their eyelashes, shout for me. I'm going to find a place to stash this lot."

I grab my mobile and find it still works, so I put it in my pocket. After a quick search of the house, I decide the bathroom is the best place to lock them in since it doesn't have anything that might help them break out. When I return to Piper, the guards are still out cold. We search them for any other weapons and confiscate their mobile phones, then I carry the blokes into the bathroom one by one and brace a chair under the door as a temporary measure to keep them confined in case they wake up.

Piper and I head for the bedroom where a single guard waits with her parents. I know there's a driver outside, and I cannae be sure Hammond doesn't have other guards hiding in the trees. We need to hurry.

I gesture for Piper to stand aside.

She plasters herself to the wall beside the door.

And I kick it open, rushing at the guard inside before he realizes what's happening. The Langs jump but don't make any noise that's louder than a gasp. I punch the guard in the gut, and when he doubles over, I ram my knee up into his chin. When I slug him in the jaw, the lad falls to the floor, though he's not unconscious. With more zip ties, I secure his wrists and ankles.

Piper sprints to the bed and sits on the edge, leaning over to hug her parents. They all start to cry, but Piper doesn't let emotion slow her down. She picks the lock on her mother's cuffs first, freeing her hands, then does the same with her father's cuffs. I find a nail file in the dresser and use it to cut the tape off their feet.

We've left Hammond alone for too long. If he's roused from unconsciousness...

I run to the office and find him still slumped against the desk on the floor.

Piper and her parents appear in the doorway. Mr. and Mrs. Lang stare wide-eyed at Hammond.

"Keep an eye on him," I tell Piper. "And be careful. He's a slippery bastard."

She trains her gun on the British erse.

I hurry back to the bedroom and carry the third guard into the bathroom, blocking the door with a chair again.

On my way out, I poke my head into the study. "Going to take care of the driver, then check for any more guards hiding out there."

Piper glances at me. "Be careful."

"Aye. You do the same. And donnae be afraid to bash him in the head if he causes trouble."

She returns her attention to Hammond. "Don't worry. I'll have no qualms about beating the shit out of this scumbag."

I know she means that. Piper is no mild-mannered museum archivist anymore. She has become a warrior, and I love that about her.

With a final glance at Piper, I rush outside.

Chapter Thirty-Three

Piper

I'm stuck in this house with my parents and three unconscious guards, but my biggest worry is the dangerous man slumped against the desk, apparently out cold. Should I trust he really is knocked out? If Hammond woke up, I have no doubts he would fake being unconscious and wait for an opening to free himself. I really, really wish Magnus hadn't gone outside, but I understand he had to do it.

My mother stares at the gun in my hand. "Would you actually shoot someone?"

"Yeah, I would."

"But you were always such a sweet child, kind and innocent."

"Things change." I cast her a sideways glance. "Did it bother you at all that I was on the run for almost two years? Did you care what became of me?"

"Of course we did."

I focus on Hammond again, because I need to keep a close eye on him. "But you walked away and washed your hands of me. I was charged with murder, and you believed I was guilty."

"No, no, Piper. That's not what we thought."

"Of course not," Dad says. "We were shocked and…we reacted badly. You were gone, an escaped fugitive, before we had a chance to tell you how sorry we are about what we said the last time we saw you."

"Three hours after you called us," Mom says, "we tried to get a flight to London, but everything was booked up. We couldn't leave until the next morning, and when we got there, you had already vanished. For two years, we've wanted to apologize and tell you that we love you."

I swallow against the lump that's formed in my throat. "Let's talk about that later. Right now, we need to concentrate on staying alive."

Do they honestly regret abandoning me? I can't think about that yet. It will distract me too much.

The front door bangs open, and Magnus jogs up to the study doorway, breathing hard—with the limo driver slung over his shoulder. "The last guard has been incapacitated. I'll put him in the bathroom with the others."

Magnus disappears, returning a moment later without the unconscious man. He holds up the device the driver had used to check us for weapons. "Turns out this also has infrared. I scanned the area but didn't see any live bodies out there."

God, I hope he's not implying there are dead bodies in the woods.

He approaches Hammond, who still lies there like he's out cold, and kneels beside the Brit. Then he slaps Hammond's face hard.

The evil mastermind winces ever so slightly.

Has he been faking unconsciousness? Or was that an uncontrolled response?

Magnus hoists Hammond to his feet and shakes him. "Look at me, ye *bod ceann*. I know you're awake."

Hammond sighs and opens his eyes. "You won't make it out of here alive. I have reinforcements on standby, and if they don't hear from me every half hour, they will storm the house."

"Will they?" Magnus sounds not the least perturbed by that fact. He shakes Hammond again. "None of us will be here when they turn up. You aren't the only one with a backup plan."

Since when do we have a backup plan? Nobody informed me of that fact. If Magnus says we'll get out of here alive, though, I know we will. But one important fact finally hits me. "Where are my parents?"

"In the living room. They seem to be in a wee bit of shock, and I think they needed to sit down. Didnae ye see them leave?"

"No. I've been kind of distracted, what with assaulting armed men and watching you throttle Hammond."

Magnus throws the Brit over his shoulder and carries him outside while I follow the Scot out of the house. I tell my parents to come with us, and they don't hesitate. Once we're all outside, Magnus halts halfway between the house and the limousine, then drops Hammond on the ground.

And Magnus just stands there.

"Shouldn't we get in the car?" I ask. "Escaping kind of requires going someplace else."

"Our ride will be here in a minute or two." He pulls out his cell phone. "But we should get rid of our mobiles right now. Errol removed the malware on them, but we can't risk it. Our devices might've been compromised since we've been with Hammond."

We both dump our phones on the ground.

If the limo isn't our ride out of here, I can't imagine what is. But I keep my mouth shut and wait—because I trust Magnus more than anyone else in the world. That fact no longer feels weird to me. Instead, it seems completely right.

The sound of an engine and the crunching of gravel alert us to the approach of a vehicle. Magnus narrows his gaze, focused on the woods and the driveway that cuts through the trees.

A big SUV rolls out of the shadows and stops alongside the limo. Inside the vehicle, I see the silhouette of a person.

"Who's that?" I ask.

"The backup plan," Magnus tells me. "Let's get Hammond loaded into the rear cargo area, then the four of us will squeeze into the seats."

"One guy is your fabulous backup plan?"

The driver steps out of the SUV, and I see it's Logan.

"No offense," I say to Magnus, "but I was kind of hoping for more than just your cousin."

"Ye donnae know Logan. But you've seen Errol in action. Do ye really want to underestimate Logan, the former MI6 agent?"

"Okay, I see your point. Is everyone in your family an expert in some kind of covert stuff?"

"No. My cousin Kirsty is a witch, and Jack is a psychologist."

Yeah, we might need their expertise considering that we're kidnapping a powerful and dangerous man. Still not sure what our plan is after that.

I still haven't had a chance to talk to my parents. We have so much to work through, but now isn't the right time. I insisted Magnus should sit up front with Logan, which leaves me alone with Mom and Dad in the backseat. So we could talk now, but I feel weird about doing that while Logan is within earshot.

We've just reached an intersection, where the dirt road we're on crosses another dirt road, when Magnus hollers, "Watch out, Logan!"

I jerk my head to the left just in time to see a big SUV barreling toward us. Logan swerves, but not quite in time. The other vehicle slams into our front bumper, which shoves us sideways. The shock of the impact stuns all of us—except Logan, who breaks his window with the butt of his gun so he can aim the barrel at the men who just leaped out of the other vehicle.

I can't see much of what's going on since the darkened windows in the backseat obscure my view. But Logan fires two shots.

The rear door of our vehicle is torn open.

Everyone else is focused on the men exchanging fire with Logan, but I hear the click of the rear latch just before the door swings open. I twist around to see what's happening. One man grabs Hammond and slings him over his shoulder. Before I can react, the man slams the rear door shut.

"They've got Hammond!" I shout.

I throw my door open and leap out, brandishing the gun I'd commandeered from one of the men back in the cabin. But I'm too late. The man who stole our hostage shoves Hammond into the other SUV and climbs in with him. The men who'd been shooting leap into the car.

And they rocket away.

I jump into the backseat, where my parents sit frozen with their eyes practically bulging out of their sockets. "Don't worry. Everything will be okay."

"Can this car make it to the airport?" Magnus asks Logan.

"Aye. We'll get there." He guns the engine, and the car surges forward. "But we need to hurry and get in the air."

"Hammond's men will be waiting for us."

"But the bastard willnae be stupid enough to let them start a firefight at an international airport." Logan swerves around a corner onto a paved road, turning so hard that I'm flung against the door. "We need to get to safe ground, someplace where we have the advantage."

"Aye."

Where can we go? I have no idea, but I trust Magnus and his cousin to know the answer. "Shouldn't we have chased their car?"

Logan shakes his head. "No, lass. Our last resort plan will be better. Trust me."

The backup plan failed, so now we've moved on to the last resort plan. Yeah, that makes me feel so much better.

Nobody speaks anymore as we pull onto a highway and hurtle toward our destination. What can we say? Things have just gotten much worse, and I can do nothing except lay all our lives in the hands of the MacTaggarts. I want to comfort my parents, but I think that can wait until we're on the jet. Honestly, though, Mom and Dad have taken all of this much better than I would've expected. Kidnapped? Held hostage? Trapped in a gun battle? Most people would've panicked and fled, but my parents didn't do that.

They stuck with me.

We reach the airport much faster than we'd gotten to the cabin earlier, thanks to Logan's expert and very fast driving. Once we reach the tarmac, we climb out of the car. I notice another jet parked nearby.

"Is that your plane?" I ask Logan.

"That's our cousin Rory's jet," he says. "I borrowed it and got in the air not long after you lot did. Evan rang me, saying you needed backup."

"And you just zipped over here based on that?"

Logan lifts one brow. "What did ye think I'd do? Sit on my erse waiting to hear Hammond had murdered all of you?"

No, of course a former secret agent wouldn't do that. But I still can't quite comprehend that a family like the MacTaggarts will do anything for each other, even jump into a gun battle or hack servers that belong to a megalomaniac.

"Why don't you ride with us?" Magnus asks. "The pilots can take Rory's jet back to Inverness without you."

"I have another errand to run."

"Errand?"

"Aye. I'm retrieving an asset."

Logan says goodbye and strides off to the other jet.

Magnus and I lead my parents into Evan's plane and offer them drinks—the alcoholic sort—since they need some serious nerve-soothing. I need that too. Magnus grabs a bottle of whisky and leads me to a set of chairs that face each other. We're far enough away from my parents that they won't hear our conversation. Mom and Dad have been through enough today, and I have a feeling the talk Magnus wants to have will involve discussing our dire situation.

Magnus pours us both a measure of whisky. He relaxes in his chair with one ankle propped on the other knee, but I sink into my seat like my spine has melted. I feel tired, yes, but also strangely invigorated.

"Where are we going now?" I ask.

"Scotland. We'll land at Inverness, then drive three hours to reach Dùndubhan. It's the safest place I know."

"Dun-where? You mentioned that name before but didn't explain."

He smiles, his eyes twinkling. "Dùndubhan. That's the name of the castle owned by my cousin Rory and his wife, Emery. She's American like you. Quite a few of my cousins married Yanks, including Logan."

"Interesting. You Scots have a fetish for American girls."

"Not just lasses. Some of my female cousins married American men." He makes a disgusted face, though it's clearly sarcastic. "But Catriona tied the knot with a Brit. He has dual citizenship in the US and UK, but still, she brought a British erse into the family."

"Don't you like him? Or are you just prejudiced against all Brits?"

"I'm not prejudiced. But I donnae know Alex well, and he's, ah, rather strange."

Can't help it. A half-stifled laugh sputters out of me. "You think he's strange? Take a look in the mirror. You dress like a member of a biker gang, talk like a hardcore killer, and use all those bizarre Gaelic phrases."

He leans across the gap between our chairs, his gaze riveted to mine. "Ye left out the most important fact about me." His voice becomes a rough whisper. "I make ye come so hard ye cannae speak afterward."

"Oh no, I would never forget about that." I sit up straighter while he pulls back into his chair. "What did Logan mean about retrieving an 'asset'?"

"The man was a spy. When he says 'asset,' he means a person."

"Who is he retrieving?"

"No idea."

I go to check on my parents, who are yawning and clearly exhausted. When I suggest they get some rest in the bedroom, they don't argue. Magnus and I lie down on the sofa together and watch TV. He wants to turn on action movies, but I inform him I've had enough of that in real life lately. He agrees to watch rom-coms instead. While we race across the Atlantic Ocean, high above the water, one thought keeps bouncing around in my brain.

What will Royce Hammond do next?

Chapter Thirty-Four

Magnus

We land at the Inverness airport after dark and climb into a Mercedes. Rory waits for us behind the wheel, and as soon as we've all gotten inside, he drives us away. After spending hours watching romantic comedies with Piper, I'm looking forward to having a conversation with my cousin, but Rory doesn't want to talk. He tells me he prefers to focus on the road and that Logan will explain everything once we get to Dùndubhan.

Piper and her parents, who sit crammed together in the backseat, stay silent for the entire three-hour drive. They must be anxious, and I donnae blame them for that. Royce Hammond is out there plotting. What, I have no idea. But I'm sure he wants Piper, alive or dead. The bastard will never get his hands on her, not as long as I'm alive.

The first time I caught Piper, I convinced myself she was nothing more than another fugitive trying to evade justice. But over those first seventeen months of my pursuit of her, I realized the museum archivist had shattered all my preconceptions about the people I hunt. She's not a hardened criminal, has no record at all except for the murder charge, and cooperated with the police until it became clear they believed she was guilty. Even then, she stayed put. Only when someone tried to kill her—the real culprit or an agent of that person—did she run.

No other fugitive ever got away from me once, much less time after time. Nothing I learned about Piper from my research prepared me for how cunning and skilled she is at hiding. So aye, maybe I developed a sort of admiration for her over those seventeen months. Not just her talent for getting away, but also her cleverness, determination, and sheer grit. If I hadn't become obsessed with capturing the lass, I would never have known just how impressive she is.

I glance over my shoulder at Piper, who smiles softly when she sees me looking at her. I smile at her the same way. Maybe I shouldn't have feelings for her considering we've only known each other for a matter of days, but that's not the whole story. I've known Piper for almost two years, known her in ways nobody else could. I understand her better than any man could simply by dating her for a month or even a year. I've seen into her soul.

That's rubbish, I know it must be. But I cannae shake the certainty that it's true.

Kirsty would love to hear me say I've seen Piper's soul. She would insist I have some sort of metaphysical connection to the lass, but that absolutely is rubbish.

I turn on the radio to give us all something to listen to besides the rumble of the road beneath us. The distraction makes the trip seem to go faster, and at last we turn onto the dirt drive that leads straight to Dùndubhan. We're already on Rory and Emery's land. The estate consists of one hundred acres with the castle almost in the middle. When we pass through the metal gate, which stands open, the dirt segues into gravel.

Rory pulls out a remote control and presses a button. The gate swings shut.

"Are we almost there?" Piper asks.

"We are," I say. "Rory shut the gate so no one can get in that easily. Tromping through the forest is much more difficult, and we'll see them coming if they try that approach."

"They? Sounds like you're expecting an army."

"No, but I'm sure Hammond will bring a contingent of armed men with him. If he bothers to show up at all. The bastard seems to prefer executing his orders from a distance."

Mrs. Lang hugs herself and looks a touch pale. Her ex-husband hooks an arm around her and murmurs something that I can't hear.

Piper's brows shoot up. Her lips twitch at the corners in an almost smile. I'm sure seeing her divorced parents huddling together for comfort is a surprise to her. But there's nothing like a calamity to bring people together.

Rory continues driving. Soon, the trees thin out and the castle comes into view.

"That's your castle?" Piper says. "Wow, Rory, I had no idea. Guess I was kind of expecting a dinky little thing that had been remodeled to look like a house."

"It is a house," Rory says. "Medieval lairds lived at Dùndubhan. Emery and I lived here until our bairns were born, and my sister Jamie and her husband also lived here for a while after that. It's also a museum, which might interest you since Magnus mentioned you're an archivist."

"Yes, I am. And I'd love to explore the castle, once the current problem is resolved."

Aye, that's a diplomatic way to phrase it. I suppose Piper doesn't want to upset her mother even more by referring to our "problem" as an imminent murder attempt. I would say that, being a terrifying *bod ceann*, but Piper's way is better.

The massive wooden gates stand open. As we approach them, Piper rolls down her window and pokes her head out to gawp at the castle. It has square turrets atop the tower and a high stone wall encompassing the compound. The grey sky above us matches the color of the stones used to construct the fortress—and the somber mood of everyone present. Piper might enjoy seeing the castle, but she isn't as excited as I know she would be under normal circumstances. She had gotten adorably excited in Barcelona when she saw the ocean.

I can show her the ocean again sometime. Scotland has plenty of coastline.

We pass through the wooden gates, and in the rearview mirror I see Lachlan and Iain pushing it closed. They drop the metal barricade to seal us inside the compound. No one has shut the gates since the last medieval laird abandoned the castle. We considered closing them a few months ago when Kirsty was being mercilessly hounded by a horde of rabid tabloid reporters, but we realized we didn't need to go that far. The uproar ended with no one even trying to reach Dùndubhan.

For the first time in modern memory, the gates are sealed. An odd chill shivers up my spine. Hammond might be coming for Piper, but she wouldn't be in this position if I hadn't led him to her. I should've guessed Hammond and his lackeys would go for Piper's parents.

None of that matters right now. Survival is our primary concern.

Other vehicles already occupy the gravel courtyard, and I know many of my family members will have gathered inside the castle itself. I take Piper's hand as we get out of the car, and her parents hold hands too. I donnae expect the Langs to reconcile and remarry, but I'm glad they're giving each other comfort. I keep hold of Piper's hand as we enter the doorway into the vestibule and Rory leads us upstairs to the great hall on the first floor.

Later, I'll explain to Piper that the first floor is not the ground floor. That fact is irrelevant right now.

I expect to find only the men in the family gathered in the great hall, where a crowd of chairs have been arranged in rows in front of a large television that sits on a tabletop. To my surprise, women are here too. Kirsty and her sisters, Isla and Elspeth, chat to Kate Wagner, my cousin Callum's fiancée.

"What are you lot doing here?" I ask as the lasses come over to greet us. "Women shouldn't be here. It's dangerous."

Kirsty laughs and pats my chest. "You are such a sweetie, Magnus, worrying about us. We lasses who don't have bairns to worry about insisted on coming here to offer moral and practical support. Kate is a physical therapist who can treat any injuries that might happen, and the Witches of Ballachulish will provide whatever other support we can."

"Donnae think your rubbish spells will work on Royce Hammond."

Kirsty raises onto her toes to kiss my cheek. "Trust us, Magnus. We're not as barmy and useless as most people think."

"I donnae think you're useless, but magic is bollocks."

She gives me her patented enigmatic smile, then glances at Piper. "This must be your lass. Will ye introduce her?"

"That's Piper Lang."

Kirsty rolls her eyes. "You are a dear sweet man, but you're terrible at socializing." She offers her hand to Piper. "I'm Kirsty Turner, Magnus's cousin."

Piper shakes her hand. "Nice to meet you. Magnus has mentioned you and said you're a witch."

"My sisters and I are devout Wiccans, which our brother Logan calls rubbish, just like Magnus does. They pretend to scoff at it, but we know they secretly believe we might have mystical powers. I'm blessed with *da-shealladh*, the second sight."

"Cool. Maybe you can foresee where and when Hammond might attack."

"Donnae see that, but I can tell you everything will work out." She glances sideways at me, then winks at Piper. "Absolutely everything."

She is barmy, but I love the lass.

Kirsty introduces Piper to Isla, Elspeth, and Kate. I try to convince them to go home, but they refuse to leave. I introduce Piper to the men of the clan, the ones she hasn't met yet—Lachlan, Iain, Evan, Aidan, Callum, and Jack. Luke Turner is also here, as are Gavin Douglas and Alex Thorne. Those blokes are married to my cousins Kirsty, Jamie, and Catriona, respectively.

"What's the television screen for?" I ask after the introductions have concluded.

Logan slaps a hand on my shoulder. "For the presentation, of course. We wanted to use a chalkboard to plot out our strategy, but Evan insisted on doing it the high-tech way."

Of course he did. The lad loves all that technical bollocks.

Piper and I sit in the first row to watch Evan's high-tech presentation. He displays a 3-D map of Dùndubhan and the surrounding forest as well as the river that gave the castle its name. Dùndubhan means fortress of the black water. I can't deny that Evan's graphics give us a better idea of the lay of the land than a simple 2-D map would. I didn't realize until he explained it a moment ago that Evan had commissioned an aerial survey to collect all the data he now displays for us.

Bloody hell. All I can do is beat up criminals.

We come up with a good plan, though we can't anticipate which direction Hammond and his men might come from, if the man himself indeed accompanies his lackeys. After the incident in his Nashville cabin, I suspect Hammond will bring a wee army with him this time, not just a few guards.

The lasses will stay in the great hall to help coordinate. We have radios and weapons, but I hope we never need the guns. I've shot men before, but only in battle. Most of the men in this room have never killed anyone, excepting me, Logan, and Gavin. We've all fought in a war.

Has Royce Hammond declared war on me and Piper? Will he drag my family and Piper's into his vendetta? I will never let that happen. If he threatens the Langs, or injures any of my cousins, I will tear his throat out and not feel even a twinge of guilt about it.

Once we have our plan set, it's time for us to take up our positions inside and outside the castle. No one will leave the compound unless it becomes absolutely necessary. Staying inside the walls offers us more protection. But Evan and Logan had set up miniature infrared cameras at strategic locations on the property outside the walls to let us monitor things from inside the dining room downstairs. The lasses will watch from the great hall using the old-fashioned binoculars and eyeballs method. Piper's parents will stay with her and the other women.

"What happened to the asset you needed to retrieve?" I ask Logan.

"You'll see. The delivery man is almost here. Couldnae join us for the strategy meeting, but he should arrive any moment." He checks something on his mobile, and his lips curve into a knowing smile. "Aye, any second."

Footsteps pound up the stairwell, and a figure rushes across the great hall to halt in front of me and Logan. Errol is almost gasping thanks to pelting up the spiral staircase at full speed. He holds up a hand in a "please wait" gesture while the laddie catches his breath.

Then he rests his hands on his hips. "It's all set. We're ready for the invasion of the bloody English bastards."

"Careful," Alex Thorne says as he walks up to us. "You're talking to a bloody English bastard."

"No offense, mate. I meant the criminal ones." Errol smirks. "But that term applies to you too, in the past tense. Eh, Alex?"

"Yes, indeed it does. But I'm semi-reformed."

Piper has sneaked up beside me, and she eyes Alex with curiosity. "Semi-reformed? What does that mean?"

"My birth parents were grifters who taught me the not-so-noble art of the con. But my adoptive parents raised me from the age of eight and molded me into a proper gentleman, though I can't say I've shed all my grifter genes."

"He's a good man," I tell Piper. "Donnae let his snarky attitude fool you."

Piper shuffles closer to me, her body almost touching mine. "What do we do now?"

"Wait and watch." I fold an arm around her, holding the lass to my side. "Sooner or later, Hammond will make his move."

"Should we be getting all your cousins involved in my mess? Hammond is extremely dangerous."

Alex chuckles. "Oh, darling, you have no idea what the MacTaggarts can do. No one stands a chance of breaching this castle."

"Listen to Alex," I tell Piper. "No one has ever gotten the better of us. Trust the clan, lass."

Errol grins. "And my land mines."

Chapter Thirty-Five

Piper

Is it legal to have land mines?" I ask. Errol had C-4 back in Istanbul, and I know that's an explosive only because I like to watch action movies. But I can't believe the authorities would let civilians buy land mines. "Is it safe to have those things? If we all get blown to smithereens before Hammond even gets here…"

"Donnae worry," Errol says. "I know what I'm doing. But if mines fash you, I probably shouldn't mention what else I've got in my arsenal."

"Aye," Magnus says. "Keep that to yourself."

Do they think I'm a pansy because I worried about getting blown to smithereens? Ugh, men. "I'm not scared. I simply expressed a legitimate concern about land mines. Those are buried underground, right? Somebody might trip one by mistake."

"No," Errol says with a laugh, shaking his head as if I've said something totally ridiculous. "These mines aren't triggered by pressure switches."

"What does trigger them?"

He holds up his phone. "An app on my mobile."

Of course. Why didn't I think of that? Everybody knows you can get an app for anything, even setting off land mines.

Errol is kind of insane, but I like him anyway.

Alex and Errol wander off to talk to Logan, and my mom hurries over to us.

She touches my arm, gazing at me with so much worry in her eyes that I feel an urge to hug her, though I don't do it. "Piper, what is going on? I know your friends explained that a dangerous man is coming to get you, but I don't understand…anything else."

"I know, Mom. I'm sorry I haven't had time to really talk to you guys."

"Should I leave you two alone?" Magnus asks.

"No." I lay a hand on his chest and look up at him. "I want you to stay, please."

He kisses my forehead.

The worry lines iron out of my mom's forehead, and she blinks slowly twice. "You're in love with this man, aren't you?"

"In love?" I laugh, but it comes out sounding a touch desperate. "Magnus and I barely know each other."

"Sure seems like you're better acquainted than that. Besides, love doesn't happen on a timetable. My parents got married after knowing each other for five weeks."

"I'm not getting married." My nervous laughter bubbles out again. "You're misreading the situation, Mom."

When I glance up at Magnus, I expect him to seem annoyed or uncomfortable. But he just smiles at me with a softness that makes my chest ache. Outwardly, it seems like we've known each other for a matter of days. But is that accurate? Magnus had hunted me for twenty months and spent all that time learning about me. I learned a lot about him too, though I haven't shared that fact with him. He stopped asking me how I kept getting away from him, but I think it's time I explained.

But not in front of my mother.

"Magnus and I need to have a talk," I tell her. "Would you mind if we continue this conversation later?"

"Of course." She gives my hand a squeeze. "I love you, Piper. I hope you know that, even if I was never good at showing it."

She walks away before I can process what she said. My family has never been the kind that expresses emotions out loud. As for showing our feelings... Well, I'm still not great at that, so I can't fault my parents for not being more expressive toward me. Honestly, it never bothered me. Every family is different.

"We need to have a talk?" Magnus says, his brows arched.

"Yes, we do. Is there someplace private we can go?"

"Aye. We can go into Rory's office. He won't mind."

Magnus takes my hand to lead me across the great hall and to a closed door. He pushes it open and leads me inside what looks like a library, since it has shelves of books filling up three walls. As he shuts the door, I notice the three tall windows along the fourth wall and the bench seat beneath them.

"This doesn't seem like an office," I say, "except for the big desk and the executive chair. It feels more like a library."

"Because it was the library, until Rory converted it into his law office. Most of the books are about legal rubbish."

"Let's sit on the window bench."

We walk across the fancy rug that covers most of the floor and sit down on the bench facing each other. I turn sideways and pull my knees up to lash my arms around them. Magnus keeps his body facing forward but twists his torso to look at me. He leans against the window frame, just like I do.

"Ye wanted to talk," he says.

"That's right. You've wanted to know how I kept escaping from you, and it's time I explained."

"None of that matters anymore."

"It does to me. I need you to understand."

He watches me for a moment, then sighs. "All right. Tell me."

My throat has gotten dry, and my fingers dig into my knees. I force myself to relax, taking a couple deep breaths that I exhale slowly. "Maybe I didn't snoop in your home or read your diary, but I managed to learn a lot about you just by paying attention. I think being a museum archivist trained me to take note of details, even ones that seem unimportant at the time. That's what I did with you. I paid attention, noted everything I could about you, and memorized your habits and patterns."

"But we rarely saw each other. How could you memorize anything? I was chasing you, but we only spoke to each other once in those first seventeen months."

"It's not true that we 'rarely' saw each other. You got close to catching me so many times that I learned a lot about you." I find myself relaxing, and I stretch one leg across the bench. My foot nudges Magnus's thigh. "You probably won't believe this, but you have a lot of tells. Little things that give you away. I doubt anyone else would notice that stuff, but I had strong motivation to study you every chance I got."

"What sort of tells?"

"For one thing, you always followed me for a while before you tried to grab me. So I developed a habit of going to pubs just to ask around and find out if anyone had noticed a big, hunky Scotsman dressed all in black. Your goatee, your clothes, and your size ensure you always stand out in a crowd."

"Bloody hell." He grimaces, but the expression swiftly melts into a smile. "You are the cleverest lass on earth. Clearly, no one else has noticed my habits. I always get my man, but you kept slipping away. At least now I have some idea of how you did that."

"I learned even more when we had sex."

He tips his head to the side, studying me while his lips slide into a sensual smile. "Which time? We shagged on two occasions when I caught you."

"The first one. That's when I got to know the most about you, though I learned things the second time too."

"Aye, I got to know you better too when we shagged. Have you always had a naughty streak? Or did that come out after you became a fugitive?"

I stretch out my other leg and set both my feet on his lap. "Never thought I'd like being handcuffed during sex, but damn, I loved it when you did that. And the first time? I'd never gotten such an intense workout in bed. Thank you for showing me that I do have a naughty streak. Nobody else would believe it."

"Glad I could bring it out in you." He lays his hands on my ankles and stares down at my feet. "You taught me something about myself too. I never realized I could have, ah, tender feelings toward a woman who isn't related to me."

He has tender feelings toward me? I've realized I have those too, but I'm stunned by his admission. The big, tough bastard of a bounty hunter has a softer side. I'd known that, but I never imagined he would admit to it.

But he's not done shocking me.

Magnus keeps his head down but lifts his gaze to me. "I have strong feelings for you, Piper. Willnae let anyone hurt you. I told ye I'll go to the ends of the earth and back to prove your innocence, but I will go down into the darkest depths of hell to stop Royce Hammond or anyone from laying a finger on you. If that bastard or his lackeys so much as look at you sideways, I will tear their throats out."

Before my time on the run, that statement would've scared me. Now, here with this rough-and-tough bounty hunter, I feel a tingle of excitement when he swears to protect me at any cost. No one else has ever done that for me. No one even suggested they might, not until Magnus came into my life.

"I know you would do that and more," I say. "You have no idea how much that means to me. How much *you* mean to me."

"Aye, I do know. Because you mean just as much to me."

"Please don't panic."

His brows knit together. "About what?"

"This." I crawl onto his lap and wrap my arms around his neck with one side of my face nestled against his throat. "Are you panicking?"

His throaty chuckle vibrates into my cheek. "No, lass, not at all."

And he folds his big, strong arms around me.

Someone knocks on the office door. "Time to come out. Get your trousers back on, Magnus."

"My trousers are on, Callum, ye *cacan*."

"Good. But give Piper a moment to get her bra back on."

"We are both dressed."

Magnus stands up while still holding me, and I keep my legs latched around him until we reach the door. Then I have to let go so he can set me down. He swings the door open.

Callum's lips twitch into a brief smirk as he surveys us, but then his expression turns more serious. "Someone is coming. One of Evan's cameras caught him."

"Him? Only one person?"

"No," Callum says slowly. "But it's complicated. Come with me to the control room."

As we follow Magnus's cousin through the great hall, I whisper to him, "Control room?"

Magnus shrugs. "I think he means the dining room."

Callum glances at us over his shoulder. "Your whispering isn't whispery enough. I heard ye. And I did mean the dining room. Evan and Errol set up their technical rubbish in that space and renamed it the control room."

We hurry to keep up with Callum as he bounds down the spiral staircase and through the vestibule, into a hallway.

"Your knee must be completely healed," Magnus says. "Considering the way you took the stairs."

"Aye, it's doing much better since Kate started giving me at-home physical therapy."

As we head down the hall, Magnus tells me, "Callum is a firefighter, and he injured his knee on the job a while ago. He met Kate when his brother Jack sent him to physical therapy in Inverness. Now they're engaged."

"A firefighter? Well, at least he can douse the blaze if Hammond torches the castle."

Callum leads us into the dining room, which has a long wooden table and chairs that clearly match it. But the men gathered in here have pushed most of those chairs against the wall, out of the way, to make room for the electronic equipment set up on the tabletop. Evan and Errol aren't the only other guys in here, though. Logan, Alex, Gavin, and Rory have joined them.

"Look," Errol says, pointing at one of several computer monitors. "See those people-shaped blobs?"

Magnus and I come up behind Errol's chair and peer down at the screen. It shows black-and-white video of what looks like the driveway, since I can see the closed gate in the foreground. Several human-shaped blobs stand out as white figures against the darker background of the woods. I also notice what seem like three cars parked behind the figures.

"Those are Hammond's men," Errol says. "I'm dead sure of that. But the man himself isn't with them anymore."

A wave of cold sweeps over me, and every hair on my body stiffens. "Anymore? You've seen him?"

"Cannae make a positive ID with infrared. But one figure separated from the others and climbed over the gate. He's heading this way now." Errol nods to Evan, who clicks away on his keyboard. The image changes, and I can tell we're now seeing the part of the driveway that's just in front of the castle wall. Errol points to a figure traipsing through the woods toward the compound. "That's him. I'd stake my life on it."

"Okay, I believe you," I say. "Now what?"

Magnus folds his arms over his chest. "We catch the bastard."

I glance around. "What happened to the rest of the MacTaggart men? Only saw women in the great hall."

"They're positioned outside," Rory says, "but still within the compound. Iain, Aidan, Lachlan, and Luke volunteered to patrol the perimeter via the walkways at the top of the walls. The rest of the lads will watch from the towers and take action at the appropriate time."

Just like medieval warriors. How did I go from being a museum archivist to needing an army of Scots to protect me from a murderous bastard? Sometimes I feel like I must be in a coma in a hospital somewhere, dreaming all of this, and any minute I'll wake up and forget everything. But I pray that's not true.

Because I never want to forget about Magnus.

Chapter Thirty-Six

Magnus

The battle is about to begin, and I'm not using the phrase as a metaphor. For the first time since the middle ages, Dùndubhan is about be attacked by an enemy bent on destruction. Royce Hammond wants Piper, dead or alive, but I willnae let him get near her. If I need to die to save her, I will do it willingly. Hammond will walk up to the castle gates any moment, which means we have no time to waste.

"Isn't it weird," Piper says, "that Hammond just waltzed up the driveway? Alone?"

"Aye, it is. We need to be hyper vigilant, and that's what we're doing."

She still seems worried, but I can't promise her there's no danger in what we mean to do.

"I'm going out there to greet our guest," I say. "The women will take over monitoring the cameras from here. Piper, go and get them. A few will need to stay in the great hall to watch from the windows."

"Let me go with you," Piper says.

I grasp her shoulders. "Please, *mo chridhe*, stay here. I need to know you're safe."

The other men in the room all lifted their brows when I called her *mo chridhe*. They know what the phrase means, but I donnae have time to explain it to Piper. If I survive this day, I mean to tell her everything I've held back about my feelings for her.

"Please," I repeat, bending my head to meet her gaze. "Do as I ask. Hammond willnae get anywhere near you. That's a promise."

"I believe you. Be careful, okay? Don't go sacrificing yourself for some heroic vendetta."

She worries about me. I worry about her too, but I need to focus on what lies ahead.

"Ahmno dying today," I tell her. Then I press my lips to hers. "Donnae worry, love."

Piper hugs me so hard I can't breathe until she lets go.

Logan hands me an earpiece that will let me communicate with the others even when I'm outside. He taps his ear. "We already have ours."

I take a step toward the doorway.

Alex grasps my arm to stop me. "I'm going with you. Distraction is a key part of any battle, wouldn't you say?"

"It can be useful, aye."

"Well, no one excels at distraction more than I do."

"Donnae know." I eye him with what probably looks like skepticism, because I bloody am skeptical of what he just said. "How are you skilled at the art of war?"

"Not war. The art of the con. Let me distract that arsehole while you and the rest of the blokes take out Hammond's men." I must seem skeptical again, because he settles a hand on my shoulder and gives me the most sincere look of determination I've ever seen from Alex Thorne. "I was a grifter, remember? I know what I'm doing, so trust me. I can help."

"Aye, he can," Logan concurs. "Catriona loves to tell the story of how Alex conned his way out of being held hostage by his birth parents and an Aussie scunner."

"Fine," I tell Alex. "Let's go. Logan, alert the lads."

Piper doesn't know the whole plan, but it's better that way.

I stalk out of the dining room and down the hall, through the vestibule doorway. Alex stays in stride with me, but we don't speak. A resolve I've never experienced before has taken hold, a decisiveness that tautens my entire body and sharpens my senses. I will stop Hammond today, one way or another. I hadn't exaggerated when I told Piper how far I would go to protect her.

To the ends of the earth, down through the bowels of hell, straight into the fires of damnation. That's how far I'll go.

And Royce Hammond is going with me.

We halt at the corner of the house, on the edge of the gravel drive. Logan assured me our earpieces will allow us to hear each other even if we speak softly. So I whisper, "Where is he now?"

"Just exiting the trees," Logan says. "Whatever Alex means to do, best get in position for it now."

"Aye."

Since Alex heard that too, I don't need to pass the information along to him. He nods once and walks up to the wooden gates. I follow, but he gestures for me to stay away. I glare at him. He rolls his eyes and makes a movement that I assume means he wants me to back away but stay near the wall. When I sidle up to the gate, but stay a few yards away from him, he seems satisfied.

A single light illuminates the space around us from its position above the gateway, at its center. Alex opens a small window in the wooden gate, which I had never noticed before. I had only visited Dùndubhan a few times, though, so I don't feel like an eejit for failing to notice the wooden window. The light above us also illuminates the driveway outside the wall.

Alex peers through the opening, then he smiles. "Good evening. Afraid the kitchen is closed. No more takeaway meals today."

He really does know how to be cheerfully obnoxious.

"Still no one else around," Lachlan says through my earpiece. "Just those cars and men we already saw, who are fanning out around the estate."

My enemy didn't bring an army. That fact makes me uneasy. A man like him has others do his dirty work.

"I'm not here for food," Royce Hammond says. "You lot know precisely what I came for."

"Scintillating conversation, right?" Alex says. "Let's discuss international affairs. Or would you prefer gardening as the topic?"

"Bring me Piper Lang."

"Piper Lang?" Alex says as if he's never heard the name before. "Sorry. I think you've come to the wrong address."

"Go on, you bloody knob, mock me until the sun comes up. But my men are encircling this compound as we speak."

"Are they? Not sure I have enough tea for everyone."

"No more inane banter," Hammond snarls. "You'll be the first to die."

"I love being first in line."

Hammond kicks the gate, which does nothing more than to produce a faint thump and probably make his foot ache. "I have eight heavily armed men. Give up now."

"Eight blokes? It's lovely to have mates, especially armed ones."

Logan's voice crackles in my earpiece. "We're in position. Neutralizing the combatants now."

Alex leans against the gate as if he's just having a blether with Hammond. He even scratches his chin casually. "Tell you what, mate. I'll let you in if you solve my riddle."

Hammond pounds on the gate. "No more games, you sodding arsehole."

"No, that's not the right answer. And you didn't let me tell you the riddle first. This is exactly how the Sphinx would test travelers in ancient Egypt."

"I don't need history lessons from a ruddy bastard like you."

"No, no, that's not right either. My official title is the British Bastard, by the way, not the Ruddy Bastard."

Hammond shoves his hand through the wee window, apparently trying to grab Alex by the throat. But Alex jumps backward, out of the *bod ceann*'s reach.

"That's cheating, you know." Alex wags a finger at Hammond. "You naughty boy. Someone needs a hug, eh? The sort delivered by a brawny chap who squeezes very hard."

"Got them," Logan says. "All combatants have been neutralized."

"Fabulous," Alex says, spreading his arms and grinning. "Now the real fun begins."

"What the bloody hell are you on about?" Hammond demands. "You're as insane as all the Scots."

Alex clucks his tongue. "No, that's not the secret password. But I'll let someone else give you a hint."

He glances at me.

I nod.

Alex unlocks the gate and swings the halves open with a mighty tug.

I rush at Hammond, kicking him in the gut so hard that the breath explodes out of him and he stumbles backward, falling to the ground. I grasp a handful of his expensive shirt and haul him to his feet, which hover above the ground. The suit jacket he had held over his shoulder now lies crumpled on the gravel.

Glancing at Alex, I say, "Get over here and search this *tolla-thon*."

I keep holding Hammond up with handfuls of shirt while Alex roughly searches every inch of the bastard, even his shoes. He discovers only Hammond's mobile phone and takes possession of it.

I spin around and hurl Hammond into the courtyard.

He thumps down on the gravel, sprawled there in the middle of the driveway.

"Should I close the gates?" Alex asks.

"Donnae bother. We've got them all."

Hammond lifts his head, clearly dazed, and struggles to sit up.

I stomp over there and plant a foot on his chest. "I can kill you with one foot. Fracture your ribs. Puncture your lungs. You'll slowly suffocate on your own blood."

Can I do that? Donnae know, donnae care. He believes me, though. I can see it on his face, and that's all I need.

Alex comes up beside me. "Are you going to kill him? I ask only because Rory might not like having his driveway soiled with blood. Perhaps we should put a tarpaulin under him."

"Willnae be any blood. He'll drown from the fluid in his lungs."

He takes two steps backward. "In that case, have at it."

The vestibule door bursts open, and Piper races up to us. She seizes my arm, her eyes wide and her bottom lip trembling. "Please don't kill him. I mean, I don't give a shit about his life, but I don't want you to go to prison."

Alex pulls a pair of handcuffs out of his pocket and offers them to me.

I squint at the cuffs. "Are those mine?"

"Yes. I might have sort of nicked them from your bag. Thought they might come in handy."

Aye, Alex is just the kind of man who does things like that. But only for a good cause. That's what my cousins tell me, anyway.

"What should we do with him?" I ask Piper. "He ruined your life, so the decision belongs to you. But I will gladly snap his neck or run him down with my car."

"No need for that. I want him to rot in prison for the rest of his life."

Hammond laughs, but he sounds hoarse. "You are fools."

"Are we?" I roughly flip the *bod ceann* over and lock the cuffs around his wrists. "We'll see about that."

I lift him to his feet and yank on his cuffs, making him hiss in a breath and grimace.

"You are wasting your time," Hammond says through his gritted teeth. "All the evidence points to Piper. You can't tie me to the murder."

"No, we can't." I lower my head to snarl into his ear, "But you are going to confess to all your crimes."

"You have no evidence, MacTaggart. I have a network of connections while you are a loner."

"Who's the fool now, Hammond? I've got more than connections." I turn around so he can see my cousins as well as Alex and Piper. "I have a family who will do anything to help me. That's what MacTaggarts do. What have you got? Lackeys who do your bidding because they're afraid of you. True loyalty comes from love, ye bastard."

"Everyone in my employ would die to carry out my orders."

"Do ye even hear yourself? Your orders." I jerk his cuffs, making him wince again. "Look at these people, Hammond. We fight for the ones we love, and we would all die for each other. Not because we're ordered to do it. Because we're family."

Hammond lifts his chin and affects an attitude of haughty indifference. He still doesn't understand, but the truth will become clear to him soon.

Eying him with suspicion, I ask, "Why did you walk up the driveway by yourself? Ye had to know we'd grab you."

He makes a face that reminds me of a wee laddie who didn't get his way for the first time in his life. "How can there be so many of you? No family is this large."

Ah, of course. He underestimated the size of the MacTaggart clan. Many people make that mistake.

Logan and Errol amble through the gates and stop an arm's length from Hammond. The laddie tips his head side to side as if he's studying the British ersehole. "I thought you'd be taller."

"You are all barking mad," Hammond says. "If you mean to force a confession out of me, don't waste your time. I didn't kill Archer Caldwell."

"I believe you," I say. "But I'm dead sure you ordered someone else to do it."

"Time to bring in the asset," Logan says.

I point to Errol. "The lad is right here."

Errol laughs. "Ye think I'm the asset? No, Magnus. We've got a much better surprise than that for this bastard."

"Bring her out here," Logan says as if he's talking to a ghost. Hammond can't see our earpieces, and he seems rather confused by Logan's statement.

At least, I assume he's talking to one of my other cousins through the earpiece. But I'm wrong.

Piper marches into the vestibule and returns a moment later, ushering a familiar woman into the courtyard. Dilara Terzi shuffles her feet and hunches her shoulders while her gaze darts wildly. The two women halt a dozen feet away from where I still hold Hammond.

"Errol?" Dilara says when she sees my cousin. "Are you all right?"

"Fine, love," he says. "But it's time to do what you promised. It's for the best. You'll feel much better once you get the truth out."

"What is this?" Hammond asks, though his arrogance is now tainted with a note of panic. "You've brought Mata Hari here to tell unsubstantiated lies about me? You lot must be desperate."

"You're the desperate one," I growl. "Haud yer wheesht, or I'll stuff a rag in your mouth—one soaked in turpentine."

Errol walks over to Dilara, though he doesn't touch her. "Go on, lass. Get it all off your chest."

She bows her head, takes a shaky breath, and raises her face. With her shoulders rolled back, she looks straight at Piper. "I murdered Archer Caldwell."

No one speaks. We're all too stunned to come up with any words.

She thrusts an arm out to point her finger at Hammond. "But he told me to do it."

Chapter Thirty-Seven

The world spins around me for a couple of seconds, and I just stand here feeling disconnected from reality. Did I hear what I think I just heard? Dilara Terzi confessed to murdering Archer and implicated Hammond in the conspiracy. That doesn't mean my twenty-month nightmare has ended, though. Not yet.

"You lot are pathetic," Hammond says, though his disgusted tone hitches as if he's not as certain of his untouchable status as he wants us to think. "If someone who works for me commits a crime, that has nothing to do with me."

Errol picks up Dilara's hand, holding it between both of his. "Go on, love. Tell them the rest."

She clears her throat. "I will also confess to helping Royce with his antiquities trafficking operation. The authorities will find his private collection, the items he couldn't bear to sell, locked in a secret room in his home in the Cotswolds. I can tell them where the hidden panel is that conceals the room, and I'll provide the combination that unlocks the inner door."

Hammond lets out a harsh bark of laughter. "Antiquities theft? I'll slip out of that noose. My lawyers will make sure of it."

"I will testify against you, Royce. And I'll also testify that you not only ordered me to kill Caldwell, but you provided the poison."

The evil mastermind bares his teeth like a wild beast. "No one will believe a murderous harpy like you."

"You've always thought I'm a fool, haven't you? Maybe I am, but I had the sense to save the vial of poison, which has my fingerprints on it as well as yours."

Hammond lets out a snarling shout. "You are all going to die. My men will rescue me soon—"

"No, they won't," Magnus says. "We captured all of them."

"Aye," Logan says. "Those laddies aren't as steadfast in their dedication to their master as you think, Hammond. They surrendered without a fight."

"What now?" I ask. "If we take Hammond to the police, he'll probably get out on bail. Then his lawyers will make sure he never serves a day in prison."

"Dilara can help with that," Errol says. "She knows all the passwords to Hammond's laptop, his mobile, everything. The computer experts at the Met will salivate over all the data she can give them. And it will prove he's the mastermind of an international antiquities smuggling cartel. With Dilara's testimony, Hammond will be punished for his part in Caldwell's murder too."

Magnus looks at me. "It's almost over. Trust me."

After evading the law for so long, I have trouble believing my struggle might end soon. But I do trust him, so much that I know in my soul he will make it happen.

Men amble through the gates into the courtyard, each one bound with zip ties and paired with a MacTaggart who keeps hold of the bindings.

Lachlan separates from the group to take possession of Dilara, leading her into the house.

"Here are your loyal soldiers," Magnus tells his captive. "How many of you will defend this man and lie for him? Nod your heads if you feel that way."

Not one of them nods. They all stand perfectly still.

"I will get you out of jail," Hammond shouts to his men. "Don't let these bastards get away with assaulting me. I'll have bruises. You can testify that this lot beat me."

His men don't speak or move.

Logan turns to address the group. "We're going to release you, but if you know anything about Hammond's illegal activities, you would do well to give that information to the authorities."

"Is it smart to release them?" I ask. "They might try to rescue Hammond."

"Donnae worry about that." Logan aims his steely glare at the men. "These lads know what they need to do. The right thing, that's what. Besides, we took all their weapons, and I had a nice long chat with them."

His tone suggests that "chat" involved lots of scary glares from Logan and plenty of graphic descriptions of what might happen to those guys if they cross the former MI6 agent.

Logan says something to the group of men, and they hurry down the driveway—heading for their cars, no doubt.

Alex is turning Hammond's cell phone in his hand as if examining the device. His lips pucker slightly, and his brows lower. "Why did Hammond bring only his mobile? No weapons. Just this."

He holds up the phone for everyone to see.

Errol trots over to him and takes the device, swiping and tapping on its screen. Now his mouth crimps too. "Cannae see anything unusual. We should get Evan to look—"

The lights go out, in the courtyard and the house, plunging us into darkness. Our eyes can't adjust to the much dimmer light of the half moon fast enough.

Scuffling erupts, like someone is struggling to get up. Footfalls crunch on the gravel as that person races away.

"He's trying to escape!" Logan shouts.

A flashlight comes on, the big and bright kind that floods the entire courtyard with its brilliance. The light spills into the walled garden just as a figure sprints past the arbor and out of sight.

Hammond is gone.

Logan and Alex race after him.

"Stop!" Errol hollers. "Donnae go out there. He willnae get away."

Alex and Logan halt just inside the garden entrance. They turn and aim puzzled looks at Errol.

He hands Hammond's phone to Magnus and whips out his own device. After a few quick swipes, he squints at whatever is on his phone screen. Then he taps one more time.

Boom.

An explosion detonates. The earth shakes, and the concussion echoes through the courtyard, but the flash of the blast erupts outside the castle walls, directly behind the garden.

Errol smirks. He taps the screen again.

Boom. Another flash, another explosion.

Someone screams out there in the darkness.

With his gaze glued to his phone, Errol detonates three more blasts. "That should do it. He's not dead or even injured. My land mines are precision targeted."

He slips the phone back into his pocket.

No one moves. We all gape at Errol.

"Well, get yer erses moving," he says. "Donnae want Hammond to get away, do ye?"

Everyone dashes through the garden and out onto a grassy area. The lights inside the house and all around the castle compound come on again, but there's no floodlight out here behind the compound. Fortunately, Logan still has his lantern flashlight. Its wide beam reveals the scene before us.

Royce Hammond lies on the ground halfway between the castle wall and the trees across from us. He's curled up in the fetal position.

Magnus and I stand beside Errol. He tips his phone screen toward us. "I tracked him via the infrared cameras. See those red dots? They mark the locations of my land mines. I set off a few of them to scare Hammond."

"But the power went out," I say. "How could those cameras still work?"

"They run on batteries, love. Told ye I have an app on my mobile that controls the mines. Evan connected it to the cameras for me too."

"Wow, you MacTaggarts sure are industrious masterminds. Glad you're all on the side of good."

"Scots are always on the right side."

Logan marches over to Hammond and grabs the man's arm to haul him to his feet. The evil bastard is crying. Sobbing, actually. He makes no effort to fight it when Logan drags him back inside the castle walls. The rest of us follow them.

"We'll take care of Hammond," Logan tells Magnus. "You and Piper should have a nice long chat with our other guest. But in the morning. Ye look exhausted."

"Aren't we going to call the cops?" I ask.

"In due time. First, we're going to make Hammond comfortable in the ground-floor bathroom with several of us guarding him." Logan gives Hammond a hard shake, but the man is still crying and doesn't react. "Think we'll bind his feet and hands, gag him too. The bathtub will become his prison cell until we hand him over to the proper authorities."

Since it's late and Logan was right about us being exhausted, Magnus takes me into a bedroom in the guest wing so we can get some sleep. We don't bother with getting undressed. Instead, we drop onto the mattress fully clothed and curl up together, falling asleep within minutes. Though I wake first, just as the first rays of sunrise peek over the horizon, I don't disturb Magnus. He needs the rest, and I have something I need to do alone.

I march down the hall and through the dining room, swerving left toward the vestibule, and hurry up the stairs to the first floor. Why am I here? Because I need to interrogate our prisoner. She owes me answers.

Once I reach the tower bedroom on the second floor, I knock on the closed door.

It swings open, and Luke Turner gives me a tight smile. "Hey, Piper. Had a feeling you'd come here." He glances at Alex. "See, I was right."

"Can I come in?" I ask.

"Yeah." He opens the door wider and steps aside. "Welcome to the Tower of Dùndubhan. It's not as scary as the Tower of London, but it holds a prisoner just as well."

I walk into the room and see Alex Thorne sitting in a chair by the window, seeming like he's browsing a magazine. But his eyes don't move with the text, so I'm pretty sure he's faking it, flipping pages every so often to keep up the pretense. In reality, he's guarding the woman who lies strapped to the bed.

Luke shuts the door.

The men did a good job of tying her up. Dilara has her hands and her feet tied up with rope, and a longer length of it secures her wrist bindings to the headboard rails.

"We fed her," Alex announces while fake-reading that magazine. "And gave her water. Apparently, we're adhering to the Geneva Convention or some such rot."

"Not the Geneva Convention," Luke says. "That only applies to war."

Dilara hasn't been gagged, like Hammond was. She watches me with dread in her eyes, as if she thinks I might pull out a gun and shoot her. Maybe I should. This woman is a killer, after all, and a co-conspirator in Hammond's illegal dealings.

"Would you guys mind if I speak to Dilara alone?" I ask.

Luke and Alex exchange glances, then both men shrug.

"Fine by me," Luke says.

Alex rises and drops his magazine on the chair he'd sat in. "I could stand to stretch my legs in the long gallery. But leave the door open, Piper."

"Okay."

The men exit the bedroom, but I know they won't go far.

I sit on the bed's edge, at the foot, and do my best to mimic Magnus's hard stare. "You owe me answers."

"Yes, I know." She wriggles as if she can't get comfortable. Good. The bitch doesn't deserve to feel comfy ever again. "I never meant for you to be caught up in this. I'm sorry for the pain my actions have caused you."

Gee, thanks, that makes it all better. I think that but don't say it because I need her to keep talking. "Why did you murder Archer Caldwell? I know Hammond convinced you to do it, but I want to know why you agreed."

"Royce can be quite charming and persuasive. When I first came to work for him, he seemed like a decent man." She bites her lip so hard it turns white. "Royce knew how to take advantage of my every weakness and draw me into his web. We became lovers, then he initiated me into his antiquities smuggling operations. I knew it was wrong, but I needed the money. My father had become very ill, and his cancer medication was extremely expensive. Royce paid for his treatments."

If she expects me to feel bad for her, she can go screw herself. I feel sorry for her dad, but not for Dilara.

"By the time Archer Caldwell became a problem," she says, "I was in love with Royce and would've done anything for him. Still, when he told me Archer needed to die, I refused to help Royce. But he threatened to revoke my father's treatments. I had no choice."

"Excuse me? That's bullshit. Murder is always a choice. You could have gone to the cops and told them everything."

"I should have, I wanted to." Tears dribble down her cheeks. "I was terrified of losing my father, but more than that, I couldn't bear the thought of losing Royce. I thought he loved me. As soon as I put that poison in Archer's glass, I wanted to take it back. But I couldn't."

"Of course you could. All you had to do was warn Archer so he wouldn't drink the poisoned champagne." I can't help fisting my hands, digging my nails into my palms. "You let me hang for his murder and never said a damn word to help me."

"I know," she sobs. "I'm so sorry. The worst part is that two months after Archer died, my father passed away. Royce ended our relationship too. I'd done it all for nothing."

Christ, this woman is a mess. She became so obsessed with Royce Hammond that she would do anything to stay in his good graces. I don't feel sorry for her, though. She let me twist in the wind, not caring if I lived or died.

"You could have confessed to the police anytime," I say, surprised by the fury in my voice. "But all you cared about was being Royce Hammond's girlfriend. I bet he lavished you with gifts and trips to exotic places. All of that mattered more to you than owning up to your your crime."

"That's all true." She aims her bloodshot eyes at me, though she's stopped crying. "I want to turn myself in and confess."

"Good. You'll get your chance very soon." I consider her for a moment. "You like earthy perfume, don't you? The kind that's a lot like men's cologne."

"Yes. Does it matter?"

"No. I was curious, that's all." But now I know I was right.

Dilara sniffles, then looks straight at me. "I know everything Royce has done. I'll confess to more than the murder. I'll give you Royce Hammond on a silver platter."

Chapter Thirty-Eight

Magnus

Piper Lang amazes me at every turn. Just when I'd thought the lass couldnae surprise me anymore, she does. After checking on Hammond, who is currently guarded by Rory and Gavin, I ask if they've seen Piper. Rory tells me she's in the tower bedroom with Dilara. When I ask if they've had any trouble with Hammond, Gavin assures me that the "slimy piece of festering human garbage" hasn't tried anything. They've given him water, but he won't get any breakfast until the detectives from the Met arrive to take him into custody. Logan and I will then go along with those blokes, both of whom know my cousin well, to ensure Hammond doesn't pull any more tricks on the ride to the Inverness airport or on the flight from there to London. We will all travel in Evan's jet.

Now that I know Hammond is secure, I head up to the second floor and the tower bedroom. Alex and Luke are walking toward me, clearly having just come down from the bedroom. They inform me Piper is in there with Dilara. I walk up the stairwell that accesses the bedroom, but I stop three steps from the top. From this vantage, I can see and hear both Piper and Dilara.

"I never meant for you to be caught up in this," Dilara says. "I'm sorry for the pain my actions have caused you."

Piper doesn't accept the woman's apology. I can tell that despite the fact Piper doesn't respond to the statement. Why should she absolve Dilara of her guilt? She shouldn't, and she doesn't. I listen while Piper interrogates the woman, getting more information out of her than I would've expected. Dilara Terzi honestly wants to confess and provide whatever information we need to nail Hammond.

Maybe I should reveal myself, but I donnae want to just yet. I relish watching Piper question Dilara and punish the woman with her words, tone, and expressions. The first time Piper got away from me, I recognized she was not an average woman. My admiration for her intelligence, resolve, and strength increased with every encounter—even all those times when I glimpsed her but couldn't catch the lass. But here today, in this room, I realize just how strong she is.

"I'll give you Royce Hammond on a silver platter," Dilara says.

Piper rises and aims a hard look at the woman. "You'd better follow through on that promise, or I will come for you."

She almost sounds like me when she says that, and the steely tone of her statement makes my cock jerk. There is nothing sexier in the world than Piper Lang in badass mode. The lass turns toward the doorway and sees me. Her brows hike up, then she gives me a sexy smile. I want to kiss her, but Alex and Luke come up the stairs to tell us Logan's mates from the Met are here to collect our prisoners. I help drag Hammond outside and into their SUV. Then Logan and I get in the car too. The two detectives, an inspector and a sergeant, climb in last.

And we drive away.

That evening, when Logan and I return to Dùndubhan, we're too jeeked to do anything except go straight to bed. I'm too exhausted even to shag Piper. We turn on the television for a few minutes to watch the evening news because I know the broadcast will include a report that Piper will enjoy.

We watch Royce Hammond being ushered out of a police car in handcuffs, on his way to a jail cell. Aye, we both wear smug smiles as we watch that video.

Once the report is over, Piper turns to me. "Gee, I wonder who alerted the media that Hammond would be arrested today."

"Must've been a wee bird that told them."

"Are you sure it wasn't a big, sexy, gruff-and-tough bird with a goatee?"

I smirk. "It might've been."

She loops her arms around my neck and kisses my cheek. "Thank you, Magnus. You saved my life. How can I ever repay you?"

"We're even, because you saved my soul."

"Aw. See, you are a sweetie."

I pinch her erse. "But you are the crack detective. Errol told me that he realized Dilara must be the killer because of what you said."

"What did I say? Don't remember."

"You pointed out that a woman might wear woodsy cologne, and that

Dilara was nervous. Errol went to see Dilara again. Said he knew as soon as he sniffed her that she had murdered Caldwell." I tap the tip of her nose. "She was wearing that sort of perfume. You broke the case, love."

"We all collaborated on the investigation."

"Aye, we did."

That night, we both sleep better than we ever have in our lives. Piper's burden has been lifted, but I still have something I need to settle. I've let the problem boil away for far too long. I know that, but it still takes me two more days to work up the nerve to deal with it. Instead, today I take Piper to my house on the outskirts of Loch Fairbairn and show her Kirsty's metaphysical shop in the village, then we have dinner with Jack, Autumn, Callum, and Kate.

Aye, I've become a ruddy coward. But on the second day, Piper gives me a kick in the erse—a literal one, with her foot shoved into my backside—to push me out the door. She will be there to support me during what might turn out to be a worse battle than the one at Dùndubhan a few days ago.

We walk up to the door of the little white cottage, and I knock.

The door opens, and a woman flings herself at me, babbling in Gaelic.

I pat her back. "Ma, calm down. Ahmno here to make trouble, but I would like to speak to Da."

Rhona MacTaggart pulls away, wiping tears from her eyes with her shirt sleeve. "Oh Magnus, we're so happy you're all right."

I hook an arm around Piper's waist. "Ma, this is Piper Lang. She's my girlfriend."

My mother starts to cry again. She grabs Piper's face and kisses her cheeks. "Oh, dearie, yer the bonniest lass I've ever seen. Cannae wait to get to know ye."

Have I walked into an alternate universe? My mother should be worried about how my father will react when he sees me, but instead, she seems overjoyed.

"Come in, come in," she says, ushering us inside. "You two are famous in the village now."

"Famous?" Piper says as we enter the living room.

"Oh, aye. Everyone knows what heroes you both are."

"Heroes?" I say. "What are ye on about?"

My father walks into the room. He halts just this side of the threshold and stares at me with the stern expression I know all too well. Any moment, he'll start telling me what a flaming ersehole I am and that I'm no son of his.

Baltair MacTaggart rushes over to pull me into a firm hug. Then he takes two steps backward and clears throat, averting his gaze. "Glad ye didnae die."

I cannae think of a damn thing to say in response to that.

My mother gestures toward the sofa. "Please sit down, Magnus. You too, Piper. Baltair and I would love to hear the story in your own words."

"What story?" I ask as Piper and I take our seats.

"The big story." Ma holds up a newspaper. "You both made headlines, dearie."

Piper and I glance at each other in bewilderment, then I take the paper and we both read the headline on today's edition of *The Scotsman*—"British billionaire's dirty deeds exposed by Scottish bounty hunter." The article goes on to describe me and Piper as some sort of heroes who broke up an illicit antiquities ring and brought a murderer to justice, along with the man who orchestrated everything. The story mentions Errol too, but no one else.

"The whole family helped," I say. "We didn't do it alone. And it's hardly heroic."

"Of course it is," Ma says. She clasps her hands under her chin, her eyes glistening as if she might cry again. "Ahm so proud of you both. And the rest of the family doesnae want the credit. They're glad you stopped a killer and that British *bod ceann*."

I've never heard my mother curse before.

My father drops onto an armchair. He winces and scratches his cheek, then finally looks at me. "I'm sorry, Magnus. I was wrong about you and your job. You bring criminals to justice and make the world a safer place, and those lads at the Met say so in that article. A killer might have gone unpunished, able to commit more crimes, if you and Piper hadn't stopped him."

All I can do is stare at my father. I think my jaw falls open too.

"I know I've been horrible to you," my father says. "Wouldnae blame ye if you never want to see me again. But if you can forgive me, I'd like us to, ah…start rebuilding our relationship."

Ma starts crying. Tears trickle down Piper's cheeks too.

Even I get a wee bit choked up when I tell him, "Aye, Da, I'd like that."

Repairing the damage we'd both done to our relationship will take time. But we decide to start with a family dinner so Piper can get to know my parents. I need to get to know them again too, and for once, I'm no longer dreading the thought of seeing my father. I'll be coming home much more often.

Over the next few weeks, we spend most of our time with my parents. But then it's time for Callum and Kate's engagement ceilidh at Dùndubhan. I need to explain to Piper that a ceilidh is a big party with music and dancing. She knows I donnae like to dance, but I make an exception this time. I get dressed in the appropriate way for a MacTaggart ceilidh, which means I wear a kilt. Piper loves it. She says I'm "too hot for words" when she sees me in my kilt, and I get the first dance with her. Then Errol whisks Piper away, and soon every man in the great hall wants a turn with my lass.

While Piper spins around the floor with Alex Thorne, I join Logan and Errol for a drink at the bar.

Logan sets a hand on my shoulder. "So, when will the bounty hunter settle down?"

"Never. Piper and I will be hunting fugitives together. That means traveling, though mostly in Scotland. Donnae get many international hunts."

"Not since ye caught Piper," Errol says with a wink. "But I think Logan was asking when you'll propose to the lass."

I smile and walk away.

Then I track Piper down on the dance floor and take her away from my cousin Iain. Together, we go downstairs and head outside to the garden. A full moon shines above us as we sit down on the concrete bench near the arbor.

I clasp her hand. "Piper, I love you."

She laughs. "Still don't understand subtlety, do you?"

"No." I squint at her. "I said I love you. You're meant to respond."

"Thank you, Magnus. It's sweet of you to let me know how you feel."

I compress my lips, squinting harder.

She laughs again and kisses me. "I love you, too, Pig-Bear."

"Feeling so good that I donnae even care if ye call me that." I drop to one knee in front of her. "Will ye marry me, Piper?"

"Yes, I will." She leans in to whisper in my ear, "And you'll never need to chase me again."

"What if I want to?"

She grins. "Well, if you want to…"

I rise and pick her up, setting the lass on her feet. "I'll give ye a head start by counting to a hundred."

"Deal. But let's confine ourselves to the castle compound this time."

"Aye." I slap her erse. "Now, run."

Piper takes off.

Wherever she goes, I will always find her—and she will always find me. My body tenses, readying for the chase, as I count down. "Ninety-nine. One hundred."

I race after her.

Epilogue

Errol
Ten Days Later

I kick the dirt and sigh, then gaze up at the clouds and wonder if I've lost my touch. Maybe it's my new temporary partner jinxing me. I should have found treasure here, but instead, we've dug a ditch and turned up nothing more exciting than an old dog bone, the sort people buy for their pups to chew on. It's not ancient. It's not even interesting.

"What's wrong, Errol?" asks my cousin Callum, aka my temporary partner. "Ye wanted my help, but now ye just keep scowling at me."

"Sorry, mate. I was hoping for a eureka moment."

"How often do ye get those?"

"Not as often as I'd like. Treasure hunting isn't easy."

Callum drops his shovel. "Are we done, then? Kate wants to go for a ride."

My cousin means on a motorcycle, not a horse or a mule. At least I think that's what he means. If he's talking about shagging his lass, I donnae need to hear about that. I've become a wee bit depressed ever since Magnus got engaged to Piper. The fearsome black sheep of the family has become an upstanding member of the MacTaggart clan. He's been hailed as a hero too, for his exploits with Piper. I'm happy for him, but for some reason, my cousin's good fortune has made me feel slightly…miserable.

No, I never feel that way. I'm disappointed that my latest treasure hunting expedition has turned into nothing. That's all.

Maybe I shouldn't have listened when Mungo Gunn told me there must be treasure in the field behind his house. The lad is not the most reliable person. Until recently, he was essentially insane. Now he's normal again, mostly, but he claims my cousin Kirsty cured his madness by taking back a cursed book that Mungo's family had held onto for ages. I shouldn't blame Mungo for my failure today, though. I haven't received a good tip in a long time, and I haven't found a solid clue either. My escapade with Magnus and Piper seems to have drained my puzzling-solving brain cells.

"Go on," I tell Callum. "Have fun with Kate. Think I'll go home and cogitate."

I want to get drunk, not think, but that willnae help me find my next adventure. My partner in crime has gone silent lately, ignoring my texts, calls, and emails. I've gone it alone before, so I have no idea why I'm in a slump now.

Callum slaps my shoulder. "Better luck next time, eh?"

"Aye, next time."

While he walks back to his Harley, I fill in the bloody useless hole we'd excavated. Then I let Mungo know we're done and drive back to my house. I live halfway between Loch Fairbairn and Ballachulish, so I could stop to visit Magnus and Piper on the way. But I find myself driving right past their street and going straight home.

I've just poured myself a dram of whisky when the doorbell rings.

That's perfect. I want to wallow in my failure, and some erse shows up to bother me. It's probably Magnus or Jack or some other family member. I shuffle over to the door while still holding my whisky glass and peer through the peephole.

A bonnie brunette stands on the porch.

I yank the door open and smile at her. "Hello there. How can I help you?"

She eyes me up and down, her mouth puckering and her brows wrinkling. "Are you Errol Murdoch?"

"Aye. And you are?"

"My name is Ashley Hartman." She offers me a business card. "I'm here to hire you, Mr. Murdoch."

"To do what?" A beautiful American woman turns up on my doorstep offering me a job? That happens to me all the time. No, it doesn't. And aye, I'm a bit suspicious.

"I want you to find something for me. Isn't that what you do?"

"Aye. But I work for museums, not individuals."

She glances down at my hand, which still holds the whisky glass. "May I come in and have a drink with you? Then we can discuss my offer in more detail."

Maybe I should say no since all my instincts are warning me to be careful of this woman, but I've never had much willpower when it comes to lasses. I swing the door wider. "Come in."

Ashley gives me a slight smile as she walks past me.

I lead her into the living room and invite the lass to sit down. She takes the sofa, and I choose the armchair. "What sort of treasure are you looking for, Miss Hartman?"

"Call me Ashley. May I call you Errol?"

"Aye."

She sets her purse on the cushion beside her and brings out a folded-up sheet of paper. "This will be the biggest hoard you've ever found, and I'm willing to pay any amount of money to find it. The archaeological value alone would be priceless."

"Ye haven't told me what it is yet."

"Could I have that drink first?"

She's delaying. Donnae know why, and donnae think I trust her. But the lass does intrigue me, so I get her a glass of whisky. As I hand it to her, she looks up at me, her lips curling into that slight smile again.

"Thank you, Errol," she says. Then she takes a sip of her drink. "Mm, that's good."

"Glad ye like it." I settle onto my armchair again. "Enough overblown hype about this treasure you supposedly want to find. Tell me what it is."

She offers me the folded paper, stretching her arm across the coffee table. "This explains everything."

I doubt that. But I take the paper and unfold it. "Is this a practical joke?"

"No. I'm completely serious." She pulls a packet of hundred-dollar bills out of her purse and sets it on the table. "This is a retainer. You will get much more when you begin the search."

"How much more?"

"Millions, potentially. I can't say for sure because you will get a cut of the treasure. How much you receive depends on the outcome."

I stare at the paper in my hand. It's a photocopy of a story in an old newspaper. At the top, it says, "Oldest Paper in Phoenix—Twenty-Ninth Year. Gazette, Monday Evening, April 5, 1909." But that's hardly the most interesting part. The headline declares, "Explorations in Grand Canyon. Mysteries of Immense Rich Cavern Being Brought to Light. Jordan is Enthused. Remarkable Finds Indicate Ancient People Migrated from Orient." I've heard this story before, and I know it's rubbish.

With a sigh, I toss the paper back to Ashley. "The Grand Canyon treasure is bollocks. People have spent their lives searching for it, and they always come up empty-handed. There are no Egyptian hieroglyphs. There's no cavern. It's a myth."

She leans forward, and her blouse falls open just enough to give me a glimpse of her cleavage. "But wouldn't you love to be the one who discovers the treasure and proves the myth is real?"

I'd love to shag her, but I do not want to go on a hunt for a fictitious treasure.

Ashley taps the packet of bills. "Keep the money. When you change your mind, give me a call. You have my card."

The lass walks out the door.

No, I will not ring her. No, I do not want to hunt for a myth.

But aye, I want her. Not enough to go on a barmy search for a treasure that never existed, though.

I pick up the stack of hundreds and flip through it with my thumb.

No, I won't do it.

Well, not today.

Errol Murdoch returns in
Incendiary in a Kilt **(Hot Scots, Book Twelve).**

Love the

Hot Scots

series?

Visit
AnnaDurand.com

to subscribe to her newsletter
for updates on forthcoming books in the series
&
to receive free gifts for signing up!

Anna Durand is a bestselling, multi-award-winning author of contemporary and paranormal romance. Her books have earned bestseller status on every major retailer and wonderful reviews from readers around the world. But that's the boring spiel. Here are the really cool things you want to know about Anna!

Born on Lackland Air Force Base in Texas, Anna grew up moving here, there, and everywhere thanks to her dad's job as an instructor pilot. She's lived in Texas (twice), Mississippi, California (twice), Michigan (twice), and Alaska—and now Ohio.

As for her writing, Anna has always made up stories in her head, but she didn't write them down until her teen years. Those first awful books went into the trash can a few years later, though she learned a lot from those stories. Eventually, she would pen her first romance novel, the paranormal romance *Willpower*, and she's never looked back since.

Want even more details about Anna? Get access to her extended bio when you subscribe to her newsletter and download the free bonus ebook, *Hot Scots Confidential*. You'll also get hot deleted scenes, character interviews, fun facts, and more! Plus you'll receive audio bonus content narrated by Shane East, Vanessa Edwin, and Ava Lucas.

Visit AnnaDurand.com to sign up.